"YOU'LL HEAR EVERY WORD I'M ABOUT TO SAY, OR SO HELP ME GOD, I'LL THROW YOU INTO THE DEEP!

"Mark me well, Tierney, for never have I been so tempted to strangle a woman." His voice was hoarse with restrained fury. "I'll not have my men laughing behind my back! You will remain Tierney Chambers, cabin boy, until we reach Charleston harbor. There it will be my greatest pleasure to dump you on the docks to fare as you will. . . ."

. . . So green were her eyes. The color of mandarin jade. And the girl's hair was not red, really; it was autumn brown. It had merely seemed red in the fireglow. . . .

What incredible fate, he thought, *that I should have worried over a slip of a girl waiting tables, who then became my cabin boy, and who is now the albatross about my neck!*

FRENCHMAN'S MISTRESS

Irene Michaels

A DELL BOOK

Published by
Dell Publishing Co., Inc.
1 Dag Hammarskjold Plaza
New York, New York 10017

Dell ® TM 681510, Dell Publishing Co., Inc.

ISBN: 0-440-12545-6

Printed in the United States of America
First printing—December 1980

FOREWORD

Any writer of historic fiction is indebted to many others, particularly those writers whose expertise is the writing of history per se. All of the historians to whom I am indebted are too numerous to list here; however, I do want to give credit to the following nonfiction works without which *Frenchman's Mistress* would have been the story of two lovers without a place or time.

The War of 1812, written by Harry Lewis Coles, and published by the University of Chicago, was immensely helpful in giving me a fuller appreciation of this little-understood conflict; *Indian Wars of the U.S. Army*, by Fairfax Davis Downey, Doubleday, enlightened me on the problems encountered with the Creek Federation during the period; and *Indians of the Southeast: Then and Now*, by Jesse Burt and Robert B. Ferguson, Abingdon Press; all presented their subject in a warm and understanding fashion. Especially delightful to me personally were *In Pirate Waters*, by Richard Wheeler, Thomas Y. Crowell Co., and *French Quarter*, by Herbert Asbury, Capricorn Books.

Although I did attempt to preserve the tone of history throughout, *Frenchman's Mistress* is fiction. Obvious historic persons included in the book, such as Andrew Jackson, were an integral part of my story; I have made an effort to portray them as accurately as possible.

I admit I took extreme license in incorporating Jean and Pierre Lafitte into the story, particularly the latter's escape from the Calaboose. But Pierre Lafitte was such an obscure man, and my heroine such an unpredictable lass, that I could not resist putting the two of them together. In any event, the pirate's escape at such a critical time has never been explained—to this day it remains a mystery.

There are others to whom I am grateful. My parents

encouraged me throughout the writing, as did my husband whose patience with my nocturnal schedule I shall never forget. My children, too, deserve a note of thanks for being less demanding than children of their ages are wont. My closest friends were aware of this, my first book, and I want to express my appreciation for their hearty approval of my efforts.

I thank also my literary agent, Arthur Schwartz, who took the manuscript under rather strange, comical conditions. And last, but foremost, I thank my editor and publisher; they, after all, breathed life into my characters and kept my story from being just a writer's dream.

*Dedicated to the memory
of my own dear Nana,
Margaret Murphy Ryan*

Part 1

A TIME OF DISCOVERY

CHAPTER ONE

The sky was radiant with the colors of crimson-brushed gold, and a cool breeze ruffled his hair as *La Reine de la Mer* slowly coursed upward on the Thames. André felt a sense of relief as he realized that London was within his reach, finally.

His emotions were mixed with triumphant pride as he approached the sprawling city and gazed at Whitehall, which stood as proud and sober as when he had last seen England. It was hard to believe that ten years had passed so swiftly. If London had not changed, André reflected, he himself had since he was eighteen, setting foot on this, which was enemy soil. Now he was captain of his own proud sailing vessel.

Then there had been a brief respite in the war when England had signed a truce in 1802 with the French Consulate under the direction of Bonaparte. Tall and thin, the young André had been a crew member on his father's merchant schooner, *Le Valiente,* and although he had even then been at sea for three years, the legendary British maritime fleet had overwhelmed him.

It was different today. He leaned over the brass railing on the foredeck and watched as the bow cleanly swept aside the waters of the Thames. *La Reine de la Mer,* the Sea Queen. There was none quite like her, and André openly admitted he loved his vessel as he could never love a woman.

She was long and sleek, her three masts almost imperceptibly bowed to the wind. The delicate angle of her masts was intentional, as were her unusual length and narrow girth. Her designers, French naval architects from André de Montfort's native Brittany, had virtually guaranteed the young captain of her superb maneuverability and speed. Smiling, he now appreciated fully the architects' skill and foresight. The designers had actually underestimated her—she was far ahead of her time. It would be years yet before the merchants of the world would understand her unique beauty and execution.

The British sea captains no longer awed André, though of course he still greatly admired them. English supremacy at naval tactics had, in André's opinion, kept Napoleon from realizing his vision of a unified Europe.

The emperor would soon reach Moscow, thought André, and widespread speculation held the forebodings of his defeat. Already there was a great deal of rumbling over the possibility of a united European front against the French emperor, with intelligence leaks reaching de Montfort from ports of call in Amsterdam, Spain, and Portugal.

Captain de Montfort knew he was risking a great deal by choosing this particular moment to return to London. But, he thought wryly, Bonaparte had for too many years now denied the merchants of Nantes and the surrounding Brittany ports of their inherent trade relations with England. The captain had decided it was an opportune time for him to take the gamble, since concentrated effort was on the Russian front and Channel surveillance relatively weak.

As it turned out, de Montfort's information sources and his own intuition had been accurate, and he now docked and dropped anchor without incident. It was all quite apparent that Britain herself was eager for French commerce, her citizens having forsaken the silks and wines from the Continent since 1806. By the time those goods were smuggled in along the rocky coasts of Cornwall to London, they were outrageously expensive.

"Capitaine. Qu'est-ce que vous avez?"

"Speak in English, Paul!" the captain ordered. "And nothing is the matter with me. I am just thinking of how we will fare here, and when we set sail for the crossing. Take your leave, man, and let me be!"

Paul Mauriac was first mate, and ten years older than his young captain. He had trained young André in the art of seamanship on board the schooner that had belonged to André's father, Maurice de Montfort. The old man's temperament had been fiery enough, but Paul silently swore that André's moods were as changeable as the seas. The first mate knew his station, but when they were alone, he was next to André and not beneath him. Paul was the only man alive who understood the young man, and could even humor him on occasion.

"Speaking of leave, sir, what about the men? They'll be wanting to go ashore as soon as you give word." But even Mauriac was taken back when he thought the captain had not heard him. "Sir," he repeated loudly.

"What's that? *Oui,* the men. I have been listening to you, Paul, if only with one ear. No shore leave until noon tomorrow. In the meantime I want them to remain on board while I assess London's reception of French sailors. I cannot tolerate any trouble in port!" Again his voice raised and he quickly added in a more moderate tone, "Paul, I understand the men are anxious. I also understand that many of them were hesitant to set sail for England. And I know why.

"If Bonaparte's Russian campaign is successful," he continued quickly, "then the spirit of victory will bring him back to the coast and his most desired conquest of all— Great Britain. At which point, my *Reine* will never again be welcome in French waters. Perhaps all of Europe! I would have to completely revise my plans, concentrating my trade in the West Indies and America."

As an afterthought, the captain added, "The crew may not be able to fathom the details of our current venture and its possible folly, but they are not at ease either." André glanced at the darkening skies for a sign of some sort, as if it might hold a portent of the future.

Mauriac agreed with André that the men were restless, and silently hoped that no fights would break out among them before noon on the morrow. He also shared the captain's hesitation about their going on shore. Unlike de Montfort and himself, who frequented the United States and were fluent in the language, most of the crew spoke only French. The first mate smiled; that was so, except for the few foreign desultory swear words and oaths that all seamen quickly learned.

The sky showed neither sign of storm nor balmy weather. "Probably a common London drizzle," André muttered. Suddenly the captain's temperament changed, and he turned back to his first mate, his eyes slightly mischievous.

"The crew will remain the night, Paul. But you and I shall go on shore. Put Pelier in command during our absence," he ordered.

"Yes, sir!" Mauriac would have liked to ask why they were going into the city at dusk, but before he could speak de Montfort was striding toward his cabin.

Alone now, André lit one of the hurricane lanterns and surveyed the small room. He took a measure of pride in his berth, satisfied that it met all his needs. Unlike the somber elegance of the *Reine*'s exterior of the dark and highly prized teakwood, the master cabin was richly appointed.

Although the room itself was small, the portholes were unusually large, lending spaciousness to the otherwise conservative quarters. The portholes were encased in shiny brass, which the cabin boy took special care to polish daily. They were covered in heavy velvet of hunter's green, and André drew them back only when they embarked on a voyage. He was something of a fanatic in his insistence on privacy.

His bunk was three-quarter in size, also covered in the dark green material. It too was well-utilized, having storage compartments below, and beneath them, a trundle type bed that pulled out at night for the cabin boy. Whereas many captains were rather elaborate in their decorations of the master cabin, André scoffed at these ship "boudoirs," preferring instead practical furnishings to extravagance. The only luxury in the room had been a gift—an Ottoman rug with colorful designs given to the captain by a grateful pasha. To André's surprise, the carpet that covered the dark waxed oak floor was becoming more beautiful with wear. It was difficult to understand how something that looked so delicate was actually very durable.

The walls that were panelled in the same stained oak had little ornamentation, with only the Dutch pewter hurricane lamps on either side of his bunk and portholes and navigational maps pinned on the wall above his desk. The desk was the only distraction in the room, and the captain did not allow anyone except Mauriac to touch it.

It was covered with more charts, the ship's logbook, and the records of all de Montfort's business transactions and commercial bookkeeping. A hidden drawer held the captain's money, as well as false identification papers essential to a profiteer in times of war. The desk was orderly inasmuch as André could find whatever he needed within seconds, but the books and strewn papers were a departure from the otherwise immaculate room.

After counting out the necessary English currency, André opened the small closet and took out appropriate apparel for the evening. He chose a white shirt of brocatelle with conservative ruffles at the throat and wrists, silk stockings of the same color, navy breeches, and a coat of burgundy-colored broadcloth with silver buttons. His polished black boots were low-heeled, unlike the high-heeled and thickly soled shoes made popular by Bonaparte.

He stood over six feet and three inches, and it was his opinion that added height was a disadvantage in business negotiations with men of lesser height. The captain's prices for his goods were quite high and the quality of his merchandise was superior and beyond question. But André de Montfort was young, remarkably good-looking, and wealthy. The men with whom he dealt were generally envious of him, if not openly wary, and he did not want to physically dominate them when a commercial transaction was at stake. He once commented to Mauriac that had he been blessed with shorter stature, he would have become far richer far more quickly.

After shaving and dressing, the man opened his trunk and removed a pistol. He did not anticipate using it, but he took the precaution that it might be needed. Although his English was fluent and bore no trace of a French accent, he sounded somewhat American in that language, and it was difficult to determine whether British sentiment was currently running stronger against the Americans or the French.

Besides, he considered, London was an unpredictable town at best. Only this summer, in the midst of Britons trying to adjust to the assassination of their prime minister, Spencer Perceval, had they learned of the formal declaration of war on them by the United States. One could never be too cautious.

He strapped on his gun and paused. Opening a small bottle, he slapped a few drops of bay rum on his face and neck. André personally despised the use of any male cosmetics, but he reasoned that his decision to go into the city was impromptu and had not allowed him time for the luxury of a bath. The trip from Nantes to London had taken less than two days, but he didn't want to chance offending his new business associates.

"Mauriac!" His voice was booming orders before he even reached the deck. Paul appeared immediately, and between the two men commands were delivered to have the deck swabbed at daybreak, crates of the choicest wines and silks opened on the deck for display, and an impressive noon meal to be readied for his expected return with several guests.

It was nearly eight o'clock when de Montfort hailed a hackney coach and directed it to the Silver Steed Inn on the Strand. Once inside the coach, André and Paul exchanged looks. The captain smiled at his friend and leaned back into the seat, stretching his long legs out to rest on the opposite seat. Paul Mauriac was looking a trifle uneasy. Clad in the dark sober colors of his Huguenot tradition, the blond-haired Frenchman was neatly attractive.

Mauriac struck the captain's boot in good humor and said, "Enough of your silent appraisals, André! What in God's holy name are we doing about London at this hour? Your sense of timing is commendable, I'll admit. But certainly you do not expect a rendezvous to materialize for you, without so much as a message sent this afternoon."

"I cannot be sure, of course. But in Amsterdam, Mr. Nagel had advised me that Phillip Thompson frequents the Silver Steed several evenings each week, and that many a contract is decided in that inn. Perhaps we will see him, and perhaps not. In the latter case, Paul, we shall find some other amusement away from the wharves with its stench and painted trollops."

Mauriac nodded his understanding. They had been in Nantes for almost a month before embarking on their current journey, and André lived a virtual celibate's life in his home port.

The captain's younger sister, Madame Françoise Loren, was actively engaged in the business of finding a suitable wife for her wanderlust brother. She now sought his betrothal to one Anne-Marie Dormaise, who, though beautiful, was rather dull and did not seriously appeal to the vigorous young man. To protect both his sister and the prospective fiancée from scandal, however, de Montfort spent his time at home mapping out further travels and enterprise, seeing Anne-Marie only socially when the situation demanded it.

It would do the younger man some good, thought Mauriac, to enjoy his stay in London before leaving on the arduous cross-Atlantic voyage to America. It was anticipated that *La Reine* would remain in London for at least four weeks; and by the time they set sail again, winter would be fast approaching on the North Atlantic.

Paul knew his captain well enough to realize without asking that they would charter a northern course for the sake of speed. Tempestuous weather might inhibit their voyage, but André would undoubtedly weigh the risks carefully and proceed north for the better currents and winds with hopes of gaining on them before they developed into the seasonal gales.

"What cargo will we sell here?" asked the first mate.

"Whatever they wish to buy. As much silk, wine, crystal, and perfumes as they can afford. This contact, Thompson, will broker the goods to local warehouses and only a few persons shall know that they come directly from France. By the time our merchandise reaches the shops it will be priced nearly as high as black market goods, but for our negotiations, a good profit will be made by both Thompson and myself." A fine mist was beginning to descend, and de Montfort was slightly annoyed that his visibility was impaired. He was anxious to see if London was as he remembered it. He silently mused that it sounded the same with the cobblestones clacking beneath the wheels of the carriage.

"And do we take on cargo here, as well?"

André turned away from the window. "I am hoping to take on at least four hundred tons before leaving. Thompson, if agreeable, will arrange our consignment of wool, linen, bone china, and perhaps furniture. As of this past summer, England is again at war with the United States. Exchange of trade is once more hampered, and we will be paid top dollar for British goods. In spite of their differences, the Americans are quite fond of the luxuries of their old mother country," he added.

As the lackey pulled up in front of the Silver Steed, a footman approached the vehicle and bowed. "Good evening, guv'nor. Sir," he said to the other passenger, opening the coach door.

Both men surveyed the two-storied brick establishment and nodded their mutual satisfaction that the place did indeed invite the company of gentlemen of means. The proprietor greeted them at the huge, oak double doors.

"Welcome, milords. Are you expected to join a party, or will a table for two accommodate you?"

The taller guest replied, "That all depends, good host. Is a gentleman by the name of Phillip Thompson here tonight?"

The owner smiled with satisfaction, as though he had anticipated the question. "Not yet, Captain. But I daresay he will arrive momentarily. If you would be so kind as to follow my wife, she will direct you to the conference area."

A short, pudgy woman bobbed into the anteroom. "Beatrice, show these men to the Chalice Room," and then added quietly, "That's a good girl, now." She sniffed in silent disapproval, and the visitors exchanged quizzical glances.

"This way, please," she mumbled and turned to leave without so much as a look over her shoulder. The proprietor, obviously embarrassed by his wife's behavior, excused himself and left.

André shrugged at his first mate, and the two followed the woman who was now on her way up a flight of stairs. They were far enough behind her retreating figure to quietly converse in French.

"André, your incredible luck never fails to amaze me! We *are* going to meet the broker our first night in London!"

"We had a better than fifty-fifty chance of meeting Thompson on any weeknight." The captain was pleased with this initial success too, despite his dry comment.

"How do you suppose the innkeeper knows you?" asked Paul.

"I don't believe he does. He didn't call me by name, you know. Simply 'Captain.' And it is not that difficult to guess that our sun and wind-burned faces have been at sea. Gentlemen of leisure usually look quite pallid in comparison. What I would like to learn is why that old battle-horse of a woman does not like us here!"

On the second floor and to the left of the stairs, she

waved them into a brightly lit room. The two men blinked to adjust to the sudden light, and turned to study the chamber. Directly in front of them was a long table with pitchers of water and decanters of amber-colored liquors. On the far left side was a fireplace with fresh logs crackling in a merry, chaotic fashion, and to their right were several pieces of heavy furniture placed about in casual disarray. Behind the sitting area was a bookshelf filled with leather-bound volumes of contemporary writings. The overall impression was one of masculine comfort.

There were three men seated here, and one rose swiftly, extending his hand to de Montfort, and smiling at Mauriac.

"Ah, wonderful! So glad you've arrived," he exclaimed. The man appeared to be in his early thirties, and his look of genuine pleasure at greeting the visitors made his otherwise homely face seem attractive.

André was about to introduce himself when the Englishman continued. "You are Captain de Montfort, I presume?"

"Yes. We have just arrived late today and chanced coming here straight away. I would like you to meet my friend, Paul Mauriac. Paul, this is Mr. Thompson." He inflected his voice somewhat, making it more a query than a statement of fact.

"Oh, no! Forgive me, my good man. My lack of manners is atrocious!" he expostulated. "I'm not Thompson. Hall is the name, Thomas Hall. Please call me Tom." His obvious enthusiasm was contagious, and a rare grin broke over André's face. Paul noticed with some amusement that the exuberant exchange had brought a halt to the seated men's conversation.

"Phil's late, as usual," Hall continued, leading the newcomers to the brandy decanter. "I am his partner. We've known for some time now that you were expected."

"Did Jens Nagel get word to you?" the captain asked. He accepted the glass Tom offered, and Paul declined, helping himself to water.

"Yes, two weeks ago we received his letter. You know, of course, that Amsterdam, while allied with Boney's empire, insists on her own trade relations. But it has been difficult. We haven't seen Jens for over three years now. Awfully good man, Jens. I'll be glad when this bloody mess is over and we can get back to normal commerce."

André raised his glass in agreement but stated, "I try to involve myself in politics as little as possible during these times."

Nothing could have been further from the truth, thought Paul. The captain was enmeshed in the politics of every country with which he dealt, and although he claimed allegiance to none, it was of paramount importance that he stay abreast of current events in all of them. His love of money, only superseded by his love of *La Reine,* depended upon it.

The extemporary host was now introducing the guests to the others. One, a Mr. Samuel Levitz, was a clothing manufacturer. He was about fifty years old, short but well-built, with a balding head. The other man was identified as Edward Byrd, thin, spectacled, and otherwise nondescript. The latter did not offer the visitors his reasons for being present.

Tom went to the mantel and returned with cigars for the Frenchmen. "They are the finest from Cuba," he explained. "But, of course, you lucky blokes have the world's best tobacco within reach." Before he could discourse further on the topic of tobaccos, his attention was drawn to the door.

A young girl, about eighteen, de Montfort guessed, had entered the room and was quietly spreading linen on the table. She had some difficulty in moving the pitchers and glasses onto the cloth so as not to spill them. When she finally had the simple task completed, she turned to make ready the service for six and struck her elbow on one of the decanters, knocking it precariously close to the edge. André tried to stifle a laugh, but the girl whirled around to glare at him indignantly.

"Careful," he said. "If you keep spinning about like that you'll get dizzy and knock yourself down!" He was smiling amicably but the maid mistook it for teasing.

"Thank you for your concern, milord," she quipped, "but these crystal jars are far more precious than my derrière!" She had not meant to be quite so brazen, but it was too late to retract the words. She blushed profusely, stammered an apology, and returned to setting the table.

André de Montfort was surprised by the fast retort, but remembering the cool reception given him by the proprietor's wife, he satisfied himself with the common belief that Englishwomen were known for their lack of warmth. Besides, he considered, the chit of a maid should have been flattered by his mild attention.

In her high-collared gray smock and starched white cap and apron, she looked rather drab. And what little he could see of her figure held questionable promise. She was tall for a woman, and slender. He liked that. But she was flat. Flat-busted, flat-hipped, and probably flat-minded, he thought ruefully. He could not see enough of her hair beneath the cap to determine its color. She was pretty enough, he supposed, but even the color of her eyes had not been discernible. She had been oddly squinting at him during her explosive reply, and what struck him as even more odd now was that he was giving the brash girl any thought at all. He suddenly felt tired, and decided he must need rest.

Paul Mauriac would not have agreed that what the captain needed was sleep. Always aware of the younger man's temperament, Paul had not missed the exchange with the serving girl. And it did not take much imagination for the first mate to realize that André's sudden pensive mood was a direct result of the brief encounter. He could see that he would have to allow more time in London for female companionship.

When the maid had gone, Tom leaned over toward de Montfort, and spoke in a low voice. "Don't mind the little twit, Captain. She's simply nervous. New one, and I'll warrant she won't last long."

"Why?" André was mildly curious.

"Well, we first saw her in the main dining area last week, and making a real mess of things, I might add. In any case, a couple of the chaps—myself included—found her charming in an innocent sort of way. We knew she'd be dismissed within a fortnight down there, so we persuaded old Dick to give her a try up here in the private chambers. We men are not so demanding, you know, as the public clientele. Besides, a bit of fresh fluff was a welcome relief after years with old Beatrice. Dick's wife is efficient, but hardly entertaining."

The young Frenchman might have disagreed that the girl in any way resembled "a bit of fresh fluff"; she was hardly that, he thought. But at least the broker's explanation of events last week might also explain the older woman's odd behavior upon his arrival. "Is that why she was so, ah, brusque this evening?" de Montfort asked. "She was hardly civil when she brought us up. I thought it was perhaps because she knew we were French."

Tom laughed appreciatively. "No, my friend. It's the girl. We've sort of retired the old lady, and she is furious with us and everyone else at the moment. I've heard she isn't even speaking to her husband. Poor Dick! Marriage has its drawbacks, especially to one like Beatrice." After a pause, the Englishman added, "Come to think of it, Dick may consider the break in conversation with his wife a blessing in disguise."

Now Paul could not suppress a laugh, and to see the usually sober first mate lose composure caused André to chuckle. Mr. Levitz, who had been immersed in serious conversation with Mr. Byrd, was not immune to the hilarity either, and laughed at Tom, who at this point was red-faced and nearly choking.

"What's all this nonsense, gentlemen? I thought we were about business tonight." The voice was not loud, but deep, and it arrested everyone's attention.

Tom Hall stood, wiping his eyes and smiling broadly. "Hullo, Phil! We were beginning to think you would disappoint us tonight. Captain de Montfort arrived today and he and his mate, Paul Mauriac, have joined us. Come meet!"

Both de Montfort and his first mate were fully recovered from the comedy now, and stood to greet the austere businessman. The captain spoke first.

"My pleasure, Mr. Thompson."

"Mine, sir," responded the broker, bowing stiffly.

"I feel most fortunate in meeting you our first night in. Should all our dealings be this expedient, I shall be able to set sail sooner than I expected," commented the captain. He hoped he had not sounded abrupt, but the sudden return from gaiety to prospective business had shifted him into being even more reserved than usual.

Thompson's face relaxed. The captain was young, but Jens had written he was also surprisingly mature—and particularly clever at his profession.

"I can assure you that your arrangements will be suitably expedient, Captain. But I insist that you enjoy the sights of London at your leisure. It isn't often that we are privileged with a visit from our neighbors across the channel, and I would consider it an honor to escort you through our old town."

"I am grateful, sir." A trace of a smile played about his lips when he added, "Should our association prove as profitable as I anticipate, we shall both have much to celebrate." The captain and Thompson were warming to one another now with the understanding that financial gain was uppermost in both men's minds.

The serving girl, accompanied by two tray-laden youths, entered bearing a platter of aromatic meat. The table was soon filled, and the gentlemen adjourned to eat. André, now seated and facing the fire, was relieved to see that the fare looked appetizing. The roasted lamb was served along with boiled potatoes smothered in butter and parsley, and a side dish of peas. Warm fresh breads, creamery butter, and a compote of fruits, cheeses, and nuts completed the menu.

The Frenchman disliked the typical English fare of meat pies, herring, chops, and the abominably heavy stews. He took pleasure in turning his now intense hunger toward the simple meal before him. He was only vaguely annoyed that the serving girl had disappeared soundlessly, and he had not yet seen her clearly.

His annoyance was short-lived, however, for she soon returned with a dessert tray of trifle, carefully placing the huge bowl next to the compote. She consciously avoided meeting the captain's perusal of her, but he was nonetheless able to study her features.

She had a high forehead and exquisitely arched brows. The girl kept her eyes lowered, but her nose, he noted, was pleasingly small and delicate. The fireglow made her oval face radiant; he was not positive, but her complexion appeared to be flawless. What few curls he could see looked red as she faced the hearth. "Probably an Irish lass," he privately mused, remembering her display of temper.

"Aren't you forgetting something, missy?" It was Tom who spoke, and his tone was mildly chiding.

"Milord?" she softly queried.

"Ale, my girl!" You have neglected to bring us the tankards of brew. What did you expect us to wash down our fine vittles with, gravy?"

"No, sir. My sincerest apologies—I forgot altogether!"
The maid was now not only embarrassed but completely
upset, as well. She gave a perfunctory curtsy and fled the
room to the immense amusement of the male party.

When she returned, her eyes were wide with fright as
she bore a heavy tray that supported a huge pitcher of ale
and six pewter tankards, the contents of which rattled
dangerously. The poor child was beside herself, and was
obviously ill-suited to her duties. However, as she proceeded to fill the mugs and pass them around, she regained
some semblance of composure.

She served Paul first, and continued in a complete
circle, reaching the captain last. Again her hands trembled,
but only the one guest noticed.

"Relax, my dear," he whispered. "I do not devour
young girls, you know." He reached toward her to pat
her arm reassuringly but before he could manage to touch
her, a full tankard of brew was jolted into his face.

"Why you little bitch!" he yelled, jumping to his feet.
"Mon Dieu, what a spastic little monkey you are!" André
was quite certain that the event was intentional after their
momentary argument some time earlier. He was enraged
at the chit's obvious effrontery.

Before she could express her contrition over the accident, de Montfort remarked in a threatening tone that he
had seen twelve-year-old cabin boys more capable than
she.

"Get out, you stupid wench," bellowed Thompson. "I
won't allow my guests to be treated so shamefully! Get
out, and by God, if you step foot in this room once more,
I'll have you in the streets tonight!"

The broker's outburst was so angered that André's own
irritation subsided. "I assure you I'm fine, Phil. Just let
the girl go without further ado so we can return to peaceful conversation." The young man could not resist casting
one more withering look at her, however, before she
quickly made to exit.

As luck would have it, though, it was not altogether
that simple. Beatrice had been eavesdropping at the time of
the incident, and flew into the room soundly slapping the
girl across the face. André winced when he heard the blow.

"Madame," the young girl stammered, "I swear to you
I meant no . . ."

"Never mind what you meant," Beatrice hissed. "Just go get some towels to sop up the mess you've made. I can promise you one thing, little high and mighty," she spat, "you won't again be permitted in this room or the dining hall either! If I can't have my way and be rid of you this night, you'll become a simple scullery maid!"

"Yes, madame. That would suit me fine, please," she responded weakly.

"Suit *you* fine?" The older woman was fairly shrieking at this moment. "You'll suit *me* fine, and none else, or I'll be done with you!"

"Yes, mum," the girl murmured, and she ran from the room before the others could see her tears.

By now André was angry again, but for different reasons. Paul raised his hand in an attempt to stem the inevitable outburst from his captain, but it was a futile gesture. Although de Montfort was usually most congenial when business demanded, his temper could at times outweigh all prudence. Paul grimaced over the expected manmade gale about to erupt.

"Mon Dieu, woman! Did you feel compelled to strike that girl?' he shouted, throwing his napkin on the table for emphasis. As he surveyed the stodgy Beatrice, standing with her feet spread and hands on her hips, André privately attempted to fathom his own irrational behavior. But her pugnacious stance now, and her cold arrogance at his arrival pushed him beyond sound judgment, and he strode across the room to stand before her.

"She deserved more than she got, your Excellency." There was a hint of sarcasm in her voice, but when she took note of the man's ill-concealed ire, she quickly added, "Me husband and me cannot afford the likes of her waitin' on gents like you. It could cost us our good reputation." She ended in a wail, thinking perhaps the brute in front of her was, in fact, the one who could destroy the Silver Steed's cosmopolitan business.

He spoke to her more quietly now, but not less menacingly. "Madame, I assure you that your good intentions have not gone unnoticed. But to preserve peace in this establishment, I suggest you do not dismiss the maid. I care not a farthing whether she's in the scullery, waiting table, or tethering horses outside! But," he added earnestly, "I cannot tolerate the girl being put out on my account.

I am certain now that you understand my good intentions, as well. Yes?" he asked quietly—too quietly.

Beatrice could not find her voice, but immediately nodded her understanding, and left.

Within seconds, the maid reappeared with towels, but stood silently in the doorway. She was evidently searching for the man who had first bid her to leave and warned her not to return. Again she seemed to be using that peculiar squint, and it piqued André for reasons he could not comprehend. "Damnedest little habit," he muttered, returning to his seat.

Tom spoke up first. "Well, come in, come in, you little minx. We haven't got all night!"

She quickly glided over toward André and he was surprised to note how graceful she could be without the burden of food-laden trays. She hesitated before him, her face blanched in fright. "Milord, I am truly most sorry," she whispered. Her sincerity was touching, and André smiled his acceptance of the apology. She pressed a towel to his chest, trying to absorb the noxious odor and wet spots. Although her hands shook, she was reasonably efficient with the task before her.

André was annoyed with himself when he realized her innocent ministrations were beginning to arouse him. She stopped abruptly when her eyes fell below the captain's waist. Much to her consternation, she could see that the ale had spilled on his trousers too. She paled.

"Here," he said gruffly. "I'll take care of the rest." The captain pulled the towel from her hands and dismissed her, saying, "Go downstairs now, lass, and do as you are bid. If you behave, perhaps you will succeed in finding some kind of reward for your efforts."

Without warning, he pressed a coin into the palm of her hand and closed her fingers over it.

"Milord, I cannot possibly . . ." she started, but was quickly interrupted.

"You can. And you will. Now be off, and steer clear of any further trouble!"

Her eyes widened in mute gratitude, she curtsied and quietly left the men's chamber. What had been the color of those eyes, he wondered? Damned stupid of him not to take notice while she was so close. But he reflected that her silent departure had once again been graceful, so contradictory to her clumsiness at serving.

The captain's thoughts were immediately squelched, however, and it was the senior broker who spoke up first. "Most gallant of you, Captain de Montfort," Thompson chided.

"Yes, indeed!" piped Tom Hall. "I was quite jealous that I had not taken the initiative to rescue the fair damsel. You can be quite the prince, eh?"

André was about to take issue with the gentlemen's interpretation of what had transpired, but he caught a smile on his first mate's face, and delivered a frosty glare.

"Well, gentlemen, we all know that Frenchmen are particularly sensitive as far as ladies are concerned. And it seems they needn't even *be* ladies," Richard Byrd drily commented. It was the first time he had addressed the group as a whole, and his remark made André shift uncomfortably.

"Enough of our humoring the good captain," commanded Thompson. "I'm sure our friend is anxious to return to his ship his first night in port, and we have yet to discuss the business before us and the cost of our venture."

"I am eager to get back to *La Reine*, sir," de Montfort agreed. It was an honest reply, for although he had hoped to find some amusement this night in one of London's exclusive brothels, his clothes were stained, and now he had no intention of arriving back at the docks in the light of day. He was not foppish, but he did not want his men to think he had spent a night in drunken revelry. Such behavior was not in his nature, and he discouraged his sailors similarly.

The gentlemen, having satisfied themselves with the supper, returned with cigars and brandy to the sitting area.

"I think all of you will be more than satisfied with the cargo my vessel carries. And although my enterprise is profitable, I am not a pirate. But you yourselves can judge me and the quality of my goods on the morrow.

"I have in mind inviting you to *La Reine de la Mer* for a personal inspection of her wares on board, and should you desire to question cost or quality, you may do so then. Do you find the arrangement suitable?"

All those present were subdued. The hour was growing late, and in spite of the confusion at the table, they had eaten and drunk heartily. There seemed to be an air of general acceptance of the captain's proposal, and Mr. Levitz, for one, was actually relieved at the postponement. Like the captain, he preferred being at his most alert, astute self where monies were involved.

Only Edward Byrd appeared mildly discontent. He mumbled something about having to cancel a previous engagement, but Thompson spoke over his muttered protest.

"Very amenable, I am sure, Captain. Quite fair!" With that, all the men nodded in agreement and arranged to meet on board at noon.

"After looking over the stock and testing the wine, I hope you will join me in a light repast. I cannot guarantee the meal will match this evening's fare, but my cook takes pride in his preparation and will enjoy the opportunity to demonstrate his culinary skill to someone other than his temperamental captain," André confessed. "In fact, I believe he has dreams of becoming a master chef!"

The Englishmen joined their French guests' laughter, for it was common knowledge that cooks never left a ship's galley to become notable on land.

Paul Mauriac gave the captain a meaningful look and they silently concurred it was best to leave on this congenial note.

André rose from his chair, and Paul and the two brokers quickly stood also. Mr. Levitz started to join them, but André strolled over to his seat and graciously bowed.

"Please don't rise, sir. I have enjoyed your pleasant company and shall look forward to our meeting tomorrow. I think you will be most pleased with the silks and brocatelle. Enjoy your smoke and drink at leisure. You have already been more than hospitable," he said sincerely. The clothier bade his good night and commented he was certain he would find the bolts of material to his liking.

Then de Montfort turned to Richard Byrd, who had made no attempt to either stand or give his farewell.

"I presume, sir, that you are the wine connoisseur," the French captain stated.

"Yes. I do hope I will find yours satisfactory."

"Moreso than you imagine," André answered, deciding

that Byrd's wine would be more costly than originally planned. Byrd would pay for his lack of deportment, and the captain would enjoy the wine master's gold much more than any social amenities the man might have offered.

It was all de Montfort could do to keep from whistling when he turned to leave.

Both Thompson and Hall insisted on seeing them to a hired cab. In the anteroom once again, the proprietor approached the captain. In the meanwhile, Paul Mauriac and Tom Hall, who had developed a mutual liking for one another during the meeting, went out in good cheer to summon a coach.

"Captain," the innkeeper began nervously, "I must apologize for my maid's clumsiness and my wife's display of emotion. Please overlook the squabblings of women, milord, and trust the Silver Steed will be honored should you visit us again!"

André could not resist chuckling. "I assure you, I never listen to women. They are a distraction beyond equal, and their bickering holds not the slightest interest for me." They walked slowly toward the door. "I find women valuable for one universal application, Dick, and only one. Else how could I sail the seas and take my heart with me?"

The three laughed and summarily agreed that the captain's was the only sensible attitude. Unfortunately, the well-meaning proprietor added as an afterthought, "The chit is in the kitchen now where I hope she can manage.' She's a flighty girl, that one. . . . And my wife, once again assigned the private parties, will be more bearable."

André was conscious of a returning sense of bemusement. Why should he give a damn, he wondered. Enough!

Phillip Thompson and the captain quietly confirmed their prearranged contract. The broker would be awarded a full tenth of de Montfort's profits. The fact that he had inflated the French market value before entering his figures on paper did not bother de Montfort in the least. He knew the broker would again plump the prices before bargaining with English buyers. It was a mutually satisfactory exchange.

Outside Tom was briefing Paul Mauriac on London's brothels and houses of questionable reputation. He quickly ticked off names and addresses of recommended "ladies," and the various current prices for such entertainment.

"You look as though you could use a bit of play, old boy!" he said. "I promise you that those I mentioned are top quality and quite discreet. After all, I am a happily married man!"

Mauriac laughingly made his thanks as the coach came to a halt before the inn. The captain, having thanked the brokers once more, ordered the driver to return them to the docks.

Paul gratefully sank back into the seat, happy that the evening was coming to a close. He was weary.

CHAPTER TWO

Tierney Chambers would be seventeen in December. She felt older than that, but so much had happened over the past few weeks that she supposed her childhood dreams had abruptly ended, leaving her no choice but to mature quickly.

But the girl, suddenly independent, unconsciously clung to many of those dreams, and her youthful body and spirit were still budding, not nearly fully bloomed. She was naïve enough, however, to consider herself a mature woman.

A month before, Tierney had discovered her grandmother still abed one lovely late summer morning. Surprised to awaken to the call of sparrows and finches instead of Nanna's gentle nudging, she had quietly slipped into the old woman's room, expecting her to be just barely snoring, as was her habit. The woman had worked unusually hard the day before because the vicar had expected important guests, so Tierney was actually relieved at first, thinking her grandmother needed the rest.

Much to Tierney's fright, she found Nanna lying quite still and silent. Too still!

The old woman had died in her sleep, and as the tears welled up in the young girl, she knew it was as it should have been. Nanna had died as quietly as she had lived, and as peacefully.

Tierney could not check the sobs, though, as she fell to her knees beside her grandmother's bed. She knelt there, clasping the lifeless hand, for a time that seemed a part of eternity itself. Finally, the girl drew her head up and heard, or thought she heard, her grandmother's voice: "All is well, child. It is good!"

The woman-child tossed her chestnut hair back and tremulously smiled. She could take consolation in the fact that her loving guardian had met death in dignity, and was now at rest. Forever.

The irony now was that Tierney felt she herself had been thrown into turmoil, and her dim prospects seemed to her young mind equally infinite in the span of time. Where would she go? There was nothing to hold her in Salisbury, for although the townspeople and parishioners were kind, no one needed the liability of a young woman on their hands, economically or morally. And Tierney had made for herself a reputation for being high-spirited, if not wild.

"Calm, child. You're too big now to go running through the fields and skipping barefoot in brooks," her grandmother would gently scold.

Tierney was tall, as her father had been. And her hair was the color of chestnuts, like his, with a few golden strands about the temples and neck to leave a trace of her mother's charm. The only features that were obviously her mother's were the fine eyebrows and luminous green eyes above the pert little nose. Otherwise, she was her father's child, and especially so in spirit. Tierney had always found it odd that Nanna, her paternal grandmother, had more reminded her of her dear mum with her genteel ways than of the woman's own son. She would not have mentioned this to Nanna, for if there had been one subject that could arouse her grandmother's ire, it was talk of the daughter-in-law she had never seen.

Sidney Chambers had been sent to Ireland as an officer in the Royal Brigade, to impose peace on what was commonly thought to be a wild and unruly group of subjects in the realm. Sidney, however, was enchanted by the spirit of the Irish, and it was here he met and fell in love with Kathleen Tierney, much to the opposition of his widowed mother in Salisbury. He took a permanent post in Belfast and enjoyed a wildly romantic marriage.

Tierney knew of at least one letter her grandmother had written to him. "My son," it read, "it is not so much her Irish blood that distresses me as it is her papist upbringing. No doubt she will insist on her children being reared in Roman doctrine, and it is this that weighs most heavily upon my heart." Nanna was a devout Anglican.

She was also correct in her prediction. Tierney was the only product of the union, and she was dutifully baptized a Catholic. Sidney Chambers' opinion was that religion was women's business, and not to be taken too seriously. Besides, he worshiped Kathleen and would have converted himself had she insisted.

Tierney's own religious preference was in doubt. She had been to confession and communion only once when the tragedy occurred. Some drunken Irish rebels had mistaken the Chambers' home for the magistrate's house, and set it afire late one night. Fortunately, one of the vandals had seen a child's face at a window and Tierney had been rescued immediately. The terrible error of mistaken identity was not discovered in time to save Sidney and Kathleen, however, and the child was orphaned.

The event was most dismal in terms of local politics as well. Chambers had been one of the very few Englishmen whom the Irish community had respected, and they themselves had been responsible for his unwarranted death.

It was then that Tierney was sent to England to meet her grandmother. It had been an immediate decision on the part of the magistrate, who declared Belfast too dangerous for the child. Her mother's parents, living in the south of Ireland, were not even notified of the calamity until after the child's departure, thus precluding them from claiming their grandchild.

So the eight-year-old little girl arrived at Salisbury much confused and grieving for her lost Mum and Dada. The child's grandmother had been overwhelmed with her own loss of her only son, and greeting the bewildered Tierney, she felt an enormous pity that within a very short time developed into love.

The child responded to the warmth and affection, and Nanna and Tierney became devoted to one another. It was often said that the girl and old woman had been one another's salvation, for the aging Mrs. Chambers had become quite embittered before the child had come to live there.

Widow Chambers had assumed the duties of housekeeper to the vicar shortly after her son's marriage. She did not need the pittance of income it brought—her deceased husband had been the town's most prominent barrister and had left her with a comfortable allowance. But learning of her son's papist state of matrimony had so distressed her that she felt it her duty to devote time to the

church. She hoped that in some small way, her personal
devotion might overcome her boy's straying.

Now before her was the task of saving Tierney. She
determined the child should be raised a proper Anglican,
and met with no argument. Tierney had inherited her
father's lackadaisical attitudes regarding spiritual doctrine,
but to accommodate her Nanna, she attended services with
apparent decorum. It was Tierney's private opinion that,
apart from Latin, there was very little to distinguish the
two ideologies.

But all that was behind her. Nanna was dead.

"Dear Reverend," she spoke sweetly, "I am honored by
your offer to permit me to assume my grandmother's post
here. Please do not think me ungrateful, but I must decline."

The vicar gave mild protest to her decision, but could
not completely cover his obvious relief. The girl was well-
meaning, he supposed, but far too impetuous to trust with
the care of a vicarage—to say nothing of his aging bachelorhood! He had to admit she was an enticing maid with
her devil-may-care love of life. She was comely enough
already, but he anticipated that she would likely develop
into a beauty in the not-too-distant future.

She interrupted the minister's thoughts, asking, "Would
a letter of introduction be too much to ask, sir? It would
be most valuable to me to have a reference in applying
for a post in London. I have assurances that there are
many such openings for working as a nursemaid or companion. But they would require some recommendation, or
proof of a respectable background. Especially since my
previous experience is limited," she mused aloud.

"Non-existent would be more honest," the vicar gently
admonished. "But I pray you will use good sense, my dear
girl. I cannot prevent your leaving us, and can only hope
you will be well received in London. Of course you can
have my letter of recommendation! It is the very least I
can do after your grandmother's many years of service.
You have enough money from her estate to travel there
and back again, should you encounter difficulty?" he inquired.

"Yes, Reverend," she lied. Actually she had only

enough to take the coach one way and find a week's lodgings. Tierney had meant to be practical, but her Nanna was so dear to her that she could not have foregone the extravagance of a fine burial and marble headstone. That had left only a few pounds and shillings to her name.

"Well, well," muttered the vicar. "It has to be, then. You are a strong-willed girl, Tierney Chambers. I can only hope that you will keep in touch, and let me know how you fare. You must remember, child, your grandmother's good teachings and my own warnings about your wild streak. You'll come back, hmm? If you find you have stepped in a bit over your head?" The girl nodded emphatically, so he sighed, "Come to my office, dear, and I'll prepare the letter."

They turned from the little garden that had been her private playground, and went into the rectory. As they walked across the polished floors and passed into the spotless study, Tierney was again poignantly aware of her loss. Never again would she see the neat little woman, and she instinctively knew that she would neither again see the orderly vicarage that had been Nanna's pride.

Never, Tierney reminded herself. If she failed to find a suitable position in the huge city, then she would simply die! Even if she were penniless and starving, she could see herself refusing to beg for bread. Despite her assumed maturity, the girl was still quite childishly imaginative.

"Here you go," he offered, passing the parchment to her. She quickly read it, her heart thumping with excitement. It would be a marvelous adventure going to London in her uninvited—but newfound—freedom!

Dear Sir or Madame,

Please know that you have my assurances that the person in possession of this letter, Tierney Chambers, is a loyal and honest acquaintance, worthy of your employ.

I have known the child for many years, and can vouch for Tierney's integrity. Orphaned at the age of eight, the child was reared by a paternal grandmother, Mrs. Charles Chambers, recently deceased. The older woman was my own faithful servant of fifteen years.

As God is my witness, Tierney Chambers, her grandchild, possesses the same qualities of good service.

In His Holy Name, I am
      The Right Reverend Matthew Richards,
      Vicar, St. James Church of England, Salisbury

The parson had not made mention of her temperamental nature, and Tierney impetuously flung her arms about his neck and kissed the top of his bald head. She thanked him profusely, and her tears were mingled with uncontrollable delight. She was free!

The old man removed his spectacles, wiped them of imaginary dust, and blew his nose. He certainly would miss the lively girl, he realized. Amid his own mixed emotions, he wished her God speed as she ran from the rectory, not waiting for him to escort her to the door.

The vicar slowly pushed himself out of the chair and directed his steps toward the church. It would take a papist miracle to keep the high-strung Tierney Chambers out of harm's way, once in London.

Tierney had not even settled in her lodgings or unpacked her trunk before setting out to find employment. She had arrived late the following afternoon, and after a light meal of tea and potatoes, fell into an exhausted sleep on a lumpy mattress in the Vestige Retreat for Young Women.

She awoke with a start, happily surveyed her drab surroundings, and went to the common toilet shared by the resident girls. After a cold bath with cheaply scented lye soap, she dressed for her first day out. She chose a high-collared watered-silk dress of dark green with leg-o-mutton sleeves. The dress was modern inasmuch as it fell smoothly over her slim hips, wide skirts having been out of fashion for some time now. But it was old, Tierney mused, examining, and the material at the elbows nearly threadbare.

Nanna had often scolded her for her unladylike posture as she read at the desk or knelt at church. Sometimes she would forget decorum altogether, and lazily prop her elbows at the dinner table. Alone now and remembering all of Nanna's instructions, she felt for a minute she might weep again.

Tossing her hair back, as was her custom, she immediately forgot her resolutions of propriety when she put a foot on the dresser to lace her half-boots.

Having laced both boots now, she unceremoniously propped a starched muslin bonnet on her head, grabbed her loose-string purse and skipped down the dark stairway. She carried only a few shillings in the bag, having carefully sewn the rest into the bodice of her dress.

Once on the street, she felt gloriously alive. The clacking of wheels, neighing of horses, and shouts of shopkeepers were a symphony of sound that thrilled her senses.

Some well-minded parishioners in Salisbury had tried to impress upon her the frightening events of noise and activity in a big city. But remembering the none-too-quiet Belfast, Tierney was struck with a rare moment of remembering her parents quite clearly. How lovely they had been, laughing and holding hands while strolling with their little girl. "Our pet," they had called her.

Shaking off her reminiscences, Tierney looked up and down the busy street. She determined that her first stop would be in a fashionable tavern where she could peruse the public notices and newspapers. Perhaps she would find an advertisement for a nursemaid her very first day!

She approached the first shopkeeper who was free of bickering clients and inquired as to where such a tavern might be located.

"Eee Gads!" he exploded. "It's another one of you, eh? You country birds are all alike. Come to London and like that," he exclaimed while snapping his fingers for emphasis, "and you expect to find bed and board for your cock-suredness!"

Tierney was not in the least dismayed by his outburst, and summarily dismissed him as she would a little bantam rooster.

Wishing he had been a bit milder in his address, he sighed audibly and called the slim girl back. "Here, now," he mumbled apologetically. "I'll give you directions, that I will, and wish you luck."

Memorizing his instructions, Tierney made her way across cobbled streets and crowded walks, happy at last to find herself in the Strand, weary but eager. The girl was resolutely optimistic, and after her two-hour trek, she was glad that the day was blessedly cool and, though dusty, her dress was not stained with perspiration.

She had some difficulty in finding the Silver Steed Inn itself. Tierney Chambers had not been blessed with good vision. It had never occurred to her that she was disadvantaged, and she innocently assumed that all God's children had trouble reading signs until they were almost on top of them. Had she known how many butterflies and blossoms she passed unwittingly, she would have been sorely distressed. The simple beauty of nature did not escape her, however blurred her interpretation might have been.

Once seated in the public dining hall she became aware of her intense hunger. Her funds were already limited, though, and she satisfied her need with tea and toast with honey. So as not to call attention to herself, she read the papers while slowly sipping her beverage and munching the toast.

Finally, after dallying for nearly an hour over her humble fare, she found what she sought. "Perfect!" she exclaimed aloud. She quickly counted the few pennies and hurried out, carelessly hailing a coach.

Once inside she whispered to herself the words she had read: "Reputable Lady to work as Charge in care of three small Children. References Required. Salary—Employer's discretion." She clutched her bag which held the vicar's precious letter. Oh, it would be so wonderful!

Her mental wanderings were short-lived, however, as the carriage halted before a three-story brick mansion that at first glance held Tierney fast in her seat. The short lawn was well-manicured with late blooming thrift escaping over the stone steps in calculated abandon. Too late the young woman realized that the home was within walking distance of the Strand, and she regretfully retrieved a shilling from her purse and bade the driver leave.

Remembering her grandmother's admonitions about her posture, Tierney threw back her shoulders, gave one habitual toss of her head, and ascended the steps. Her fingers trembled only slightly when she raised the brass knocker and sounded her arrival.

The door opened within seconds, and she was ushered into the foyer by a stiff, unsmiling butler. "Miss Chambers, Miss Tierney Chambers to see the lady of the house," she proclaimed a bit too loudly for the silent hallway.

He bowed his acknowledgment and left silently on the thickly carpeted floor. Tierney barely had time to take note of the wallpaper or painting above the settee when an older woman's voice addressed her.

"Miss Chambers?" The woman looked to be in her fifties, and in comparison, the butler now seemed jovial. She looked much too old to be the mother of three children, and Tierney belatedly noticed her starched uniform.

"Yes. I have come to inquire on the position advertised for a nursemaid."

"Charge," the woman corrected. "I fear you are much too young, miss. The mistress is looking for an experienced woman, preferably widowed."

"But, madame! I would like to have at least the favor of an audience with the mistress, and I do have a written recommendation." Her voice was strained, and Tierney blinked back the tears that threatened while she fumbled for the valuable paper.

The older woman softened a bit. "Recommendation or reference?" she asked quietly. Tierney could but look up from her fumbling in mute appeal. "Yes, yes. I see. A recommendation, and probably from your local pastor. I am sorry, young woman. Truly. But you see I have my instructions, and we do see at least a dozen young girls like yourself each week. I am merely the housekeeper, you understand, but my orders are firm."

Tierney imagined her chest would burst as she fled down the steps. What folly, she moaned. What absolute folly! And she had thought herself so ingenious at having obtained the vicar's letter. Clever, indeed.

In her walk back to the Strand, she took a more leisurely pace. She would not give in so easily, she vowed. Her spirits revived, she boldly stepped back into the Silver Steed, pretending she had left behind a book of sonnets. While the proprietor dutifully searched the public room, Tierney studied the notices posted on a bulletin board near the entrance. No, she would not give in! When the man returned to apologize at not having found the book, Tierney imperiously replied that she would return again until it was discovered.

The girl in the watered-silk dress did return—many times. She was quietly giving up to despair. It had been more than one week by this time, and each time she approached a prospective employer, she was met with the same bleak response. "It seems to me," she thought angrily, "that every post in London has either been filled or requires an ugly old maid to meet its needs!"

Old Dick, the owner, was not oblivious to the young girl's situation, and when it appeared that she had not eaten for days, his pity overtook his common sense and he offered her a position to wait on tables. She would earn two shillings each week, he said, and all the food she could eat on the premises. He had a soft heart, but not a soft head, and knew of many a servant who stole from the pantry to feed other hungry mouths.

Tierney gratefully accepted the job, too hungry now for one of her typical demonstrations of emotion. It was a good thing, too, for Dick Johnson already had some difficult explaining to do to his wife. It was Beatrice's immediate opinion that the wench was a good-for-nothing slut toying with the old man's sympathies.

If Beatrice was wrong in her prediction that Tierney was wanton, she was at least accurate in her estimation that the girl was good for nothing. Worthless, in any respect, to the Silver Steed Inn.

Waiting tables in the public room had been a dire mistake. She forgot what people ordered, tripped over her own feet, and generally speaking, botched the simplest task. When she stepped on Mrs. Kipling's foot and simultaneously overturned a tray—Beatrice swore it was deliberate—that was the final straw. Had Tom Hall and some other gents not been present and found the entire circus hilarious, Tierney would have been dismissed on the spot. But the gentlemen insisted she be given another opportunity, and Dick agreed to let her serve them upstairs. Beatrice gloomily predicted that that would be the end of their elite business.

She might have been right, had it been any other night. But the righteous Captain de Montfort had played the gallant officer, undoubtedly to impress his English hosts. Beatrice had been furious, but bowed to the client's wishes. The captain might never again step foot in the Silver Steed, but the brokers and their other guests were impor-

tant to their livelihood. Beatrice could be stubborn, but
matters of money always predisposed her to good judgment. Besides, her only concession had been in assigning
the clumsy chit to the scullery. Once there, it would be
only a matter of time before the girl proved her ineptness
in kitchen duties, also; she could then be given notice
without the gentlemen's knowledge. She would soon be
forgotten.

Tierney was not happy with waiting tables, to be sure.
But she was glad to have any income at all, and the meals
were an advantage to her paltry budget. When she had
been directed to serve the private parties upstairs, she
tried to improve in both the delivery of service and her
personal deportment.

But she would never forget the night she had been so
disastrously awkward. It had been an evening filled with
new experiences for her, and she had not been able to
overcome her unusual shyness. If the young man with
dark hair had not been present, if only he had not spoken
to her! So many factors contributed to the fiasco, and she
reasoned that without even one of them, her enormous
embarrassment might have been avoided.

But her saucy retort was due to his mocking manner,
which she could not endure in silence. At times she
thought that had been her ultimate mistake—talking back
to a person above her station in life. Nanna would have
told her that she had only received her "just desserts."
Unable to restrain herself, she knew before she turned to
look that it was the handsome one who had spoken. She
had to strain to see him clearly, and he was even more attractive than she had previously determined. She was inexplicably drawn to him and to hide her confused embarrassment, imprudently answered a quick retort. What
was it she had said? She could not remember anything
except making reference to her behind, and she blushed
now to merely remember it.

What had followed was even worse. She had intentionally delayed serving the ale to him, hoping to regain
her composure before coming to stand near him. But he
had spoken to her again, this time saying he might devour
her or some such nonsense; and what little grace she had
mustered fell away completely, and with it, the ale!

His shouts and the ensuing argument with Beatrice had

all but sent her flying. When she was ordered to return
and mop up the mess she had made, Tierney almost gave
notice of her leave on the spot. But despite her aggravated
nerves, she did owe the man an apology, and Nanna would
never have excused her had she not the courage to make
one.

While wiping his shirtfront, she experienced a sensation
so strange, so foreign to her, that she thought for one confused second she would faint. She tried to recall the details of the experience now. It began with the tingling
at the base of her spine that slowly crept upward toward
her neck, almost like fear, she reflected, except the feeling
was deliciously warm instead of cold.

Her work in the kitchen had been every bit as unsuccess-
ful as her duties in the dining halls, and her less than desirable career here ended within a fortnight. Much to old
Dick's chagrin, and his wife's delight, she had been unceremoniously let go without so much as severance pay.
Admittedly, they had let her keep the gray smock and
apron, but that had been only because Tierney had abused
the garments beyond repair; she had sloshed gravy all
over the apron and stained it permanently. Later, standing
on a stepstool to reach for a platter above the ovens, she
had unwittingly caught the hem of her dress aflame. The
uproar that followed was unprecedented in the Silver Steed
Inn, and it had been this final incident that prompted her
dismissal.

It had been two weeks now since Tierney had earned
a ha'penny, and her prospects for the future were glum.
It was clear to her now what her fate must be. She would
die of starvation, quietly and with grace, to join her beloved Nanna, Mum, and Dada in heaven. The image of
her winged spirit being greeted by the Heavenly Host and
her departed family consoled the girl, and she would de-
voutly pray to those above to give her courage during these
last days.

But she was awfully hungry, as any young girl of sixteen would be in such straits. Although she could not
bring herself to beg a meal, she did have the coin given
her by the man she still clearly remembered. There had
been many an occasion in which she had been tempted to
squander it, but she clung to it in romantic, girlish fashion.

Now that her impending death was at hand, she thought, it would be foolish not to enjoy what it might purchase. She scribbled a note to the management of the rooming house to the effect that she had no money with which to pay her last week's rent, but was leaving in its stead her trunk and all its contents. Tierney accurately believed this was more than ample recompense for her dreary accommodations.

Excited now, she quickly stuffed her most important belongings into her purse: the prized gold piece, her grandmother's brooch, and two miniatures of her parents. She paused momentarily to study the portraits. She had not seen them before her grandmother's demise. For reasons unknown, Nanna had never told her of the small paintings, but Tierney had found them, along with a long-ago letter from her father. He had written his mother that one Charles Robertson, an Irish miniaturist, had painted them, and he would like her to keep them as a fond remembrance.

The letter was dated 1792, before Tierney's birth. Nonetheless, the tiny oil images were exactly as she remembered her parents. She drew the purse closed and tucked the vicar's letter into her bodice.

Perhaps some kind soul would take note of it, and write to the reverend. She would be remembered, if only by the good people of his parish directing their prayers to her salvation. But, she told herself righteously, she would need no prayers. Her present circumstances were in her estimation more than adequate penance to gain her immediate entrance through the pearly gates!

She stood up proudly and walked into the sunshine. Tierney would not see the Vestige Retreat or her discarded possessions again.

CHAPTER THREE

October 31, 1812

André de Montfort was more than pleased with his success in London. His profits had been even greater than he had anticipated, for despite her wars, England was undergoing a period of prosperity, and the rather drab but popular architecture of the Georgian period was, in the captain's opinion, merely a façade against the ever-increasing opulence of the structures' interiors.

The added markup of his exported wines to Byrd had been rewarding to both his pockets and spirits, but that had been only a slight portion of his current financial status. Thompson and Hall had excelled as brokers for the cargo, and André reminded himself to post a note of thanks to Jens Nagel for the reference.

Even Mr. Levitz had proved quite profitable, for although the captain had made the silks as reasonable as he had promised, the astute clothier recognized the additional value of the various laces, cording and ornaments made popular by the Empress Josephine.

The real boon, however, had been in his negotiations to take on more than four hundred and seventy tons of English exports that would bring a marvelous profit to him in the United States. He mentally ticked off columns of figures, from francs to pounds to dollars. *Mon Dieu,* it was grand! Already he could anticipate his return to London. The American rice, cotton, and indigo would bring a price heretofore unknown.

There had been little difficulty with the logistics of French crewmen in London, as well. Commanding his men to remain near the wharves, the month had passed with few disruptions. Paul had reported a few noisy brawls, but fortunately, no arrests had been made. Fights were to be expected, especially where Pelier was involved. Although third in command on *La Reine,* Pelier was a temperamental brute and only his seafaring prowess kept him in de Montfort's employ.

All taken into account, André could be proud of his men. They had been satisfied with their limited shore-leave, and the pubs and the inevitable whores were the better for it. Only one aggravation was still unresolved, and under different circumstances, even this would have been minor.

The cabin boy had apparently jumped ship. In any event, he had disappeared, and they were scheduled to leave on the morrow with the first tide. The captain was only slightly perturbed that the boy was missing, for the crew had told him it was deliberate. The lad had relatives living here, and had been frightened at the prospect of sailing to America. The short trip from Nantes to London had been his first voyage, and he had not yet managed to get his sea legs. Therefore, André had given up the search and arranged for notice to be sent to his parents via Thompson to Nagel to home port.

The chances of taking on a new cabin boy were slim. There were political altercations involved. Persuading an English youth to work on *La Reine* was doubtful indeed. A French captain and vessel en route to America when Britain was at war with both were not likely to entice the wharf boys.

So the captain had resigned himself to doing without personal service until they reached Charleston, and ordered only a single notice posted on the dock beneath *La Reine*'s resting bow. Paul Mauriac was given the dubious honor of meeting applicants and determining one's hire, should any happen by.

Reflecting on his last week in London, André discarded the problem of cabin boys. The month had been such an enormous success that he had enjoyed the past several days at leisure, and Phil Thompson had proved himself to be a most amiable host.

They had been to the theaters, attended memorable parties that had been the scene of London's most beautiful ladies—whom André had successfully held at bay—and gambled unencumbered by women. The parties had held unexpected pleasure for the young man. His tall and muscular frame, dark hair, and brilliant blue eyes had not gone unnoticed, and the twenty-eight-year-old Frenchman was not immune to the inviting looks and comments that invariably accompanied his presence at the gatherings. Also, he was surprisingly good on the ballroom floors, and all this combined to create quite a stir among the ladies, young and old alike.

He had been particularly tempted to pursue the obvious advances of one striking girl by the name of Clarissa Townsley. But he had smoothly disengaged himself of her, gallantly swearing to her that he must uphold her honor. But in truth it was his long-standing code that a sailor must avoid serious relationships to avoid catastrophe on land. And involving oneself with a young woman of means always invited complications.

The self-imposed sacrifice had not been very trying, in any case. He found extreme satisfaction in a privately operated brothel, where the girls were dressed and scented expensively, and undressed in elegant, secluded rooms. Nancy, a voluptuous brunette, had been delightful; and the madame, Bernice Lewis, had given him many a good laugh over her unique interpretations of the politics of the day.

Thinking further on the matter, he decided his last night in London would be best spent with Nancy. It would be three, possibly four weeks before he got to Charleston.

Charleston was a most remarkable city. Unlike the other noisy American harbors, it was not sprawling with rat-laden docks. The city itself was clean and quiet, sparkling in the bright Carolina sunshine. Its people seemed even cleaner and more quiet. Reputation was paramount in this Southern town; and although it, too, had its share of harlots, André assumed the pious attitudes of his associates while there.

Slavery was the mark of a man's wealth in Charleston, but in André's considered opinion, this spoiled the beauty of the city. He consciously avoided the topic, however, during his visits there.

Yes, it would be a long time before he found sensual delights again. Commanding Paul to make the final preparations and check again to be sure the ropes would secure the hold, de Montfort set off for his last bantering with Mme. Lewis and bedding of Nancy.

*   *   *

Tierney Chambers had greatly enjoyed her feast the day before, which had consisted of ale (her first taste of the stuff), roast duck, rice, kidney pie, breads with jam, boiled custard, and a cherry tart. She was now sick, and again thought herself to be dying—not of starvation, but of the opposite!

The gold piece given her by her handsome prince—for that is how she thought of him, not knowing his name—had been worth more than she had imagined. It had paid for her over-enthusiastic appetite with much left to spare. Before feeling the effects of the meal, she had wandered through London, even hailing a carriage to take her in grand style over the bridge.

When within a few hours she did become ill, she paid in advance for one night's lodging in the closest hostel— a grim, dilapidated structure near the wharves. Besides the stench and crude room to which she had been assigned, the premises included a tavern below. The bawdy songs and oaths had kept her awake most of the night, and when she discovered that whores as well as sailors participated in the pub's activities, she became immediately inquisitive.

She perched at the one small window and squinted toward the streets below. She perceived very little in spite of her efforts. Twice she heard couples bickering over payments, and once she strained to see what she thought was a woman actually raising her skirts in the street! She attributed the latter episode to her own overactive imagination.

Her present nausea, however, was not imagined. She felt in dire need of a bath, a tonic, and some fresh air. Straightening her soiled dress, she angrily scolded herself. Besides being threadbare, it was now stained with the jam and gravy. "Good thing you're gone, Nanna," she thought, "else you would disown me!"

She quickly ran her fingers through her unkempt curls and took up her purse. Giving one light toss of her head, she airily stepped out of the ugly building into the crowded street. There was one pound and a few shillings left, so she went out in search of the tonic.

To her amazement, some prostitutes were hawking already. Tierney did not know the time, but remembering her hours of watch from that grimy window, it occurred

to her that she had overslept and it was probably after
noon. Now *that* was a career of sorts! She had never before
considered the obvious solution to her state of poverty;
and even now, the idea of selling her body struck her as
preposterous.

Just at that moment, a painted woman of buxom proportions laughed raucously and passed by Tierney, her
arm flung casually about a seaman's waist. Had the young
girl given any serious thought to embarking on this sullied
means of survival, her hopes had been instantly dashed.
Glancing down at her own sparse bosom, she sighed. That
would never do.

Trying to make some sense of it all and where to go
from here, she did not mind her steps and presently fell
over a barrel filled with pitch. She brushed her skirts, ran
her tongue over her bruised lip, and swore. "Jesus, Mary,
and Joseph, sure and I'm in a fine fix!"

The Irish brogue had completely deserted Tierney years
before except in moments of sheer exasperation, which
seemed to happen frequently of late. She stamped her foot
furiously, and squinted about her in an attempt to get her
bearings. To the left was a small sign posted, and she
walked toward it, carefully stepping over a pile of chain.

She was disappointed. It did not tell her where she was,
only the name of some ship. *La Reine de la Mer.* Latin,
perhaps? She read on: "Position available for cabin boy.
La Reine sets sail for the North American continent November 1, 1812. Experience preferred. Direct inquiries
to Paul Mauriac on board. Pier 24 beyond."

"Wouldn't you know that it says 'experience preferred'
for boys, but it's always 'required' for girls!" she said
angrily to no one but herself. She looked down at her
small chest again, and for the first time ever was delighted
with its size.

Why not? There had been escapades of stolen identity in
The Arabian Nights, her favorite reading. A fairy tale
come true!

She was growing more excited by the minute now, her
nausea completely forgotten as she tried to remember the
day's date. She was so eager as the plant took root, she became frenzied at the thought of losing the opportunity
altogether. October thirty-first. "Perfect!" she cried. All
Souls' Day, a sure sign her masquerade would succeed.

she thought; for although her speech had all but lost its lilt, vague Irish superstitions lingered.

She literally ran toward the street from which she had come, the details of her scheme whirling through her mind. She searched frantically for a shop which would carry the necessary costume. At last she found one and hurriedly explained to its manager that she needed boy's breeches, shirt, pullover, and cap.

"Why, missus?" he asked, curious.

"What's that?" she asked in return. She must think quickly for she had not considered any inquiries on her purchase.

". . . and breeches, for whom? And what size?" he ended. The wench was quite a spectacle tearing in here like that, thought the storekeeper. He was still irked that she had almost overturned his display counter.

"My brother, sir. He's about my size."

The man looked at her doubtfully and was about to ask why the boy had not come himself, when Tierney added, "He can't come, sir. Mum don't allow it." She signaled the man to lean down, and continued in a whisper.

"The lad's an idiot, sir. We kept 'im at home, away from the streets. Me da, now, he wants to put poor Lennie in Bedlam, but Mum won't have no part of it!" Tierney felt little remorse for the lie, for since she had no brother, mother, or father, she reasoned that little harm could come of it. She had sounded so convincing, in fact, that she could have wept for the unfortunate Lennie.

The owner, too, had taken pity and presently patted Tierney's hand. "Never you mind, missy," he mumbled sympathetically. "We'll fix the poor lad up just fine, we will!" He found all that she had ordered and only when she made to pay him did she realize that her disguise was not complete.

"Sir, I have forgotten what else I was sent for, thinking about me brother and all . . . Do you have a seaman's bag?"

The man once again looked suspiciously at her, but shrugged it off. What the girl wanted to buy was her affair; what was sold was his only concern. Nonetheless, Tierney babbled on about her father being a sailor whose duffel had been stolen on his last voyage.

The buying now complete, she hurried from the shop,

determined to accomplish the next step of her plan. Tierney expected some difficulty in returning to the hovel where she had spent the previous night, but decided that despite this, it was what she must do. "Please, sir," she said upon finding the rough-whiskered innkeeper, "I have left behind a book of sonnets. May I go back up to the room and search for it?"

The bleary-eyed owner muttered something about never having seen her before, but she looked harmless enough and he waved her his permission to go upstairs.

Once alone, Tierney flung her clothes off and donned the new clothes. To her dismay, she realized that it was inadequate. Her ladies' half-boots were far too conspicuous, although her black stockings might serve their purpose. Most distressing of all, her heretofore unnoticeable breasts poked out defiantly against the rough wool sweater.

Pushing her arms out of the pullover and leaving it bunched about her neck, the girl added the shirt and nervously buttoned it up. She shoved the shirttail into her breeches, and struggled back into the sweater. Even with the shirt underneath to give bulk to her torso, her true gender was evident.

Panic rising, she looked about the room for an answer to her dilemma. Quickly she grabbed the sheet and began ripping it into broad strips, fingers nimble with her excitement. After that task was completed, she doffed her clothes again and began wrapping the torn strips of sheet under her armpits and continued encircling her torso until the cloth reached her waist. She added more strips to the upper binding and, tucking them neatly in the folds, she presently stood up erect to accustom herself to the peculiar restriction. Her waist was sufficiently thickened by the material to completely diminish her slim hips and buttocks.

For a moment she was distracted, thinking herself a half-petrified mummy, and laughed appreciatively at the spectacle she must make. Her amusement quickly vanished, however, as she remembered that she had spent more than the allotted time for her disguise, and she hurriedly threw on the boy's clothes again. This time, with her prosthetically broadened chest appearing flat and the waistline widened, she realized with satisfaction that she had the figure of a youthful boy.

Tierney checked her purse, and with only a few coppers remaining, sadly admitted she would have to go barefoot. She shrugged with resolution, unceremoniously tossing the stockings into the duffel, along with the contents of her purse, and determined it was time to pay a visit to the docks in search of one Mr. Mauriac.

She used the cut drawstring from the purse to tie back her unruly hair. Although it was the current style for boys to wear their hair cropped short, Tierney believed it unnecessary to cut her own as she was anything but stylish, boy's garb or not.

She perched the beaked cap low over her forehead, shadowing her brow, and with a quick toss of her head, straightened her shoulders and left the room. She exited the inn by way of the back, and slipped around to the street unnoticed.

Her feet stung with the bite of cold cobblestone, and she proceeded to run in the direction of the wharves. Encumbered only by the nearly empty duffel, she felt enormously relieved to be running. She had not had an opportunity to do so since leaving Salisbury. A neighbor once remarked to her grandmother that Tierney was much too athletic for any decent girl, and her grandmother had replied that it did her old heart good to see the child enjoy herself so.

Presently, however, Tierney found herself short of breath. The binding was uncomfortably tight for exercise; and by the time she reached the pier, the girl was panting.

She located the same barrel of pitch, and pulling a heavy rope to it, sat down to rest. She rubbed her icy feet and pondered what she must do next. How were cabin boys supposed to behave? Tierney was unfamiliar with a sailor's mannerisms, per se, but she had often been accused of acting like a young jackanapes. That part of the ruse should not prove too difficult, she reflected. In fact, she would enjoy playing the role of a sex whose greater freedom she so envied.

Squinting up at the posted sign, she could not recognize the lettering. She leapt to her feet again to refresh her memory. Pier 24, the captain's name was Mauriac, and experience was preferred . . . Suddenly Tierney remembered the vicar's letter which she had inadvertently tossed in the duffel along with the miniatures and brooch. The letter which gave her true identity might prove her downfall if discovered. She quickly pulled it from the bag and scanned the paper, hating to discard it.

She read it, and read it again. It did not in unqualifying terms identify her as a girl. To Tierney's interpretation, it did indeed imply that she was female in describing "the older woman." That, in so many words, suggested that Tierney was "the younger" one, but it did not explicitly state so. The girl closed her eyes and clutched the letter to her breast. "Dear God," she silently prayed, "thank you!"

She walked down the pier, the letter again concealed in the seaman's bag. Tierney would not volunteer the letter, but should she yet meet with unforeseen misfortune, some-one might learn her true identity.

Mauriac was disturbed by the fact that the boy was bare-foot. More than this, he was suspicious in that the narrow feet bore no calluses. There was something amiss here, but he could not put his finger on it. The lad had toppled over himself on the boarding plank, and it had been Pelier's bellowing laughter that had brought the first mate up from his cabin to the deck. So it could be summarily assumed that the youth was awkward and without ex-perience.

Paul Mauriac was not in a position to be too discrim-inating, for before him was the only lad who had ventured to seek the position. Correcting the misnomer of "Captain Mauriac," Paul led the boy to his quarters.

"You speak only English?"

"Yes, sir," Tierney responded, trying to lower the pitch of her voice.

"You have never been at sea, I presume," said the first mate noting the new duffel.

"No, guv'nor." Tierney thought it might be to her ad-vantage to sound somewhat illiterate.

"What's your name, son?"

"Tierney Chambers," she replied honestly, grateful at last for her unusual name. It had always been a point of mild embarrassment before, especially here in England.

"Tierney, you say? Odd. How did you come by it?" Paul was beginning to feel uncomfortable, and suspected the boy was looking to escape London under an assumed name.

"My mother, sir. She gave me her maiden name to preserve my Irish heritage. Not a very likely name, to be sure." This was wonderful! she thought. She had not had to tell one lie, at least not yet.

"What is your age, Tierney?"

Lie number one, she told herself ruefully. "Fourteen, excellency!" using the last form of address in hopes that flattery might soon end the interrogation. She did not think that she could pass for an older boy, despite her height.

It did not stop the questions. Mauriac persisted, and Tierney eventually admitted that she had been born in Ireland, orphaned at an early age, and reared by her grandmother in Salisbury. She also had been obliged to say her shoes had been stolen.

When Paul inquired about her previous working experience, she was able to honestly report that she had waited tables in a London tavern. Then came the final blow.

"Do you have anything with which to identify yourself? Any papers, for instance, with the name Tierney Chambers on them?"

The young woman held her breath as she reached for the duffel. "Dear Lord," she thought, "don't let me fail now, when I am so close!"

"Yes, guv'nor. Here it is, please." She handed over the vicar's letter and thought wildly the end to her masquerade was at hand. He seemed to study the words for an eternity.

Paul Mauriac could find no justification for his gnawing indecision. The lad was not experienced in sailing by his own admission, but he had worked as a servant. Not much more could be expected the night before setting sail. The bare feet? The boy had explained this also. Paul's original idea that the boy was lying about his peculiar name was altered entirely by the letter. And here, a man of God was vouching for the boy's honesty and fealty.

As a final attempt to dispel his suspicions, Mauriac warned the boy that he was taking a grave chance by leaving his homeland when Britain was at war with both the vessel's native country and the ship's destination.

At this, Tierney had simply shrugged, stating, "My homeland is truly Ireland, milord. And since my grandmother passed away, there is naught to hold me here."

Paul Mauriac, it appeared, had nothing to fear. Tierney appeared honest enough, and a good-sized lad for fourteen. "Well, then," he said, after what seemed to Tierney an hour's silence, "I think you will do, son."

Tierney restrained herself from leaping up to hug the man. During the trying session, the first mate had won her admiration; despite her victory, though, she felt quite humble, and humility was an uncommon emotion for her. She had not failed!

Mr. Mauriac was such a solemn man. Tierney firmly committed herself to faithfully serving this symbol of strength. Captain de Montfort (such queer names!) was to be her master, Mauriac said. He himself had described himself as "merely the first mate." Well, Tierney decided, even if he was not the commander, she swore she would always be in this man's debt.

"Thank you, milord," she said quite simply. It was most difficult for a girl of Tierney's nature to restrain her tumultuous feelings. But she must, or all would be lost. "I won't disappoint you, sir, and that is a promise!"

"Good lad. I must warn you that it won't be easy. You're English. Our crew, for the most part, speak only French. You know nothing about sailing now, but soon you'll learn. And a virgin voyage is hard. The men won't go easy with you."

Tierney was startled with his comment. A virgin? He could not have recognized her sex, she thought nervously. Virgin voyage—it must refer to the ship's name. Perhaps *La Reine de la Mer* meant Virgin Mary, or whatever a boat named after the Holy Mother would be called. There were so many questions, but she dared not interrupt him.

". . . or they might try telling you to fetch them an item that does not even exist. But you should not take their tricks too seriously, Tierney. Every good sailor remembers his Davy Jones, as you Britons call it."

Who was Davy Jones, she frantically thought. "Oh, I must pay very close attention to what he says!" she considered nervously.

"Now, the captain is a different sort entirely. You'd best get to learn his temperament on your own. But I can tell you this: he never plays the fool! He speaks English to perfection, and whatever he says to you, he says in earnest. He will expect immediate response to his orders, and demands the utmost of every man on board.

"He will give you time to adjust to your new duties, lad, but be quick about them. He is not a tyrant. But he is no saint, either." He felt compelled to tell the guileless boy all that might win him acceptance with André. There would be ample time to detail the lad's duties tonight, but now, there were more immediate problems.

"You must have shoes," he stated abruptly.

"Sir, I have only a tuppence to my name. Might I use rags to bind my feet?" Why hadn't she saved the sheet remnants? Fool, she thought, now you must beg rags! "I promise you," she continued, "I won't complain."

"Nonsense! You haven't any idea of what you are asking. Wet cloth, freezing on the deck . . . You would lose your feet before we reached the first port. We must buy you basic provisions."

He held up his hand to stay any further argument.

"No favors, Tierney. It will be duly noted to the captain, and he will deduct the sum owed him from your wages. Now, come along," he commanded, standing. "We haven't time to dally. I will expect you to obey all orders from this point forward—without question!"

The shoes were marvelously comfortable. She felt overly clumsy in them at first, but soon concluded that boys' shoes were decidedly more comfortable and serviceable than ladies'. They were thickly soled boots laced tightly above her ankles, and her toes were warm as toast inside the woolen socks purchased along with them.

The first mate had jokingly suggested a razor, as well, saying a first voyage put whiskers on any man. But then he had tweaked Tierney's nose and gave her a slap on the back that almost sent her to the floor, and she knew he was chiding about the shave. In addition to the socks and leather shoes, the only other purchases had been a heavy woolen jacket and knitted cap that would pull down over her ears.

Sitting in the captain's berth for the first time now, Tierney peered about the cabin trying to discern its details. She had been admonished not to touch anything until the first mate returned from seeing to the crew. He promised he would then instruct her in her initial responsibilities.

Tierney was kneeling on the floor, tracing the intricate pattern of the carpet when she heard someone approaching.

The cabin door swung open.

"What's this?" a voice mocked. It was not Paul Mauriac's! She held her breath.

"Where in the hell did Paul find you?" he exclaimed, and proceeded to continue the assault in French.

Before she could even see him clearly, Tierney knew it was the gentleman from the Silver Steed. The deep resonant voice, the inflection of mockery . . . Then the terrible truth struck all her senses at once. The captain! Captain de Montfort, her master, was the very same man who had teased her at the inn, caused her those embarrassing sensations, pressed the coin into her hand that had eventually been spent to buy the very costume she now wore. Oh, God! she thought wildly, I must be going mad!

He was standing before her now, legs spread, and a look of genuine disgust on his face. "Get up," he demanded in English. "Were you praying, perhaps? A Moslem on all fours? Well, then, lad, face the East!"

Behind him a woman giggled. As Tierney scrambled to her feet, she felt utter dismay. Married! Tierney unaccountably feared she would start crying. It was all too confusing for her. This day of frenzied activity, her excitement at winning the new post, seeing *him*, and now . . . But she warned herself that discovery would endanger the nice Mr. Mauriac, and she knew that, if possible, the ruse must continue.

André had not meant to scare the boy. But he was in a sour mood at having capitulated to Nancy by bringing her on board their last night in port. He had not expected to meet with a cabin boy at this late hour, and now realizing how green the youth was, regretted that Paul had found one before Charleston.

The lad was obviously scared out of his wits, pale and trembling. Turning to Nancy, he offered his apologies for the outburst and ordered her to shut up, all in one breath. Nancy inclined her head in compliance, and greedily took in the furnishings while André dealt with the boy.

The captain turned to eye his new cabin boy. The lad was thin, but tall. "Looks a bit like me at his age," thought de Montfort.

"What's your name, boy?"

"Tierney Chambers, master," she said rather loudly.

"Captain," he corrected. "How old are you, Tierney?"

"Fourteen, sir. But I'll be fifteen soon, sir—Captain!"

"Ever sail before?" Tierney had no recourse but to answer him as she had Mauriac. No, she had never served on a ship. No, she did not understand French. Yes, she understood the word "expatriate." And so the questions went, quickly and with little opportunity for her to respond with further explanation.

"How did you bruise your lip, boy?" André finally asked, trying to conceal his amusement.

"I fell over a barrel, Captain."

The woman, Nancy, started giggling again, and even the captain now smiled. "Watch your step, lad, or you might stumble over the rail and meet your end in the deep!" he chuckled.

Tierney blushed deeply as she remembered her last retort to his chiding, and stammered a reply. "Yes, Captain. Quite right. I'll be more careful in the future."

Presently, Nancy silently approached the captain and boldly pressed her body against his back. Tierney was resentful, telling herself that wives were supposed to handle themselves with greater reticence, and especially before strangers. But to her complete amazement, the captain turned around and caressed the woman.

"Patience, my little vixen," he said smoothly. "You are the one who pouted to come here, and for your trouble you must wait while I attend to business."

Tierney felt physically ill. Her prince was no prince at all. Just a mere man, and a despicable one to boot! A part of one childish dream sharply cut itself away from her heart, and she wanted very much to be someone other than Tierney Chambers, in some other place and time. Before she could dwell on the possibilities further, Tierney was startled into reality with his sudden command.

"Tierney, some wine for the lady. And brandy for me."

Mauriac had shown her the galley after they had returned from shopping, and Tierney quickly made to exit. So far he had not recognized her from the Silver Steed

Inn, and Tierney was anxious to remain out of his sight until the tide. But before she could get through the door, the captain's bark arrested her.

"No! There—on my desk. The glasses are there also," he added more quietly. André reminded himself to go gently for the time being or he would find himself with two jumped-ship entries in his log.

"Didn't Mauriac brief you on your duties and show you the cabin?"

"No, Captain. The first mate was not expecting your return until morning. He said he would tell me tonight."

"Aye. I did tell him not to look for me until dawn," he remarked, soundly slapping Nancy on the buttocks and gesturing her toward the bunk.

Tierney was doing her utmost to prevent a mishap with the glasses. Finally, promising herself that she would carry the masquerade successfully until they reached America, she turned and walked slowly toward the woman who was busily unlacing her ribboned slippers.

"Put it there, love," said Nancy, jerking her head in the direction of the nightstand.

"Yes, milady." Tierney caught herself before the curtsy, and deferred a slight bow in its stead.

Then coming to the captain, she stiffly bowed again from the waist, in a more respectful manner. "Your brandy, Captain."

Taking the snifter, de Montfort nodded his thanks. "Thank you. You are dismissed," he said. "Find Mauriac and tell him I want a word with him." Looking to his bunk, he added, "And hurry. I haven't got all night!"

Tierney hurried from the room, dreading the news she must tell Mr. Mauriac. She had not been employed for half a day, and already she had been dismissed! "I am a dismal failure at it all," she thought woefully.

Stumbling up the ill-lit stairwell, she fought to control her fears. She could explain everything to the first mate; he would agree to return the duffel and her personal belongings, she would give back the shoes, and a barefoot boy would die in London before Christmas, his true identity undiscovered until it was too late. Perhaps it was best, after all. Tierney told herself that sailing under this captain might very well have been a fate worse than death;

and she had, only the day before, looked forward to meeting her departed loved ones.

By the time she reached the deck, Tierney had once more regained control of herself. Mauriac was there counting all hands. He turned when the cabin boy called.

"Sir, the captain wants to see you!"

As he passed her mumbling in French, she lightly tapped his shoulder and requested a word with him in private.

Mauriac shrugged with annoyance, but said, "Well, be quick about it, boy! The captain doesn't wait his word for that of a stripling."

"Yes, sir. So I understand. Already the captain has found me . . . er . . . incompetent, sir. I have been dismissed," she confessed.

"What?" he growled. The first mate was incredulous. André had never, to his knowledge, passed such quick judgment on anyone—man or child. In deference to the first mate's own initial doubt of the boy, Paul had finally considered him a sound prospect. And the captain at least owed him an explanation for the boy's sudden discharge.

"I've been let go, sir," reaffirmed Tierney. "Can't say as I blame him. I was slow to understand his orders. Don't worry, Mr. Mauriac. There'll be more ships in need of a boy like me. I might even join the Royal Navy." Tierney almost choked on the words. Such a nice man to be in the service of one so cruel! Had Mr. Mauriac been with the captain at the Silver Steed Inn that night? She couldn't remember. It was too late now, anyway, to really matter. It was all in the past. Like Mum and Dada and Nanna . . .

Paul paused a moment in disbelief. What on earth had Tierney done to antagonize his captain? he thought.

"Sir, I would ask one favor, if I may. I didn't think to bring my duffel. It has some important items in it, sir. Miniatures of my parents and the vicar's letter and . . ."

"Dear God," thought Mauriac, "the boy is going to cry!" Aloud he said, "Don't worry, son. I'll see to it." Slapping the cabin boy's shoulder, he told him to stay put and bounded down the steps toward the master's cabin. "See to it, indeed," he silently fumed.

Not awaiting André's answer to his knock, Paul threw

open the door. The captain was leisurely stretched across
the bunk beside the harlot, and jumped to his feet at the
abrupt intrusion.

"What is the meaning of this?" de Montfort roared.

Paul was in no mood for protocol. "I was about to ask
the same of you, *Capitaine!*"

The two men stood face to face, and continuing in
French, abandoned all thought of the woman in their
presence.

"Why have you dismissed the cabin boy?"

"Dismissed? I dismissed him for the night, you stupid
ass! I told him to send you to me—I want an account of
the men. What the hell is your problem, barging in here
like that, Paul? Sometimes I think I don't know you at
all! And you, you know me even less if you think I'd send
a lad like that flying without due cause."

The first mate momentarily relaxed; and then, realizing
his bizarre entrance, felt compelled to box Tierney's ears.

"Sorry, André. The lad misunderstood you, and I concluded that you doubted my judgment. Really, André, I
feel like a fool!"

"You look like one, as well," laughed the younger man
as he poured a brandy for Paul. It was unusual for the
first mate to indulge in hard liquor, but then, it was even
more unusual for the two to argue.

"Wherever did you find him, Paul?"

"He literally stumbled on board. I know he seems to be
a simpleton, André, but I think he will be suitable. The
poor lad did not even have on shoes when he came. An
orphan. His grandmother recently died. And he has a bit
of the Irish spirit in him. Cares not a *sou* whether he sets
eyes on England again." Paul debated whether or not he
should entrust the captain with his own reservations, and
decided it would be in the best interest of all concerned
for the master and servant to acquaint themselves.

To further her own ambitions, Nancy had been extremely patient during the foreign discourse. Presently,
however, she coughed in a demure manner, then yawned.
The first mate immediately took note of the none-too-
subtle signal, and changed the topic of discussion.

"All are present and accounted for, Captain," he said,
returning to English.

"Very good, Mr. Mauriac. Now please see to it that

our clumsy new crew member learns his duties. Since I am . . . preoccupied tonight," he added with a wink, "why don't you permit him to share your cabin and devote the rest of the night to the boy's instruction. I have dined already. I won't need his services till morning, at which time I'll expect a breakfast for two."

The captain's attention drawn once again to his wench, Paul took his leave and quietly closed the door. The couple's laughter followed him up the gangway where the cabin boy had waited as ordered.

Tierney did not dare ask why it had taken the first mate so long to return, nor did she ask why he had failed to bring the seabag. The blackguard had probably demanded she leave it behind for her incompetency. She defiantly thrust her chin forward. She would fight, if necessary, for the brooch and pictures.

"Tierney, follow me to my cabin. There has been a misunderstanding, and we shall see to it that it does not happen again. Captain de Montfort expects you to start your responsibilities in the morning, and we have only a few hours left for instruction and sleep."

Once again, Tierney Chambers felt herself hurled into a state of turmoil. Having accepted for the second time in twenty-four hours abandoning all hope for the future, she dully realized as she followed the first mate back down the stairs that she would indeed remain on board, and sail on the morrow.

She was speechless. Too much was happening to her, and much too quickly. She still felt weak at hearing his voice again. When would she grow up and stop her foolish fantasies?

Paul Mauriac lit two lamps in his room and decided it would be best not to humor the lad. He was already confused, and teasing him further would only upset him. Paul wanted to get directly to the point. He was exhausted.

"Tierney," he started in a low voice, "when the captain 'dismissed' you, he meant simply that your services would not be needed anymore tonight. Dismissed means you are to take your leave, temporarily, until called again. Do you understand, boy?"

"Yes, sir," she answered tonelessly. She understood perfectly. Mr. Mauriac had persuaded the captain to keep his cabin boy, and now she felt she was even more in this man's debt. How could she tell him the truth of it all— that she no longer wanted to sail—without risking his own position with the irritable captain?

"Now, we shall discuss what the captain expects of you."

Tierney listened as attentively as she could in her distressed mood, and learned that she would serve the captain his meals, clean and polish his cabin daily, follow his direct orders without delay or inquiry, and take orders from senior crew members in his absence. If she were quick to learn, she would be permitted to give a hand on deck, when needed, and the first mate promised increased wages would be commensurate with her ability.

Tierney mentally weighed the risks of her assuming another sex, and found difficulty asking those questions that must now be answered, ones that she had previously overlooked in her excitement. She had no choice but to ask now.

"Mr. Mauriac, where do I sleep and bathe?" She hoped she would have a private cabin, but thought that if she were to sleep in the common quarters, she still might avoid discovery. She would simply have to be very cautious. Bathing would be difficult unless she did not indulge herself at all. The girl hoped that how she might attend to her other personal needs would be made clear to her now, without having to pose such a delicate question verbatim.

"Bathe? Why, you won't wash at all before Charleston, except, of course, for minimal purposes." As Tierney happily accepted the first response, Mauriac shuddered at the youth's obvious ignorance. "And you sleep with the captain," he added nonchalantly.

Tierney's growing confidence faded altogether. She could only stammer her frustration. "But, but . . . Oh, how can that be? His wife! Surely she . . ."

"His wife!" bellowed Paul. "His wife? That scantily clad wench he has brought on board?" The first mate could no longer disguise his agitation, and presently indulged in what he considered a due chastising of the cabin boy.

"You nincompoop! André's a bachelor. That woman is a common slut, and I'll warrant he has paid well for her charms! No, lad. You still leap to conclusions without so much as minimal information." Paul continued his barrage, but eventually finding the amusement in the lad's mistake, started to laugh.

"And that reminds me. Your first duty tomorrow is to serve breakfast to the captain and his woman. Try to carry out that simple order without a commotion," he chided more gently now.

Whatever was the matter? he wondered. The boy was pale, and trembling as though he feared for his life. Could it be that the child had been abused since arriving in London? Many young boys did fall victim to lascivious seamen, too long without the comfort of women.

"There now, Tierney. If it is the captain you are worried about, you've nothing to fear. He isn't one of those who likes the looks of young boys! Not in the least, as you'll likely find out for yourself in the morning." The lad did not even appear to hear him, and Paul was furious with the thought that he had actually fallen victim to some scurvy sailor.

"You don't actually sleep *with* him, lad. Beneath him. Your berth pulls out from under his bunk, and there is where you sleep at night.

"André—rather, the captain, is well aware of the abuse some poor lads suffer at the hands of salty seamen, and for that reason and space conservation, you sleep in his cabin. It's for your own protection, son. I assure you."

Paul shrugged at the boy's lack of trust. He would find out for himself. "And speaking of sleep, Tierney, it's time you and I got a few hours' rest. I shall have too much to do tomorrow to check on how you are faring, but you'll need your shut-eye too." He tossed Tierney a blanket, and continued to talk.

"The floor here is no softer than the deck, but you will at least stay warm. You can have a hammock in common quarters if you so desire, but I don't recommend that," he added. "Have you any questions before I turn in?"

"No, sir," she said meekly. "That is, I am sure I will. But at the moment I cannot think clearly."

"Well, you are tired. And right you should be. A big day for a fourteen-year-old boy!" he said while turning down the lanterns.

In deference to the cabin boy's apparent encounter

with homosexual men, Paul removed only his coat and shoes and got into his bunk. He wanted to ask after the lad's comfort, but decided it was best to remain silent, and presently fell into snoring.

Tierney Chambers was miserable. She was physically exhausted, and the binding about her and the hard floor beneath lent little to her comfort. But her thoughts were far more disturbing than mere bodily distress.

Sleep with him! Mr. Mauriac's description of her lower berth did not detract in any measure from her genuine fear of such close physical contact with the captain. The girl could not decide whether his bachelorhood was a virtue or a vice, but in either case, the young man was certainly a scoundrel. Not so the first mate.

His rhythmic snores were solace. She had not heard a man in sleep since that last terrible night in Belfast. "Oh, Da!" she murmured sleepily, "what am I to do?" Her father did not answer, nor did any solution come to mind. Prayer seemed the one alternative always at her disposal, and for the first time in many years, she began silently reciting the rosary using her fingertips in lieu of beads. "Hail Mary," she repeated for the sixth time, "full of grace, the Lord is with thee. Blessed art thou, among women . . ." She slipped into a blissful sleep, void of dreams.

CHAPTER FOUR

The ship was gently rocking, with only the occasional muted bumps of her hull against the pier, when Tierney awakened with a start. It was still dark outside the porthole, but a low-burning lamp dimly lit the tiny cabin. Shadows played with the slight movement of the anchored vessel, and the girl reluctantly remembered where she was now, and why.

Yesterday, she now realized, had been sheer lunacy, and she was seized by the desire to escape. At first she looked frantically about the room for a pen and paper, but within minutes she knew that leaving a letter of gratitude or apology for Mr. Mauriac would be of little benefit to him. He was kind, but the most she would be able to offer him were her own silent blessings and fond memories.

It had been a long time since she had seen to her private needs, and presently she discovered she must find a solution to her problem. The first mate's cabin had a chamber pot, and although Mauriac still slept soundly, Tierney could not bring herself to make use of it in his presence.

Perhaps the urge could be delayed until she escaped the ship. Sighing at the now unavoidable loss of her miniatures and brooch, she crept toward the cabin door.

It creaked when she opened it, and the first mate's snores stopped. Tierney waited breathlessly, and finally he returned to the patterned heavy intake of breath. "God speed," she wished him silently, and closed the door behind her.

She squinted and looked past her shoulder to the captain's cabin. Silence! Cautiously making her way up the stairs, she approached the deck. To her right was the gangway and freedom.

Her quiet steps were brought to a sudden halt by someone yanking at her tied-back hair.

Before she could scream, her head was roughly pulled back against a man's chest and a hand was clamped over her mouth. Despite her mounting terror, she thought quickly and did not struggle. It would have been useless, she knew, and probably only resulted in the man inflicting more pain. But she could not control her quaking arms and legs.

Just as suddenly, he relinquished his grip and spun her around to face him. He was a bandy-legged muscular man, not too old, and no taller than Tierney herself. He was toothless. At first she thought it was his gums that prevented him from speaking clearly, but then she realized that he was addressing her in French.

"I am sorry, sir. But I don't understand a word you say. But, of course, you cannot understand me, either," she added helplessly.

She was trying to decide the best means of explaining to him her intended departure when she was startled by his next words.

"You bastard," he said without menace.

Tierney felt like striking him across the face, but thought better of it. "I most certainly am not!" she cried indignantly. "I am the new cabin boy. Cabin boy," she repeated slowly, hoping to educate the surly ape. "I work for the captain."

"Yes," he responded simply.

The situation was improving. He might understand her, after all, and she could convince him that she must be allowed to leave.

"I have the captain's permission to go on shore. He wants me to deliver a message for him," she lied cheerfully.

"No," was his only answer.

"But I must," she insisted.

"No."

Tierney began several other explanations for her exit, and after telling the sailor she was to suffer the captain's wrath; she was running away; and finally, that she was the king of England, it was obvious the brute understood nothing. As a last attempt to flee his persistent refusals, she turned to go back toward the cabin.

When she saw him turn also and walk toward the helm, Tierney sprinted back for the gangplank.

She was lifted in midair and flung onto the deck with a loud thud.

"No, you goddam son of a seawhoring monger!" he thundered in perfectly comprehensible English. Tierney slowly got up, and literally spat at him as she rubbed her bruised backside. "You horse!" she hissed. "I'm no boy to be tossed about like that. I am Tierney Chambers, daughter to Mr. and Mrs. Sidney Chambers!" She broke off her outburst before the tears spilled down her cheeks, and turned to leave what she considered an abominable man, beyond all reason.

In truth he was simply on watch and following his orders—no man could either board *La Reine* nor leave her without the captain's direct approval. He now shrugged, satisfied this feisty cub would be about his own business and go below.

That was precisely what Tierney intended to do. She could not escape, as her aching bottom reminded her, nor could she postpone attending to her bladder. Walking toward the aft, she espied a commode at the far end of the deck. Much to her relief, she found it cleaner than the one in her sordid room the last night on shore. Once she had made herself comfortable, she cautiously returned to Mr. Mauriac's cabin.

Dawn was stealing upon London when she stretched across the blanket again. It did not trouble her that the hour was so late, for she knew she would not return to sleep. Too much weighed on her mind. She hoped the forthcoming activity for their early departure might distract her from dwelling further on her dilemma.

She barely heard him approach before his fist pounded the door. "Mauriac!" he shouted as Tierney scrambled to open the door.

The first mate was up when de Montfort entered. They began talking, but the French exchange was lost to her. Finally the captain turned to look at her, as Paul Mauriac passed between them on his way out the door. They could hear the man second in command barking orders as he retreated toward the deck.

She felt a blush creeping toward her cheeks as he sur-

veyed her from her new boots to her dishevelled hair,
which she had forgotten to tie back again after her tussle
with the night watchman. The captain seemed altogether
displeased with her appearance, and she dropped her gaze
and stared at his own polished boots.

"Cut your hair," he said suddenly.

She looked up in surprise now, and met his stony glare
with silence.

"I do not tolerate slovenly habits in my men," he continued testily, "nor do my commands go unanswered."

"Yes, sir," she said, controlling her own temper. It was
difficult. Tierney wanted to tell him what she thought of
his questionable lady and sailors, as well as his unreason-
able demand that she should shear her last semblance of
femininity.

"Now take breakfast for two to my cabin. Tell Cook
to make it quickly. We haven't time to dawdle," he added
before following the first mate's steps toward the deck.

His swift exit did not leave her time for the perfunctory
"Yes, Captain" or "Aye-aye," so she stuck her tongue out
at his retreating back.

There were a very few rewards to her role as a boy:
one had been spitting at the guard before dawn, and the
most recent was her vulgarity just now. It would have sent
the gossips flying in Salisbury, but here, none would take
notice. She fairly skipped down to the galley.

Tierney tapped lightly on the cabin door, precariously
balancing the tray on one uplifted knee.

"Entrez," she heard him say, and paused before opening the door.

"It's the serving boy," Nancy said as Tierney bore in
the tray.

"Good lad. Put it there on my table and pour the lady
some tea. I take coffee. Always coffee," he instructed.

"Yes, Captain," she said, catching herself again before
she bobbed a curtsy. She nodded vaguely in his direction
instead. "Will there be anything else, sir?"

Before the captain had a chance to respond, the woman
interjected, "Yes, dearie. Your captain is in a foul mood
this morning, probably because he dreads our sad parting." Even Tierney did not miss the obvious sarcasm in
her voice. "Be a love, lad, and help me with my dress."

The captain was glowering, but had not yet given

Tierney her leave, so she did as she was bid and proceeded to hook the prostitute's costly gown. "Thank you, love," murmured Nancy as the last loop was fastened.

André de Montfort had taken his seat and was piling ample portions of baked eggs and sausages onto his plate. There was also a pastry that was unfamiliar to Tierney, but made her mouth water. Dragging her hungry eyes away from the feast, she now looked at André in mute appeal.

He took notice of her expression, and washing down some food with a huge draught of the steaming black coffee, winked at Tierney.

"All is fine here, lad. Go get some breakfast with the crew, and be back to clear this away in twenty minutes. I shall be escorting Miss, ah, Nancy to a hackney then, and I'll want the cabin orderly when I return. We sail in three-quarter an hour's time."

Tierney did not go to the galley for food. She was hungry, true, but not enough to confront the man with whom she had struggled a few hours earlier. The gaping seaman might call attention to her and threaten the temporary peace she felt.

A sixteen-year-old girl of Irish descent was leaving—Belfast, Salisbury, London—all that she had known. The adventure of it thrilled Tierney, in spite of her hazardous arrangement with this French captain, his ship, and his men. What had she to lose now? Her virtue? Not as long as she could continue the disguise; and now, in her second day as the other gender, no one had even suspected the ruse.

It would be grand, she thought. If it were less than that, less than her dreams, what had she lost? And if she gave up the fairy-tale adventure at this late hour, what had she gained?

When she returned at the appointed time, Captain de Montfort had gone. The room was in chaos.

The woman's teacup had evidently been flung across the room, and now lay shattered on the floor, its stain slowly spreading on the exquisite carpet. Nancy's eyes were kindled with anger, but all she said was, "Your fine master is hailing a coach!"

"Yes, mum." Tierney was in no mood to tangle with the fiery woman, and quietly began picking up the pieces of broken china. Her eyes averted from those of the harlot, she silently swore at the brazen woman. "Bloody bitch!" she fumed, trying to determine how best to remove the stain. Perhaps Cook had some mild soap or vinegar she might use.

"Listen, you little brat!" snapped the woman, tapping her stockinged toe toward the spilt tea. "You did that, if André asks! Do you understand me?"

"Quite, milady," drawled Tierney.

Nancy was so vexed she mistook the tone for sympathy and presently became demure. "I haven't much time, love. Be a good boy now, and help me lace my slippers."

She sat down on the bed and coyly raised her skirts as Tierney knelt to tie the ribbons. The younger girl was so furious she was red-faced, but the tart mistook this also.

"There now, don't be embarrassed, handsome!" she teased. "We don't bite, as you're sure to learn soon."

Tierney stood up to retort, but before she could manage the first word, Nancy took her hand and pressed it inside her bodice. "Feel how nice it is, my boy? If I had more time I promise you'd be delighted with your manhood."

Tierney pulled her hand away and struck the woman's face with all her strength, sending Nancy against the bunk's headboard.

"Why you bloody son of a bitch!" screamed the woman. "Fancy boy, are you? Well, I never would have guessed it of the captain!" she shrieked with a thin laugh. "André and you? What a friggin' joke!"

Tierney was almost as appalled with herself as the brazen brunette. Hitting her had been an impetuous mistake that would probably cost her more than her job.

Panic seized the young girl and she raced toward the door, Nancy's laughter and vulgar obscenities ringing in her ears. She collided with Paul Mauriac as she sped into the passageway.

The first mate caught her to keep her from toppling and gave her a puzzled look. When he heard the prostitute's now smothered giggles, he scowled. "Best get yourself on the dock, missus!" he called out to the woman. "Carriage is waiting and the captain's stewing. We're pulling anchor."

To Tierney, he said quietly, "When she clears out, laddie, get back in there and clean the cabin. Our captain is in bad enough humor, God knows. Don't you provoke him, as well. And don't mind the whore," he added, nodding toward the open door. "They're all born teasers."

When she was back alone in the cabin, Tierney pondered all the sexual implications she had heard in the past twenty-four hours. Tierney Chambers knew next to nothing about the ways of men and women, but the idea of men and boys was startling, indeed! She had not known such a liaison was even possible.

By the time she had the room orderly, she heard the captain approaching. She stood up her full height and faced the door, bracing herself for whatever consequences she must pay for striking de Montfort's woman.

"We're off!" he beamed as he threw open the door. "Come up on deck, and bid a proper farewell."

The girl was stunned by his obvious pleasure. The prostitute had evidently not mentioned the incident to him, she thought happily as she followed him back out into the morning mist.

They pulled away as the breeze ever so slowly tugged at the white canvas above. Tierney felt a sudden surge of joy, childlike in her wonder at beginning a new life. Watching the cityscape recede, however, she closed her eyes and fervently said a silent prayer for all the faceless waifs of London. She, at least, had escaped.

André de Montfort drew in a deep breath. In no time at all he would feel the invigorating salt air that was like a drug to him. The man could not long go without it.

Looking to the youngest crewman's face, he hoped to see the same sense of awe and admiration. André wanted a young protégé of his own, one he could mold in the same manner in which Paul Mauriac had once trained him.

What he saw was a look of humility about Tierney, and he was not altogether disappointed in that. The lad was already learning respect for the elements, he thought. He would look forward to seeing the cabin boy's first impression of the most treacherous mistress of all—the open sea.

His squinting! There was something vaguely disquieting about the boy's eyes, but André could not identify it.

CHAPTER FIVE

The week had been splendid, thought Tierney. If only her current bout with nausea would end, and the throbbing in her back might ease, she knew she could enjoy the brisk wind and the frisking of dolphins alongside *La Reine*'s starboard.

"Virgin Mary!" Captain de Montfort had laughed when Tierney had inquired on the ship's history. He had laughed so heartily that tears twinkled in the corners of his sun-lined eyes, and slapping the cabin boy's back in a jocular manner, he sat the lad down in the cabin late one night and proceeded with an hour-long discourse on the love of his life—*La Reine de la Mer*.

"Sea Queen, or Queen of the Sea, if you will," he had translated for Tierney. He told her of their many voyages, he and his fair ship, and his tone was almost reverent when he explained the vessel's fine points.

That evening and in conversations since, Tierney learned that *La Reine* was designed to carry fourteen hundred tons, and could sail at top speed four hundred miles—over six hundred kilometers, the captain explained—in a single day under optimum conditions! Part of her success was due to her three innovative masts that were slightly crooked toward the aft. "It sends her flying into the wind," he had said.

Tierney believed him. When they reached the Atlantic, Captain de Montfort had ordered all sails hoisted. The billowing white canvas (another innovation, he later told her—cotton canvas from the United States, much improved over the European flax sails) had seemed to the impressionable girl veritable wings that sent the ship skimming over the shimmering waters.

* * *

That night of *La Reine*'s glowing accounts, Tierney was able to learn more about her captain too. He was not a prince, certainly, but she reached a silent admiration for the young man. He was determined, forthright, and courageous. Not so respectable a person as Mr. Mauriac, she concluded, but he was not the scoundrel she imagined, either.

Tierney was performing most of her cabin duties in an exemplary fashion. The brass shone, the walls and polished floors gleamed, the captain's meals were delivered hot and efficiently and to date, she had managed to stay out of trouble.

She had even been able to remove the tea stain from the carpet, a simple task that had not gone unnoticed. The captain congratulated her for restoring its original beauty. "And a lesson for you, lad!" he grinned. "Never get too involved with a woman. They are cunning little creatures, Tierney, but you will find that all that soft flesh and frailty is simply a disguise for their cold and treacherous hearts. Make use of their vulnerable shells, but never tread on the iron core beneath!"

Tierney had not been able to find any response for his comment, so she asked instead, "Where did you come by this rug, sir?"

"An act of heroism, and one any imp your age would find greatly amusing!" de Montfort chuckled. "I'll tell you the story tonight, but I must see to our course right now. I'm afraid we are moving headlong into a broil."

Glancing at the porthole now, Tierney found it difficult to imagine that the current calm would become a thunderous storm soon. But she knew better than to disturb the captain further. He was at his desk, with a chart at his feet and another under his elbow, and peculiar gadgets resting above on the book-lean.

Tierney sighed as she cleared away the dishes and made her way toward the galley. Now her forehead joined her back in synchronized throbbing, and her stomach lurched when she entered the steaming kitchen. "Cook, Captain wants coffee," she managed. "Coffee."

He turned toward the cabin boy, muttering in French, so she repeated, "Coffee." She sank onto a stool while she waited, and bent forward to ease her back, mindlessly rubbing her scuffed boots with spit on a napkin.

The cook handed her another tray, clucked at her again in unintelligible words, and put his hand to her forehead. Shaking his head, he gestured her to go back to the cabin. Tierney shrugged, slipped off the stool, and left to the sound of his continued grumbling.

By the time she reached the captain's door, Tierney was dizzy. "Peculiar," she thought. "I was told if I had not been seasick within the first forty-eight hours, I could consider myself one of the lucky few." It was true that Tierney had not felt the nausea that accompanies a maiden voyage, and she had gained her sea legs the second night on board.

She loved the roll of the waves beneath her, and felt that *La Reine* was one enormous cradle under its sea-sprayed deck. "But just now," she mused irritably, "I could do with a bit of solid ground under my feet."

When she lifted her knee to balance the tray, as she casually did now when opening the latch, her abdomen and back wrenched simultaneously.

"Aagh!" she yelled as the door swung open. The captain retrieved the tray before it could drop, and led his cabin boy to a seat.

"Here now, lad. You're looking drawn as a mule!" The boy looked sick, and André for a moment worried about an ague starting among the crew. But despite the sickly pallor and beads of perspiration on his brow, Tierney did not feel feverish.

Her backache was becoming more severe, and she wondered if perhaps she had injured it the day before when Mr. Mauriac was showing her the rigging and allowing her to hoist one of the sails. It had taken more strength than she had ever needed, but she had been pleased at the first mate's compliment. "Well done," he had said. Not an overwhelming commendation, to be sure, but one that the young girl held important to her self-worth.

She winced at the sharp pain, and opened her eyes to see her captain holding a mug of steaming coffee beneath her nose. "Drink up, Tierney," he ordered.

She involuntarily wrinkled her nose with distaste. "Please, sir. If I put anything on my stomach right now, I'm sure to lose it!"

"It's a little late for this, boy," he lightly scolded. "Are you in pain?"

"No, Captain." Tierney had told so many lies in the past week that they slid off her tongue unaware now. "If I could only get this blasted binding off!" she swore to herself. "It's a bloody nuisance."

A lot of things had been a nuisance lately, she reflected angrily. Always having to make certain the captain would be away while she used his privy—emptying it, as well, before his return. No baths. Picking up *his* discarded clothes, carrying *his* meals, restlessly trying to sleep in *his* room beneath *him*, while *he* soundly slept and without the lull of Mr. Mauriac's snores. And on the few occasions when she had erred, being called a jackanapes by *him*.

"Damn them all, anyway!" she muttered.

"What's that?"

Captain de Montfort had returned to his desk and was already immersed in the charts again.

"Nothing, Captain. I was just saying I hope we can circumvent the damned squall!" She had given up her forced cockney accent the second day, and with all the French conversation about her, she surmised it had been of little consequence anyway. She took to blasphemy now instead, and was privately delighted with her liberal spicing of her own native tongue.

The captain did not notice this either, it seemed. "In fact," she pouted, "he takes little notice of anything but the skies and sails!"

It had been a week—eight days, to be precise—and not once had the captain looked at her with anything but indifference. Although she had every intention of remaining the puerile servant until America, it would have been most flattering to her feminine ego for the man who had pressed the coin into her hand at the Silver Steed to at least take the time to study her.

But she sadly realized that what to her had been an extraordinary experience, was an easily forgotten moment for him. She wanted to scream at him this very minute, hunched over his bloody papers!

The cry she issued sent a chill up André de Montfort's spine. He immediately rushed to the cabin boy, who was kneeling on the floor, back arched like a cat.

"Sorry, Captain," she managed weakly.

"What the devil's wrong?"

"It's my back. I guess I pulled it on the rigging yesterday. It will be all right in a minute."

"Tierney, you're obviously in a great deal of pain! Don't
lie to me! You need bed rest," he exclaimed as he pulled
her to her feet. "I'm going to pull out your berth now,
and I want you to get some sleep. Take off your clothes,"
he demanded.

Icy fear clutched at her innards now. "No, Captain. If
you order me to bed, I'll go. But I'm too cold to undress."
She could think of nothing else to say to him. Undress!
God, she prayed, I promise to quit blaspheming if You
will only protect me now!

"Nonsense, Tierney. I have some warm nightshirts in
my trunk. They will be too big to fit you, lad, but much
more comfortable than breeches and that infernal sweater
you wear."

Glancing toward the cabin boy's shock-stricken face,
André grimly smiled. He had been warned by Paul that
the boy had apparently fallen prey to some wayward
sailors and had an unnatural fear of men. "I admire
modesty in any young man," he told her quietly. "But be
reasonable, lad. You need one good night's rest, at least.
I've heard you toss and turn during the night, and if there
is one thing I do not need on this voyage, it is a consumptive crew member."

To her enormous relief, he turned to leave as he tossed
her a huge flannel nightshirt. "I'll be back shortly, and I'll
expect you to be in your bunk with the covers drawn!"
he gruffly announced.

Tierney made quick work of her change of clothes.
Trousers and socks aside, she pulled off the rough sweater
that she now secretly despised. She hesitated. As sorely
as she desired to remove the binding, she dared not. "Oh,
dear Lord! To have a soft chemise against my flesh
again. . . ."

Except for the boy's shoes which she still greatly admired, Tierney Chambers was thoroughly disgusted with
her costume. She wanted a chemise, above all else, and
pantaloons and skirts about her legs. She threw aside the
shirt with disdain, donning the nightshirt and long under-
wear the captain had provided.

The sleeves hung well past her fingertips, the hem lay
crumpled on the floor, and she had to roll up the under-

garment's legs and draw the string tightly to hold them above her hips. She giggled nervously, for in spite of her soreness, the feel of fresh, soft clothing was so welcome she felt nearly intoxicated with relief.

"I must look like a tent!" she mused gaily. The girl inhaled deeply against the material on her arm, and was pleased to discover it bore no scent of salt air. She slipped beneath the covers without further ado, and decided that had it not been for the blasted binding, she might never have been more comfortable. She closed her eyes with a grateful sigh, secure that her change of clothes had been a wonderful respite after all.

"That's a good lad, now," he said. "Sit up and drink a bit of this potion. It will settle your stomach, and kill the ache in your spine." Captain de Montfort was effortlessly pulling her up to the brown vial.

"What is it?" she asked suspiciously.

"Just an eastern remedy that cures what ails you. You are groaning in your sleep, and I think you should indulge in a taste of oblivion." Noticing the boy's hesitation, he added, "Unless, of course, you prefer a good draught of brandy!"

Tierney shook her head at the alternative, and accepted the tiny bottle. It was so bitter she thought it must be poison. "Captain," she sputtered, "I promise you that I'll be up and about my work at dawn."

The captain's amusement was not well-concealed. "We'll see, Tierney. Now you just lie back and relax. The stuff is foul-tasting, I'll admit, but you can be sure that you will be pleased with its results—and the sweetest dreams you've ever dreamt!"

The young man's smile was reassuring, and although she searched for a hint of malice, she found none. "Tell me about the carpet," she said abruptly.

"The hell you say!" he mocked. "I need my sleep too, boy. Now, turn in." But his tone was unconvincing, and she pressed him further.

"You promised me, sir. This afternoon. You said it was a tale of heroism any youth like me would admire. I'll probably fall to sleep soon, anyway. I'm already drowsy," she yawned.

"All right, you'll have your way this once. But listen

well, for I'll not tell you again. And I may drop off to sleep myself before you!" With that, he swung over her small berth and bounded into his own bed.

"Every commodity in this world has its price," he began, "and acts of courage are no exception. Always remember that, Tierney." He went on to explain that he had procured some exquisite silks and Italian tapestries for a wealthy Turk, and upon delivery, found the man beside himself with grief. The Turk's only daughter, Miruka, had been taken captive by Mediterranean pirates—a band of men long sought by martial forces in Greece.

"I was bound for Athens, anyway," he continued. "We had sailed in and out of several obscure Greek islands attempting to find their stronghold. At last we did, and returning to the inlet by night in a small dinghy with Paul . . . Mr. Mauriac," he corrected, "I entered the stucco fortress silently."

He described the elaborate treasure the thieves held stored, and Tierney envisioned sparkling gems and shining gold reflected in dim candlelight. The pain in her back had altogether disappeared, and she presently slipped into a state of semi-consciousness. She was hearing her father continue the tale from *The Arabian Nights* as she drifted off to sleep.

"She was beautiful beyond compare, lad," he said. "Her eyes were black as night, and soft as velvet. *Mon Dieu*, what a woman! Olive skin, an hourglass figure . . . as handsome as any I have ever laid eyes on," he murmured huskily.

"There was a battle, a vicious hand-to-hand assault on Paul and me that resulted in death and maiming. I killed several men myself. I had never before slain any man, and I have not again since. I pray to God I never do!" he growled. "Young boys think nothing of their war games, but I can tell you honestly that killing another man is rarely a proud deed."

He considered it best not to describe the gruesome details. "We don't talk about it, Tierney. And I will not have you make mention of it to him." The captain turned from the memories of the hideous fight, and proceeded to paint a picture of the joyous reunion of father and daughter. He told the cabin boy about the riches heaped upon them by the grateful pasha, explaining, "Paul refused even a token for his participation in the slaughter. I would have gladly received it all had it not been for his damned sensitivity!" Chuckling with the remembrance of his friend's disdain for reward, he added, "So I merely accepted this Ottoman carpet to keep from offending our generous Turk!"

André leaned over the side to peer down at the sleeping boy. He was growing fond of this English youth, he admitted reluctantly. The lad demonstrated spunk, and had not balked at the most menial of his duties. And André took inexplicable pride in his quickly attained seamanship. He was punctual, sturdy-legged, and not terribly clumsy for a boy of fourteen years.

An orphan. The young captain was genuinely moved by this Tierney Chambers, and wanted very much to represent to him the dependable and stable male character a lad raised by an old woman would need to face the vagaries of life.

The boy was sleeping soundly, but André found he was now restless. What if the cabin boy were seriously ill? Perhaps he could find a physician in Charleston . . .

André pulled himself from his bunk, and poured a brandy. Enough of this mite of a crewman! There must be a course that would eliminate the forthcoming gale that André sensed was nearly upon them. He lit the lantern above his desk, and once again studied the strewn charts.

Tierney was drifting on a sea of pleasant dreams. She had been captured by pirates who held her for ransom. A handsome young prince—no, she unconsciously altered, a handsome young captain—was rescuing her.

Safe in his arms, the dark-haired Adonis proclaimed her beauty. Her fair skin, her coppery brown hair frosted with gold, her tawny green eyes were the most exquisite in all the world! He would carry her to the far corners of the earth, never to be set adrift alone again.

But wait! she cried in her dreams. My father! I must say good-bye to him. I never even kissed him good night the night of the fire, she wept.

The sudden sobs brought André to his feet and back to the bed. He quickly turned up the lamp above the sleeping figure. The boy had evidently kicked away the blanket in his struggle with the dream, and André started to pull the covers back up about him when he stopped his hands in midair.

Blood! A stain was spreading on the sheet under his young friend. "Jesus God," he muttered. "The boy is injured!"

He reached down to probe the boy's back and felt the bandage. The child had obviously bound a wound to conceal it from everyone. "You stupid little monkey!" he exclaimed.

He was back at his desk in one swift stride, tearing through a drawer to search for the scissors. "Where the hell did he put them after cutting his hair?" the captain wondered furiously. Finding them at last, he returned to the cabin boy's side and began anxiously snipping the nightshirt and bandage up his middle.

Tierney was immensely relieved as the binding was finally being removed. Nanna had scolded her for dressing like a boy, but was now handing her a lovely cotton chemise. "Put it on, Tierney," she admonished. "And never, never again pretend to be something you are not. God made you a woman for a reason, though I cannot guess why with your foolhardy ways! And it is an effrontery to the Lord to doubt His judgment."

"I am sorry, Nanna. Please don't be angry. It was only a game . . ."

André was so confused he could only sputter oaths in every language known to him. Not a boy at all, but a girl! Nearly a woman!

How could he have been so easily duped? "And I'm worried about an orphaned boy who is bleeding to death!" He laughed mercilessly. "Just a little bitch in her time of month!"

He kicked at her hip with his bare foot, but none too gently. "Wake up!" he shouted. "You have some explaining to do, you little trollop!"

Why had Nanna told the vicar? She had never heard him yell so, and he was actually trying to push her down the stairs! She tripped, and began to tumble down the steps, striking her right side at the bottom.

"Get up, I say!" he roared.

Tierney opened her eyes and the nightmare continued. She had not meant to spill the ale! He would kill her for her carelessness. She struggled to sit up, and was roughly shoved to stand. Her knees shook. She must eat, she thought, and starve later. Where was the coin?

She felt the sensation of wetness as she regained consciousness. Must he shout so? "I can hear you," she said. "Please stop screaming at me."

André let go of her and permitted her to sink back onto her berth. He knew the effects of the opiate had not worn off yet, and mentally warned himself to control his anger. He was irrationally embittered as he realized a number of unrelated things . . . that Tierney's shorn hair was so raggedly cut, for instance.

"All right, you brazen idiot," he said menacingly. "We will attempt once again to conduct an appraisal for—for cabin boy!"

Tierney was slowly regaining a semblance of cohesive thoughts now. She was on *La Reine*. This was Captain de Montfort. And she had been rudely awakened by him. Something was terribly wrong, though.

"Dear God!" she cried aloud. "Where is my sheet?" Clutching the torn nightshirt across her bared breasts, she shuddered violently. He knew! He had seen her body, perhaps abused her body. She would certainly not be able to face him now.

Taking her hands from her flushed cheeks, she cast her eyes down on the bunk, and for an instant her heart stopped with the realization of her living hell. Eve's curse! The blood was real, her cramps were real, and the captain glaring down at her was most definitely real. "God, let me die," she begged in silence. "Sweet Jesus, Mary, and Joseph, grant me death!" She could no longer endure the agony of her embarrassment. Had she so fooled herself into playing the part that she could forget her sense of feminine decency? Never had any human being suffered such ignoble misery and humiliation, she was certain.

"I'm glad to see you finally recognize your state of wanton neglect, young woman!" he spat.

It was too much. The girl's throat was constricted and a dry sob wrenched from her heart. There was nothing to say, nothing to do. She absently pulled the blanket over the incriminating stain, and ran her tongue over her dry lips. Tierney could not even attempt an apology.

André was becoming more frustrated by the second. Never had he been forced into such a ridiculous confrontation, and he, too, was embarrassed, even if he re-

fused to admit it. Suddenly he threw the shorn binding
at her lap and said, "Here, sit on this . . . or whatever
the hell you're supposed to do with it!"

He went to his desk, and turned his back while she
noiselessly made the necessary adjustments. Pouring a
short glass for her and a liberal one for himself, he returned to his bed and sat down, bottle and glasses in
hand.

"Here," he said gruffly, handing her the glass. Tierney
could not yet raise her eyes to meet his, but accepted the
glass with a silent nod. It was like swallowing fire to the
miserable girl, but she enjoyed the scorching drink, telling
herself that this would just be the start of life-long penitence for her horrible carelessness.

André downed his snifter in one long draught, and threw
the empty glass across the room, shattering it against the
wall. Then he pulled out the stopper and presently began
pulling long, calculated swigs from the decanter.

Except for the muted sounds of the improbable pair
swallowing the cognac, the room was silent.

At length, Tierney began to weep, sniffing and sighing
at irregular intervals. André's nerves snapped.

"As I have said," he began in a nasty tone of voice, "we
will again pursue an investigation of sorts, and determine
the outcome from there." He paused for another sip.
"First, what is your name?"

"Tierney Chambers," she said tonelessly.

"Your true name," he demanded.

"Tierney Chambers, Captain. Tierney Maureen Chambers, given me by my parents. It says so on my baptismal
certificate."

"Have you that paper with you?"

"No, Captain."

"But Mauriac claimed you had identification!" he
threatened. "I'll have his skin for this, by God."

Tierney forced herself to stay calm and remain alert.
Dear Mr. Mauriac must not suffer for her treachery! "I
do have identification, sir," she interjected into his tirade
of French rumbling. "A letter from my home parish in
Salisbury. The vicar was kind enough to provide a reference for me in London. Mr. Mauriac was deceived by
that letter, and I pray God he will forgive me—" she broke
off emotionally.

"Let me see the paper!" he ordered, ignoring her penitent tone.

"My duffel, sir. It's in the bottom of your closet," she said hopefully. She could not rise, else he would witness again the stain on his very own nightshirt!

André perceived the extended awkwardness of their ludicrous position, but told himself he cared not a whit for the girl's embarrassment. Nonetheless, he begrudgingly went to the closet and delivered to her the small bag.

"Thank you," she murmured without looking up. Opening the duffel, she espied the token symbols of her deceased family and wept anew. "Oh, they would never forgive me," she groaned inwardly. "It is I, and not poor Lennie, who belongs in an asylum for the feeble-minded."

She handed the letter to de Montfort, who irritably took another draught of brandy before studying the parchment. "Why the hell did he fail to mention you were a girl!" he expostulated.

"I suppose, sir, it never occurred to him that a person might assume I was anything else," she ventured with a shrug.

"And that's a wonder in itself," he taunted, "with your meager proportions. It's preposterous that you bothered with that damned sheet—you've little enough to disguise there!"

Tierney was immune to his cruelty, but his tone was frightening, so she put her hands over her ears to block the vehemence behind his words.

He flung himself across his bunk and smacked her hands back into her lap. "You'll hear every word I am about to say, or so help me God, I'll throw you into the deep!" he barked. "Mark me well, Tierney, for never have I been so tempted to strangle a woman." His voice was hoarse with restrained fury. "I'll have my day with the first mate for ever falling for your ruse, but for the time being, you will remain a boy. I'll not have my men laughing behind my back for this tomfoolery!"

He lowered his voice, but each word clipped off his tongue like grapeshot. "You will remain Tierney Chambers, cabin boy, until we reach Charleston harbor. There, it will be my greatest pleasure to dump you on the docks to fare as you will, male or female!" He looked meaningfully at her slight bosom and laughed.

"What a little ass you are! How old are you truly?"

"Sixteen, Captain. Seventeen this Christmas, St. Stephen's Day, to be exact."

"But you are orphaned, as the letter states?" he asked with feigned indifference.

"Yes, sir. My parents died in a fire," she answered in a whisper.

He got up abruptly and threw on his trousers, boots, and jacket. "Then I'd advise you to keep up your little game until we lay to port, else you'll be prematurely joining your parents and the late vicar's housemaid from a watery grave."

Unlatching the door, he turned to glare at the girl. "Your first order, cabin *maid*," he spat, "is to get rid of those soiled linens. Burn them, bleach them, drown them. I don't give a tinker's damn! But have this room spotless by the time I return. And one more thing, Tierney," he added. "Don't replace that goddamned corset. You'll injure what little God gave you!" With that he slammed the door shut, and took the steps four at a time to the deck.

The big sailor, Pelier, approached him immediately, asking if something had gone awry.

André glanced at the clear skies and brilliant winter stars, shaking his head. "No, my man. I just wanted a breath of cold air."

Pelier remained in front of his captain, apparently eager for conversation. "Back to your station, man," ordered de Montfort. "I wish to think in peace."

Tierney gathered up the sheets, and piled them in a corner. Next she whisked off the captain's longjohns and flannel shirt, momentarily regretting the loss of their comfort. "Jesus, Mary, and Joseph!" she swore. "I cannot imagine why I am beset by woman's curse at a time like this!"

Her determined spirit would not dwell too long on her woeful predicament, however; and presently she squirmed back into the boy's clothing to which she had accustomed herself.

Dragging the soiled bedclothes to the porthole, she struggled to unlatch the brass lock. Her head was throbbing, but she pushed aside such a minor inconvenience now. He might return any minute, and the room must be put to order.

His return! "How on earth can I face him?" she asked her dim reflection in the glass. She discarded this worry also, confident that an answer would make itself known to her. She finally undid the latch and vehemently flung the clothes away.

She tidied his bed, searched the bunk drawers for more clean linen, found some, and remade her own small berth, sliding it closed with a decided kick of her boot.

The captain did not return.

She proceeded to pick up the broken glass, the disorderly but treasured charts, and then straighten his desk. She returned the treasonous scissors to its drawer, and set the smaller glass and near-empty decanter back in place.

Still, he did not come back.

Dawn was breaking when he finally did return, chilled to the bone. In his swift escape from the cabin, the captain had neglected to take his cap or gloves and now his fingers and ears were numb from the North Atlantic's cold winds.

"Coffee!" he boomed, "and a hot breakfast right away."

Tierney had startled when the door was thrown ajar, but at his sharp command she jumped to her feet and ran toward the galley. She had not been given a chance to evaluate their first crucial encounter after discovery, but remembered that she must have looked directly at him. He had been scowling at her, while stamping his feet and rubbing his hands.

When she returned with the steaming tray, André was changing from his fog-dampened garments into warmer ones. Tierney turned her back to him in consideration, but was rewarded with more accusations.

"No need to feign modesty now, Tierney. That's all over, remember? You have lived with me for over a week now, and though I've respected your precious privacy, you left me little room for my own!"

It was true. At first, Tierney had felt compelled to leave the cabin when the man was dressing, but finding little opportunity for excuses, had soon settled herself into viewing his various states of dress and undress as natural. In fact, when the captain's own back was turned, Tierney

had often caught herself squinting across the room at him
in mindless curiosity. Unfortunately for her, her weak
eyes had betrayed very little.

It would be different from this point on, she thought
nervously. He could stare at her now, with little chance
of seeing what he hadn't already viewed. Tierney could
not squelch the indignant blush that reddened her cheeks.

He ate in silence, and Tierney paced the floor back
and forth, next to the bunk and then along its footboard,
then back again in a monotonous L-shaped pattern. She
chewed her lip, which had only recently returned to its
normal size after her bump with the barrel of pitch.
"What to do, what to do?" she drummed mentally to the
rhythm of her steps.

"Sit down, for God's sake!" he broke.

Obediently, she dropped into a chair opposite him and
was surprised to find some of her dignity restored. Her
chin held high, she steadily met his gaze now, remaining
silent until called upon to speak.

André studied her intently and was vaguely discom-
forted by the chit's outward composure. She had no right
to feel settled, when his own nerves still flickered with the
absurdity of his position. He looked her up and down,
and remembering the lurch he had felt when cutting apart
the binding last night, his eyes burned through the rough
woolen sweater she now wore.

Tierney could not visibly discern where her captain's
eyes wandered, but she sensed the intimacy of his perusal.
Much to her distress, her young nipples responded to the
uninvited study and presently made themselves defiantly
evident under his unabashed stare. She was immediately
made confused again, and squirmed on the bulky strip
of sheet tucked between her legs.

He laughed. "Well, I'll be damned," he said softly.
"The makeshift corset did have its purpose!"

"Milord, please!" she begged. "Do not torment me so.
I would gladly offer my most humble contrition for this
foolishness if it would but help."

"Well, it would not help, now, would it?" he agreed
drily. "But some discussion of this 'comedy of errors'
might prove useful. Did you know me before boarding
La Reine?" he demanded suddenly.

"No, Captain," she said simply. And as if to verify his

growing suspicion, she added, "Milord, I did not know you were the captain!"

"Then you did know me! I thought there was something familiar about you. How do you know me? Where?" When she hesitated to answer, he slammed the table. "Speak up, damn you!"

"Damn you, too, you ill-mannered brute!" she shot back without pause, no longer able to tolerate his disposition in silence. But she regretted her sharp response as soon as the words fell upon her own ears. "Captain, I'm sorry," she whispered. How could she be so irresponsible when the man before her held her very life in his hands?

The captain barely heard the stammered apology, so engrossed in thought was he. Where had he heard that fast retort before? Her sudden vehemence reminded him of something . . .

That was it! The stupid little serving girl who had splashed ale on him. How could he have overlooked the obvious? The nagging annoyance of that habitual squint, the arched brows, the chestnut hair . . . What a fool he had been!

Her eyes were wide with fright now as she felt the glowering temper in him build. "You are that sorry little maid from the Silver Steed Inn, aren't you." It was not a question—his voice was flat, expressionless. Only his eyes betrayed any emotion, and Tierney's faulty sight prevented her the advantage of knowing what he might next say or do.

"Yes, milord," she barely admitted.

So green were her eyes, he mused thoughtfully. The color of mandarin jade. And not red, really; the girl's hair was autumn brown. It had merely seemed red in the fireglow, he recalled. "What incredible fate," he thought, "that I should have worried over a slip of a girl waiting tables, who then became my cabin boy, and who now is the albatross about my neck!" He suddenly laughed aloud.

Tierney Chambers failed to share his amusement, however, and began to drum her fingers on the table between them. She wondered why he refused to divulge his thoughts to her. There was little to be gained from being secretive now.

She might have been pretty, he thought. He tried to picture her with long soft curls and shoulders bared, a

touch of perfume at her ears and throat, and a sparkling
diminutive jewel on her little finger. He stopped himself
there, and saw with disgust her calloused, chafed hands.
"Well, enough," he thought. "She managed to get this far
on her own. The tart will have to pull someone else's
strings once we reach the Carolinas."

He stood abruptly and reached for his gloves and coat.
"Finish making my bed. We have rough weather ahead,
and I'll be lucky to be down for supper tonight."

"Can I give a hand on deck, sir?" she cautiously volunteered.

"You'll get in my way!" he barked. Tierney wanted to
remind him that while he thought his cabin boy was a
male youth, he had never indicated she had been anything
but useful. Thinking further on it, she decided to remain
silent.

"Unless I call for you, remain below. You might try
catching a catnap yourself," he added brusquely. He felt
a fleeting twinge of guilt for her ordeal the night before,
and the lass did look ghostly pale.

Alone in the cabin, Tierney returned to her pacing to
and fro. Finally with determination, she sat again at the
table and nibbled at the captain's barely touched plate.
She shuddered at the cold coffee, but forced herself to
drink the brew, thinking it might settle her nerves as tea
would.

She was hungrier than she would have believed possible,
and soon finished the entire meal. Tierney had not felt
secure enough this dreadful morning to take her customary
meal along with the captain, and now wished she had.

She hurriedly gathered up the plates, mug, and silver and
took them down to Cook. Upon her return, she precisely
tucked in the captain's blankets and spread the beautiful
green velvet coverlet over it. Routinely polishing brass
and hanging his strewn clothes before the coal-burning
pipe heater, she presently found her hands idle.

Absently she browsed through the captain's desk for a
book she might read. Most of them were French, but
eventually she found a small leather-bound volume in
English print. It was a collection of modern English poetry, and most of them were unfamiliar to her. But the
captain did not seem poetic in nature, so she thumbed

through the first few pages for a signature. Her trouble did not go unrewarded.

A beautifully written inscription lay on the inside of the cover: "With fond memories, Clarissa Townsley."

Was there no end to that man's appetite for women? There was that Mediterranean beauty, she thought furiously, with the peculiar name—Miruka! And his shameless mistress, Nancy. Now, Clarissa! "Oooh!" she fumed.

Not much to get in a boil over, she silently cautioned. The captain was just a man she had met in passing. He would soon be forgotten once she landed in the American states, when an entirely new set of circumstances would demand her complete attention. "Besides," she pouted, "the way he looks at me, there is little chance of rape, never mind seduction!"

Picking up the book again, she flipped through the pages, pausing to read several short pieces. William Blake's London was so sorrowfully true, she thought as she read aloud:

> "I wander through each chartered street,
>   Near where the chartered Thames does flow,
>   And mark in every face I meet
>   Marks of weakness, marks of woe . . ."

Finding another, she read Kubla Khan. She found it vague, although admittedly exotic. But the damsel with a dulcimer, this "Abyssinian maid," reminded her of the captain's adventure with the Turk's daughter and she quickly took up another poem. "Elegy to the Memory of an Unfortunate Lady" struck her immediately as befitting her own sad state of affairs.

Alas, Alexander Pope's meaning was lost to her, as well. Two stanzas she memorized, however, for these seemed most poignant:

> "O, ever beauteous, ever friendly! tell,
>   Is it, in Heav'n, a crime to love too well?
>   To bear too tender or too firm a heart,
>   To act a lover's or a Roman's part?
>   Is there no bright reversion in the sky
>   For those who greatly think, or bravely die?"

And then:

> "By foreign hands thy dying eyes were closed,
> By foreign hands thy decent limbs composed,
> By foreign hands thy humble grave adorn'd
> By strangers honor'd, and by strangers mourned!"

The more often she read the words, the sadder she became. Thinking of her father's burned remains buried in foreign soil contributed to her dolorous mood, until the tears fell unchecked. She closed the book and curled herself upon the captain's bed, her sorrows suddenly too heavy to bear.

She was awakened by a knock at the door. "Strange," she mumbled, rousing herself, "he never knocks."

It was not de Montfort, but Paul Mauriac. "Here, lad. I've brought you some hot tea. Captain says you're a bit under the weather," and gesturing toward the porthole, added, "No wonder, either. We have quite a storm brewing."

The day had grown bleak, indeed. She thanked him for his thoughtfulness, and the first mate left with as little ceremony as that with which he had come.

"Such a wonderful man," she sighed as she poured a cup of the heavenly drink. If she had but a drop of fresh cream, her delight would have been complete. Despite Nanna's gentle persuasion that ladies of decorum preferred their tea with a bit of lemon, which Paul had considerately provided, Tierney had a definite preference for serving it Irish.

"Now there is a man a woman could easily lose her heart to," she thought aloud. "Nothing like his ill-humored captain." Tierney decided it would be best not to think too much on the subject of André de Montfort.

After having her fill of tea and biscuits, the girl rose and looked out of the window. A dense mist had gathered around *La Reine* now, and it was impossible to discern their direction or even the time of day. "If he really wants me to act the part, he should have me on deck doing something!" But shivering at the porthole, she had to admit she was too tired and tense to be anywhere but here.

She found a deck of cards and tried to amuse herself with solitaire. As always, the game bored her. Next she tried playing whist, but her imaginary partner was dealt the best cards each round and she grew irritable with the nonsense. Finally she returned the deck of cards to the desk drawer where she had found them, and spied another book in English, *Gulliver's Travels*. She had heard a great deal about this incredible tale by Jonathan Swift, and eagerly turned up the hurricane lamp above the captain's bed. He had told her that it would be very late before he came down again, so she plumped the pillows and happily settled herself onto his berth to read.

The captain's return after dark did not disturb the sleeping girl. She slept soundly and dreamlessly, her unconscious mind clinging to the temporary serenity, grateful for its moment of utter solitude.

André made to roughly rouse her, but changed his mind when he saw the total complacency of her face that was lost to slumber. She was curled up like a kitten, her lips barely parted in soft breathing. "Why, she could be a beauty after all," he mused.

Shaking off his wet clothes, he laughed and said aloud, "But you're mistaken, wench, if you think I'll share my bed without returned favors." He pulled open the lower berth, and turned down the fresh covers. Gingerly reaching to pick up the fully clad girl, he was surprised at how slight she felt in his arms.

André nuzzled her cheek curiously, and was disappointed that the only scent she bore was that of a faint sea breeze. "No matter," he said. The man was exhausted himself, having lost all of his sleep the night before. He gently lay her in the smaller bunk, careful to cover her slim form with the heavy blanket.

CHAPTER SIX

It had not been a gale after all. Mauriac explained to her that it had been merely a squall; and now, several days later, Tierney was truly frightened as the first seasonal gale moved in on *La Reine*, sweeping in from the northeast.

On that night, a week before, the squall had been vicious enough to tumble Tierney from her berth. She had not asked how she had been removed from his higher bed without awakening—to do so would have invited another insult.

But when she was bumped to the floor, she awoke fully, and the captain's mockery still stung her pride. "Here now, lass," he had laughed, "come into my arms and I promise you a more enjoyable ride than the one you suffer alone!"

She scorned his offer, of course; but as she struggled to stay put in her own bed, he had added gently, "I'm sorry, Tierney. If you want to join me, I shan't hurt you." In truth, she was sorely tempted to come up because the howling winds and treacherous waves had scared her, but she did not answer him that second time, pretending to be already asleep again.

This storm today was different, black and far more menacing. The icy rains had not yet begun, and André excitedly ordered several more sails aloft. The breathtaking winds would quickly push them westward, and the captain was determined to gain as much speed as humanly possible before the full-fledged gale broke upon them.

The ship lurched unmercifully as Tierney struggled toward the deck. She commanded herself to remain as steadfast as the rest of the crew in this hellish weather, though, and forged her way across the slippery deck to empty the privy. So strong were the winds and high-pitched the waves, she felt certain that she would be blown into the angry waters. But clinging to the frigid rail on the starboard side aft, she managed to throw the waste matter into the wind.

"My God!" she cried as she realized her mistake. She had tried to empty it against the wind instead of with it. How could she be so stupid! Her very first lesson on board had been learning the leeward side of the ship.

Before she could turn to go below, someone grabbed her from the rear and flung her to the deck. It was Pelier, and from her horizontal view, he loomed bigger than a giant. He was yelling at her in French, on his face a look of sheer hatred.

With a brutal kick to her side, Tierney rolled toward the fore in agony. He abruptly spun her to her feet, and now she could see his flashing white teeth as the chamber pot's contents dripped down his face. He looked murderously enraged.

Her pleas of apology went unheard as the whining winds whistled through the canvas. She struck out at him in an attempt to flee, but his powerful grip held her fast.

Several crewmen now gathered about her in a menacing circle, and she wished with all her being that the French raving about her would make itself clear. But all she understood was the toothless ape who kept her on board that first night in London. For the second time in her life she was charged with being a "bloody son of a seawhoring monger." In her hysteria, she fought the hideous urge to laugh.

Suddenly Pelier released her, and she tried to escape down the hatch. But this move, too, was futile, for she was then ignobly snatched by the seat of her pants, and amid their roars, was led to the foremast. The shouting and shoving continued, and at last she was made to realize they wanted her to scale the ropes.

Tierney was enveloped in a fear unprecedented in her young life. Desperately she squinted at the men for a kindly face: Paul Mauriac, Cook, the captain . . . Anyone who might intervene in her behalf. Instead she was met with a sordid variety of angry, menacing, or amused grimaces.

Slowly she took hold of the rigging. Pelier gestured

into the air, but she could not see to what he was pointing. At each step of the precarious rope ladder, she cried,
"Hail Mary, full of grace . . ."

At times the wind at her back made her lose her breath
completely. She felt naked in the damp cold. Once she
lost her footing, but her bleeding hands tenaciously clawed
the ropes above her until she found a rope to heel. "Dear
Lord," she thought in terror, "is this how I must die?"

Captain de Montfort and his first mate were finished
securing the valuable cargo, and Paul agreed to join his
friend in an uncommon snifter of brandy before the pair
braved the stinging tempest on deck again. He was chilled
to the bone.

André unlatched the door and ordered the spirits. But
the cabin boy did not answer. "Where the hell is Tierney?"
he barked. "I told her to stay below!"

"Her?" Paul queried. However, the mate's question
went unanswered as André spun around and angrily strode
toward the deck.

As he leaped up the stairs and out into the inclement
weather, his attention was immediately drawn to the
gathered crew. "Ah, Christ," he moaned, "an accident!"
But the jocularity of his men quickly put to rest that fear,
and it was then that the terrible truth struck him. The
girl was swaying dangerously aloft, and his foolish men
were laughing.

Thundering in French, de Montfort grabbed two of
them by their necks, demanding an explanation for the
deadly game. Before either could respond, however, the
captain espied Pelier and knew who could be held ac-
countable.

Later, he decided, he would deal with the bastard, but
now he must get Tierney to safety. It was miraculous she
hadn't been thrown into the churning deep by now, a girl
of her thin strength. The rain began to pelt his face as he
looked up toward the crow's nest.

Several sails must be reefed to keep the ship steady
with the crashing force of intensified winds and rain bearing down on them now. But he knew that a sudden change
in the rigging about her would frighten the girl more,
probably sending her to certain death. He had no choice

but to first risk the climb himself, and two aloft was a fatal gamble.

Paul had broken through the ring of men and shouted to his captain. "Let me take it, André!"

But the younger man looked over his shoulder in denial and began the dangerous ascent.

Tierney had found what Pelier had destined her toward: the crow's nest. She could no longer feel the bite of cold or sting of water, nor hear the whipping sails or creaking of masts beneath her; but she clung to the wooden post that rocked her in a huge pendulous swing, left to right, right to left. She was reciting the Confiteor now, the Latin prayer of contrition, suddenly familiar on her tongue. *"Confiteor Deo, omnipotenti, beatae Mariae semper virginae. . . ."*

André nearly slipped when he reached to grab her.

"Mea culpa, mea culpa, mea maxima culpa," she continued in a dazed, cracked voice. She was oblivious to his arrival.

André had no time to argue with her, or bring her to her senses. One sail had already ripped in the tempestuous wind. Inside the nest with her now, he shouted into her ear, "For God's sake, Tierney, hang on to me! Else you'll kill us both!" With that warning, he lifted her and swung her onto his shoulder.

She must have understood him, for she dug her hands into his back, and did not struggle. With one arm gripped about her thighs, he began the agonizingly slow and perilous descent.

Tierney buried her face into the back of his coat and felt nothing more.

Still holding her, de Montfort made the final leap to the deck. Several of his sailors rushed to assist him now, but he screamed at them to stay back. For the first time in his life, he wanted to kill his own men.

He spun around and found the man he sought. "Aloft, Pelier!" he roared. "You ride the gale out in the safety you offered my servant!" Pelier read the malice in his captain's eyes, and dared not challenge the order. His gloved hands gripped the ladder.

Paul Mauriac was silent. He, too, knew better than to reason with the young man at a time like this.

After bellowing at his men to reef several sails, André turned to the first mate. "My friend, can you take command?"

Paul gripped the captain's shoulder in mute agreement and gestured André to take his human cargo below.

In the cabin, the young man made quick work of taking off Tierney's freezing, wet clothes. The coat had been little protection, he worriedly knew, for she was soaked through to the shirt. Stoking the small fire, he wrapped her shivering bare body in the green velvet bedcover, and lifted her into a chair before the meager warmth of the heater.

He quickly doffed his own wet garb, and returned now to kneel before her and briskly rub her feet and legs. She said nothing. Indeed, she seemed unconscious of his ministrations. Groaning, he noticed her scratched and bleeding hands. "Can you feel them?" he whispered hoarsely.

Tierney opened her eyes and gazed at the hands he held in his own. She dully realized that he was asking for a reply, and she shook her head.

The captain threw on a robe and ran to the galley. He returned minutes later with four pans of shallow water, two of which he placed on the pipe heater. Taking her hands gently, he lowered them into the first cold soak. She felt nothing.

He then stood behind her and rubbed a towel across her short-cropped hair. Satisfied it was as dry as he could get it, he began massaging her neck and shoulders, casually readjusting the velvet about her waist. Her bared breasts were rigid with cold, and he slipped his hands around to cover them and gently rubbed her chest, as well.

Tierney did feel this, and was remotely aware of the warmth and tingle she had first experienced in the Silver Steed on Southampton. It occurred to the girl that she was indecently clad and needed to put a stop to it, but her body welcomed the sudden distraction from pain and she said nothing. But as his hands grew warmer with their work, and her conscience grew stronger, she knew she must say something.

"My hands sting now."

"That's a good sign," he answered her, relieved that she could feel pain in them. He draped the cover about her shoulders again, and turned to gently dab the reddened hands. He next exchanged the first pan for another, and explained, "This one is tepid, *cherie,* and the next will be warm. But we cannot rush the process. To restore circulation properly, we will slowly change the temperature. The fourth soak will be hot; and by then, your hands will feel almost normal. Do you understand, Tierney?" he added.

Tierney nodded her understanding and closed her eyes, sinking back into the chair. What spurred his kindness? He must not have been advised yet of her clumsiness, which had angered the sailors in the first place, she thought. But she was too tired to explain it to him.

The captain, too, was tired. The mental strain had been much greater than the physical exertion, and he only once remembered with bitterness the thug he had sent up to the crow's nest. "Probably freezing to death," he considered without regret. He returned to the floor in front of her, and began to rub her feet.

Tierney felt a delicious warmth creep into her loins and smiled serenely at the pleasant change in sensation. Her hands smarted steadily now, but so soothing was the captain's attention, she barely noticed the pain.

André was fighting to control the warmth in his own loins when he noticed the meaningful smile about her lips. Enough!

Abruptly standing, he went to his closet and dressed in heavy clothes. As he pulled on his boots, he spoke. "I have to go above and see to the men."

Tierney's eyes flew open with the bang of the door, and she blinked about the room to recover her senses. She wondered vaguely what was happening now, and what had prompted the sudden change in the captain's mood.

"Well," she shrugged, "sure, he's about to find the cause for my punishment, and the pleasantries will end soon enough!" Snuggling down into the luxurious cover, she sighed. The only time she had worn velvet before was her last Christmas in Ireland with her parents. Presently she drifted into a light slumber, the hurling waves mesmerizing her to sleep.

"Steady as she blows, Captain!" shouted Mauriac. "No reason to worry. I can sail her as well as you any day—if not better!" he teased. The two men always addressed one another in English when being familiar before the other men. "Go on back, André," he continued. "You've been spared your foolish neck once already this day. Let's not ask too much of Neptune!"

The captain nodded. As usual, Paul was making good sense. Besides, the older mate loved to be first in command, having as great an admiration for the ship's maneuverability as her own captain. Scowling at the sky, de Montfort tried to make out the figure of Pelier.

"Where is he?" he yelled above the thrashing waves.

The first mate narrowed his eyes at André. "He's in the hold, bound to a post!" Holding his hand at the younger man's chest, he bellowed, "Don't fight me on this, Captain! You know as well as I that if you killed him in a fit of temper, you would live to regret it!"

But de Montfort was in no mood to spare the man's life. "I'll have him flogged to death on the morrow," he threatened. "Or yardarmed!"

Mauriac did not push the point further. "So be it!" he returned above the noise, and turned to steady himself back at the helm. He knew that de Montfort could, if he wanted, have him flogged too. The first mate had never known the captain's wrath; but then, Paul had never been guilty of insubordination all these years.

Tierney's nap was soon interrupted.

The captain threw open the door with his foot and lurched forward with a tray in his arms, nearly losing his balance altogether.

"Careful," she teased. "You keep spinning about like that and you'll knock yourself down."

André turned toward her irritably, but caught the joke in time. "Thank you for your concern, milady," he mimicked, "but your goddamned tea is far more precious than my derrière!"

At this, they simultaneously broke into laughter. André shoved the teapot beside her and threw himself on the bed, unable to control the sudden burst of levity. He laughed so heartily, in fact, that the girl sobered quickly. "I don't understand the man at all!" she mused silently.

Presently, the captain sat up and shrugged off his wet

boots. "Well, miss," he said, "I see that you are feeling better."

"Yes, Captain. Thank you."

"Nothing I wouldn't do for any of my men," he replied. "How are the hands?"

"Quite sore, to be honest. And they are growing stiff again in the water. Might I change to a warmer pan now?"

"Mon Dieu!" he exclaimed. "I forgot." He once again took up the hand-soaking ritual, but when he reached for her foot to return to his previous massage, she tucked them demurely up under her legs in the chair.

"They are fine now," she stated simply.

"Good," was the toneless reply.

André retrieved the teapot from beside her, and delivering it to his table, poured a cup. He lifted the replenished brandy decanter too, and filled a snifter for himself.

Presented with the cup and saucer, she raised her hands from the water and shakily accepted the offer. "Wait," he ordered as he put the drinks on the stovetop. He took up the towel with which he had dried her hair, and tenderly patted the bruised fingers. "You'll need liniment." She winced but said nothing.

Now handing her the tea, he raised his own glass in salute. "You are a remarkable young woman, Miss Chambers!"

She raised the cup to her lips, but stopped. "What are you giving me?" she asked suspiciously.

"Tea, you little ass!"

"But it doesn't look right," she started when he rudely cut in.

"It's a special blend, if you must know. Rose hips and hibiscus blossoms. Expensive too," he added.

"Oh," she responded weakly, sipping the steaming red brew. Her eyebrows lifted in surprise. "It's delicious!"

He laughed humorlessly. "You trust no one, do you?"

"Yes," she answered quickly. "I trust Mr. Mauriac."

"You sullen wench!" he muttered, not pausing to wonder at his sudden anger. He raised his glass to draw in the welcomed cognac when he heard her hiss back.

"I've had all I can stand of your name-calling, you . . . you . . ."

She had not the time to search for an appropriate insult, for he roughly pulled her to her feet. The velvet slipped to the floor as he shook her.

"I'll call you anything I damn well please, you conniving bitch! Why, you're lucky I don't beat you for the trouble you've caused." His voice died in his throat as his eyes ran over her naked body. "Dear God," he choked. "Did Pelier do that too?"

He was pointing toward the side of her back, and Tierney twisted to see what provoked his French curses. She could not see what had arrested his attention, but reached back and touched the area. It was painful, very painful, and she now reluctantly remembered the seaman's vicious kick. "Dear Lord," she thought wildly, "must I suffer this man's open gawking as well as injury?"

The captain was circling her now, as cautiously as a cat. He studied her naked limbs unabashedly, intensely. She bent over to pull up the coverlet, retrieving the upturned teacup as well.

She stood up, wrapping the velvet around her.

He ignored her protestations, and picked her up in his arms like a child. Gently placing her on his bed, he went back to his chest, alternately muttering in French and English.

He returned with a jar, and put it next to her. Quietly and efficiently, he pulled back the makeshift cloak and then instructed the girl to roll over on her stomach.

Tierney knew she was about to be raped, but found no hope of deliverance. She lay deathly still. She knew he was still fully clothed, but dared not open her eyes to see what would happen next. Why was he taking so long? she anguished. Be done with it!

Slowly and with great care, he dabbed the salve on the huge bruise. She cried out with fright, so he leaned over her to whisper soothingly, "There now, *petite*. This will only take a moment, and you will feel far better for it."

So he wasn't raping her! "Thank you," she murmured into the tear-streaked pillow, "thank you!" His surprisingly supple fingers moved rhythmically up and down her spine, vigorously on tensed muscles and gently on sore spots. The salve smelled of cloves, and Tierney finally relaxed, submissive under his persuasive hands.

The ship was rocking quite a bit, but Tierney stirred

when a sudden lurch threatened to toss them onto the floor.

The captain spoke then, but his voice was husky and the words foreign. She did not hear him get up.

André put the jar back into his trunk, and picked up his unfinished brandy. His knees were trembling, from whether his sexual restraint or hour-long ministrations he could not decide.

Presently seated at his desk, he pondered the unbelievable plight into which this nymph of a girl had forced him. When he had drained his glass, he went back to the bunk and cautiously lifted her under the sheets, securing a blanket around her.

Then he gathered the pans, strewn towels, and dishes, and returned to the galley. There he met Paul who was bent over a cup of hot coffee.

"How goes it?"

"Fine, Captain. She's been through worse, and the gale will soon blow over."

"Well, you have had enough. I'll take her the rest of the night."

"If it's all the same to you, Captain," Paul answered slowly, "I would prefer to finish out the night, and have an entire day of rest tomorrow."

André glanced at him for a sign of exhaustion. The first mate rarely took a day off even in port, and never had he requested a twenty-four hour rest during a voyage. "Very well, my friend. I'll get some sleep myself then."

As he turned to go, the older man stayed his arm. In English, he said, "André, I must ask you something. Perhaps I misunderstood you, but I thought I heard you refer to the cabin boy as 'her'! Am I wrong?"

"No, Paul. You heard me well, though I did not intend it. Tierney Chambers is a woman! She deceived us both," he flatly stated.

The first mate's jaw dropped open in awe, but before he could pose another question, André stalked out of the galley.

He knew Mauriac well enough to understand the secret was still safe from the crew. Later he would explain further, perhaps even chide the first mate if ever he saw the humor of the situation. But at the moment, he was in no mood for conversation or comedy.

* * *

Stripping to the waist, he slid beneath the covers beside her. He tried vainly to sleep, but the precious relief would not come. Her unconscious proximity intensified the growing discomfort.

Suddenly the ship pitched, and Tierney rolled onto her side. He could see her eyes were still closed, but quietly turned himself fully to face her, studying her relaxed countenance. His urge could no longer be denied, and he cautiously slid down to kiss her taut little breast. He was rewarded with a throaty moan.

Encouraged now, he quickly and silently untied the drawstring about his waist. His fingers lightly traced her thighs, knees, and back up to her spine. *"Mon Dieu,"* he groaned fervently. He was growing impatient.

Tierney was very slowly responding to his caresses, and presently began to unconsciously undulate her hips to the rocking motion of the vessel. Ever so gently, he eased her onto her back, simultaneously pushing apart her thighs. She awoke fully now, and the pulsations she was feeling from head to foot clamored in her ears. "No!" she cried.

But André de Montfort knew her type, knew every type. He had not forgotten the seductive smile he had seen on her face earlier tonight. Although she now tightly pressed her knees together, her thighs were so slender that his hand slid easily between them. She was warm and willing. "Well, perhaps not willing," he silently warned, "but it won't be long."

He manipulated his fingers in much the same way he had massaged her backside—gently here, vigorously there. Tierney thought she might burst with the confusing conflict of joy and fear. Tears welled up inside her, but she could not force them out, nor find any words to stem the flow of what was happening to her. "I am happy and sad at once," she thought wondrously.

Her body's response was as contradictory as her thinking. Although she persisted in tightly pressing her knees together, her impetuous hips had a will of their own. Finally, she could endure no more and the involuntary release spread through every limb. She feared the feverish throbbing in her loins would never cease.

André was greatly relieved to see the simple struggle

end, and lifted her now lax legs apart. He mounted her comfortably and thrust inside, at last resting himself across her shivering body.

Alas, the peace was only momentary. The minx *was* a virgin! He should have guessed as much, or at least asked the girl, he admitted to himself. But she had seemed so eager, he thought frantically, and the business with her stubborn thighs just more evidence of her play-acting.

The damage was done, however, and he was beyond controlling his own long-awaited passion. Gently he proceeded, murmuring to her in his own beautiful language, and tenderly kissing her ears, throat, and tear-streaked cheeks. He withdrew suddenly, thrusting his tongue between her teeth as their muted cries entwined.

At last he rolled to his side, cradling the still trembling girl in his sinewy arms. *"Je regrette, ma petite,"* he whispered. "I am sorry, little one."

Tierney was too bewildered to speak. It was too much to comprehend all at once. So much pain, so much joy! Such peace, and yet such anguish! She wondered if this was what was meant by damnation.

Finally, she managed a weak "You have no reason to be sorry, Captain. It was not your fault. The guilt rests on me . . ." And indeed, she thought it had not been his fault. Had she been more discriminating in London; had she been more careful here; had she refused his gentle ministrations this very night . . .

But André de Montfort did not hear her forgive him. He was asleep. Tierney Chambers turned and quietly wept into her pillow.

The dawn stole silently upon a two-hundred-mile stretch of North Atlantic waters, and *La Reine de la Mer* crept slowly eastward under a blanket of dense, gray fog.

Tierney awakened uneasily, and remained rigidly still until the man's rhythmic breathing at the back of her neck assured her that he slept. Silently she slipped from beneath his arm, and rolled out from under the crumpled sheet. Later she would try to recall last night's disturbing chain of events. She knew that she had not imagined any of it, but for the time being, it was much easier to assume that everything—every moment since Nanna's death— was a series of fantastic hallucinations.

Shivering in the chilled cabin, she reached for her clothes. The yet-damp trousers and sweater were real enough, she reflected, but they, too, might be a part of this pretense—this nightmare. Her shirt, at least, had dried before the heat. Having stoked the coals, she now buttoned her trousers, laced the still sodden boots, and left the cabin.

She hesitated before climbing the hatch. The men might still be angry, and she dreaded her first encounter with the Frenchmen. But she had to retrieve the privy, that abominable article that had brought about her ordeal.

Remarkably, she thought, the men took no notice of the insolent cabin boy. Indeed, they moved about in the cold mist without the usual morning exchanges, and except for the creaking of ropes and endless song of the ocean beneath them, the deck was quiet.

She returned the commode to the captain's cabin, careful not to disturb the slumbering figure on the bed. She wondered what she must do now, and how she should behave since this latest twist in events. "Well, I suppose I must carry on as though nothing has happened," she decided. "I'll speak only when spoken to, and pray to God the lout will conceal the second half of this dimwitted play!"

In the galley, Tierney gathered the routine breakfast for de Montfort, sullenly adding a bowl of steaming porridge and freshly-brewed tea for herself, vowing the captain would not interfere with her own hunger again. She thought angrily of the many meals she had lost because of his unpredictable moods, and added a few more names to her list for André de Montfort as her stomach grumbled in agitation.

Making her way to ascend to his quarters again, she stopped abruptly as the first mate entered. "Egad!" she exclaimed suddenly. "You look like the devil himself, Mr. Mauriac."

He made no comment to her criticism, but queried, "Captain still abed?"

"Yes, sir," she answered noncommittally.

A scowl crossed his face. "After delivering Captain de Montfort his morning meal, I'll see you in my cabin, Miss Chambers!" he whispered hoarsely.

"Saints preserve us!" she moaned as she scurried to the

master cabin. He knew! The good Mr. Mauriac had been told by that seafaring scoundrel de Montfort, and now her treasonous ruse was known to the one person she trusted. How could she ever win his forgiveness? she dismally wondered.

To her surprise, the captain was awake and fully dressed when she entered the room. She said nothing—could say nothing—and noiselessly prepared his table.

André was similarly mute, but he regarded her with an intensity that made her flesh pucker. Finally, he took his chair and lifted the scalding coffee to his lips. Spewing the hot beverage and sputtering in French, he grabbed her by a sleeve and demanded, "Have you seen Paul?"

"Yes, Captain," she blushed.

"I promised to relieve him at dawn. Why didn't you wake me?" he accused.

Tierney fought her own rising temper. "You said nothing last night to indicate this morning's duties, milord," she answered haughtily.

André shoved her away and stood. Without so much as one French oath, he stormed out of the room.

She would have to tidy the cabin, she thought, but now the girl looked about the disorderly room and shrugged. She must not keep the first mate waiting. Even her impending humiliation, however, could not dispel her pronounced appetite. Sighing at the meal before her, she plopped one dried date into her mouth and resolutely marched toward Mauriac's cabin.

André reached the deck and began ordering more sails aloft immediately. He was determined to get with the wind as quickly as possible, and make up for any delays caused by the storm. He was told that the first mate had gone below to rest, and would report to him at noon.

There was much to be done. He commanded two of the crew to check the hold, and retrieve an alternate sailcloth for the hewn fore topgallant sail. Inspecting the gaff, spankers, mainsail, and crossjack, André satisfied himself that the spent gale had caused no further damage. He turned to what he considered the most pressing task of all.

The derelict Pelier was unceremoniously hauled onto the deck and roped by the wrists to the foremast. An example must be made, the captain determined, and with the exceptions of Cook, cabin boy, and first mate, all hands were ordered on deck.

André de Montfort personally despised the use of a whip, and in his estimation floggings were usually barbarous extremes meted out to undeserving seamen by sadistic captains. But Pelier was guilty of paramount disregard for the lives and safety of the crew, and as the captain now remembered the bruise on the girl's back, his rage mounted. It did not cross his mind that his own violation of the young woman was more permanent than the ugly welt above her hip.

"Yes, Tierney, the captain has told me." A persistent headache was becoming more unbearable, and Paul could no longer remain standing. He sat on his bunk heavily, and pressed his eyes shut to ease the pain.

"Mr. Mauriac," she began solemnly, "would there were something I could do . . ."

"Well, there isn't, you foolish child!" he interrupted. "Have you any idea of how preposterous this is, to say nothing of what harm you have invited to your own person?"

"Sir, had I given more thought to my actions, I never would have endangered your own good standing with the captain, and it is the jeopardizing of your post that really grieves me." Her voice was strained with emotion now, and she wanted to take his solid hands and kneel before him for forgiveness. Never since Da had she so loved a man!

Paul Mauriac would have laughed at her naïveté had he felt better. But his eyes were scorching now, and his mind weary. At length, he said quietly, "Tierney Chambers, lad or lass, you have much to learn. The captain and I are . . . Well, it is hard to conceive of anything, even a jinx like you, severing our friendship."

Vaguely he told himself that he must rest. If ever André needed his counsel, it was now. Before surrendering himself to sleep, however, he gently questioned her once more. "Has André, that is, has the captain hurt you, lass? Touched you in, ah, an unseemly manner?"

"No, sir," she lied. "He has been considerate in every . . ." but the words died in her throat as the man before her collapsed.

Tierney raced toward the crowd on the deck. "Captain!" she screamed, "Captain de Montfort, come at once!"

Blindly breaking through the clustered men, she suddenly stopped and caught her breath. "God's death," she murmured in disbelief.

The scene before her was ghastly. Pelier was slumped forward, his back torn and bloody. Before he could deliver another lash, Tierney attacked the captain from behind leaping up on him like a monkey, her legs securely wrapped around his middle. He raised back an arm to strike off the mutinous bilk when she stayed his arm and hissed in his ear. "You bloody bastard! Would you murder this man while your only friend lies dying?"

He dropped the whip immediately and she slid off his back. Barking a command to release the prisoner and take him down to common quarters, he turned to seize the girl.

"Now, what are you talking about?" he demanded. "Where is Paul? If this is another attempt at girlish strategem, I'll have *you* drawn and quartered!"

Tierney hated him. In the past six hours, this man had proved himself the most vile of humanity. He had ruined her only chance of a moral life and was now threatening to kill her! And while the only person for whom she cared lay feverish and delirious, André seemed more interested in dealing torture than in saving his loyal friend.

"Captain, Mr. Mauriac is indeed very ill. I have just left his cabin. He's unconscious. Do with me what you will, but for the love of God, come with me now!"

CHAPTER SEVEN

André de Montfort's every move had been thwarted by the stubborn girl. Never, he swore, had he been so tempted to drop a person overboard. No one dared to consistently disregard a ship's captain! But Tierney was apparently oblivious to protocol on the high seas for dared him she had. The captain's only consolation was that their heated exchanges were in a language incomprehensible to his men.

Her first direct disobedience had been in removing herself from the master cabin to sleep on the floor near Paul. She seemed to have forgotten altogether their night of lovemaking, and was completely engrossed in the first mate's recovery.

After they had gone into his cabin that desolate day, Tierney had changed dramatically. She was assertive, bold, and wholly unresponsive to André's simplest needs. To complicate matters further, the young man felt a growing attraction for the girl and a gnawing jealousy of his friend.

Even Pelier had won the chit's attention. She had said nothing further about the flogging, but her accusation of cruelty was made clear by her silent disdain. Again disregarding his command, she had gone to the galley to prepare a concoction for the sailor's lacerations. Ordering lime water, linseed oil, and laudanum, she mixed these with pure tallow and applied the liniment to his wounds with a soft linen cloth. The sailor, still believing the servant to be an English lad, suffered her ministrations in abject silence. André had not yet regretted the discipline, and considering his frustration with Tierney, he refused later to translate Pelier's apology to her for the breakneck episode in the crow's nest.

The preparations she dictated for Paul's struggle to regain strength were more complex, and obviously of tremendous concern to her. She applied mustard plasters to his chest; forced cough remedies of honey, lemon and brandy down him; and regularly administered a vile-tasting compound for fever made of muriate of morphia, bismuth, and carbolic acid.

The captain was covertly astonished at how quickly his first mate progressed under Tierney's peculiar, albeit effective, methods. He was happy to see the man recover, but once when he witnessed Tierney laying atop the length of Paul during a delirium of chills, he was unaccountably resentful. Such was his confusion that he spent free time gambling with the crew in common quarters.

"I understand you are hungry, Mr. Mauriac," she said soothingly, "but I must insist you limit your intake of food to this lovely beef tea I have made. It is not as pleasing as it is when made with fresh meat, but the dried concoction is quite palatable," she urged.

Paul sighed, and allowing himself to be propped in a sitting position, accepted the strong broth and bitter tea she offered.

"Tonight you may have burnt toast," she said gaily, "and on the morrow, we shall add some jellies!"

"Tomorrow," he croaked, "I take orders from only André—and tonight, you go back to your own berth, Tierney."

The young woman had prepared herself for the argument, but had not expected it to come about so soon. Paul gestured her to silence before she could even open her mouth.

"Now, lass, listen to me well. You have put us both in precarious positions, as we have already discussed. André is my captain—your captain, too. I took your hire under admittedly false pretenses, to be sure. But you, Tierney! You knew full well what you were getting yourself in for as his cabin boy, and *his* servant you will remain!

"I understand your quandary, my girl. Truly I do. But you have already assured me more than once that he treats you with respect, despite your insolence. And I'll warrant that no nobler a man ever mastered a ship!"

Why was it that God decreed one lie must spin a web of lies? "Dear Lord," she mused, "he is not honorable. And here, this God-fearing man would have me believe otherwise. . . . Oh, Paul! If only I could tell you. . . ."

But the first mate continued his preordained lecture to the girl. "This business with Pelier—you must see it as it truly exists. It was fear for *your* life, anger at what had been forced upon you, that prompted the captain's discipline. A flogging!" he spat. "Bah! Had you any idea of how justice is generally met on the high seas, my girl, you would be amazed at André's merciful nature, and I am certain that Pelier himself shares that sentiment!"

The somber Frenchman could see the girl was not convinced. At least he now understood her initial contempt for the ship's sleeping arrangements. No instance of sordid child abuse at all, he realized, but a frightened young maiden. And a lucky one, as well. Had she been allowed to sleep in common, and one of the sailors had forced his way with the new cabin boy. . . . Well, the outcome of men at sea finding a vulnerable young girl in their midst was too licentious to contemplate.

"There now, Tierney," he said. "If you do meet with difficulty, that is, if André"—he cleared his throat—"if Captain de Montfort attempts to . . . you understand, my girl . . . well, just come to me and I'll handle him. But perhaps if I tell you a little tale about your fearsome master, it will lay to rest your worries."

As Tierney listened to the account of André de Montfort and his propitious regard for his betrothed, Anne-Marie Dormaise, she became inexplicably incensed. "Another!" she silently fumed. The Turk's daughter, the English trollop, the woman who had bequeathed the book of poems, herself—and now a French fiancée. His lust for women was insatiable, she thought furiously.

Paul mistook her silence for acquiescence, and presently drifted into a comfortable slumber. Tierney listened wistfully to his gentle snores for a few moments, then tenderly kissed his brow. She left the room without a sound.

Outside in the chilled afternoon air, Tierney began pacing the deck. Fore to aft, aft to fore. She would simply return to the master cabin, she decided with resolution, and perform the duties of cabin boy—strictly male duties. She wondered, though, why she should be so nervous. Never again could she fall prey to his seductive ways. Not now that she understood what an abomination the captain was, and how very much she loved another. Paul.

André watched the girl from his vantage point behind

the staysail. When she finally gave up her anxious stroll and leaned to peer into the waves beneath them, he stole upon her from behind.

"Jesus, Mary, and Joseph!" she squealed. "You gave me such a start!"

"My apologies, milady," he answered with a condescending bow. Straightening himself, he searched her eyes. They seemed to take on various shades with her surroundings, and this day appeared sea green. But she had lost weight, as he silently noted. "Are you feeling well?" he queried after a moment's pause.

"Yes, Captain. That is, until today I felt fine."

André raised his brow in concern, but she brusquely continued. "Mr. Mauriac has ordered me from his quarters, and says I must return to my duties as cabin boy."

"You mean cabin girl," he growled in a low voice. "I won't be paying you a single copper for the time you've wasted this week! It's high time you took up your servant functions again. There is much to be done in your master's cabin.

"This sea air quickly tarnishes brass and mildews the floor," he continued archly. "Besides domestics, I have a sailcloth that is in need of repair. I presume you do know how to work a needle!"

There was an air of smugness about her when she answered. "Good Captain, you remind me of a nursery rhyme taught to me as a child. Permit me to recite it:

"I saw a ship a-sailing, a-sailing on the sea;
  And, oh! it was all laden with pretty things for thee.
  There were comfits in the cabin, and apples in the hold;
  The sails were made of silk, and the mast was made of gold.
  The captain was a duck, with a packet on his back;
  And when the ship began to move, the captain said, 'Quack, quack!' "

Captain de Montfort had no further reply for her insolence. He delivered an icy glare, and turning on his heel, stalked toward the helm.

Tierney was delighted. She giggled as she skipped toward the hatch, confident she could now handle the proud captain of *La Reine de la Mer*.

* * *

"It's true," she remarked, "I've never seen the place so untidy!" She began picking up the strewn clothes and mentally scolded the man for becoming so lazy, when she knew from Paul that the captain was habitually careful with his wardrobe. "Probably his cocky way of teaching me a lesson,' she fumed.

After cleaning the room and polishing the brass and woodwork, Tierney cautiously approached the bed. Again a peculiar contradiction struck her. She shuddered with revulsion and tingled with pleasure at the memory of her last night spent here. Shrugging off the strange reaction, she began the perfunctory straightening of sheets. Her hand brushed a hard object, and she stopped short.

It was the English book of poems. "Probably crooning over his ladylove, Townsley," she thought with disgust. Nonetheless, she searched the pages looking for what poems had especially appealed to him. Two were marked at the corners: "Kubla Khan" and "The World Is Too Much with Us."

"It must be the dark-haired Mediterranean girl who haunts him," she glowered.

Throwing the volume to his desk, she spread the green velvet on his bunk, careful to smooth each soft line.

The captain was greeted with cold hostility when he came down to supper. Tierney seemed not to look at him at all as she served him the soup, and a side dish of dried meats and rice. It looked wholly unappetizing, and she plopped down in her own chair in a desultory manner.

"If you insist on behaving like a buffoon, you may take your meals in the galley with the rest of the crew," he drily commented. "It's fried rice. Quite a delicacy in eastern countries. You will like it, I am sure. There is much you have to learn yet, Tierney. Especially when it comes to worldly pleasures," he added.

The girl did not reply; in fact, she appeared not to have heard him at all.

Tierney silently hoped that the rice mixture would be so distasteful that she could spit it back on her plate, thereby insulting him further without having to talk. But the dish was truly delicious, and she had to agree with him that there were many things she still had to discover.

Finishing the last morsel, she now eagerly attacked the fish chowder.

André watched the young woman devour her food. It pleased him to think her appetite was returning, and with it perhaps, the much-needed flesh on her bones. But he was growing more impatient by the minute with her haughty silence.

"If it is worry over a babe that has your tongue," he said, "you need not concern yourself. I don't make a habit of spreading brats through the world!"

Tierney choked on a bit of fish. With his help, she finally coughed it clear and sputtered, "What the devil did you say?"

"Quite simply, I was telling you not to worry about being pregnant."

"But, but . . . Oh, my God!" It had never occurred to the girl that an unmarried woman could get with child. Nanna had been nebulous enough in explaining her menses, but never had the facts of life been further expounded. "And me, an ass," she raged within, "never even asking!" Sheltered childhoods had their disadvantages, it seemed.

André was convinced the girl was pulling another one of her tricks. Certainly she must have realized `. . . But as he studied her changing expressions, and finally the look of sheer bewilderment on her face, he reluctantly admitted the girl was pathetically naïve and lacking in counsel. Gently now, he queried, "Do you honestly not understand me, *cherie?*"

Tierney looked up at him, her eyes wide with the startling news. "But, of course," she stammered. "It . . . it only makes sense."

Had anyone witnessed the exchange, he would have been hard pressed to determine who was more greatly embarrassed or distressed. It was Tierney, however, who broke the uncomfortable silence.

"Well, Captain de Montfort," she said with forced gaiety, "it was you who pointed out my lack of education in worldly wisdom. So it is you, I suppose, who must explain it to me. I already know, at least," she giggled, "it is no cabbage patch that sprouts a babe!"

"The packet on my back is you!" he chided and, at her blank expression, added, "The nursery rhyme? The duck had a packet on his back. This captain's burden is a girl who pretends to be what she is not!"

Tierney's nervousness faded, and she laughed. "Quack, quack!"

"Don't get too giddy," he warned. "Clear away this supper now, like a good girl. I'll be back to discuss things with you tonight." With that, he got up and left the cabin.

Standing under a canopy of winter stars, André gripped the rail and inhaled a deep breath. He must think clearly. The absurdity of his position with Tierney was becoming more complex daily. He was captain of a fine ship, above all else, and an opportunist for profit in war. What was happening to him?

Tierney was no raving beauty in her ill-fitting garments and with her pale complexion, to be sure. And yet, this girl was turning his head from important matters to trivia, for what was more commonplace and trivial than sex? Now that she was discovered and deflowered as well, he ought to be using her for his own amusement, not playing nursemaid to her!

He preferred knowledgeable women. The only virgin he had ever taken before Tierney had been an Arab maiden, and for that doubtful pleasure he had paid mightily. But this Irish lass was somehow different, he mused.

She was too slight in proportion to be physically appealing, he told himself, and her haircut lent little to improve her questionable looks. She had not been imaginative nor shown much talent that first night, and yet she had unquestionably responded to him, he remembered with a marked degree of conceit.

Struggling to overcome the uncertainty of his feelings and his genuine affection for Tierney, André turned his thoughts back to the matter at hand. How best could he educate the girl without threatening to seduce her again? It would be difficult, he realized, but promised himself that accomplish this he must. Otherwise, leaving her in Charleston would be disastrous. Perhaps he could secure a position for her there as a housemaid with some family of his acquaintance.

When he returned to his cabin, André walked to his desk and poured himself a glass of Madeira. "Care to join me?" he asked.

Tierney started to decline, but then decided that dulling her senses might make such intimate conversation more bearable. "Yes, please." She was considering asking him to delay this supreme awkwardness. The forthcoming discourse on male and female behavior was making her jittery already. But she realized that perhaps allowing the captain to explain things to her was the best alternative. He already knew more about her than any living person, she reasoned. And she could think of no greater humiliation than his discovery of her womanly period, nor his easy seduction of her. What could be more insufferable than these?

Even if she befriended another woman in the New World upon her arrival, how could she broach such a delicate subject with someone she barely knew. And now, knowing that procreation could result from her indecency, it was vital she learn. The captain was the only person . . .

They drank in silence. As he refilled the glasses, he solemnly embarked upon the most ludicrous voyage he would ever venture.

"I think perhaps it would be best to describe this objectively. We will take an imaginary girl who has reached puberty, and proceed from there," he began.

"What about boys?" she whispered.

"You can speak up, Tierney. The walls haven't any ears! We will get to the male species later," he said drily. "But at the moment, dear girl, you are in dire need of knowing more about your own propensities."

It went more easily than he had imagined it would. The wine helped, for he soon dropped his formality and she relaxed enough to pose several questions.

"And that, *chérie*, is how conception takes place. It has obviously been going on for time immemorial, for never have we run short of people. Babies are born every minute, and for every single birth, I'll warrant there are thousands of couples making love."

Tierney was fascinated. Never had any fairy tale, poem, or play been more enthralling to hear. But she was also remotely frightened. "Then how can you be certain that I am not with child?" she asked doubtfully.

"I am a firm believer in coitus interruptus. Unless, of course, the woman is a paid professional," and noting her flushed expression, he quickly added, "And you, *chérie*,

do not fall into that category." After explaining the
method of delayed ejaculation as a means of preventing
conception, he started to describe how she might prevent
it herself if she would time her own cycle. But he thought
further on it, for already he conceded that he did not
want Tierney Chambers knowledgeable enough to choose
her own men. So he covered the slip of the tongue, saying,
"A woman's cycle is important. Missing a month is the
first indication that she carries a child. Though you probably do not believe me, there is much yet I have not explained. Childbearing is another education in itself, and
I'll admit my own understanding of the process is lacking.
But when the time comes for you to understand this, I am
sure a woman would more readily be able to answer your
questions." At long last, André got up from the table and
stretched out on his bed. It had been a trying two hours.

Tierney was aroused, and wondered at the cause. The
captain had neglected to mention emotion in his clinical
dialogue, and the girl, tipsy from three glasses of Madeira,
was mildly perplexed. First the coin he pressed into her
palm, then his massage and final seduction of her, and
now his soothing voice caused pleasant scintillations.

While he lay on his bed motionless, Tierney got up herself and humming a tune, began a light dance in her
stockinged feet. "Black is the color," she sang softly, "of
my true love's hair. His face so soft and wondrous fair.
The purest eyes, and the bravest hands . . ."

Such a true little voice, he thought. But when she sang,
"I love the ground whereon he goes," Tierney fell into her
own berth in a fit of girlish giggles. The young captain
groaned into his pillow, as he heard her laughter dwindle
into blissful sleep.

Another week passed and Paul, fully recovered now,
took up his regular night command. The captain's nights
were filled with erotic dreams, invariably with his serving
girl as the focal point. He could only be grateful that they
were now only two days out of Charleston harbor, and
the vexing ritual of sleeping next to sweet innocence would
end. He even went so far as to solemnly swear that a
wharf prostitute would meet his urgent need. To hell with
propriety in Charleston!

It was that night that something irrevocably changed in André de Montfort. He was awakened from his own fitful sleep by the girl's screams. It was a nightmare, he realized, as he stumbled from his bunk to kneel by her.

"Wake up, *chérie*. Wake up!" he ordered softly. "You're having a bad dream."

And indeed she was dreaming she was a child again; her parents were kissing her and tucking a blanket about her. Then flames crackled, and she felt the smoke choking her lungs. She could hear her father screaming for her to wake up and get to her window. "Tierney," he cried, "Tierney, my lass . . ."

André was shaking her gently, and calling her more loudly now. Finally, the dream disappeared and she clutched him. "The fire!" she sobbed. "I could hear Da yelling to me, and Mum crying!"

"Ah, *ma petite*," he whispered. "It's over now." But her every limb quaked with the terrifying memory, and presently he picked her up in his arms. Holding her against him as he would a child, he began rocking her and humming a French tune.

The tears eventually subsided, and she grew silent. Now André grew tense, as Tierney put her arms about his neck and mutely kissed his cheek. He returned the kiss to her lips, slowly at first, but when he became demanding in his tongue's search, she did not struggle.

Softly and wordlessly, he laid her on his bed, and their gentle caresses developed into passionate embraces. He moved deftly, untying a string here, loosening a button there. When their naked bodies finally entwined, Tierney sighed and tremorously began a search of his body.

André was desperate to enter her, but checked his own inclinations while the girl silently moved her hands in cautious investigation. When she touched him most intimately, he moaned. *"Bon, chérie. Do not stop, little one."*

But she stiffened in surprise and removed her hand at once. André could no longer refuse his own heated desire, so he kissed her thoroughly, and stretching one long leg across her thighs, eagerly spread kisses to her throat, arms, and breasts. When her hips began their instinctive motion, he knew she would surrender.

Never had Tierney experienced pleasure of such immeasurable proportion. The lovers were bound to one another, and won the ultimate reward that only two people acting as one can experience.

André, too, was enormously moved by the intensity of their mutual performance. He was pleasantly surprised by Tierney's active response to him, and in his state of complete abandon, he was stunned to find real lovemaking a more intense rapture than the casual amusement to which he had become accustomed.

Before drifting into sleep, however, one worry lay heavily in each of their minds: Tierney knew she had sinned, and there were no excuses in her heart this time. She felt damned; André's concern was more in the present. He realized that in the height of his excitement, he had completely forgotten delaying his climax. He knew that his seed lay waiting in the helpless girl's belly.

CHAPTER EIGHT

Winter was upon the Carolinas, but the sun shone brightly on Charleston harbor as *La Reine de la Mer* docked and lay to port.

Tierney had been despondent over her capitulation two nights before. How could she behave so wantonly, so despicably? Her family—thank God they were gone—would have been scandalized, reviled!

She was still naïve, but only to a point. Tierney knew very well that it was she who'd encouraged the interlude; in fact, had almost demanded it. The captain was a mere pawn, she reflected, for her own willful desires.

That was just it. Tierney had discovered her own passionate nature and was humiliated to learn that she liked very much what had happened—and more shockingly, wanted it to happen again! She had betrayed Mr. Mauriac and her love for him, but found some consolation in the fact that she had never confessed to him that love. She had also betrayed herself, her very heritage and proper upbringing. Had it occurred to the young girl that her parents had been passionate lovers, she might have found some explanation for her own impetuous nature, but, alas, Tierney was too preoccupied in her own troubles to consider this.

The captain had been of little help, she decided. He seemed wholly unconcerned with the incident, even blasé the following morning. And last night, he and Paul had gone over the details of their forthcoming business in Charleston. Tierney had been so perturbed at their apparent dismissal of her, she had gone aloft and sat amid the lower rigging of her own volition.

Now, viewing this new country from the deck, she felt the burden lighten, if only by a small margin. Soon she would set her feet on solid ground, never to see either the captain or first mate again. It would be the first step in unraveling the monstrous web she had unwittingly spun.

"Hopefully," she worried, "he will offer me my wages. If I have to ask him, I'll feel no better than a paid cockatrice!"

Tierney began to absently pace the deck planking. "I must have enough money to buy decent clothes. This boy's costume is so wearisome, and oh, dear God, to have a bath!" She dared not look into his small closet mirror again. Only once since shearing her locks had she ventured to look at her own image, and that had only been curiosity, not vanity. She had wanted to see for herself if lost maidenhood was visible to the eye.

Remembering the ghastly visage that awaited her in the glass, she now winced. Dear Mother in Heaven, she agitated, what a spectacle I make! She knew she was too thin, and with little but her eyes and hair to help her, she had sorely regretted losing her curls. Tierney silently prayed that the cut delivered to her brow by one of the rough sailor's blows that night had healed without a scar.

Looking down at her hands, she sighed. Though not permanently damaged, they were scored and chafed. The sailcloth hadn't helped, she sadly reflected. Tierney did repair the torn topgallant as she was ordered to do, and in the process had stuck her fingers many, many times with the huge whalebone needle.

It will be good, almost too good, to get off this damned ship, she thought.

André de Montfort, however, was a man of changeable moods. He no longer wanted to set Tierney adrift in Charleston, nor anywhere else, he dourly admitted. There was no point in leaving her here, at any rate. Even if he could find employment for an unpredictable girl, he did not yet know if she was pregnant.

It had been only two days since he foolishly risked making their tenuous relationship more permanent. If there was anything that André openly despised, it was permanence, especially where women were concerned. And the simple girl still knows not what to expect, he thought with some amusement. She has probably already forgotten what little I have told her, for she did not even question my thoughtless indulgence of her.

That was not precisely true. Tierney did wonder if coitus interruptus had been employed, but dared not ask. She could not bring herself to pose such a personal question to him. She had gone to great lengths to get here, she believed, and God in His generally confusing manner would provide for the child, should one make itself known. The child, after all, would be born innocent of its parents' sin.

As André dressed to go ashore, Tierney impatiently shuffled the deck of cards. She was already packed to leave herself—had been for the entire voyage, she rudely reminded herself glancing at the flimsy duffel. Now all she needed was to summon the courage to ask for her pay. He evidently had no intention of offering it, the rogue!

She envied him his striking attire, and sullenly waited for him to dole out her wages or admit he had no intention of paying her for the trouble she had caused. She would not be able to afford such fine clothes, she knew, even if she were to receive full compensation for the voyage. Nonetheless, any feminine clothes would be heavenly, no matter how cheaply made.

Seizing on her sudden impulse to flee, she stood up to face him. "Captain de Montfort," she began more bravely than she felt, "if you would be so good as to pay me my wages, I shall take my leave now."

"Would that were possible, love," he said cheerfully. He seemed more intent on adjusting his cravat than he did in dismissing her. Damn him, anyway!

"What do you mean, you bloody pirate! I have just seen you count out more money than you would owe me in a year's time!" she stormed. "It is possible—it is!"

"Watch your language, Tierney," he answered her smoothly. "You won't be a sailor much longer, and you are intelligent enough to realize that if anything carries you well in your reentry into womankind, it will be your polish and decorum."

He looked at her abominable clothing and with absolute amusement added, "It seems to me, *chérie,* that you'd best get busy washing your tongue and polishing your manners."

His laughter hurt more than she would have deemed possible. She honestly believed that once embarked, she had no choice but to play out this charade, and now his insensitive chuckles bit her pride. Her anger had fled, however, and now she simply pleaded with him. "Captain," she started, but then: "André, please! You promised me my freedom at the first port and we are here. Spare me any further insults if you have any heart at all. My earnings were to buy a dress and a few nights' lodging. But if truly you will not pay me even a token, then I will gladly leave your ship for naught!"

It took considerable self-control to keep from striking her. "Never! Never—do you hear?—never speak to me again in such a pious, demeaning tone. It sickens me!" he spat.

Tierney was so upset, she completely mistook his meaning. Anger had turned to begging, begging now remorse. "I'm sorry," she sobbed. "I did not intend to call you by your first name. It is simply that I must leave now. If you put me ashore later tonight, I will lose my way! Captain," she wept, "I am so scared!"

"It isn't your use of my name," he sighed, coming toward her. "I hate beggars. Their mewlings only serve to make a cold heart colder." He reached for her now, and pulled her close. "Tierney, Tierney," he whispered into her hair. "Do you know me so little?" She was scared, he knew, for her body was stiff against him.

Releasing her, he lightly held her shoulders. "Look at me, Tierney," he demanded. She lifted her eyes and found his handsome face and piercing blue eyes.

"I cannot leave you here, Tierney. The night before last, remember? *Chérie*, I failed to take precaution! Do you understand?" he queried softly. She nodded her understanding, and he added in a more relaxed manner, "I said I didn't believe in spreading my brats around the world. Too many already!" With that, he strode out of the cabin, and through tear-stained eyes, she watched him leave *La Reine*.

"So that was it!" she thought morosely. She really might be with child—and he knew it. Despite her desperate desire to be on solid ground and end this preposterous carnival, Tierney was frightened enough of the prospect of motherhood to dutifully remain on board. She was not sure what the captain had in mind, should such be the case, but she was not foolish enough to pilfer his money drawer (assuming she could pick the lock!) and make an escape.

"What would be the use?" she sighed. "I know nothing of this American city, and he would surely find me—that is, if he looked for me." She wondered if André de Montfort would send out a search. There was not much hope in any case. Tierney could not determine whether getting lost in this foreign place or facing his wrath would be better.

She shuddered involuntarily, and looked at her grimy, salt-laden clothes. "Phew!" she cried. "I must at least have a bath and wash these things."

A knock at the door interrupted her musings. Brushing away the curls that had already started creeping down her neck and tickling her ears in complete disarray, she opened the door.

"Mr. Mauriac! I thought surely you had gone with the captain."

"No, lass," he said glumly. "The captain asked me to stay behind and see to your comfort."

Had André been so insensitive that he had confided their intimacy to the first mate? It was awkward enough already.

Her fears were pushed aside by Paul's next remark. "Tierney, he isn't trying to impress you or in any way force you to remain on the ship. He merely believes that the adjustment to life in America would be easier for you in a new territory, like Louisiana. There, more of the people are newly arrived with backgrounds that are, ah . . . well, family is of little consequence there. I have to agree, lass, that Charleston would not be an ideal place for a young girl alone to settle."

"Tell me about Charleston, please, sir. And this territory—Louisiana, is it?"

Mauriac and she took the chairs where ordinarily Tierney and the captain sat to bicker or dine. It was so much more genteel and comforting with the blondheaded man, she sadly reflected.

Paul told Tierney fabulous tales of the first settling of the colonies, the impoverished and the rich men, women, and children who braved the wilderness and savages to build a new world. The French came also, and the Dutch, Irish, Scandinavians, and already even Italians were com-

ing to this land of plenty. But here in Charleston, he explained, the credit belonged to the English.

He compared the American Revolution to that which
had occurred in France, but she found the political aspects
of establishing a youthful society not nearly as intriguing
as the accounts of its people.

She was disappointed to learn that the savages—Indians,
they called them—were not much in evidence along the
Eastern seaboard. "Then I will see them in the territory?"
she asked hopefully.

"Yes, there are many tribes in Louisiana, but for the
most part, you will see Choctaws. You will see much more
than Indians, my girl. Louisiana is a strange land, almost
tropical. And its history is as rich as the states themselves.
It has been French, Spanish, and French again. Most
recently it was purchased by the Americans. It was their
President Thomas Jefferson, I think, nine years ago. Fifteen million dollars, Tierney, to double their holdings! A
remarkable bargain, to be sure, but these Yankees are
shrewd with their money."

More politics! "Tell me about the people there. Do they
speak English?"

"Yes, many do. And French and Spanish as well as several peculiar dialects common to the Santo Domingan
natives, Indians, and Cajuns. The Creole people, those
descended from the earliest French and Spanish settlers,
are the aristocracy there."

It was too fantastic, thought Tierney. A land full of
strange animals, plants, and people. Like Homer in the
Odyssey, she would marvel at the world's wonders. She
asked about the Cajuns.

She would have been disappointed, had not the first
mate so beautifully narrated his picture. "Like the Poly-
nesians, they are a lovely sight to behold. The women, in
particular, are handsome. They are a delicate blend of
French, Indian, and African blood, and generally, they
are a warm, friendly people. Their language is most odd,
though. French patois. Sort of a combination of French,
English, and Negro dialects."

The women were handsome? Well, no matter. She had
found no evidence of a Cajun paramour among the captain's veritable harem! It pricked her to realize that she

had yet to experience the same twinge of jealousy over Paul Mauriac.

The first mate was rambling on about exotic Louisiana food, but stopped short when he noticed the girl's interest had waned.

"Well, miss, I must be about my duties. Can I get you anything?"

Tierney paused only a second. "A bath!" she exclaimed. Then more calmly, she added, "Would that be possible, Mr. Mauriac?"

"Well, we cannot go ashore. But perhaps we can make some other arrangements. We merchant sailors are not often met with the particular needs of ladies on board, and we are apt to be neglectful." With a bow, he took his leave while Tierney graced him with a smile.

"Mon Dieu," he breathed as he escaped up the hatch, "would she were a few years older, or I a bit younger. André must be blind!"

It was past dinner when Tierney eased her body into the warm water. Her flesh goosed in surprise at first, then melted in sincere appreciation. She sighed and slid down to submerge her face and hair.

It was thus, ungraciously posed, that André saw her, feet rudely hanging outside the wooden tub, and head underwater. He was startled at first, thinking her drowned in despair, but catching her toes wriggle in obvious pleasure, he chuckled. The nymph was still so much a child.

Tierney could have held her breath longer, so great was the tranquility. But his laughter pervaded her solitude, and presently she shot up, sputtering and blinking water from her eyes.

"Well, my little water lily," he teased, "you look happier than I have ever seen you!"

"I was, you mean," she hissed, reaching for a towel.

"Don't let me disturb you, chérie."

His nonchalance could be maddening. She stood, but before she had affixed the cloth about her, he snatched it from her hands. "Relax, will you?" he growled. "You look more like a skeleton than any tempting morsel. Sit down, you little fool."

Tierney was too mortified to make an adequate retort, so she splashed back into the bath in silent rage, crossing her arms to cover her small breasts.

André began unraveling packages he had brought back
with him, but for all the girl's straining her eyes, she could
not see what he was planning. Still eyeing him with suspicion, she watched him candidly approach her. Slowly,
so as not to draw more criticism, she slid further down
into the water.

He laughed aloud and pulled from his coat a small
envelope, sprinkling its contents over the girl and surrounding water. "Bath salts!"

Tierney could not disguise her genuine pleasure. "Oh,
André! It's heavenly . . . the scent is—don't tell me—
damask?"

"Precisely," he responded. "Attar of roses."

"Mmm . . . I've always wanted some. My mum used it.
I never had any perfumes because Nanna said it was
frivolous. But she did keep lavender-scented soap." Without further ado, Tierney ignored him altogether and busily
swished the water to dissolve the fragrant crystals. "Such
elegance," she sighed, and closing her eyes, drowsily
soaked in her first return to femininity.

André sat in his bunk now, content to watch her. His
amusement was somehow touched with sadness too. How
had such a spirited girl been reduced to such a dismal
future; and more importantly, what was he to do with
her?

Tierney regretted having to spoil the serenity of her
soak, but she had yet to thoroughly wash herself. She
would have been grateful for solitude, but she could not
muster the courage to order the captain from his own
cabin. Besides, she reasoned, the man had just graciously
enhanced her long-awaited bath, so she could not find
it in her heart to be angry with him. A seed was taking root
in the young girl's soul, a philosophy of sorts. Life was
becoming a series of compromises, and in order to survive,
one must accept that premise.

Dutifully, she reached for the soap Paul had procured
for her along with the wooden tub.

"Wait!" he said suddenly. André quickly got up from
the bed and began to fumble through more packages.
"Here, catch!" he called, and tossed across to her a smaller
bar of soap. It slipped from her fingers and plunked into
the water, splashing Tierney's eyes. "Rose-scented, as well,"
he said noncommittally.

The girl was speechless. He was being far too kind, she warned herself. But before she could question him, he interrupted her thoughts.

"Hurry, *chérie*. There is more, and you and I have a supper appointment on shore at seven o'clock. If you dally, I'll have to leave you behind."

Tierney needed no further encouragement. To set her feet on land! She frantically soaped her sponge and sudsed her body from head to toe. Dunking again to rinse the soap from her hair, she then quickly struggled to stand and open her burning eyes.

When she did open them, André was standing at the foot of the tub, holding open her towel. She was so excited and fearful of being left behind that she lightly sprang out of the water into his waiting arms.

André worked quickly, running the towel over her small frame and paying particular attention to her dripping ringlets. While the towel was thus draped over her head and face, he heard her squeal. "My clothes! They are filthy!"

When he laughingly pulled the towel from her face, he was met with a mournful gaze. "Am I to act your manservant tonight?" she asked dismally.

"The play is over, Tierney," he said quietly. "You are a young woman, tonight and from this point forward. I'll expect you to use all the proper decorum as befits your true station. Do we understand one another?" he warned.

Tierney was a bit confused, for truly she did not know her station in life anymore. Did he mean that she was to behave as his mistress? But she answered him positively, afraid to change his uncommonly good humor. "Oh, yes! Certainly, Captain." Then, in a wild sprint of new-found freedom, she asked, "Did you bring me a dress as well? Oh, did you, really?"

André chuckled in agreement, and to his genuine amazement was rewarded with a hug from her bare body and a sophic kiss on the cheek. Had the young man known the similarity between this exchange and the kiss bestowed upon the vicar, he would have been gravely disappointed.

Tierney quickly recovered her senses before encouraging him further, and meekly encased herself in the damp towel. André, too, switched moods and went to retrieve the purchases from their boxes. He was impatient now, and already doubting his wisdom in being extravagant with her.

Tierney waited in exasperated silence. It had been so long since she had felt womanly. Had she ever? she wondered incredulously. She already felt nearly intoxicated with the glow of damask emanating from her warm flesh. Never had she so delighted in her very being!

He held up a chemise. "Oh, God," she thought feverishly, "it would have been worth wearing the dreadful binding this whole voyage to merely see it!" Holding it gently in her hands now, she examined the garment carefully. It was satin, eggshell-white in color, with beige satin ribbons entwined in the delicate white lace shoulders and hem. Wriggling it over her arms, she sighed in utter joy. "Perfect!" she cried.

André didn't think so. It fit her small bosom to perfection, he acknowledged, but it fell short along the hem, and only lace reached her navel. Soundly commanding himself to proceed with the frivolous ordeal, he tossed her the matching pantaloons. She climbed into them unceremoniously, oblivious to all but her ecstatic debut into her true gender. As she daintily tied the satin bows above her knees—they, too, were a bit short—he handed her silk stockings and lace garters. She was too busy to notice his quandary. Which dress? he wondered. God knew he had never been so beguiled, so stupid, so foolish with his money. He had gone into the most elegant of Charleston's modistes and purchased several gowns off the model's back, and paid a particularly outrageous price for one that had been made for a Charlestonian bride's wedding trousseau. But he had pictured it on Tierney, and now the Southern belle must wait.

Finally he chose a rich velvet gown of burnt orange. Tierney gasped in utter joy at seeing it. She shook so he could barely slip it over her head, and now as he hooked the back, she managed a very weak, "Oh, what a pity!"

"What's the matter now?" he exclaimed.

"The bodice," she wailed, believing this her only choice. "It doesn't fit. Look!"

He turned her around to face him, and restrained himself from caressing her in open admiration. "You silly goose," he teased. "It's intended to fit like that! It is called an Empress waistline, I believe, and Josephine has made it quite the rage in Europe. It fits here," he said, tracing his fingers along the narrow sash, "under the bosom. Turn around and I'll tie it," he added gruffly.

"Oh, I wish I could see it on me," she moaned.

"You look fine," he flatly answered.

She did. The dress was demurely cut, emphasizing the girl's graceful, slender lines. And the fashionable bustline enhanced her diminutive bosom. Although it was daringly cut to expose the slight cleavage, dark brown lace modestly covered her chest and narrow shoulders to the neck; and satin cuffs, buttons, and the sash of the same brown completed the gown. He studied her with open satisfaction until he noticed her watching him. "Do something about your hair," he ordered her abruptly.

While the captain busied himself with his own attire, Tierney fretted over her hair. Not bothering for permission, she finally reached for his own silver-crested brush and comb. André took notice, but said nothing.

Tierney did the best she could to control her unruly curls, but they sprang into a pattern of their own, heedless of her ministrations. Her hair twirled carelessly around her ears, neck, and high forehead. She stamped her stockinged foot in dismay.

"Lucky for you," he commented, "that Josephine also wears short hair. You ought to post a note of thanks to her."

Tierney giggled and danced about the room, spicing the display with exaggerated curtsies and imaginary toasts of wine.

"Oh, I almost forgot," he interjected in the midst of a pirouette. "Slippers."

Finding them, he presented her with the dainty satin slippers, also brown. She sat down on the bed coyly, and remembering the tart Nancy, asked his assistance in their lacing.

Amused, André knelt before her and tied the ribbons. They were too small, she knew, but dared not admit it. "I feel like Cinderella suddenly transformed into the ugly stepsister with big feet!" she silently mourned.

"Well," he stood. "We are ready to take our leave, mademoiselle." André de Montfort was more pleased with her attire than he was with his own. He had not been able to resist choosing for himself a complementary brown coat and cravat, white shirt, and fawn-colored trousers. Now he regretted his own youthful indulgence, for he thought they must look like a pair of matching Dresden dolls. He was rather embarrassed, but there was no time for a change of clothes by either of them, and Tierney looked as though she would die before taking off the gown!

He threw a soft shawl about her shoulders and they left the cabin without being seen.

As he hailed the clarence coach, he noted that even under the soft streetlamp, her bright curls shimmered a coppery brown. She looked so winsome, in fact, André found it difficult to believe he had ever been duped into thinking her a gangling boy.

He congratulated himself at having selected such appropriate attire for her, and fingering a jewel in his side pocket, he was pleased, too, that he had remembered this final touch. The only criticism of her, he thought, might be the length of her dress. He had misjudged it on the model, and presently saw that her ankles could be seen when she walked. The soft, flat dance slippers did somewhat balance the effect, however, and he could not but admire the pleasing show. "Unfortunately," he mused, "it is doubtful that she can dance."

André smoothly handed the girl up into the carriage, and took his seat opposite. Tierney was surprised that he chose not to sit next to her, and pushed aside her vague irritation at the slight. Others might find her beautiful.

"Where are we going, milord?"

"To the home of a prominent Charlestonian, Charles Pinckney. Several guests, all of them important, will be there. Tierney, I want your word of honor that you will be charming, gracious—if that is possible!—and above all silent, except when called upon to speak." His voice was so stern that it bordered on being threatening, but the young girl was far too excited to make a desultory reply.

"Of course, Captain! I shall behave exactly as you say."

"Good girl. Now, I shall make the introductions. Listen well to what I say, and you should not find much difficulty."

Reaching into his pocket, he added, "And I have something else I would like you to wear, Tierney. It was my mother's, and I shan't make a gift of it, but I think it would be most becoming tonight."

Tierney squinted at his upheld hands in the dim light. She could not see it.

"Do stop that abominable habit!" he chided. "Now close your eyes, and I'll put it on you."

Tierney did as she was bid. She felt his hands go around her neck and knew it must be a necklace.

André was sorely tempted to kiss her, but restrained himself. "There now," he said, sliding back toward his seat, "take a look."

"It is exquisite," she whispered. Never had she owned anything so lovely. Nanna's brooch seemed pinchbeck in comparison. A striking topaz, about the size of a thimble, was secured in a gold pendant that hung from a fragile gold chain. It suited her attire perfectly. Before becoming too enamored of the simple gem, she reminded herself that it was hers just for the evening.

It was futile to peer out the windows of the coach. Tierney was unable to distinguish residential districts from forests except for the occasional fleeting glimpses of lighted streetlamps.

"Here we are," he suddenly announced. "Take care to remember what I have told you."

In a whirl of activity, the carriage came to a halt, the door was opened, and Tierney saw the back of the captain hunch to get his broad shoulders out of the vehicle. Tierney's heart was beating furiously when she overheard a strange voice.

"Evenin' suh. Massa Pinckney 'spectin y'all. You go raht dat way," then a deep chuckle. "But sho', cap'n, you knows de way."

To her amazement, when André handed her onto the ground, she saw who had been speaking. It was a tall, thin, gray-haired man. But his skin was black! Never had she seen a black person, and it was impossible to conceal her absolute awe of him. No Indian, she knew. This man must be African! A tingle crept up her spine as she fantasized the first episode of her odyssey unfolding.

"Nathan, you will have to excuse Miss Chambers. It is her first day in the country," he said with amusement.

"Yassuh . . . ma'am," he bowed, and followed them to the entrance.

"Is that the Yankee dialect?" she whispered.

"God, no! It is an African interpretation of the American Southern drawl, equally difficult to learn. Now be silent," he quietly ordered.

Tierney was beside herself with anticipation. The mansion loomed before them, white-columned and well-lighted, with an expansive portico. Never had she entered such an aristocratic home. It made the English manor where she had first been denied employment seem a mere cottage.

"Good to see you, Massa Mon'fort!" It was another black servant, whose rich costume matched that of the footman. Tierney was finding it difficult to imagine wealth that provided such beautiful uniforms—starched white shirts, green gabardine jackets, and black pants and boots.

A maid took her wrap, a beautiful girl of toffee-colored complexion. Tierney was most anxious to hear her voice also, but the girl merely bobbed when Tierney gave her thanks.

"Ah, André! So good to see you again! You must be doing well, indeed. It has been two years since you have graced our little town," he smiled. "And who is this lovely little belle?" Tierney looked at the gentleman, careful to keep her eyes wide so as not to offend the captain. Never had she heard such slow, deliberate English spoken, and the inflection was almost musical.

"Miss Maureen Chambers, Charles," and turning to Tierney, he continued, "Miss Chambers, this is Mr. Charles Pinckney." Tierney dropped a low curtsy.

"Very pleased to meet you, milord," she murmured.

"Milord!" he chuckled. "Now, Miss Chambers, here in these United States we don't take to titles of nobility. Yes, child, you have a lot to learn . . ."

André interjected an explanation. "Miss Chambers is new to your country, as you can see. She is sailing with us to New Orleans where her kinspeople await her arrival."

"What brings you here, Miss Chambers?" the older man asked. But before she could respond, the captain spoke again.

"Miss Chambers is recently orphaned, Charles," he said quietly. "She has no family left in England, so her relatives in Louisiana have requested she join them."

The host frowned and turning back to the girl, said,

"Well, I'm really sorry about that, sweet child. Truly sorry."

Leading them into the parlor, he took Tierney by the elbow and explained to her that once she had accustomed herself to it, she would forever love her new home. But Tierney was preoccupied with Captain de Montfort's tale of her travels. The web had grown bigger. At least using her Christian name, Maureen, had not been a lie. She wondered how the captain had remembered it.

The room was filled with ladies and gentlemen of elegant bearing, and equally elegant dress. Had she worn anything less splendid than what the captain had chosen, Tierney would have felt sorely out of place.

"Captain de Montfort," said the host, "I would like you to meet my cousins, Mr. Charles Cotesworth Pinckney and his brother, Thomas Pinckney. Folks, this is Captain André de Montfort from France, and his passenger, Miss Maureen Chambers, lately from England."

Everyone graciously welcomed the new arrivals, and André smiled leisurely. "My pleasure, gentlemen."

The first Mr. Pinckney continued, "André, you know, of course, my wife. If you would be so kind, honey, show the little lady around."

Having relegated the ladies' protocol to his wife, he turned back to the captain. "There is someone most anxious to meet you. James Gadsden. If I am not mistaken, James was at college during your last visit with us.

"James," he called, "why don't you and André here have a little chat before dinner?"

Tierney had never met so many wives with the same name before. She was careful to address them in the local abbreviation of "ma'am," but found it impossible to remember which wife went with which Mr. Pinckney. There was one other young woman, a Miss Anna Leah Williams.

Anna Leah and Tierney quickly engaged in girlish conversation, and the two spontaneously warmed to one another.

"Is he your beau? The captain, I mean."

"Beau?" queried Tierney. "I don't think so. We are not close, personal friends, if that is what you mean."

The blond girl giggled. "That's exactly what I meant, Maureen. I'm so relieved," she confessed in a whisper.

"He is absolutely the most beautiful man!" Sighing, she added, "Not that it matters. James is my escort. We aren't engaged, you realize, but I imagine he will propose to me soon. That is, if this nasty war ends soon," she pouted.

Tierney looked across the room at the two young men. She squinted momentarily, but remembered herself and turned back to the pretty girl at her side. "Your young man seems attractive too," she commented, although she had not seen him clearly.

"Aw, he's all right. But he is so terribly serious all the time. You would think that a Yale graduate would be a little more, um, romantic," she confided.

Tierney had not the vaguest notion what a Yale graduate was supposed to be like, but she was spared making a reply by the announcement of supper. James immediately strolled over toward them, glancing at Tierney, then quickly averting his eyes back to Anna Leah.

André followed, and the couples adjourned to the spacious dining hall, preceded by the host and hostess and their older guests and cousins. Mrs. Pinckney directed everyone to their assigned seats, and Tierney sat with the captain to her left, Mrs. Thomas Pinckney to her right, and James Gadsden directly facing her from the opposite side of the table.

Two Negro servants began serving the meal, with a creamed clam chowder and corn muffins opening the course. That was followed by a fruit salad with a sauce that Tierney decided tasted of honey, vinegar, and celery seed. The taste was foreign to her tongue, but she very much enjoyed it, especially spooned over the banana and pineapple chunks. These particular exotic fruits were new to her, although she had seen them in the Silver Steed's kitchens.

What followed was the largest array of dishes she had ever seen delivered to one table. There was baked ham, *faisan en crème,* and chicken pieces that she thought had been sorely abused in baking. Quietly asking André if the distortion was deliberate, he laughingly explained that it had been fried! She sampled a small piece, and to her surprise, found it was delicious. The vegetables were equally varied and well-prepared, and Tierney soon found it difficult to take but a mouthful of each delicacy.

The conversation at the table was serene but formal. Tierney was quickly adjusting her ears to this sonorous English dialect, and only twice did turns in the social amenities confuse her.

André, for the most part, devoted his conversation to Mr. Charles Cotesworth Pinckney. He had long waited to meet the man who so aptly reflected his own sentiments. " 'Millions for defense, but not one cent for tribute . . .' Did you really say that, sir?"

"Well, words to that effect. But since my infamous visit to your country some years ago—you were a mere child then, Captain—I have thought perhaps I was a bit too inclined to leap to conclusions. The XYZ Affair and subsequent document may have been, as Napoleon claims, a complete misunderstanding. You know, of course, that your emperor denied any knowledge of the French agents. That may or may not be so. Perhaps we were duped. But at any rate, I am happy to say, sir, that your country and ours are once again on amiable terms."

And that was a wonder in itself, André considered. The United States had just as many reasons to declare war on France as on England. In truth, both European countries had done their utmost to impair America's neutrality through punitive tariffs imposed by each. An American merchant dealing with France was supposed to pay a penalty fee to Britain, and Napoleon reciprocated by charging the same fees for an American vessel bound for an English port. The French captain wryly perceived that money, the source of virtually all conflict, was the real reason behind the United States's declaration of war. He accurately assumed that the final decision by Congress to choose England over France was the matter of impressment.

André de Montfort admired the American statesman present, and when Mr. Pinckney confessed he might go down in history as a great fool for his role in America's early international intelligence efforts, the captain took issue. "Not so, Governor! The French themselves can only support your position of refusing to buy allies!"

"I thank you, Captain. My greatest fear was that our country was young and vulnerable enough to succumb, thereby setting a precedent for generations to come. It is my fondest hope that the United States never stoops to pay for friendship!"

Meanwhile, Tierney was immensely bored with the conversation at her side. She and Anna Leah chatted occasionally across the table, Tierney commenting on her first taste of American cuisine, and the Southern counterpart describing other unique dishes.

"I wish you had been able to join us for Thanksgiving, Maureen. It's quite an experience for a newcomer, sort of our national harvest day to honor our first founding fathers; Englishmen, as you might expect," she smiled. "We roast turkey and stuff it with dressing and have pecan and sweet potato pies. Everything is just scrumptious!"

Tierney was about to ask if turkey resembled other wild fowl when one of the older women asked rather abruptly, "My dear, are you traveling to New Orleans alone? Certainly a young woman your age should be chaperoned!" she added with a sniff.

Young Mr. Gadsden grinned and was about to make comment when de Montfort broke off his political discussion and said, "Miss Chambers has escort to the new territory, I assure you." Then turning to his hostess, he added, "Mrs. Pinckney, please forgive me! Mrs. Taffey, the young lady's traveling companion, begged me to excuse her tonight. I fear the woman is rather old to journey abroad, and she has not recovered from her first voyage. I completely forgot to extend her apologies earlier."

The hostess nodded graciously and replied that she hoped the lady would soon feel herself. James Gadsden, who could no longer subdue his admiration for the comely Miss Chambers, added, "No one doubts, Captain, that with such a lovely woman on one's arm, any man would fail to remember social amenities from her chaperone!"

When the laughter died down, André addressed the young man. "Mr. Gadsden, I hope you will find this current riff with England short-lived so you can return to your busy schedule here as one of Charleston's most promising merchants."

"I do, too, Captain," he answered seriously. "But our revolution was for naught if we bow to British domination now. I personally have volunteered my services to the army's engineers." Then to Tierney, he added, "My apologies, ma'am, if I offend you."

Tierney said quietly, "Sir, my true homeland is Ireland, so I assure you that my sentiments have not always been entirely British."

The company at large relaxed, and after having been served dessert, the couples retired to the parlor. A beautiful rosewood pianoforte graced the room, and it was soon discovered that both Tierney and Anna Leah were familiar with the instrument. The girls shyly agreed to perform for the small gathering, and after a whispered conference and a few embarrassing starts, soon began to play and sing a medley of ballads. Their voices and fingers complemented one another surprisingly well, and with Anna Leah as soprano and Tierney singing alto, they sang "Greensleeves" and "House Carpenter" in memorable fashion. The entertainment ended with Anna Leah's clear solo performance of American songs.

André de Montfort never took his eyes from the girl in orange velvet, but only James Gadsden noticed. He suspected the French captain had lost his heart to his Irish passenger.

CHAPTER NINE

Tierney did not understand why she felt so annoyed with Captain de Montfort. He had been more than generous with the clothes and toiletries he had purchased for her. The girl imagined that the gifts were far in excess of the wages she could earn in a year as cabin boy, let alone one month. The captain, however, did not make mention of the cost.

In fact, she reflected, he had been more than respectful in every manner. That night after the supper party, he had returned her to *La Reine*; seen her to the master cabin; shown her the rest of her wardrobe, including a silk negligee and a flannel nightgown; then left the ship again—alone and without explanation.

Tierney's pride was pricked that he had shown no further interest in her, especially considering she had never felt so beautiful before in her life. The clothes were enticing enough to make a scarecrow irresistible, she thought. Besides, she pouted, it would have restored her self-respect to deny his advances. Tierney could envision the dramatic scene, telling the captain that she, Tierney Chambers, could not be bought! She, of course, imagined she would have to return all the gifts if indeed they were gifts.

All she had managed to return that night, however, had been the topaz pendant. At even this, de Montfort had merely shrugged, asking her to put it back into his trunk when she retired.

The carriage ride back to the docks had been no more flattering. The only time he had spoken was to comment, "You were beautiful tonight, Tierney. And your musical talents combined with those of Miss Williams were a delight to everyone. Thank you."

It was a rather disappointing end to an otherwise enchanting evening for the young girl. She silently undressed, donning the new flannel gown. "Ah, well," she had sighed, climbing into her berth, "I will learn his game soon enough."

It was now two days later, though, and still Tierney had not fathomed what the captain's plans were. Paul had informed her that they would be setting sail in the morning before dawn. The captain, he explained, had finished his negotiations, and would sell only furniture and wines, waiting for his return voyage to take on a consignment of cotton. However, she had not seen de Montfort since the night of the party, and Paul Mauriac's visits were of little comfort these days. She missed André.

There was much activity this afternoon, and Tierney was growing impatient with her virtual imprisonment in the master cabin. She paced, began a diary which she later tore into shreds, and read more of Jonathan Swift. "I should be happy for this respite from him!" she scolded. Suddenly, she kicked off another pair of new ladies' slippers (also too tight), and threw herself onto the bed. She searched her heart in vain for how she truly felt about handsome André de Montfort.

It was after dark when the captain returned with the box under his arm. Paul greeted him on the deck, and fully aware of André's eagerness to reach New Orleans before the new year, assured him that *La Reine* was ready to embark.

"The British have not yet blockaded any American ports, Paul. To date, reports of action are limited to the northern seaboard and Great Lakes region. I am told that no surprises await us at dawn."

Paul heard the muffled whimpers and thumping, and to his surprise recognized the noises as coming from under Andre's arm.

Seeing Paul's expression, the young man grinned at his first mate. "It is a surprise for Tierney," he winked. "A chaperon for our lady traveler!" Without further hesitation, he bounded down the hatch toward his cabin.

Tierney turned her head away from what tried to disturb her, but the annoyance was persistent. A cold, wet nose nuzzled her cheek and small teeth chewed her earlobe. It tickled, and the girl giggled, still half asleep.

A sharp little yap awoke her fully, however, and her eyes flew open to see the puppy's soft brown eyes staring into her own. She sat up and as she stroked his soft, light beige fur, the pup's tail wagged at a furious pace.

"Well, little muffet!" she whispered happily, "however did you get here?"

"Must be a stowaway, like yourself," said the captain. Tierney jumped at his voice. "Where did you find him?" she queried, turning back toward the frisking animal.

"Are you asking me where I found the dog, or vice versa?"

"My, you are flippant! I was asking this lovely little cocker spaniel how he came upon a scoundrel like you, of course!" she teased.

"Then I'll let him answer you," sighed André, pulling off his boots.

Tierney was presently so preoccupied with the dog, she once again forgot her all too easily forgotten sense of propriety. Kneeling on the bed with her back to the captain, she slapped her hands on the coverlet this way and that. She soon had the puppy in a short frenzied chase from left to right, growling in mock attacks upon her fingers. "Oooh, you little darling," she cooed, "Watch those baby teeth or your mistress will thump your nose."

Watching her thus, hips swaying invitingly in her innocent play, André silently swore. She was making it damnably difficult to control his own urge to play—not so innocently.

Suddenly aware of the captain's view, Tierney jumped from the bed and brushed her skirts into place. She turned then and squinted toward him. "May I keep him, sir?" she asked in a guarded tone.

"Yes. Why the devil do you think I bought him?" he replied gruffly. "For the rest of this voyage, you will have to remain below except when the majority of the crew sleeps and when Paul or I are on watch. And those occasions will not be as often as you would have it, I am sure.

"I thought it would be easier on all of us if you had some amusement here in the cabin. And later, in New Orleans, if you don't ruin the dog with too much affection, he will be of company to you there. Maybe even some protection, though that is doubtful," he ended.

"Of course!" she cried. "It is most generous of you, Captain. I am grateful, sir, truly I am," she murmured. Picking it up, she nuzzled the puppy.

She put him down on the rug then, warning him not to wet it. "What shall I name you, little one?" she whispered. And then it struck her. The captain had called her fictitious chaperon Mrs. Taffey, a silly name really, but she had not the nerve to tease him about it. But the pup's blond-and buff-colored curls reminded her of the candy, so she quickly concluded that a dog so rare could only be Lord Taffey. "Lord Taffey," she repeated aloud. "And I shall call you Taffey or Taff for short, milord," she giggled. The puppy responded with a cheerful bark and the incessant wagging of his short tail.

André was privately pleased that the dog was so happily received. He had given Tierney and their precarious position a great deal of thought. More consideration, in fact, than he had given his trade negotiations in Charleston— an unprecedented turn of the head for him. He dared not examine his motives, but merely told himself that once she was in Louisiana, he could again sail with a free conscience. "That is, dear God, if she is not with child."

Even if she weren't pregnant, he mused, something about her played on his hitherto stalwart heart. He decided it must be simple human pity that he experienced for a girl so young, adrift without friends or family. André de Montfort knew that a mere pet was no compensation for loved ones lost, but he genuinely hoped the dog would bring some comfort to his young mistress.

"I'll take Taffey on deck for his walks," he said. "The men will not be happy, but they will not complain except among themselves."

"Do they know about me? I mean, rather, are they aware that a woman is on board?"

"Yes, Mr. Mauriac told the crew yesterday. I instructed him to tell them everything about your disguise, and I am quite certain the common quarters has been the scene of numerous accounts by now of how *La Reine*'s foolish captain and first mate were duped by a mere slip of a girl. So we are the laughingstock, as I predicted we would be," he muttered irritably. "But I see no point in continuing the masquerade all the way to Louisiana. Besides, I

demand honesty from them and to offer them less would
be a mistake in the long run."

"Then why," she timidly inquired, "can I not take Taffey
on deck myself?"

His face darkened, but he answered her quietly. "*Chérie*,
would you tempt my good men into brawling for your
attention? Surely you realize a sailor is sorely beset with
weeks, sometimes months, without a woman to ease him!
No, Tierney. You stay below," he commanded. André
studied her. It was tempting for him, too, having her in
such proximity. But he was damned fond of her, he admitted, and for her own good he promised himself to
think of her as a child.

She picked up the now sleepy puppy and whispered,
"You will be careful, sir? He is so small, so defenseless!"

André walked over to the girl sitting on the floor with
the dog in her lap. Tousling her curls, as she herself
might scratch her pet's head, he said gently, "Tierney,
your little Lord Taffey will be safe, I assure you. If it is
the men you worry about, take rest. When Paul told them
of your identity, they were quite embarrassed by their
rough handling of you the night of the gale. I hear Pelier
is most abjectly apologetic, and now delights the men
with stories of your gentle healing of his wounds. Wounds
well-deserved, I'll warrant!" he added more sternly.

"Has Taffey eaten?" she suddenly asked.

André did not conceal his amusement. "Well, lass, he
sleeps. Does a mother wake her babe to nurse?"

"No," she giggled. Then she remembered the captain
himself and asked whether he had yet dined.

André explained that he had taken his supper at a
Charleston inn before coming on board. It would be a
long day, he told her, and an early start.

He undressed then, and turning his back to Tierney
who still sat with the pup motionless on the floor, he said,
"If you are worried about me, and think that I have
bought your charms with a few simple gowns and a pet,
fear not. I have never forced my attentions on anyone,
Tierney, and you are no exception."

Tierney finally was able to put into words what had
weighed on her mind all day. "Then may I forfeit my
wages in exchange for your generosity?" she choked out.
"I have nothing else to offer."

André sensed the girl was on the verge of tears again, and rather than throwing back at her that her accumulated earnings would not even cover the expense of her undergarments, he cautiously answered her. He did not think he could endure any more of her foolish weeping.

"I don't want your wages, Tierney. And you are correct, they would not be enough, in any case." Sighing and adjusting the blanket about his bare shoulders, he continued. "I bought the clothes and dog on impulse, if you insist on knowing. I cannot explain it further. Consider them all Christmas presents, if you wish, and your birthday present, as well. You did say Stephenmass, on Christmas Eve?"

"Yes," she said, "but . . ."

"Well, now, *chérie*. It is settled then. We shan't be anywhere but on water, nor doing else but work come the holidays. So enjoy your Christmas now. You said you would be seventeen this year?"

"Yes, Captain."

After warning her about the morrow's early approach, André ordered her to open her berth and get to sleep. He heard the pup whimper when she kissed and put him down. While he listened to the rustling of her dress as she took it off in exchange for the flannel nightdress, the young man wondered at his lack of common sense. Why had he given in and bought the damned dog? He didn't need to bother commanding her to keep it on the floor. He knew as soon as he fell to sleeping, the girl would tuck her little prize under the sheets with her!

Tierney was busily unwrinkling papers from the boxes and carefully spreading them in the corner near the privy so that another stain might be avoided on the colorful carpet she so admired. She had now incorporated into her daily chores brushing the pile vigorously with a broom, and delighted in the multiple hues that made themselves more evident with each grooming.

Surprisingly, the puppy accepted the papers for what they were, and as soon as he had made use of them, Tierney picked him up and rewarded him with muffled congratulations and a gentle squeeze. Taffey responded with another yap. Tierney held her breath, anticipating an angry curse from Captain de Montfort, but none came.

Smiling, she pulled her berth out and lay down with

her warm, wriggling gift. Lord Taffey. She sighed drowsily, and confident that the man above her slept soundly, whispered, "Thank you, André, for the puppy. And thank you, Lord, for André de Montfort."

He was not asleep, and only after Tierney fell to quiet dreaming did he sit up. Opening the drawer of his bedside table, he withdrew a cigar and lit it from the lamp above. As the pungent smoke swirled through the air, André looked down at the sleeping girl beside him. He must reach New Orleans before she played too closely on his once steadfast heart.

La Reine de la Mer's massive hull creaked as if in agreement. No mere girl must come between the ship and her captain.

André awoke before the sun cast its first rays over silent Charleston harbor. To his amazement, he found the dog curled outside the covers at his feet. He chuckled and in a low voice called the animal. "Here, boy. Come, Taffey!" The puppy roused himself and, frisking his short tail, leapt up on the man's curly-haired chest. "That's enough now," scolded André. "What's the matter with you, pup? You're sorely mistaken in trading my big feet for the warmth of your mistress's arms! And women are a jealous sort, m'boy. She'd be sure to resent it if you prefer my company."

Getting up and silently slipping into his trousers and sweater, he softly whistled to the dog. "Come along. You'll take some fresh air, and we'll put you back into bed with her before she even misses you."

Taffey made a valiant effort to jump clear of the lower berth where Tierney still slept, but fell short of his mark. He landed on top of her buttocks, and the girl awoke to the startling sensation of paws on her backside and André's laughter ringing in her ears. Scrambling to her feet, she smacked the puppy and whirled to face the captain.

"You!" she sputtered.

"No, *chérie*," he said, still laughing. "I assure you the little Lord took that brave dive on his own initiative!" He couldn't stop smiling, but his manner made a subtle switch from mirth to pure pleasure. Although she wore the cotton garment laced to her throat, the light was spreading from the east through the porthole behind her. She had not the vaguest notion that the captain could see clearly distinguished her entire form, from her gold-tipped hair to her slender bare ankles. André drank in the sight at his leisure, momentarily quite confident about the future and whatever it held.

A knock at the door interrupted his perusal. Tierney jumped at the sound, and swept the blanket around her as she sprinted for the closet, the puppy close at her heels.

"Entrez!"

Paul appeared in the doorway looking as though he had spent the night without sleep. He scanned the room suspiciously, apparently searching for something amiss. "She's ready, sir. All ready to sail whenever you give the command."

"Good. Now stop peering about like an old spinster. The girl is fine . . . I told you I wouldn't harm her. As a matter of fact, she's hiding from you," he chuckled. Still speaking in French, he added, "There by the closet door. She is quaking like a little church mouse. No, don't look! She isn't an idiot, Paul, and will know we speak of her."

"André," the first mate started worriedly, "I have a proposal for you."

The younger man frowned slightly. "Well?"

"I was thinking. Although *La Reine* has no accommodations for passengers, and though Tier—the girl—is not a passenger, as such . . . well, I would be more than happy to surrender my cabin to her, and bed myself in the common quarters." Paul Mauriac was justifiably worried about the girl's well-being. He knew better than anyone what a rogue André could be, and suspected that if the captain had not already taken the girl's innocence, he would now with his decided change of behavior since arriving in Charleston.

"No, Paul. I have my reasons. I'll handle this my way!"

The first mate was prepared to argue the point, but André cut in, "Do not bring up the subject again, Paul! That's an order!"

He was mildly perplexed as he watched his friend of thirteen years turn on his heel and angrily stalk toward the deck. André made to call his man back, but thinking further on it, slammed the door and seated himself at his desk.

Swearing vehemently in several languages, he jerked on a boot. As he reached for the second one, Taffey attacked

it from behind. The brief tug-of-war with the man yelling
in French, and the pup's growling brought Tierney to
tears of laughter.

"Oh, stop it, you two!" she finally managed. Taffey
merrily raced to her with a mischievous bark, and began
licking her still bare toes. Despite his ill temper with Paul,
André smiled.

Before leaving the cabin with the puppy, André instructed Tierney to once again don her boy's garb. Noting
the expression of disappointment on the girl's face, he
added, "My apologies, love. But we must take precautions
should the reports on British naval movements be errone-
ous. There may be a blockade out of land sight, in which
case *La Reine* will need a foolproof stratagem to outfox
John Bull.

"If we are searched, you are to be my English cabin
boy again. Do you still have the priest's letter?"

Tierney nodded. She had been unaware that political
considerations were indeed vital to the safety of the ship
and her crew, but she was now beginning to realize the
gravity of the situation. She had heard rumblings of impressment in London, and Paul Mauriac had described in
detail some of the problems between the United States
and England in naval confrontations. He told her that
this very issue of American merchant marines being
forced to serve the Royal Navy had led to the war.

Noting her serious attention, he continued. "Good girl.
If we are boarded, listen carefully to what I say, and if
addressed, speak that damned little accent you attempted
to use when first disguising yourself here. We fly the
Dutch flag, and my crew will remain silent. Only you,
Paul, and I will be able to converse with them." Seeing
Tierney's genuine concern now, he added gently, "Don't
worry, *ma petite*. I have assurances that no blockade will
surprise us, but it is best to prepare for the unexpected."

Then removing the neutral flag, André left the cabin
accompanied by the diminutive Lord Taffey.

Tierney made quick work of doffing her gown and putting into place the now reprehensible disguise. She wrinkled
her nose in disgust, and remembering André's instructions,
practiced a Cockney tongue to the walls as she put the
cabin to order.

After a light meal of fresh fruits and boiled fowl at

noon, André poured two glasses of Madeira. Without asking Tierney if she cared to join him in a drink, he handed her a goblet and gestured her to remain seated. "I appreciate your willingness to play a boy again, Tierney. But we seem to have managed to circumvent a blockade— if, in fact, any have yet been arranged.

"Drink your wine, *chérie,* and get dressed however you want." His voice was suddenly thick with desire as he remembered his first encounter with her in bed. He now felt it would be impossible to continue this mockery of chastity when his own body clamored for release. His restraint was wearing thin. Pouring himself another drink, he was surprised by Tierney's raising her glass for a refill of the heady wine too.

The silence was deafening. They drank, looked at one another, and looked away again at intervals. André thought about their first meeting in London, his bemusement over a silly young girl even then. He thought of her honestly, not pretending to be annoyed anymore. Here was a truly remarkable young woman. She had the ambition to leave unhappy memories of her lost family, and that ambition had taken her so far as to forsake her own identity. He had to admit she was clever enough to completely fool him that first week, and he had to admire her for it.

But she was touchingly feminine too. He wanted to think of her as a child, his ward, perhaps, until they reached Louisiana. But he must be careful, he warned. Having enjoyed such intimacy with her, it was no simple task thinking of her as either a child or his ward.

André was frankly confused. He wanted more of the relationship than he could afford to give and more, he believed, than he had any right to ask of a girl of such tender age. "Still," he thought, "she is lovely in her own, impish way. No," he corrected himself, "Tierney is more than that. She is lovable."

Tierney, too, was confused. She wanted Andre's approval now, wanted his attention. She wanted *him.* She wondered if lovemaking caused a girl to fall in love, or if the reverse were true—that loving a man resulted in lovemaking. It was truly perplexing to her.

She sensed that combined happiness and sadness again. She thought about her fanciful dreams of a "prince"— someone who had pressed a coin into her hand and stolen

her heart. Such childishness! Looking at him now, his
steady gaze not revealing his own thoughts, Tierney felt
as helpless as when Nanna had died. How could a handsome wealthy man who had traveled the world ever return
her love? It was futile, she believed. To André, she was
a mere nuisance.

It was André who started to speak when they heard the
pounding at the door.

It was Paul, but the French words were lost to her.
André yelled back, and muttering a vivid oath, he abruptly
pulled himself away from the table and ran to his trunk.
He strapped on a pistol.

"Tierney, we were mistaken. A British frigate has been
sighted! Stay below and remember what I said earlier.
If you hear shots, however, disregard everything about an
English cabin boy. Put on your best finery, and quickly. If
they break into the cabin, you are an English maiden
taken hostage off the coast as protection for a French
crew. Tell them you have been sorely abused, and feared
for your life.

"They will take pity on you, and you will be returned
safely to your homeland." He stopped and stared at her
for a moment. "Do you understand, *ma petite*? If all is
quiet, you play a boy. Otherwise, make quick work of
presenting yourself as a lady in distress. Don't fail me,
Tierney. Promise me!"

She nodded her comprehension. If André de Montfort
failed to dissuade His Majesty's Ship from seizing *La
Reine,* then she, Tierney Chambers, was ordered to charge
her captain with more crimes. Tierney nodded, but silently swore that she must disobey him in the latter case. She
could not bring herself to treason against the one she
truly loved.

As she picked up the barking puppy and sat on the floor
to rock and soothe them both, she heard the boom of the
first warning cannon fired, and felt her house in Belfast
collapse before her eyes.

"Andrew Montfort, sir. And this is Paul Morris, my first
mate. Welcome aboard, Lieutenant!"

The naval officer gazed about him suspiciously. Seeing the
crew standing at attention, he barked, "Men, you are all
ordered to lay down your arms by His Majesty, King

George!" The crew remained politely silent and did not move.

"Sir," André interjected quietly, "my men are not armed. And they don't understand a word of English. I don't mean to rush you, Lieutenant, but I have my orders too!" Glancing at the other two officers who accompanied the frigate's inspector, he whispered into the Englishman's ear, "As I have said, my mission is secret. If you would be so kind as to follow me to my cabin, I shall be happy to show you my identification."

The lieutenant turned to his men. "Remain here. Hold this Mr. Morris until my return." The two saluted their superior officer and stood on either side of Paul, their bayonets pointed menacingly at the crew at large. Nine others sat at attention in the dinghy, bumping against the ship's hull below.

"Mr. Montfort," the officer said sullenly, "should any surprises await me below, not one of your men will survive to tell it!"

André smiled calmly. "Let's go, Lieutenant."

She heard the voices approach. Then André laughed, dispelling her fears. He evidently had everything under control. The door opened, and Tierney stood rigid as Taffey rushed the stranger with a single leap at his foot. The lieutenant automatically drew his pistol, and Tierney clamped her mouth shut to stifle a scream.

André laughed again. "Surely, sir! You do not feel threatened by a mere cur."

"By Jesus!" the man exploded, "Why the devil is a dog at sea?"

"It is to be a gift, Lieutenant. Token appreciation for a lady friend of mine." Grinning broadly, he added, "Now, any man at sea can appreciate that!"

Neither man took notice of Tierney's sudden vexation. "He can be such a cad with words," she thought angrily.

The intruder relaxed somewhat, but stated haughtily that he wanted to hear the captain's explanation, not his romantic exploitations.

"Of course. Let me retrieve the documents." Opening a drawer of the desk, André handed him false papers of identification, with a seal and a complete list of pseudonyms for each crew member. "What's your name, lad?" the lieutenant asked without glancing up.

"Tierney Chambers, your lordship."

"I don't see a Chambers here," he responded to de Montfort.

"We picked him up in London last month. Get your letter, Tierney," he ordered. "You see, our other cabin boy jumped ship in your fair country to join his English family."

Tierney ransacked the duffel, and finding the now-worn parchment, awkwardly presented it to the naval officer with a stiff bow. "Here, guv'nor. Hope it's what you be wantin'."

"Do you miss your homeland, son?"

"Yes, sir. That is, I miss London a bit. Not much in Salisbury for a boy without a trade. The cap'n 'ere, now 'e's teachin' me just fine. Says I'll be seaworthy as 'imself someday!" Tierney responded with mocking flattery.

The man turned back to André. "Talkative whelp, eh? There's mick blood there, I'd warrant! Still and all, if the lad's as good as he says, we might have some use of him. There's no doubt but that he's an English subject, so these bloody Americans can't accuse us of impressing one of their own."

Tierney reddened and narrowed her eyes. It had not occurred to her that she might be impressed by the frigate! With André's next words, she was even more stunned.

"I'd be more than agreeable to that, Lieutenant. Tierney here is not all he says he is, and I never said he would be seaworthy. Not in twenty years, if I'm any judge. We've caught him pilfering more than his rations from the galley too. So I won't brook any argument if you want to take him with you . . ."

The lieutenant was having some second thoughts about impressing the boy. Studying Tierney now, he decided the cabin boy looked a bit consumptive and privately considered he would look the fool bringing only this poor specimen back with him. "I didn't say I was positive I wanted the lad, Captain. Now, what about this nonsense of a secret mission? Do you have any proof?" he asked doubtfully.

"Keep your voice down, Lieutenant," warned the sinewy Frenchman. Turning to Tierney, he commanded, "Be off, brat! And take that damned dog with you! If he soils this cabin once more, I'll feed you both to the fishes!"

Tierney swept out of the room with the yapping puppy in her arms.

Presently, André turned to the officer with disgust. "I might ask you, sir, the very same proof. I cannot believe you are acting under orders. I was assured no English vessels patrolled this area, else I would have refused the assignment."

"What the devil are you talking about?" demanded the Englishman heatedly.

"I am talking about you, man! And I am sorely tempted to report your insubordination to the Admiralty. I am working in behalf of your government, by virtue of the prime minister. My contacts are to remain absolutely anonymous and I am furious with this apparent breach of contract," the captain muttered angrily.

The young officer was at a loss for words. The turn in conversation had completely taken him off guard. "I . . . I am sorry, Captain Montfort. But I assure you that I, too, am under orders."

"Perhaps so," admitted de Montfort, "but it merely goes to prove the ineptness of British intelligence maneuvers. Wait," he said.

Returning to his desk, he removed the first drawer and reached behind to retrieve a smaller one that was hidden. "This may help explain my precarious position," he continued, handing another document to the lieutenant.

After studying the configurations briefly, the man looked up in confusion. "But I do not understand a word of this!" he exclaimed.

"Of course you don't understand it!" he exploded at the lieutenant. "It is coded. I have already explained to you that my mission is highly secret. Do you think for one moment I, or your own government, for that matter, would risk carrying instructions in English?" André was fairly shouting at this point.

The Englishman, however, was unconvinced. "You must understand my position, Captain. I'll need to know more if I am to forego searching your ship. From what you have already told me, I am tempted to believe you. But factually, you have presented nothing concrete. For all I know, this may be a ruse!"

André paused only a moment before responding. "You must swear to me, then, not to repeat what I say. Very few, only those highest in command, know of the secret allegiance."

Goose flesh crept up the officer's neck. He reasoned that something this confidential would best be left that way, but his curiosity got the better of his judgment. "You have my word, Captain."

"There is a man in Charleston," André began quietly, "but I will not give you his name. He is the sworn enemy of Talleyrand and Bonaparte, and it is he to whom I delivered part of the message. As you well know, your government is far more concerned with the growing French empire than this ridiculous squabble with the United States."

The lieutenant nodded, silent in his envy of the handsome man before him. His own career seemed quite dull in comparison.

"Now, take the Dutch," André continued. "We are a simple people really, wanting no more than free commerce and respect for our desire to remain neutral. Unfortunately, Boney refuses to see it our way. In any case, I am merely a merchant sea captain, working incognito for the time being, for the freedom of our mutual trade benefits.

"It is just rumored, of course, but I have heard some reports that—no, I shan't say. Even if I had proof of those rumors, I would not be at liberty to speak of them." André silently wondered if his fictitious rambling was just outlandish enough to dupe the wide-eyed lieutenant in front of him.

"What? What is rumored?" cried the Englishman. "Surely you can say! I have given you my word of honor, sir!"

André was privately amused. The nincompoop was completely baffled now. He signaled the man to lean closer. In a low voice, he said, "I have been informed—quite confidentially, of course—that this war between your country and the Americans is purely a stratagem designed to hoodwink Napoleon. Only the very highest on either side are privy to the secret allegiance between the two. The hope is that Napoleon will believe the Crown sufficiently demoralized by another confrontation with her old subjects to take the bait and attempt an all-out offensive against the English. Whereupon all of us, Americans, English, Dutch, and even Spain, will surprise Boney with a unified front to overthrow him!"

The story was so outrageous that the poor lieutenant was speechless.

"I don't quite know what to say, Captain," the visitor finally managed.

"Say nothing," André warned. "Or else I will report you to the Admiralty." As a final thought, he added, "I was correct when I told you that your frigate was not supposed to patrol these waters?"

"Yes, sir," the other admitted. "We are actually on a return voyage from the Honduras. But we knew war had been declared, and my commander . . . Well, sir, we did take it upon ourselves to stop you."

"Well stop me, you have! And I must be on my way. Remember, say nothing of our conversation."

"What shall I tell my commander, Captain?"

André shrugged. "That is your problem, Lieutenant."

Tierney had attempted to speak to Paul, but was prevented from doing so by the two bayonet-bearing guards. The crew also were not allowed to converse, and only Pelier dared smile at the girl, once again in her boy's costume.

One of the sailors from the dinghy had inquired as to their comrades' safety. Assured that everything was in order, he asked about the dog barking. Tierney happily held Taffey for the men to see, and laughingly told them, "He isn't for sale. He's the captain's . . . Bought him for a ladylove!"

A muffled outburst of chuckles was heard from the rowboat. "You be English!" cried one sailor. "And the ship?"

"She's Dutch!" returned the girl. "Me, now, they picked up in London. I'm the cabin boy," she added as if this were the grandest occupation in the world, cocking a thumb in her belt loop in an absurdly proud gesture.

Even the guards were now amused by the youth's guileless conversation, and Paul could not smother an impulse to laugh. No one heard the captain and lieutenant return.

The latter announced to his men they would take their leave, but André had already dismissed the delay. Instead, his eyes followed Tierney and he watched as she leaned over the taffrail to wave at the departing sailors. Remembering the interruption in the cabin, he swore under his breath.

It was not likely that he would find her so pensive tonight. "Well, what I might have told her is best left unsaid," he mused. Thinking on the Arabic bills of lading he had employed as coded English intelligence documents, he threw back his head and laughed. As the frigate with her bemused lieutenant disappeared over the horizon, the captain whistling now, strolled toward the helm.

When he returned to his cabin after nightfall, his nostrils were scintillated by a familiar scent. It was the perfume he had purchased for Tierney; turning, he found her standing before the heater, her back to the door.

She was clad in the sheer silk negligee he had hopefully included in her wardrobe. From his vantage point, the soft material clung enticingly to her slim hips and long, shapely legs. The sight was so fetching that he stood rigidly by the door, speechless in his surprise.

"I thought perhaps we might enjoy a quiet supper," she said tremulously. She, too, stood motionless. "Where is my courage?" she thought dully. "I am dressed to play the adulteress. Surely, I can turn to face my correspondent!"

But she was spared further decision-making as she felt his arms embrace her from behind. When he turned her around to press her willowy body close, she burrowed her face into the hollow of his broad shoulder.

"*Chérie*," he whispered. "My lovely pet!"

He lifted her chin to look into her eyes, and found instead tear-streaked cheeks and quivering lips. "Open your eyes, Tierney," he demanded huskily, growing impatient with her inordinate penchant for tears. "I'm not so frightening, am I?"

Tierney looked at him then and shook her head.

"If not me what, then, do you fear?"

"Damnation," she replied meekly.

André was tempted to laugh. Pregnancy, yes. The fear for her future, he could understand that. Even the threat of a soiled reputation should their liaison be discovered; he could appreciate a girl's apprehension. But damnation? In his opinion, something that remote was preposterous.

Nonetheless, he stopped his caresses and wordlessly led her to the table.

She had obviously gone to great lengths with the supper before them. The crystal twinkled in the lamplight, and the fruits, cheeses, and cold meat were appealingly arranged on a sideboard. Pouring the wine, he handed her a glass.

"A toast, mademoiselle . . . to the only woman who ever bewitched me."

Tierney looked up in candid surprise. Surely he was joking! "It is you, sir, who has bewitched me!" She drained the glass in one breath, and gasping, asked for another.

"Whoa!" he laughed. "Sit down before you . . ."

"Yes, yes," she interrupted impatiently. "Before I . . ."

". . . crack your derrière!" he finished.

The couple retired to the chairs, but the joke was forced and uncomfortable. André refilled both glasses. Neither felt like eating, but the captain politely sliced meat for them and began the meal in silence. Tierney nibbled absently at the cheese and salted pecans.

"Quite thirsty," she mumbled some time later.

"*Oui*," he replied, and getting up, he left the cabin. When he returned moments later with two more bottles of wine, he found Tierney attempting to bribe Taffey into rolling over for bits of food.

"Don't let her fool you, boy. Your mistress merely teases, you know. Don't expect a morsel for your efforts!"

"Stop it, milord!"

"André," he corrected.

"André, then. I want him to learn some tricks. I have heard that the younger they are, the easier it is to teach them. But I have never had a pet of my own."

"Neither have I," he muttered under his breath. "More wine?"

"Please."

Well into their second bottle, André began talking. "I don't understand you, Tierney. I do not know why you began this nonsense, posing as a boy in the first place. Now, you greet me tonight, dressed for seduction. I think to myself, 'Finally, she welcomes me. She wants me— just as I want her.' Then you cry. You prepare a delightful repast, but refuse to touch it. What do you want?"

When she did not answer him, he gritted his teeth. "God's blood, Tierney! What is it you want?"

"I don't know," she sighed miserably. "Truly, I don't. I want, at least, I *think* I want you. Love you," she whispered. "Then I tell myself that I cannot. My Nanna, my very mother would shudder in her grave to know the depravity to which I have sunk," she moaned. Before her second time in bed with him, she never would have believed such passion even existed within her. But the urge was so strong, she now constantly battled to regain a faltering sense of virtue.

Presently in her state of semi-inebriation, she looked down at the silk bodice in despair. What did she want, indeed? Whatever was she doing?

André was duly disturbed by the girl's self-reproach. As far as he was concerned, she was guiltless. And he doubted seriously that there was anything between men and women to feel guilty about, anyway! He reminded himself, however, that virtue was of paramount importance to most young women, and he had taken advantage of the girl the night of the gale. The second incident was different, he realized; but again, he might be held liable for awakening the girl's passions in the first place.

Suddenly he stood up and handed her to her feet, as well. "Tierney, hear me out. I'll not repeat this. As I have said, I have never forced a woman against her wishes. And I do not yet know what it is you want. That God would eternally forsake you for following what in nature He decrees, I sincerely doubt. But that is a decision that you alone can reach. Even your mother could not help you, *ma petite.*

"So I'll not force you. But never again trick me into believing you do know what you want from me. If I find you scantily dressed and obviously scented again, I'll not hesitate. I'll put you in my bed and enjoy what I want! *Comprenez-vous?*"

"*Oui*," she giggled.

She was filled with relief. She had another chance to revive her weakening defenses and return to propriety. Thank God he was a decent man, after all. She must consider herself very fortunate, and pray for guidance.

André watched as the fleeting expressions of gaiety and

guilt and gratitude swept over her face. Smiling, he quipped, "I believe you are besotted, milady."

"Nay, sir," she bantered. "I am merely giddy with the discovery that you, milord, are a gentleman and a prince in truth!"

André de Montfort laughed appreciatively. He had been called many things by ladies of his acquaintance, but never these. "I never said I was either. Remember that, *chérie*."

Picking up their goblets, he said, "But I will propose a final toast this night before retiring to my empty bed. To you, Miss Chambers!" he exclaimed. "And your hopeful return to chastity."

Tierney winced at the blatant rub, but dutifully downed the last glass. She felt light-headed, but not so much so that she would stumble. Carefully, she turned her back to him, and made to open her berth. She should be wearing flannel, she thought; but shrugging her bared shoulders, decided it would be best to quickly get into bed and cover herself with blankets. Bending over was dizzying, and she thought she might be sick.

"Is it terribly warm in here, or do I imagine that?" she queried.

André was satisfied that he had drunk himself into indifference now. But when he turned around in his own state of undress to answer her, he saw the shimmering silk emphasize the small roundness of her hips as she bent over the lower bunk. His heart pounded in his ears and his loosely strung undergarment did little to conceal his plight.

"It is very hot," he managed. "I'll open the portholes."

"I'll get this one," she offered amicably. And climbing over her bunk and onto his, she reached for the brass lock. It was not the most graceful movement he had ever witnessed her make; in fact, she was decidedly clumsy with the effects of wine. But it was enough to entirely turn his thoughts away from gallantry.

She swung open the circular window just as he lunged for her. "Oh, my God!" she cried as she felt herself flung upon the bed.

André was senseless with desire. He ripped the nightgown apart, rudely sliding his hands over her. She tried halfheartedly to slip out of his hold while he made quick work of stripping off his only garment, but the attempt was futile for he then threw himself on top of her.

She wriggled, laughing, a few more minutes, her world becoming a swirling kaleidoscope of shapes and colors. "I can scream," she thought giddily, but when she opened her mouth to do so, he quelled her with a long passionate kiss. The scream died in her throat, and became instead a low anguished groan.

They both lay silent for a long time.

André felt wretched. Never had he acted so impetuously, so thoughtlessly. "Damned stupid of me," he thought. Now what was he to do? Anxiety had altogether sobered him.

The girl hoped he would say nothing. She felt a tremendous void in her spirit, and only occasional twinges of self-condemnation made her aware that she still lived— still held tenuously to her soul. What had he said earlier? That she had bewitched him . . . Was that it, after all— she was a witch? "No," she scolded herself, "nothing that theatrical or imaginary. I am simply a wanton woman, no better than Nancy. Perhaps I am worse," she reflected. At least the prostitute was honest in her intentions, not trying to fool herself or her lover into believing she was above her trade.

"It must be what happens," she thought dully. "This must be part of losing your soul." For the girl remembered only the sliding kaleidoscope. She had not enjoyed the immense sensuality of their last encounter, nor the pain and bewilderment of the first. She felt numb. Only the reproachful guilt penetrated her senses.

She could not blame the captain for what he had done. She had been submissive the night of the storm; encouraging the second time; and tonight, she had played the whore's part, tempting him unmercifully.

André de Montfort, had he read her thoughts, would have been surprised. He was certain she must blame him, and rightly so. She would probably despise him now, he mused unhappily. Rolling onto his side, he reached for her slim body and pulled her close to him. "Chérie," he started, "I am unhappy for you. Please do not think too badly of me . . . For the first time in my life, I find I am weak. I swear to God, it will not happen like this again!"

To his surprise and relief, he listened to her even breath and realized she slept. "Thank God for wine," he murmured. He snuggled up closely now, and buried his face in her soft curls. *"Mon Dieu,"* he prayed, "please, I haven't time to love a woman or take a wife." He gently stroked her belly and then lightly surveyed her breasts. They seemed larger, heavier in the dark.

Perhaps it was only her coming time of month, and not a babe, he thought. He was slightly annoyed to find that, in either case, he was not extremely anxious. Time would take care of them all. "What a besotted fool I am becoming," he reflected before sleep overtook him.

CHAPTER TEN

Christmas was fast approaching. Tierney was feeling the anticipation of the holidays—her birthday, the Nativity and the New Year—and felt confident that 1813, whatever it held, would be a momentous year for her.

The fact that this was her first Christmas without any family did not entirely dispel the magic of the season for her young heart. Even the idea of celebrating it on unknown waters without a yule log or carolers or church services did not dash her spirits. What more suitable a place, she thought, to marvel at Bethlehem's miracle than here, perhaps under the very star that guided the Magi.

The week before, that abominable morning when she awoke from the captain's bed with nausea and an insufferable headache, André had kissed her gently on the forehead, propped her against pillows, and delivered to her a steaming cup of plain tea. He could be so nice, she thought, and then, like the swat of a cat's tail, his manner would change. The first thing he had said to her, for instance, was, "This morning you must gather your belongings. I am moving you to the first mate's cabin.

"Stop looking at me like that, Tierney. He is moving, too. Into common quarters, an offer he made voluntarily. *Mon Dieu,* my head aches! Don't ask questions . . . just do it!"

And that was that.

Only once had he visited her, and then briefly. He inquired after her health. Tierney replied that she felt quite well and rested in her private cabin.

"Well?" he asked suspiciously.

"Well, what?"

"Tierney!" he exclaimed impatiently, "I'm wondering if you're with child."

The color drained from her face. She was still to be

embarrassed! "Why, no. No, Captain. I presumed that unless I mentioned a problem to you, you would know that you had nothing to fear."

André had stood motionless, staring blankly in front of him. "I did not fear news of any nature," he said quietly. "You are certain?"

"Quite."

Almost certain would have been more honest, she now reflected. But she was not in a position to impose upon him further. The menstrual period had been uncommonly light. In fact, she lost only a few drops of blood over a two-day span. This the girl attributed to the change in her status, assuming that once a woman lost her maidenhood, it altered forever her natural cycles.

But presently, she pushed aside these thoughts. Although André had come only that one time, she knew whenever he passed. Taffey would immediately race to the door, scratching and whining. She felt sorry for the pup, but he, too, must become accustomed to surviving without him. The girl seldom dwelled on the subject herself. Pretending the animal would miss his master more sorely was easier for her to accept.

Besides, Paul came to see her regularly. He would sit with her and explain their whereabouts, describing to her when the various islands were discovered and by whom. He often brought in her meals, and sometimes would join her at dinner.

It was at her first dinner with him that she had cautiously asked what *La Reine* had in the hold. Not the obvious bulky things in crates and barrels, she had said, but the smaller and less valuable items. Needles, threads, old sailcloth, perhaps linen? Paul had answered he could find those things, but why did she want them?

"It's a surprise," she answered him in hushed tones. "I am quite bored, as you can imagine. And you know what they say about idle hands and the devil's work."

Tierney did not need to expound further on the topic. Unbeknownst to her, André had finally confided to his friend that he had, indeed, taken the girl's innocence. The first mate had not been surprised: He had long suspected it. His first worry had been the same as the captain's—that the poor girl would be pregnant. André had laid to rest that fear after his visit with Tierney, so now Mauriac concluded that providing the girl with the few notions she requested was cheap recompense for keeping the young couple from further trouble.

"I'll get them for you, sweetheart. And I'll not breathe a word of our secret to anyone."

Quick work must be made of her plans if the gifts were to be readied by Christmas. Paul had returned that very night with the materials and threads. Now Tierney had spent the past four days sewing late into the night, and was impatient to finish them. Her only problem was that she tired too easily and often drowsed with the thimble on her finger and needle in the fabric. She had laughed at herself the first time, but now she was growing increasingly agitated with her unwelcomed naps.

She had already finished André's shirt. She knew it was not much—plain linen with a wide open collar; long, cuffless sleeves; and crude wooden buttons she had whittled in the shape of leaves and polished herself. The only design was a diminutive trail of embroidered ivy. This she created as trimming for the shoulder piece and down either sleeve, a solitary vine of dark green.

She now held it up to inspect it before wrapping it in what little paper she had saved from his gifts to her. She sighed. "He'll probably never wear the blasted thing!" Giggling at its peculiar cut, she added, "Can't say as I'd blame him, though. I have never seen anything like it, and I doubt he has either!"

Tierney had tried it on several times, gauging it against his nightshirt that she had worn once. She did not often think of the night of her discovery, but remembering it now, she was relieved that much of her initial embarrassment had diminished with the passing of time.

After wrapping the shirt, she turned back to the sailcloth. She had carefully considered what she might do especially for the first mate, and finally decided upon a biblical verse. The cross-stitching was complete now, and she spread the canvas on the bunk to admire it before putting on the final needlepoint touches. Tierney had to admit she was more pleased with her efforts for Paul, despite the hours of eye strain.

For I was hungry, and ye gave me to eat;
I was thirsty, and ye gave me drink;

I was a stranger, and ye took me in;
Naked, and ye clothed me;
I was sick, and ye visited me;
I was in prison, and ye came unto me.

Matt. 25: 35, 36

Christmas Eve began with an eerie fog-laden dawn. The waters seemed silent, and Tierney awoke to the chittering of dolphins. Thinking them squirrels at first, she stretched and lay drowsily on the bed. Salisbury in autumn sounded like this, she thought. Squirrels and the fleeting sparrows bickering in the elm outside her window, and Nanna clinking china teacups in the kitchen.

But this was not Salisbury, and there was no elm. She rolled onto her side and stroked the puppy. "Time to get up, Taffey. I am seventeen, and today begins my new year. We have much to do." On impulse she picked him up, and he wriggled against her neck.

"Oh, we shall have such adventures, Taffey. Together, you and I," she whispered. But all of a sudden the girl was overwhelmed by sadness and sank back on her pillow. She wept for no apparent reason, but all the self-control she could muster did not stop her tears. Tierney felt the same desolation as when she had found her grandmother that morning; grief-stricken and yet full of anticipation.

When she finally was dressed in the blue gown she had never before worn, she noticed the dolphins had ceased their greeting and in its place, a solitary cry rang out. Tierney ran to the porthole and squinted into the gray mist. "Why, Taffey!" she exclaimed. "I could swear that was a seagull. We must be near land!" Before she could catch sight of the bird to verify its call, however, a light tapping sounded at her door.

It was Pelier. Never had she expected to see this bullish man at her cabin, and her initial reaction was to retreat. But his expression was almost sheepish, and after shuffling uncomfortably for a few seconds, he spoke.

"*Excusez-moi, mademoiselle. Conviens, s'il vous plaît.*" The man reddened considerably, and then tried again. "Come," he stammered. "Please."

She nodded her agreement and followed him with Taffey close at her heels. He led her down the other flight of stairs toward the galley, but her several attempts for an

explanation went unanswered. As they approached the long
kitchen and dining hall, Tierney noticed it was unusually
quiet. Cook was always either in a state of grumbled frustration or singing to himself this early in the morning.
Perhaps Cook had taken ill!

She anxiously sped ahead of the huge man in front of
her, and ran toward the kitchen, afraid of what she might
find.

"Miss Chambers!"

She spun around to face the captain, and was surprised
to find him amid all his men. He rarely broke bread with
the sailors, she knew; and then was startled into comprehension as a roar from the crew went up around her.

"*Bon anniversaire!*" they shouted. "'Appah beerzday!"

The dog was barking excitedly at the cheering crowd as
Tierney blinked at them in disbelief.

"What they are saying, *chérie*," André laughed above
the din, "is happy birthday."

Still unable to speak, Tierney ran toward the captain
and first mate, throwing her arms around them and exchanging kisses with each. "Thank you," she managed.
Turning to the others, she added, "*Merci. Merci beau-
coup!*"

The breakfast party was delightful. Tierney was toasted
with champagne, and Cook delivered the finest meal he
had prepared during the entire voyage. Eggs were poached
and covered with a sauce—hollandaise, André said—
with smoked meat and biscuits. He also proudly produced
an assortment of pastries; some almond, some cherry and
apple, and a delicious cheese and sesame combination.
Tierney ate heartily, and though she understood little of
the men's table talk, the tone was cheerful and polite. The
crew, she noted, were at their best behavior and all of
them endeavored to demonstrate their long-forgotten sense
of etiquette. Not a single argument was in evidence and,
most remarkably, they were all dressed in fresh shirts.

The day grew light as if in response to the mood of *La
Reine,* and Tierney took full advantage of her day on the
deck planking. She strolled for well over an hour after the
party, and later returned with a ball of twine to play fetch
with Taffey. The pup, too, had over-indulged at the morning's feast. It was impossible to guess who more needed the

exercise or played the harder, André mused as he watched the unlikely pair frolic.

Her presence seemed to put his men in good humor too. The captain was relieved to see them noticeably relaxed; and instead of the expected hoots and catcalling when the girl virtually danced at a game or raced her spaniel from fore to mizzen, André only heard the whistling of folk tunes.

Captain de Montfort was glad the men were in such fine spirits for he regretted not having reached Santo Domingo in time for them to celebrate on shore. They were not too far out, André knew, but the wind had died and it would be afternoon on the morrow before they docked. Christmas Day.

Tierney was feeling better than she had in months. The breeze of the Caribbean Sea was refreshingly warm in comparison to the long stretch of Atlantic they had traveled. "I only wish this salt air did not affect me so," she sighed sleepily as she sank into her second nap of the day.

When she awakened, it was already dark. Taffey whined and scratched at the door, and she stumbled toward it to let him out. The dog now knew the ship and sailors well enough to romp about freely when the seas were calm, and he had won the affection of the men as had his mistress.

"Good evening, mademoiselle."

Tierney wondered how long he had been standing at her door. "Good evening, Captain," she said. The dog gave a friendly greeting by leaping against André's legs, and then hopped up the steps toward deck. After watching the animal retreat, she turned back toward the man. He really was startlingly handsome, she thought. Aloud she said, "What brings you here, milord?"

His white teeth flashed in the dim lamplight, and she was immediately put on guard. "The pleasure of your company, milady. Why else?" he drawled. He had been evidently drinking, she thought, and her heart quickened as she moved aside to permit him to enter. He closed the door.

She had waited so long for this moment that now she could not remember her practiced response. The captain studied the quarters as if for the first time and, at length, said, "Paul has nòt a single drop of brandy here, has he? He can be so abominably rigid and straight-laced."

"I find him a wonderfully warm-hearted man. One of the few, I imagine, who needs no drink for false bravado!" Inside, Tierney faltered. Why was she being unkind to André? He had been as generous in his own way as had the first mate . . .

"He is humorless! Dispassionate!" André countered.

"I disagree, sir. Mr. Mauriac comforts and amuses me," she started. She wanted to turn the conversation to a friendlier tone, but the captain was in a mocking mood, forcing her to defend his own friend. Before she could make things right, André clenched his teeth and continued.

"Yes, I thought so. So that is how it is, eh?" Then mirthlessly laughing, he stretched out upon the bed, his arms thrown back of his head. His length dwarfed the smaller bunk and cabin, and Tierney was caught between wanting to flee the room and comfort him.

"Shall I move him back in here with you? Yes, I quite think that would please you both. Perhaps then you will 'comfort' and 'amuse' him, as well! And Mauriac, the Protestant saint, will feel quite vulnerably human," he sneered.

"Oh, André, do stop!" she cried, rushing toward him. She clasped his long hands in her own slender ones and knelt at his side. Her stricken face studied his stony features, and she continued. "You are mistaken, André. There is none other than you. There never will be!" she exclaimed, no longer caring what she said. The words spilled from her lips like the first rains of spring—not torrential, but long sought.

"André, please listen . . . What I feel for Paul is love, yes. I cannot deny it. But it is not the same love I have for you. It does not even approach what I feel for you. The . . . the intimacy!" she stammered.

"You are my first, and you will remain my only love in that sense. I wish things were different, André. I must admit that. I dreamt all those dreams any girl will. A home of my own, a family . . . But things do not always happen as we would have them. I shan't marry now, not ever. But God, surely, will direct me toward whatever plan He has laid out for me." She paused before continuing. "And

I do love you, above all else. Nothing can ever change that!"

André was now sitting up, bewildered by what he was hearing. He tried to interrupt her, but she raised her hand in mute appeal and went on.

"What God wants from André de Montfort, I don't pretend to know. But I can say what he does not want—for you and Paul Mauriac to find fault with one another! He is a wonderful man, André. And so are you. Should animosity between two good men arise over me, I would have only myself to blame. Please," she cried, "please do not speak against your friend. I could not bear it!"

She was sobbing as André pulled her to his lap, lightly caressing her and brushing away the tears and unruly ringlets from her face. "*Je regrette, ma petite,*" he mumbled into her hair. To his utter amazement, he felt tears welling up in his own throat and struggled to maintain his composure.

He had come here this evening to verify his growing doubts about Paul; that was all. Since the party that morning, the first mate had moped about, increasing the younger man's suspicions. The captain was certain his own mate was in love with the girl.

Tierney had calmed down now, and only silent rivulets of tears rolled down her face. "You are the only one, André," she whispered brokenly. Tracing her fingers across his heavy knitted brows, she breathed, ". . . and I will show you."

André realized the impact of her last words and shook his head. "No, *chérie.*"

"But why not?" she moaned. "I will never understand you."

"Nor I you, I fear." Suddenly he grinned at her wickedly and explained. "Tierney, love, we won't tempt fate again. I find I am unable to resist you, once begun, and you so distract me that I am quite sure I would fail again to prevent a possible mishap."

She knew he was referring again to an unwanted child, and involuntarily shuddered at his obvious relief that their previous encounters had not produced one.

"Besides, *chérie,*" he lightly added, "I also fear you will enjoy lovemaking so much you will become a common slut once I leave you in New Orleans. Either that, or you will burden yourself with so much grief that you will enter a convent to repent the rest of your life! I cannot honestly say which I would dread more."

Tierney angrily pushed herself up to stand. "Why, you scoundrel!" she hissed. "How can you make a joke of me? I ought to love Paul instead. He consoles me, and you do nothing but prick my heart."

"Yes, Tierney, yes," he laughed amicably. "I must apologize." André needed to put her in good humor again, and at the same time, put aside his own desires. "But it is Christmas Eve, not just your birthday," he continued. "The men were good to you today. Now, what say you return the favor? Will you grace us all with your lovely voice? I daresay it has been many years since any of them have heard the songs of the season."

Tierney was duly flattered and her anger subsided.

Christmas morning! Tierney awoke to the sun high in a dazzling blue sky. The evening was well remembered with her renditions of old English carols, and the sailors in turn singing their songs of France. She had been astonished to learn that some of the men were familiar with a number of musical instruments, and there had been harmonicas, a flute, and one guitar to accompany the singing. It had been a beautiful night on deck, with the stars so close Tierney thought she might touch them.

Now it was morning, and that already half-spent. She threw back the covers and quickly shirked off the silk gown.

She was glad that she had not discarded it after André ripped it apart on her last night in his cabin. She had not repaired it immediately, but tucked it away as a token of their love—severed also. But alas, the nights had grown too warm for flannel and it had to be put to practical use. So she stitched it loosely, and had worn it for the past two nights.

"Are you awake now, lass?"

It was Paul. "Yes, sir. But I am not yet dressed. Does the captain need me?" She bit her tongue. How could she possibly be so naïve still, and so obviously eager for his attention? Tierney stamped her foot in frustration.

"Yes, he does. That is, we both want to see you. Might

we have a word with you in the master cabin? At your leisure, of course."

At her leisure? "I am almost ready now," she called back. Perhaps they had decided to leave her on this island they were moving toward, rather than putting themselves into New Orleans with a strange woman on board. If that were the case, Tierney did not know what she would do. Dear God! Even if they took her to the new territory, what was she to do?

Tea and sweet rolls awaited her in the captain's quarters. André invited her to sit down and relax a bit, explaining that he and Paul had already eaten. Before she could reach the chair where she had so often had conversations with him, however, she became dizzy.

"*Mon Dieu!*" André cried, racing toward her to break her fall. Paul, too, reached for her, and together they carried her to the bed. They were visibly shaken, and the first mate demanded to know what had upset her.

"Jesus Christ! I don't know, Paul! But look how pale she is!"

What seemed an eternity to the men was actually less than two minutes. Tierney came to as suddenly as she had fainted, and presently sat up. "What happened?" she puzzled, fingering the velvet bedcloth she had missed.

"I was about to ask the same of you, *ma petite*." It was André who spoke, and never had she heard his voice sound so soft.

"So that is a swoon!" she laughed weakly. "I've always wondered what the parish ladies meant. Now I know," she added, looking into their faces for a reassuring smile. She was met with their anxious eyes and grim expressions.

"I am fine, gentlemen. I assure you. See?" she teased, standing up. "I must have had too much champagne last night. Before my birthday celebration yesterday, I had never tasted it, you know. I'll be more cautious next time. Truly," she insisted.

When she walked toward the table this time, she surprised herself by feeling quite normal. "Such an odd thing, swooning," she thought. The pastries smelled too rich for her, however, so she chose a biscuit and sipped at her tea.

At length, the captain and first mate relaxed.

When she finally finished her light meal, she looked

back toward them expectantly. "Well, gentlemen, what is
it you need to discuss with me? Please don't dally. I am
quite capable of handling news of any sort," she added
imperiously.

Chuckling, André shook his head in disbelief. The first
mate stood and put his hand on her back. "No discussion,
Tierney, *Joyeux Noël!*"

Now André came up. "Merry Christmas, *chérie*," he
enjoined and kissed her lightly on the lips.

"Oooh," she purred. "You two! You make me feel like
such a ninny! I thought . . . Well, no matter what I
thought. Merry Christmas," she returned, hugging first
André and then his friend.

"Tierney, it isn't much, but please accept this with my
fondest wishes," Paul said, awkwardly holding forth a
package.

"No, wait!" she cried, running from the room to the
amusement of the men.

When she returned seconds later with their gifts, they
stood and each gave a deep bow. "Welcome back, milady,"
Paul teased.

"Your servant forever," said the captain.

"I daresay that is what you tell all the ladies," she
chided. To her complete delight, she witnessed André color
slightly.

"Well now, me hearties," she chattered, plopping herself and bundles on the carpet. "You must open yours
first, Captain. I insist. Here," she said, and patted her
hand on the floor. "Come down here with me and we will
all feel like children after a visit from St. Nicholas!"

They did as they were bid, and Paul, for one, did feel
as though he were amid children. What love he felt for
André had always been an odd mixture of paternal and
fraternal emotion. What he was learning to feel for the girl
was a more confusing combination. But now, he forced
himself to forget his anxiety and enjoy the other two at
play.

The first mate could not help but chortle at the captain's expression when he opened his package. The shirt
was enormous, and its only salvation was the embroidered
greenery and polished buttons.

Tierney made no excuses, but shrugged in a casual manner and tossed her head defiantly. The latter move was

incongruous, for although her hair fell below her ears now, there was still too little to effectively toss.

"It is, ah, unusual, *chérie*," André admitted. "But beautiful." When he noted the restrained anticipation on her face, he smoothly added, "It is similar to an open-sleeved garment the men wear in Ceylon. I have never owned one, but I do admire the style. I like it."

"No you don't," she said simply.

"Yes, *chérie*. I do," he whispered and kissed her again, this time his lips lingering on hers.

Blushing at being watched by Paul, she finally broke herself away. She lifted the larger box, and sighed. "And this, dear Mr. Mauriac, is for you."

Paul read it before holding it up for André to see. He smiled, and despite his appreciation, Tierney sensed an inner sadness. "Thank you, Tierney. It is extraordinary. You must have worked very hard, lass."

"Well, yes. As you may have guessed by some of those stray stitches, I am not too talented with a needle. And that canvas was heavy! I think it will look nice on the wall of the cabin, though. It's something to remember me by," she added, blinking back tears.

"As if I could forget," he mumbled in French, but only André heard.

Now it was the gentlemen's turn to deliver their gifts, and André spoke first. "*Pour mon cœur*," he said. He handed her a tiny velvet pouch.

She lifted the contents, and breathed, "Oh, André! I cannot accept this . . . It was your mother's and you must keep it within the family." But she did so want the topaz pendant! It brought back fond memories of them together, dressed up and looking like a betrothed couple as they walked into the Charlestonian mansion.

"A simple bijou, *chérie*. And one my mother would have wanted me to give a lady so rare."

Tierney was too touched to answer. What would she do without her only friends, once in Louisiana?

Paul Mauriac understood her pensive mood, and opened his gift to her himself. It was a small satin-lined jewel box with a tiny oval mirror inside the lid. It played "Greensleeves," and the tinkling melody filled the girl with melancholy.

"Thank you, Paul," she managed. "*Merci*." She kissed

him gently on his brow then, grateful for too many things to say more.

Suddenly the older man got to his knees and patted both Tierney and André on the back. "A nice Christmas, truly. Now, Captain, if I may have your permission, I would like to relieve Pelier at the stern."

"Yes. Thank you, Paul. And tell the men that they will be granted shore leave as soon as we dock."

When the door closed behind them, the young man and girl sat quietly on the floor, each waiting for the other to speak first. Tierney fingered the topaz absently, and André motioned her to move closer.

As he closed the catch of the necklace at the back of her neck, the scintillating warmth of his hand traveled the length of her spine. "Oh, André," she began nervously, "I do love this pendant. I would have preferred exchanging gifts with you and Paul on Epiphany, but I suppose we shan't be seeing one another again come the sixth of January.

"Besides," she rambled on, her back to him, "you and Paul do seem like family to me now, so Christmas Day feels appropriate anyway. I don't really expect you to wear the shirt, you know. I am sorry it turned out so miserably . . ."

André put his arms about her tightly, and pulled her to lean against his chest.

"Dear Lord," she murmured impetuously, "How will I ever manage without you! André, I know that . . ." She wanted desperately to say that she loved him, but she could not bear to have such a declaration go unreturned. How many times had she heard him say, while still thinking her a boy, that "The only woman in my life is my ship," and "Never love a woman, lad. They have their place in your bed, but not in your heart."

"What do you know?" he encouraged tenderly.

"I know that I shall never forget you," she sighed disconsolately. If only he would tell her that he loved her also, or that he at least cared. She wanted to love him, make love with him, and it was becoming increasingly difficult for her to feign nonchalance.

"Tierney," he whispered hoarsely. His breath was hot against her bare neck and shoulder, and she welcomed that warmth. "*Mon cœur,* Tierney," he continued, mumbling into her hair. His hands now lightly traced her arms, shoulders, and throat. If he did not stop himself soon, he warned, nothing in heaven or hell could! Her breasts, now under his supple touch, felt velvety smooth and looked creamy white in the shaft of morning light that spread across the floor. "Her lovely bosom, so young and firm and . . . round," he finished mentally. Remembering now her fainting spell earlier and noting the increased bustline, he asked aloud, "Tierney, do you play games with me?"

His voice was so suddenly sober that Tierney felt she had been taken from the tranquility of a bath and plunged into an icy pond in the breadth of a second. Shocked, she sat up abruptly and adjusted her bodice. His constant change of temperament was enough to drive her to distraction!

"Who plays games with whom, Captain?" she asked indignantly. She jumped to her feet, then, and glared down at him. Her Irish temper was flaring, and she wanted to pounce on him and beat him to a pulp.

He remained on the floor, his blue eyes piercing her to the core. She had the disconcerting feeling she was being objectively studied, like the night of the gale when he had searched her for bruises.

When he spoke, his calm tone both surprised and angered her further. "You are certain that you are feeling well?" he asked softly.

Tierney tapped her foot furiously on the carpet, the buffered thumps keeping pace with her quickened pulse. "I am fine, *mon capitaine,*" she mimicked. "Except in my mind, where you seem to delight in torturing me! I am sick to the death of you!"

André appeared wholly unperturbed. "And you are sure," he proceeded quietly, "that you are not carrying our child?"

The girl was livid. "So that's it!" she shrieked. "You care not a whit for me. In truth, your only concern is that your seed does not ripen in me! Me! A mere trollop, a whore, a . . ."

A stinging slap to her cheek checked her speech, and tears sprang into her eyes. So quick had he jumped to his feet and struck the blow, she had not even seen him move.

But now her eyes were as dark as forest pine in a storm, and violent anger fought heartbreak as she stared into his own inscrutable face.

"No," she managed at length. "I am not with child. Do not trouble over it again. Why," she added snickering hysterically, "my very womb spat out your seed as soon as it recognized the source. You don't honestly believe, do you, that I'd bear the bastard of a mongrel like you!"

Before he could open his mouth to speak, she ran from the room and locked herself in the first mate's cabin. His dreadful expression, however, could never be erased from Tierney's memory.

Part 2

A TIME OF INDECISION

CHAPTER ELEVEN

January 2, 1813

So this was New Orleans! Tierney leaned over the prow and squinted at the teeming quay, the smells of steaming clams and oysters, over-ripe fruits, and men hard at work assailing her senses.

Not nearly the size of London, or even Charleston, and yet something in the very air vibrated growth, activity, and yes, blood. She fought a rising queasiness. Her first day in her new homeland was far too important to give in to sickness. But she had become so accustomed to the rolling waves and sounds of sea that presently the easy bumping at the riverdock and noise of street merchants dizzied her.

Never had she seen so much flesh, and of so many colors. The rich blacks, browns, and reds of glistening backs made the white men dreary in comparison. André, she mentally revised, was an exception. The sun and salt had permanently branded him a dark copper, and beneath his thick black hair, only flashing teeth and light eyes brightened his shaded features. "I must not think of him!" she agonized in silence. "I won't!" Not since their last awful argument had he spoken with her. Such a sad, dismal Christmas it had been, and after such a promising start.

"Well, now we are here," she mused. "And they'll be wanting themselves rid of me as quickly as I can get my feet down that gangplank." Resolutely turning back toward the hatch, she squinted into the noonday sun. The day was muggy and warm, and it was hard to believe a new year had begun. It felt more like springtime. "Come, Taffey," she called. "Come, boy!"

In her cabin, she glanced around to once again determine that the room was as she had first seen it. It was, but the quarters shone brighter for her care as she lovingly

polished Paul's smaller desk and closet for the last time.
She would not weep—she knew that. Her remorse and
frustrations were spent Christmas night, when after locking herself here and crying until her eyes stung and swelled
shut, she had fallen into an exhausted sleep. She never
even went on deck during their two-day layover in Santo
Domingo.

And now she doubted she would ever cry again.

"Lord Taffey," she forced gaily, "the choice is yours.
You may stay here with your master, Captain de Montfort. He will treat you well, I'm sure, for I suspect he is
quite fond of you himself. Or come with me. I cannot
promise you a roof over your head or meat in your belly,
but oh, Taffey, I do love you!" she sighed, and she held
him to her bosom. Already the pup was becoming somewhat heavy to carry about, and now she was wont to kneel
on the floor to hug his wriggling body.

The dog danced around her feet all the while she packed
the duffel. She put the music box in first. Paul's gift now
held the miniatures and brooch, as well as the pendant
from André. Hesitating, she considered whether to return
the topaz. She wanted to keep it because wearing it beneath her bodice oftimes brought her token relief when
her heart ached for André.

It was difficult to decide whether the captain wanted it
back or would prefer she take it. Certainly she did not
deserve it, not after their last fight when she had called
him vile names and intimated as much about his own
family. On the other hand, she wondered if leaving it behind would now be an unwelcomed remembrance of her.
"Well, I know I want it." She shrugged and dropped it
back into the box.

"Whatever shall I do with these gowns?" she asked
pointlessly. "I haven't room for them in this seabag, and
since I am leaving without any wages, I am bound to need
them." Not knowing what the prospects were for a nursemaid or house servant in New Orleans, she assumed she
might need the expensive wardrobe to barter for lodging
and meals until a position was found. Tierney was determined never to sell the topaz, no matter how long it took
to find suitable work. "What *is* suitable work for a woman
like me?" she wondered dismally.

Finally, she managed to box some of the gowns, and

tied a cord around them. She tested how to balance the three tied boxes and duffel, and then left.

André de Montfort was nervous.

He had looked forward to reaching New Orleans when they first left Charleston. He could see his friends' surprise and envy of him as he escorted her to the New Year parties in New Orleans.

Tierney had been so delightful at the Pinckneys, André had not doubted she would receive the same warm welcome here from the various families. The Magazines, the Poydras, even Madame Gravier would find the girl enchanting. "But now I know what she thinks of me," he considered. "Any hopes I had for us . . . Well, be damned!"

It would be best under present circumstances for him to merely arrange her boarding at the convent at Chartres and Ursuline streets. It had been years since the sisters had taken in *filles à la cassette,* decent girls sent to the colony and put under the care of the good sisters until marriages were arranged with frontiersmen and settlers. But the young captain felt certain the Mother Superior could be persuaded to accept Tierney. He would simply play on her charitable sympathies for a young woman without a home or family, and privately arrange for regular tuition payments as well as annual donations to the Ursuline order.

Simple.

Now there were more pressing matters at hand. Granulated sugar, which had been first processed here by Étienne de Bore over a decade before, was now popular worldwide, and de Montfort was anxious to arrange bulk tonnage of the product before his departure. It had been two years since his last visit to the territory, and with the advent of another war to contend with, he could not be certain when next he would return.

"All the better," he thought bitterly. "Perhaps on my return I will find the temperamental bitch wed and bred to another. The Ursulines will no doubt be anxious to be rid of her, as well, and will arrange a suitable marriage soon enough!" His jaw twitched angrily as he scanned his cargo sheets.

Besides sugar, he would take on indigo and rice, and possibly a few crates of Indian baubles. Eccentric Europeans still paid a fine price for such nonsense. By the time

La Reine's hold was depleted of its European wares and took on the Louisiana cargo, there would only be enough space for the consignment of cotton and tobacco from his backtracking to the Carolinas.

Money, profit, power . . . He well knew how rewarding these could be and what pleasure they could bring. But genuine happiness? That could only be derived by a permanent commitment that afforded one peace of mind—like André de Montfort's commitment to the seas and his splendid ship, he wryly reminded himself.

He dressed par excellence for his first night on shore. If there were one city above all others where the young man felt comfortable, it was the bustling and ever-changing New Orleans. The very streets rumbled life beneath his feet, and here he felt the same vigorous energy as when he strode the length of his deck on the rolling oceans. With a final glance at the mirror, he left his cabin.

He stopped before her door. Unaccountably, he wished to speak with her again—quietly this time, sanely. He tapped lightly. "Tierney?" He paused again, wanting to knock harder.

To hell with it! She could damn well wait until he was ready to take her to the convent before receiving an explanation. And trying to explain himself to her . . . well, it was futile. She was too young, he reasoned, to understand a man and his—his what? Pride? Ambition?

Of course, pride! Was he to stand here begging at her door? She was wounding him again by refusing to answer it. And he, still her captain, despite the carnival this voyage had become.

Perhaps she was not refusing to answer the door, but was sleeping again. The girl drowsed far too much lately, he reflected as he joined Paul at the gangway.

As always, the man felt a sense of disgust when crossing Camp Street. Although the importation of slaves was now prohibited, this area had been the scene of the bartering of wholesale human livestock. Slavery had always struck André as a despicable business, its traders irresponsible and unthinking men. There were profits to be realized, of course, and de Montfort could appreciate that. But it was such an ignoble trade, left to unfeeling sea captains and businessmen who probably had no souls.

Even amid the nomadic tribes of the desert, where slave trade was always prevalent, the process did not seem so ruthless and calculated. This en masse degradation based on the color of African skin did not adequately compare to the ancient practices, whereby the victor of battles won all and the defeated were forced into servitude regardless of race.

Shouldering their way across Common Street toward the warehouse district, André remarked to Paul about the surging new numbers of people. There were more Creoles, mulattoes, and more European immigrants.

André de Montfort was grateful he would never have to confront the moralistic problems of taming a new land. In achieving progress modern man here defied justice, for the plantations that fed this burgeoning populace could not be prosperous without the blight of slavery. Thank God he was a sea captain, and a damned good one at that, he mused. He was master of a willing ship and an oftimes willing crew. In any case, they all freely boarded her plank and accepted the consequences thereof, including one little English damsel with a wide streak of Irish brass!

The day had turned from warm and humid to cool and rainy.

André and the first mate were well pleased with the goings-on that afternoon. After personally surveying the warehouses, they had arranged a meeting with three brokers in the new commerce section above the Vieux Carré. The brokers advised them there would be some delay in procuring the indigo. Several crops had failed and production was down, market value up. However, considering the bargain they had struck for the crucial sugar cane and granulated substance, the two men were immensely satisfied with their day's work.

They now sat relaxing over brandy and cigars after a memorable meal of French and Creole cuisine. André looked about the formidable room. The Place d'Arms was his favorite square on the entire continent, he decided. He found the walks and gardens reminiscent of Versailles, and yet the atmosphere was at the same time quaint and casual. Even his only visit to Montreal had not so intrigued

him. Here, in New Orleans, the French formality was
softened by Southern warmth and the montage of cultures
that permeated the air.

Leaning back into his chair with his long legs stretched
almost to the next table, André pondered his anxiety. It
was his dilemma with the girl, of course, but something
more. Throughout the day, transient worries had nagged at
him, alternating between his conscious contemplation of
them and a more subtle kind of irritation.

It struck him now as abruptly as a blast of frigid air.

Taffey! When he had knocked at her door, the dog
had not barked. And he had hesitated there several min-
ues. Surely, the pup would have responded! He whined
and scratched at the least sound, even when André merely
passed by the door.

As he shot out from his chair, he overturned the table,
shattering the decanter and fine crystal to the floor. A
buzz of confusion rose up around him but he took no heed
of it. Throwing a roll of money onto the spilt remnants,
he shouted to Paul. "I have to get back to the ship. Something is wrong. It's Tierney!"

She was drenched to the bone and shivering. Earlier
when she walked up Canal Street, her spirits had been
high with the intrigue of another adventure. Even Taffey
had sensed the fun of it, crazily wagging his tail and running in circles about her feet as they made their way
toward the center of the city. However, the poor animal
had long since given up the game and now plodded miserably at her side, whining and stopping often to shake his
sopping coat.

At first, the people had been most entertaining. Some
were resplendent in rich attire and fancy carriages, others
were kerchiefed and soiled, and still others were half-
naked. The babel of unfamiliar tongues and accents had
sent Tierney's imagination whirling. It was too grand. "If
only Paul were here," she reflected. "He would explain
everything to me, and still I'd feel the magic of it."

At the moment, however, she wanted André de Montfort. Desperately. Tierney Chambers, self-proclaimed
woman of the world, was frightened out of her wits.

Even when the rains had started, she had not felt
daunted. She cautiously made her way toward the business

district, confident that there she would find an inn like the Silver Steed and, hopefully, lodging for the night.

But the night had fallen suddenly, and with a chill that shook her to the core, she could well believe it was wintertime in Louisiana. Tierney had left behind the cape, conscious of what she might carry and remembering the first mate's description of a semi-tropical climate. She was wearing only the pale blue gown. Not at all appropriate, she now considered, for seeking work or strolling the unpaved streets! Too late, she vainly wished she had brought along her boys' boots. All of the slippers that André had purchased were too snug, and at the moment, she did not think she could take another step in them.

She was too tired also to think clearly. It would be marvelous, she thought, to get in a ditch and protect herself from this inclement weather with more of her lovely gowns. She could already imagine resting her head upon the soft duffel. She had not had even one of her customary naps today, and it was all she could do to stay awake.

She could not afford the luxury of sleep, however, not even in a nearby ditch. She was being followed! At least, she suspected someone had been tracking her for some time now. Twice she had been approached by drunken rivermen, and the last encounter she had barely escaped. Had it not been for Taffey making a valiant effort to protect her—causing such a ruckus that two windows flew open to check the disturbance—she certainly would have met with calamity.

The fact that they were boatmen who pestered her was worrisome. Miraculously, she had managed to leave *La Reine* unnoticed. Could she now be redirecting her steps back toward the wharves? God forbid! She had resolved herself to tearing away from the ship and her only friends, and to unwittingly return there would admit failure.

Tierney squinted into the dimness behind her but could not see anything. Nonetheless, she sped up her steps, vaguely conscious of the figure that followed. The little spaniel could no longer keep pace with his mistress and a pitiful cry issued from him as he dropped down, his muzzle spattered with mud as his head rolled into a puddle.

"Taffey! Oh, my God!" As she fell to her knees, she caught a glimpse of the man. He was there! Indeed, he

was racing toward her now and shouting through the din
of thunder and rain, pelting stucco and tin roofs.

A bolt of lightning struck something overhead, and
Tierney shrieked in terror. Throwing down the boxes and
duffel, she picked up the limp dog and started to run,
blinded to direction.

Her lungs ached and her feet were numb. For one dizzy
moment she thought herself back in London. The binding
was too tight, and she was racing, racing. Where was the
ship? "Dear God in Heaven," she cried, "where is the
ship?"

She felt one hideous scream escape her throat as the
man's arms went about her.

"Drink this."

"Oh, André! It was so awful. I thought . . . I thought
you were going to kill me!"

"Thank you for such unquestioning trust," he muttered.
She was slowly regaining her senses now, and the brandy
would soon warm her.

"I mean, I didn't know it was you. I was certain it was
a madman who followed us. And when the lightning
struck . . . It was ghastly!" She shuddered.

He was relieved at any rate to find her safe. And with
this recent near disaster, André determined to get her to
the Ursulines as soon as possible and out of harm's way.
"I still don't understand why you left the ship, *chérie*."

"Didn't you and Paul find the letters?"

"Not until an hour or so after we discovered you missing. We formed a search party—the entire crew—thinking
the worst. And had we not found you, Tierney, my men
would have torn apart this town. How could you be so
foolhardy?" he persisted.

The girl sank back into the pillows and rubbed her
hand over bleary eyes. How indeed? It would be painful to admit the truth; that she had fallen helplessly in love
with a man who could not love her in return. No, there
was no point in confessing this to him. She was alone in
the world, was destined to be so, and must now face the
reality of her situation.

Suddenly she remembered her pet. "Where is Taffey?"
she asked anxiously. "André, he saved me. Yes! From a

sailor who accosted me in the dark. You see? He is a loyal animal. But I never should have taken him with me. He was so tired, the poor darling. He's too young, and the weather . . ." She chattered incessantly, afraid to hear what he might tell her should she stop talking. "I think he should stay here, André, on *La Reine*. Would that be too much trouble? He's a good dog, and he's devoted to you and the men. Even Pelier approves of him. Could you . . ."

"We shall see," he answered quietly. André knew at this very moment the little dog might be dead. He was struggling for breath when they delivered him to Cook. But another shock might send the girl back into hysterics, and his throat was already taut with worry for Tierney. He did not think he could calmly bear seeing her so distressed again.

"He is dead, isn't he, André?" Her voice was dry and toneless.

"No, Tierney. Not dead. But he is a very sick pup tonight. Cook is keeping him warm by the stove, spooning milk to him. He is being carefully nursed down there, so don't worry. Cook knows how much you love him. We all do, *ma petite*."

Tierney felt the last of her stamina crack, and she gave in to fretful weeping. She must be a witch, she thought, for everything she touched—loved—died. Poor, innocent Taffey now lay suffering for her witless actions! The young woman anguished for her world of lost parents, Nanna, and friendships rare.

Had it not been for André's uncompromising strength, she surely could not endure this trial of spirit. But he held her firmly and rocked her until finally, to the soft sounds of his whispered language, she slept.

Taffey survived. And although she sincerely regretted leaving him behind on *La Reine*, the fact that he still lived and would be with André gave her an unusual sense of relief, hope.

"My gowns!"

"They were ruined beyond repair. Only the few that you left on board remain, but at least the duffel kept safe your music box from Paul. We shall get you more gowns. Ones suitable for your stay at the convent. When we visit the modiste, Madame Richet, you can be assured of nice-fitting garments, and you will have your own choice of colors and material."

"That's a bloody joke! I can't very well enter a nunnery dressed for a ball!"

"For the last time, Tierney, guard your language." But despite his stern voice, André could not conceal his amusement. She could be so delightful when the saucy vixen inside her overtook the saddened girl. He loved her when she spoke outright, like his initial impression of her that first night in London. His mental wanderings—those that were wont to travel from the Silver Steed to stained sheets to a pianoforte in Charleston to the incredible irony of it all—stopped suddenly.

"I love her?" he wondered. Could it be that this intricate web of emotion was love? It was confusing. Anger, joy, pity, passion, and chilly disdain all rolled into one enormous lump in his heart.

"Tierney, I want to make up for your having to leave behind Taffey," he said. What he meant was that he wanted her to take a part of him that he was uncertain about having her leave, but this was too difficult to speak. "Is there anything, besides clothes, of course, that you would have?"

Her usually soft features and inquisitive eyes were inscrutable. "Yes," she quickly answered. "There is something. I would take a book." At his look of surprise, she explained. "The idea of sitting amid holy sisters with naught to read but the Bible and prayer books strikes me as singularly boring."

André chuckled appreciatively. "What then? Jonathan Swift?"

"No, I finished that." She sucked in her breath. "The book of poems."

"Which is that?"

"The one from London. From a Miss Townsley."

His eyes glittered with suppressed mirth. So she could be jealous, as well! "Certainly. I am not often tempted to read else but maps and journal entries."

The men all stood at attention in the bright morning sun. Parting was difficult, indeed, and as she squinted into the group of men, she spotted Pelier at the back. On impulse she ran up to him and kissed his rough cheek, receiving a bear hug in return.

The first mate, who already had hailed a hackney, smiled and stood quietly at the quay. "Oh, Paul," she sighed. He held her lightly for several seconds, then kissed her brow.

"Now, lass," he began hoarsely. "Take good care of yourself and stay out of trouble." He winked, and in spite of his own dismay, gave her a big smile. "That's a big order, missy! Think you can manage to sail clear of the reefs?"

"I'll try, Paul. That I will," she choked. Kissing him on the lips, she turned and gave a quick toss of her head. André handed her up into the carriage.

CHAPTER TWELVE

Mother Superior was quite direct in her address after the captain took his leave. Her voice was soft, but there was nonetheless an undercurrent of firmness in it.

"You understand, child, Miss Chambers, that our cloister is no longer accustomed to casket girls." The lean woman shuddered slightly. "Such an unfortunate term.

"Regardless, what I am attempting to explain is that I am not in a position to ask our good sisters to conform their duties and standards to a practice that ended decades ago. Perhaps the captain has arranged an announcement of your stay here, I do not know. But if that is the case, we will take the measures necessary to provide opportunities for a chaperoned courtship. However, under no circumstances will we endeavor to assist you in a formal engagement. We Ursulines have rather firm regulations, and even in the last century, we did not procure marriage contracts. We were simply, and in good faith, a means for early settlers to secure for themselves the blessed sacrament of matrimony."

Tierney was too stupefied to speak. She peered into the coiffed face before her. Lined gray eyes, a fine aquiline nose, skin light almost to transparency . . . it was impossible to determine the woman's age. Marriage! What did she mean? André had assured her that she would be under no pressure, no obligation to join the order, but the girl had never considered that he meant the opposite extreme would be discussed. Never . . .

"So you will virtually live the life of a novitiate while you are here. You will attend mass daily, matins and vespers. You were baptized in the Faith, I presume?"

The girl nodded. Such a lovely young face to express such sorrow and turmoil! She must warn the sisters to go gently with her. She was obviously in a state of confusion, and therefore lacked proper respect. "Yes, Mother," the nun corrected softly.

"What's that?" Tierney found her tongue at last, and was appalled at its high pitch.

"When you are addressed, you respond accordingly. Yes, sister; yes, Mother; yes, Father. And so on. You must remember that a religious community is founded on love of Our Lord and mutual respect for His children."

"Yes, Mother Superior."

"I am relieved, Miss Chambers, that you have been baptized. Has your instruction included the other sacraments?" she asked cautiously.

"Well, I have been to confession once, Mother. And I did receive my First Holy Communion . . . right before the fire."

Captain de Montfort had privately explained the death of her parents, and the older woman was now grateful that he had given her a brief account of the child's background. Everything except why he, a seafaring bachelor, happened to deliver to the convent a vulnerable young girl. This part, she reflected, was highly questionable. But personal, too, and a matter best left to a confessor.

"Have you received your Confirmation?"

"Yes, Mother. That is, I was confirmed in the Church of England. I have been a practicing Anglican for almost nine years now."

The nun was dumbstruck for a moment. "I see," she managed.

"But please don't worry, Mother Superior. I am a Catholic, too. I shall be happy to live in accordance with Roman doctrine," she shrugged. "I really can't see that it matters."

The convent matron silently recited a quick prayer, hopeful of guidance. It was going to be more difficult than she had first imagined to manage this girl.

"I assure you, dear, that it does matter. And I pray that in time you will see the truth. It is your birthright, after all, and, God willing, my chosen duty to assist you."

"Yes, Mother."

"As I was saying, you will attend services and novenas with the sisters. You will take your meals with us, as well, and sleep in the postulants' dormitory. Your prefect will be Sister Mercedes, and she will be in charge of assigning you your chores and singular duties. I am sure that I need not remind you that obedience is essential. And during your stay here, you will find that service to the Lord is work of the highest reward."

"What kind of work do you do here?" she queried. The convent was so still it was difficult to believe they did anything but pray and sleep.

The woman studied Tierney. She could well imagine what she was thinking. It had been years—too many to number—since as a girl, Melissa Ann Benedict, had left her home in Philadelphia for a religious vocation. But Mother Superior never lost the memory of her worldly youth. The gowns, the parties, the love of a young man killed in the Revolution. All these were vividly remembered. And although she fondly recalled her girlhood, she never regretted her decision to leave it all behind.

"We are a teaching order, Miss Chambers. The Ursulines were founded in 1537 at Brescia, Italy, by Saint Angela Merici. Here we teach also. Charity Hospital—you have seen it—is another of our corporal works. We help the Sisters of Charity in the preparation of bandages and the like. But by chores, I mean domestic duties, such as cooking and housecleaning. We all share in the responsibilities."

Tierney's relief was evident. Housework, no matter how haphazardly performed, was something to which she was already accustomed.

"Captain de Montfort assured me that your practical education is adequate, but I do not expect you to teach or nurse; at least not immediately. For the time being, you will be required to attend school rather than teach it. You will take instruction in religion, history—including American history to acquaint you with your new country —French, and Latin. Yes, that should do nicely to start, I think." She lightly tapped a pen to her chin. Why had the girl startled at the mention of her benefactor's name?

As they walked down the silent corridor, Tierney whispered to the other woman who was even taller than herself. "Mother? May I speak?"

"Yes, Miss Chambers. But quietly. We mustn't disturb the others at devotions."

"No disrespect intended, Mother Superior, but do you think . . ." She paused. "Could you call me by my given name? Tierney? It feels so peculiar to call you 'Mother' when you address me so formally!"

The nun smiled. "Well, there is no harm in that, is there? I shall be happy to call you Tierney."

Sister Mercedes was a short, stout woman with a cherubic face. Her dark eyes twinkled merrily, and it struck Tierney that here was a person at odds with her somber black habit. Her beads perpetually jingled against her plump form, and the young visitor thought it strange that the short woman found the same solace in her commitment to a religious life as did her stately counterpart, Mother Superior.

"Well, Tierney! Welcome!"

"Thank you, Sister."

The prefect studied her charge. She wore a green velvet dress, simply cut and trimmed with a modest amount of lace and ribbon. Her shoes, however, were frightful. Kid slippers that were soiled and torn were a departure from the rest of her appearance, but Sister Mercedes knew they must have been costly at one time.

"I see you are carrying only a light bag. Come with me, and I'll show you to your room, Tierney. I am sure you will want to rest after unpacking."

"Yes, Sister. I really will have little to unpack, though. You see, my clothes were lost in the storm the other night." Noting the nun's look of surprise, she hurriedly added, "But I would very much like to rest."

The room was not a room at all, she mused, but a cubbyhole. It contained only a narrow cot, one wooden straight-backed chair, a small table that held a simple candlestick and single book, and under the table was a porcelain wash basin. The walls were barren except for a solitary crucifix above the bed. A small window high above permitted sunlight, but no view of the garden below.

Sister Mercedes saw her disappointment, and after pointing out the closet, took her leave. "Three bells will alert you to the dinner hour, Tierney. Someone will meet you here your first night with us. And Tierney," she added with a smile, "we are very happy to have you here with us."

Tierney turned to thank the prefect, but the jingling beads already sounded down the hall.

All the while she put away her few things, she thought how sad it was that she could not look out to the garden. The room, however, was immaculate in its nakedness. The scents of beeswax and lemon oil lightly perfumed the air, and these appealed to the woman in Tierney. It was a happy alternative to salt air and the malodorous wharves.

A bird took up chirping as she lay on the cot. Its mate answered excitedly, and soon the carryings-on grew intense outside her window. "They bicker, too!" she whispered happily.

Pulling the woolen blanket up about her ears, she snuggled down to sleep. Not since living with her grandmother had she felt so safe.

CHAPTER THIRTEEN

"Miss Chambers?" came the brittle voice.

It was the postulant, Amanda. She was only twenty, Tierney knew, but her hard eyes and raspy speech belied her youthful features. Ever since that first evening, when she had come to the room to fetch Tierney to dinner, the younger woman had found it impossible to win her favor.

Amanda had evidently taken an immediate dislike to Tierney, and now, only a fortnight later, Tierney was beginning to distrust and resent her equally. The postulant did everything to distract Tierney from her work and prayers, criticizing her inability to see clearly a spot she had missed in mopping, or delivering a withering stare in chapel that invariably disconcerted the impious newcomer.

"Miss Chambers!"

"Yes, I'm coming." When Tierney opened the door, she was met coldly. Amanda's lip ticked nervously.

"Mother Superior wants to see you. And be quick about it!"

Who the hell did she think she was, Tierney silently raged as she sped down the hall. But her anger faded as she descended the stairs. The old boots were as utilitarian on polished convent floors as they were on the deck. André had been mildly dismayed when she insisted on bringing them, but already they had proved useful in tending the garden and feeding chickens. In fact, she had altogether discarded the kid slippers.

Should her clothes from Madame Richet's shop or her shoes from the bootery ever arrive, she sincerely doubted she would put them to good use. Besides the green velvet dress and cape that had escaped the rain, Sister Mercedes had provided her with the novitiate's black smock she now wore, only without the abbreviated coif and veil.

She slowed her steps somewhat to enter the office gracefully. Mother Superior had twice reprimanded her for running down corridors, and once for racing into chapel! Tierney was invariably late for matins, never for meals, as Amanda had painfully reminded her the day before.

Tierney dropped into the perfunctory curtsy. "Good afternoon, Mother. I was told you wanted to see me."

"Yes, dear. Or rather, there is someone here to see you." Her tone was indecisive as she nodded toward the library. "It is Captain de Montfort. He has brought the rest of your belongings. Do you wish to see him?"

"Oh, no!" Tierney exclaimed, almost taking a seat without permission. "Pardon," she muttered absently, quickly shooting back up. "I mean yes! I want to see him, it is just that I did not expect him, anyone . . . I am not prepared!" Her heart thudded within her breast, and she did then drop into the chair.

The nun smiled. "Of course not. But a lesson in humility to be learned, if you refer to your habit. You may join him now," she said decisively this time. The girl evidently wanted to see the captain again, to be sure. "He awaits you in the study. Visit with him in our garden, if you prefer." At the girl's hesitation, she added, "Don't worry, child. You are well protected here."

"Yes, Mother. Thank you."

As Tierney approached the small library, she could not help but wonder at the irony of Mother Superior's mild chastisement. Humility? The nun had not the vaguest notion that humiliation was second nature to her now, especially where André de Montfort was concerned. And to protect her—from whom? Tierney Chambers had learned repeatedly that her own impudence was her greatest threat.

André turned to face her when she entered. He immediately began to laugh. "Tierney, your choice of costume never fails to amuse me!"

She ignored the rub. "Why are you here?" she asked suspiciously, straining her eyes to try and discern whether he was intentionally antagonizing her or merely in good humor. "I thought the clothes would be delivered by the modiste."

"So did Madame Richet, and she begs her apologies. I was asked—no, commanded—to say that should any of these gowns not meet with your approval, please get word to her and she will come herself." He leaned against the enormous mahogany desk in a leisurely fashion, his trousered legs somehow shockingly seductive.

But he seemed to be at his best behavior, and she smiled. "How nice of her. But surely they will fit."

"Let us hope so, m'dear. I brought your shoes, as well," he added, pointedly looking at the scuffed boots she wore.

Tierney bristled slightly at his tone, then tossed her head. The chestnut curls now reached her shoulders. "You are too kind. But tell me. How is it that you knew of the modiste's shop. It seems to me that ladies' apparel would be a far cry from most men's wanderings!"

"That depends on the man, *chérie*. Some men are highly versatile at meeting all a lady's needs and interests."

"I have heard of such gentlemen, but alas! I have never had the good fortune to know one," she quipped. Tierney could not bear seeing André so arrogant when she felt so ill-at-ease and looked so dreadful.

"Ch-ch-ch!" he mocked. "We can't very well have a row at it within these sacred walls, now can we? They are listening, you know."

The girl almost shrieked in frustration. Fighting a rising urge to hurl insults into his calm face, she managed to rein her temper. "There is a garden and walk where we may have some privacy."

"Privacy?" he grinned.

"Don't misunderstand, Captain. Where we can converse in private!"

"Ah! So I thought . . ."

The day was unseasonably warm and a few ignorant jonquils mistook the weather for early spring. Tierney sighed at the minuscule yellow blossoms. "By tomorrow they will have died," she mused aloud.

"Who?" He had accompanied her outside expecting the usual argument, certainly not to see her face and body pensive.

"The flowers . . . André, why am I here? More importantly, why are you? We agreed that when you brought me to the convent, it would be best not to see one another again."

"You are here, *chérie*, because it is the safest place for you in a new city. Are you unhappy?"

"No. In truth, I like it. The sisters are most considerate

and the food is plentiful. They allow me enough time to myself that I am not overly bored with the routine. I study a lot," she shrugged. "It's needed, I suppose, but it does bring back my least fond memories of Salisbury and Nanna's scoldings. I never have been much of a student, I'm afraid." Suddenly her face brightened. "And I'm studying French, too. *Quelle heure est-il?*"

"Your accent is quite good!" he laughed, pleased that she was trying to learn his native language. "Is your teacher French?"

Tierney nodded. "He is so striking," she began musing. "It is a wonder that no woman has snared him." How did one subdue a man with wanderlust? Now that he would be leaving, probably for good, Tierney felt her composure slipping.

"*Il est quatre heures.*"

"What's that?"

"The time. You asked in French what the time is, and you didn't seem to understand when I answered you. In English, it is four o'clock."

If only he would tell her that he would return, or that he would miss her! She wasn't prepared to give up this easily. Perhaps a bit of coquetry . . . "Yes, well, I suppose I ought to be going. Devotions start soon, and we're bid to silence except in prayer." Her voice drifted off as she searched for something else to say. Certainly he would detain her . . . It wouldn't be the first time she was late to chapel.

André stood up and respectfully offered his arm to escort her back into the convent. When it struck her that he was actually ready to take his leave, she froze.

"Since when did you give a bloody fig for prayer and devotion?" she snapped, remaining seated on the marble bench.

"Since when did *you?*" he countered.

"Oh, André! Please let's not argue . . . I cannot bear it! Stay, please. God only knows when I'll see you again. I will see you again, won't I, André?"

He did not know how to answer her. He wanted to say, "Yes!" But could he? André de Montfort had suffered the past several days alone aboard *La Reine*, and found little satisfaction in the profits reaped the while. He had not once been tempted to visit the choice brothels of New

Orleans; in fact, he found himself scorning such cheap amusement. But he sorely missed this slip of a girl, and unwillingly admitted it was she whom he wanted most.

Now studying her grave features, the green of her eyes darkened in anticipation, the lips firm and chin determinedly thrust forward, her lovely white face aglow in the soft light . . . He found it difficult to look at the hope etched upon her, and yet more difficult to turn away. Somehow, he would have to explain to her what he himself did not understand.

"You asked me earlier why I came here today," he began huskily. "I will try to answer. Tierney, I had to see you again! These past few days I have questioned my senses, and wondered if the whole crazy lot of it is true or my imagining. Everything! The ale in my face . . . did I lose my wits then?

"Or was it when I first discovered you had tricked me into believing you were a boy? Was the night I feared you would fall to your death from the rigging real enough? Did I bed you, or merely dream it? Damn it all! Do I make sense to you now? For I daresay *I* don't understand!"

He was nearly shouting, and Tierney shook her head in silent confusion. Calming a bit, he seated himself next to her again.

"Tierney, *ma petite!*" he said softly. "I do not know when we will meet, if we will meet, again. I am a rover, *chérie*, and you know that as well as anyone.

"You will ever be on my mind. I knew when I searched for you, thinking you gone from my life, I was beside myself in worry. I will miss you greatly, that much is true. But in spite of what I feel for you, I know more certainly now than ever that I cannot give up my ship. *La Reine* is my world, Tierney. I don't expect you to understand." He added quietly, "But I am relieved to have said it."

Tierney choked back the sobs that threatened. So he didn't love her! The girl was determined to make another attempt, however difficult. Her voice, pleading, was abhorrent to her own ears, but the pain in her heart overwhelmed all pride. "But André! I do not ask a promise from you! And I am not fool enough to ask you to forsake your ship for me. Can we not arrange occasional visits?" she asked tremulously. She wanted to cry out, "You. You and Paul are all I have!" but the words died as quickly as they were thought. He looked resolute. He would not have heard them, she dully believed.

"No, Tierney. We shan't 'arrange' anything. I watched my mother grow old before her time, waiting for a man always gone. And I witnessed her die brokenhearted while the man she loved was still at sea! No, I will not be like my father, though he loved her in his own way."

He tore his eyes away from her pained expression and looked beyond the convent wall toward the great river. He must be off before she obliterated what sense he had left. Taking a deep breath, he continued. "A man cannot have a wife and family and still sail the seas. Some try, and they fail at both. He is either married to one or the other, and must choose between them. I have already chosen."

An angry chill inched up Tierney's spine. She was done begging! She controlled her temper, however, and in its stead spoke in a provocatively haughty manner. "I presume, sir, then that is why you came to leave me here, as a casket girl. *Oui?*"

"Yes," he answered flatly. André found himself at once relieved and disturbed at her cold response to his resolution. Her voice was shockingly unemotional, and the captain found this unaccountably disappointing.

"Ah, then what Mother Superior explained to me was correct! I don't know quite how to express my gratitude . . ."

"I don't understand," he answered cautiously. Tierney had never looked so wicked. Her eyes were narrowed and nostrils flared; she looked like a tigress ready to strike its prey. "What did she tell you?"

A glint in Tierney's green eyes belied her own distress. "Why, Captain, that you have arranged suitors to come a-calling me! I appreciate your assistance, milord." Sliding closer to him, she boldly pressed her thigh to his. Her hand slipped onto his leg, and she maliciously dug her fingers into his taut flesh. He did not flinch, but he had the uncomfortable feeling she might actually claw his leg. "Truly, were we alone rather than under the watchful eyes of the nuns, I would demonstrate to your tremendous satisfaction just how grateful I am. To think that Captain de Montfort would so extend himself as to find for a simpleton wench like me a respectable gentleman to wed," she spat. "How kind, good sir! How considerate you are!"

Now it was André's turn to take up the charade. The undercurrents of anger and vindication were equally evident in either voice, and bitter words were chosen with deliberation. "Milady," he drawled, "I, too, would have us elsewhere at this very moment to enjoy the pleasure of your demonstration of gratitude." He sighed with exaggeration. Then turning to her with a menacing smile, he added, "But, *ma petite,* such is not the case. I have no choice now but leave you. When I return—and I assure you, I have decided that I will—you shall then uphold that promise of gratitude, married or not! Demonstration, you said? Think of it, Tierney, for it had best be worth my return!" With a deep satirical bow, he turned on his heel and left the garden by way of the wrought-iron gate.

She knew it was inappropriate, if not downright ill-bred, to chase him. But Tierney was not one for propriety. "André! André!" she called out.

He did not turn to retrace his steps. He did not even turn to look at her. But he stopped, waiting to hear what she might say.

Tierney looked at his tall, erect figure, hoping to memorize it in the span of this moment: his shoulders squared, his raven hair glinting in the setting sun. He was so proud. Too proud, perhaps . . .

"Hug Taffey for me, will you? And the mates—I'll miss them all!"

André raised an arm to signal he would, and began walking again, his steps no longer hurried.

Tierney was alternately dismayed and delighted. True, she had once again permitted her temper to get the better of her judgment. But he would be back. He promised.

He did not love her. "Certainly," she thought, "he would have admitted it. But I have time on my side. I'm just now seventeen. When next he sees me I vouch he will be unable to resist loving me with all his heart."

With this in mind, she skipped back into the convent, late though she was for devotions.

She had not been forced to do this, she realized. So why was she kneeling here on this hard wood in total darkness behind the heavy purple curtain? Had Mother Superior subtly pressured her into the sacrament of penance, or was it her own growing turmoil over all that had transpired on board *La Reine de la Mer*? Tierney was not certain, but she suspected the latter.

She could barely see the dim gold crucifix above the screen. But she reached up and touched it, lightly tracing her fingers over the minute statue as a blind person might investigate an intricate treasure. She knew, of course, that the crucifix was a mere symbol of salvation, and yet she felt a tremor of hope at the touch.

Suddenly the screen's covering slid open, and although the sound was not severe in the confines of the confessional, it was a rude interruption into the silent darkness.

"Gracious!" she exclaimed. "You startled me!"

No one answered. She felt rather than saw the movement on the other side of the screen. It was Father Donavan, she suspected, an elderly Jesuit who was confessor to many of the sisters here. Despite her squinting, she could not determine even his silver hair, but hearing the soft Latin prelude to the sacrament, she felt certain now it was the old Irishman.

The voice finally addressed her, "You may begin now, daughter."

She paused momentarily. It had been ten years since she had made her only confession, and she did not remember how to begin.

"Hello, Father," she started uncertainly. "My name is . . ."

"Stop right there!" he cautioned, his voice rising above the customary whisper. "I do not want to know your name. Is this your first confession?"

"No, Father, but it has been a long time, and I have quite forgotten what to say. I am truly sorry."

"No need to be sorry, child. A flaw in memory is no sin. And that is what we are here to do—confess your sins before God and beg his forgiveness." Why hadn't the Ursulines prepared her to receive the sacrament, he wondered grimly. "State how long it has been since your last confession, to the best of your recollection. Then, simply begin, 'Bless me, Father, for I have sinned . . .' Tell me in your own words what sins you have committed, great and lesser, and with what frequency. And remember, child, you confess to your Lord, Jesus Christ. I am merely a means for your direct supplication to Him, and He is all-merciful."

"Yes, Father." Her voice was weak, but she knew it was not fear. Rather, she felt deep contrition and humble recognition for those things which she had too long forgotten: her God, her church, and her own immortal soul.

"Bless me Father, for I have sinned. It has been ten years since my last confession." Tierney spoke of what few acts she had committed that brought her shame and remorse during her years in Salisbury. Lies told to Nanna, none serious, but nonetheless worrisome to her since her grandmother's demise. Disobedience. During her early adolescence she frequently absented herself from the girls' school to throw dice with the town's truant boys, and was wont to neglect her studies.

She told the priest about her years as an Anglican Protestant. Did she do so of her own accord? he asked. Did she believe that by forsaking Catholicism she had risked salvation? She gave a negative response to both questions.

"Then I fail to see any great sin committed by your lapse, except in the lack of faith. You express little faith in either doctrine, and that is a serious matter. Indifference to the word of God, albeit from a Protestant pulpit or a Latin Mass, is a severe effrontery to the teachings of Jesus Christ. Do you understand?"

Tierney knew the priest was sincere; moreover, she believed he was right. Only in times of crisis had she turned to God. It was not that she had intentionally forsaken her love of Him: It was perhaps better said that her faith had lain dormant all these years.

The grave matter of her erring ways since posing as a cabin boy weighed heavily upon her heart. As she confessed these, she realized that the priest did not take the matter lightly, either. He seemed concerned about all of them, and even commented upon the vicar's letter.

"Although you did not overtly lie about your gender, you intended for the letter to be misunderstood. More importantly, you abused the reverend's trust in you. What is done is done. Your acts of adultery do not go unnoticed by God, and the breaking of his commandments is always wrong. But you are forgiven through your penitence and faith in His mercy. Do not trouble yourself further on it, child. Remember the sinner turned saint, Mary Magdalen. She was the first person to whom Jesus appeared after His resurrection, for He loved her greatly."

"Yes, Father." She tried to think of what offenses she might have committed since André's departure. Nothing. Well, she had on occasion rather unkind thoughts toward the irritable Amanda . . .

"We all have our burdens, large and small," he answered. "But it is wise to remember that our neighbors may carry burdens too heavy for them at times. Bitter thoughts and actions are born of the unhappy heart. Pray not only for your loved ones, but your enemies, as well, that they might find peace within their souls.

"For your penance, offer your first communion to world peace, for we are much in need of it in these troubled times. And say a rosary every night to Our Blessed Mother that she will protect you and keep you pure of heart."

As Tierney knelt by her cot that night, the only light was the enormous full moon that filled her small window. To her thinking, the glow spread across her like grace itself, and she sighed contentedly. She felt at peace, and the serenity was rich and soft, as though it might be touched.

Only one slight distraction kept her from sublime happiness. André's return.

She wanted to see him again, now more than ever. But what of his threat, and her foolish game that had prompted it? To think of it! That she would dare to promise the gift of her body. "Oh, when, dear Lord, will I learn to silence my silly tongue!"

CHAPTER FOURTEEN

Tierney had little opportunity to wear the seven gowns that Madame Richet had designed for her. She had only one gentleman caller at the convent, a Mr. Charles Bolier.

When she had first tried them on, several weeks ago, Sister Mercedes had clucked with delight, her dark eyes fairly dancing. "Oooh, Tierney!" she had clapped at the dark blue velvet. And all the others had drawn similarly happy responses; all, that was, except the beige silk ensemble.

That particular design and material was chosen by André. It was almost flesh-colored with just the barest hint of peach in the color. Although it was demurely cut, it fell to the floor in soft folds that accentuated Tierney's every curve and movement. "It is . . . well, it's certainly not indecent." the sister had stammered, "but, well, I think it is a bit too mature for a girl your age. Ah, perhaps when you are older, dear, and married."

This afternoon Charles was expected at three o'clock. Tierney had been granted permission to serve him tea in the main parlor. No one would be about except Mother Superior who had just embarked upon an early "spring cleaning" of her office files. Mother had admitted to feeling a bit edgy about this war with England. Louisiana, indeed the convent itself, had been under the secular jurisdiction of so many governments, she said. The aging woman did not welcome the threat of British domination, and of late, she had suffered many dreams of the early Revolution and that young man so long ago dead at Valley Forge.

"I don't doubt but that Congress will settle this peacefully. But in any event, we must keep the motherhouse records in order."

Not that Tierney wanted privacy with Charles. She would have welcomed several of the sisters to join them

for tea if they would accept such an invitation. Only
Amanda was a nuisance, snooping about the garden when
Charles was visiting, or pretending she had misplaced
something so she could poke her head about the tables
in the study.

Charles Bolier was not much to look at, Tierney thought
wryly. He was short and stout, and his dull brown hair was
already thinning.

Charles was a timid young man of twenty-four years,
and he had been prompted to visit the newcomer by a
friend of his mother, Madame Deneuve, who had been
advised of the girl's stay with the Ursulines by that pri-
vateering rogue, Captain de Montfort.

To the matron's relief, the captain had confessed to her
that the young lady's reputation was not impugnable.
"Why, Madame," he had teased, "I made every effort to
win her favor myself! It is not often I am so neatly dismissed. Ah, it is at moments like those that I wish the
temperamental seas had not stolen my heart! This Tierney
Chambers will make some fortunate Orlean a happy man,
I am certain . . ."

Tierney did not know the details of how Charles had
come to call on her, but she could guess at least part of it.
Madame Deneuve was a name she had heard mentioned
by both André and Paul Mauriac.

When she surprisedly received his calling card the
month before, she had agreed to his visits out of spite.
And when she had first seen her would-be suitor, she had
been riled at André's obvious attempt to insult her. As
the weeks passed, however, she came to like the awkward
bachelor.

"Now," she decided as she drew the dark burgundy
dress over her arms, "I am truly fond of Charles."

His most redeeming quality was patience. He never appeared even slightly miffed at her tardiness. He never
reprimanded her for losing her temper, which now only occasionally emerged as a direct result of Amanda's prick-
ing. And most importantly, he listened with interest to
Tierney's stories about her past. Ireland, her parents,
Nanna, even London became topics of discussion. She told
him everything short of her adventures aboard *La Reine*.
Tierney saw no advantage in confiding such personal history to him when she had already avowed herself to

spinsterhood. "I shall never marry," she dismally reminded herself.

Suddenly she stamped her foot with impatience. "What the devil!" she muttered to herself as she attempted to hook the watered-silk gown. Tierney was becoming increasingly exasperated over her gain in weight. She had deliberately chosen this particular gown because it had been the easiest one to close around her slowly spreading middle, being in the Empress design. But now, even her bosom was becoming enlarged and this dress, too, posed a problem.

"I simply must quit eating so much!" The convent's fare was simply prepared, but wholesome, and Tierney found it much to her liking. It reminded her of her mother's plain Irish cooking: hot porridge, cross buns with butter and honey or preserves, stews and boiled vegetables. The greatest difference was the substitution of rice for potatoes. "How I would love new potatoes smothered in gravy!" she dreamed, her mouth watering at the very thought.

But enough of food, she thought irritably. Her present desire was sufficiently important. She had just managed three hooks at her neck when she heard the light tapping.

"Sister Mercedes! Thank goodness you've come. Is Mr. Bolier here?"

"Yes, dear. I heard Sister Margaret Térèse admit him. And I wanted a word with you . . . Tierney, you really must make an effort to be more prompt. After all, he is a nice young man. And he can only stay three quarters of an hour. You're getting worse, child! The last time he spent only ten minutes in your company before the call to vespers. Perhaps a novena . . ."

"Yes, Sister," Tierney enjoined abruptly. "I must apologize. But I'm late again today. Please, could you help me with this dress?"

Sister Mercedes had grown so fond of her lay student that she found it virtually impossible to be strict. Tierney Chambers was not like her other girls, those who sought the cloister as a way of life. This one had not the markings of a nun, but her genuine attempt to conform along with an infectious streak of humor had won many hearts here. Even Mother Superior sought Tierney's company for her heretofore solitary walks in the evening.

Now the prefect smiled, and gestured her to turn so that she might be hooked and off to her little soirée.

"Why, I do think you have put on more weight! I can hardly manage this . . . Isn't this the gown that was nearly too big before?"

The girl blushed profusely as she adjusted the sleeves. "Yes, Sister," she murmured. Only this morning Amanda had smirked at her in the dining hall after morning Mass. And now the material was stretched so tightly across her bosom she could barely breathe! For one shocking moment, Tierney vividly recalled André's impertinence upon discovering the binding.

"Mr. Bolier, please accept my apologies. I do hope I haven't kept you waiting too long."

The young man dabbed a handkerchief to his neck and bowed. "A year, mademoiselle, would not be too long to wait for a moment of your company. But I daresay that each minute without you seems an hour."

"You are far too generous, sir."

Never had the bachelor been so bold in speech, and for a few awkward seconds, the young hostess was at a loss for words. She hoped that no one had overheard his flattery, for it was understood the parlor doors must be kept open during his visits. No one had told Tierney this, but she instinctively knew now most of the Ursulines' regulations for protocol.

"Do you take lemon, Mr. Bolier?"

"Yes, thank you. And two sugars, please." He took a seat in one of the armchairs while she served the tea. "Miss Chambers," he continued nervously, "would it be presumptuous of me to request that you call me by my first name? I would be honored."

"Okay, Charles," she quipped. Occasionally, the formality of these meetings grew tiresome. Okay, she had learned, was American slang. It was actually a Choctaw Indian word, o-keh, meaning "so be it."

"So be it," she said aloud. "And you may call me Tierney."

Charles literally let out his breath. He had not expected it to be so easy. "Thank you. I dearly love your name, Miss . . . Tierney!"

"In public," she warned, "I think it best to maintain

our formal address of one another. Don't you think so, Charles?"

"Oh, yes. Yes, of course, Tierney."

What a simpleton he could be at times, she mused. Whenever were they in public together? Not that she was eager to attend any social functions with Charles Bolier as escort. But she did, at times, long to roam the city alone. The weeks had diminished the fright she had experienced her first night alone in New Orleans, and she was eager for a bit of excitement again.

For a while she drank her tea in silence, her thoughts traveling to the glistening colored backs she had seen that morning, and the pungent smells of a dock at morning.

Where would *La Reine* be now? Had André really kept his promise to take care of Taffey? Tierney hoped he had at least kept the pup until his return to Charleston. That young girl with the lovely voice—Anna Leah Williams, was it? She would take good care of Taffey should André think to give him up.

Poor Charles! He was so kind to permit her daydreaming. He had not once attempted to interrupt her mental wanderings, but merely sat quietly across from her, gazing sadly at her out of his watery blue eyes.

"Did I ever tell you about my dog?" Tierney asked. "He is a darling cocker spaniel, buff-colored . . ."

Tierney had moved as many hooks and eyes as possible to ease the now all-too-tight gowns; that is, the three of seven gowns with Empire waistlines. There was no longer any pretense of altering the others, for the seams were not generous enough to accommodate fitted designs, and she dared not contact Madame Richet.

"Ouch!" she muttered nervously. The thimble Mother had given her only protected one of many sore fingers. But she was determined to finish the intricate needlework before her now.

The poem was quite long, forcing her to use a tiny cross-stitch to complete each word on her medium-sized sample. The capital letters were only the size of her smallest fingernail. Tierney had designed the needlepoint border herself; it alternated white-capped waves, silver dolphins, and pink and purple seashells on a dark blue background.

Although she was angry with André, and rightly so, the girl felt compelled to complete the task she had started the week of his departure. If she herself could not be with him upon his return, she reasoned, something of her would await him.

She was miserable at the thought of never seeing his dark face again. Presently, she could almost see the rare glimpses of tenderness in his eyes, the bold determination in his very stride; she could feel his hands. Tierney shook her head and sighed. "Hail Mary, full of grace . . ."

Oh, why had he so deceived her, she thought despairingly. There could be no mistaking it now. She was with child!

Tierney recollected her unlikely discussions with him about such intimacies. Had he not said that the cessation of her menses was the first sign? He lied! And yet, even now as she remembered it, he had appeared quite confident that it was so. Perhaps the worldly captain was not as knowledgeable as he professed to be, she considered with a touch of cynicism.

Twice since leaving the ship, she had experienced the same spotting of blood during her time of month. She had presumed all along the change in the length and severity of her cycle was due to her lost maidenhood. But March was now fast closing, and nothing whatsoever had occurred in seven weeks.

There were other indications too. She had joined the other women in their Lenten fast, eating sparsely once daily and fasting the other two meals. Tierney felt herself nearly starving, and still her waistline grew. Her bosom now was fuller than she had ever imagined it could be.

True, her abdomen had not stretched greatly, and it was this that she had clung to during the past few worrisome weeks. But now, Tierney knew, there could be little doubt.

The night before last, as she recited her rosary, something within her stirred. It was a faint movement, almost imperceptible, and lasted only a breath of a second. Nonetheless, it was a momentous event for the girl. "Blessed is the fruit of thy womb . . ." It was more than coincidence, she knew, and in spite of her obviously circumspect situation, she was happy.

She was nervous about her unexpected maternity, most assuredly, but she was also joyously in anticipation of it.

She, Tierney Chambers, would always have a part of André de Montfort—a living part! She sighed. The needlework was not much as an exchange for her remembrance of him; but then again, she was not certain he would want even this token.

Holding it up now, she surveyed her work. It was undoubtedly the finest piece she had made, for Mother Superior herself had shown her many of the more intricate stitches. She read it aloud as she sat cross-legged on her cot:

THE WORLD IS TOO MUCH WITH US

The world is too much with us, late and soon,
Getting and spending, we lay waste our powers;
Little we see in Nature that is ours;
We have given our hearts away, a sordid boon!
The sea that bares her bosom to the moon;
The winds that will be howling at all hours,
And are up-gathered now like sleeping flowers;
For this, for everything, we are out of tune;
It moves us not. Great God! I'd rather be
A Pagan suckled in a creed outworn;
So might I, standing on this pleasant lea,
Have glimpses that would make me less forlorn;
Have sight of Proteus rising from the sea;
Or hear old Triton blow his wreathed horn.
                    Wm. Wordsworth, 1806–1807

Satisfied that it was indeed becoming and suitable for the young captain, Tierney proceeded to tack it on the light pinewood frame.

She had decided upon this poem after perusing André's gift to her of his book of poetry. This one had evidently been a favorite—or one that had caused him some study—for the page was the most worn in the newly printed edition, and the corner was turned down to mark it.

"Sister Mercedes, I beg permission to accompany Sister Matilda to the marketplace. Please, Sister. I do so want to see the city again."

"Spring fever, Tierney? Well, I suppose it is all right. Sister needs someone to go with her each week, and it is true that you have only once accompanied her. But re-

member, dear, there is some unrest these days. Besides
quarrels over British patrol barks, I have heard that the
Indians are behaving suspiciously. Speak to no one, my
dear, unless you come across Mr. Bolier," she added with
a twinkle. "And stay within sight and sound of Sister
Matilda at all times."

Tierney hugged the pudgy little nun. She still found it
hard to imagine such a merry little woman at peace within
the cloister. "Yes, Sister. And thank you!"

The prefect watched sadly as Tierney hurried down the
corridor toward the kitchens. It had been her hope that
the girl would have favored Charles Bolier with her hand
in marriage.

"But it was not to be," a tear-streaked Tierney had confided to her late one night after a visit from him. The
bachelor had, indeed, proposed to her, but Tierney had
declined, refusing even to consider the engagement. It
was a downcast young man who left the garden that afternoon, and for three weeks now the convent had been void
of a gentleman caller.

Sister Mercedes loved Tierney, but in spite of that
affection, wanted the girl to leave. The confines of a convent was no place for her to mature into womanhood. The
irony of the situation was that the postulant, Amanda,
had left the convent. She had confessed her desire to go
home to her parents, and Mother Superior had granted
her that wish with the blessings of her former Ursuline
sisters. Surprisingly, Amanda had not gone away embittered or disillusioned. In truth, her departure had been
warm and lighthearted. She was so happy that she embraced Tierney as she left the front gate! "How mysterious
are the workings of the Lord," the nun wondered as she
padded toward the chapel to light a votive candle.

The city was already abustle in the early spring sunshine
as the women drew up the horse-drawn buckboard. Sister
Matilda, a Spanish-looking woman of medium stature,
descended the trap and tossed the reins to Tierney. Before
engaging in her weekly haranguing with the hawkers and
merchants, she patted each horse affectionately and murmured into their tattered ears.

Tierney glanced anxiously about as the nun bent over
sacks of flour, rice, and cornmeal. This would probably

be her only chance to formulate an escape. She would not again go off hurriedly without plans or a destination. London and her near-death fright here had taught her better.

As much as she hated leaving the solace of the Ursulines' care, Tierney was set on going, and soon. She felt no guilt about her unintended plight. She had already confessed her adulterous acts to the kindly old priest; and as he had reminded her, she must keep faith in God's mercy and forgiveness. What caused her pregnancy was already done and behind her. There was no guilt. Surely God in His wisdom had approved the conception, if not the act.

Even so, the girl did not want to pose any embarrassment to the convent. She was certain that somehow news of the scandal would escape the convent walls, and the nuns would undoubtedly be blamed for dereliction of their duties in properly chaperoning their visitor. By the time the child was born, proving her misbehavior had occurred before Tierney's arrival, the damage would have already been done to the convent's good name.

She must leave.

"But how?" she wondered helplessly. "Who would hire me or take me in under such dire circumstances? I must think of the baby first, and before leaving, I must be assured that the baby won't suffer."

She hoped the baby would be born a girl. Tierney would have preferred a boy under different conditions, but she knew that a girl would be less difficult to rear without the benefit of a father.

"Well, time enough to think on that!" she admonished herself. It would be a long wait until August.

Squinting toward the crowds, Tierney suddenly spotted a familiar face. Charles was strolling through the tobacco stands, rolling and smelling in his palm a long, thin cigar.

Looking over her shoulder, she was confident that Sister Matilda was now out of earshot. The nun was shaking her head over the fishes and shellfish, probably refusing the asking price, Tierney thought cheerfully.

"Mr. Bolier?" she called. "Charles!"

He spun around with his mouth agape. "Why, Miss Chambers!" When he reached the side of the trap, he wiped fussily at his brow. "You're the last person on earth I would expect to see here!" He consciously avoided staring at her. He had never seen her less suitably attired, and he did not want to embarrass her.

How gentlemanly he was compared to the taunting sea captain, she thought. Tierney was acutely aware of what a spectacle she must make with her black smock, dusty and ill-fitting; the boys' boots were unmistakable, protruding beneath her hem. But there was no time for social graces or explanations.

"Charles, I was wondering if perhaps you might do something for me . . ." To her dismay, she watched him color with pleasure. To Tierney, he looked for all the world like the cartoons of Boney in the *London Times* as he threw back his shoulders which, in effect, pushed out his paunch above comically short thin legs. She half-expected he might salute her, and she struggled not to laugh. It was a successful effort when she immediately realized how silly she herself looked.

"Anything! I would consider it an honor to assist you. What can I do?"

"A newspaper, Charles." At his look of puzzled disappointment, she added, "You see, I would have a better idea of the people here and their customs if I could read the local news. I won't always be there, in the convent, I mean. And I would like to study more about New Orleans so that I might feel at home. Besides, Mother Superior is really quite distressed over the war with England, and would like to study the current news, as well."

"She need not worry, Tierney. Tell her that. The British are barely affecting the states, let alone a frontier territory. This war will be over long before it reaches Louisiana. I don't doubt that by summer peace will have been declared."

"I hope you're right, Charles. Truly, I do."

When he returned with the tabloid, Tierney smiled timidly. Even if she could have married Charles, he was far too sweet and kind to have to spend his life with her Irish temper and whimsical moods. Tierney would have liked to make him understand that, but it was useless. His face reflected blind adoration, and he would never have been convinced. This, too, was best left unsaid.

* * *

Tierney remained true to her word and delivered the political columns to Mother Superior. It wasn't any sacrifice; the girl remained immune to current events.

That night, alone in her room, she perused the society page before turning to the advertisements marked "Wanted." A name caught her attention in a brief description of a recent charity ball. Among the debutantes was one Amanda del Rindo Drake. Tierney was momentarily stunned. It was impossible to paint a scene of the starchy postulant laughing and dressed for a dance. But the very idea made her unaccountably cheerful; and despite their fractious relationship, she took a moment to silently wish her former antagonist a happy future.

CHAPTER FIFTEEN

It had been easy, a ltitle too easy, thought Tierney.

She shrugged. Perhaps God, her guardian angel, her sainted grandmother—someone—was looking out for her after all. Even André's unexpected support was going to prove highly useful. When Tierney announced she was leaving, Mother Superior had given her the three hundred dollars he had left her. According to the nun, André had called it "Tierney's mad money."

She had written to Mr. and Mrs. James Redding the very night she returned from the market. It had seemed to Tierney then, and still, that her chances of gaining their employ was as doubtful as her first attempt with the vicar's letter in London. But this time, to her tremendous relief, fate had smiled upon her. She paused to lightly touch her abdomen. "And you, too, little one. See? The angels already protect you."

Fortunately also, the babe had still not made itself evident to anyone but its mother. Although her slightly rounded belly was well-concealed by the loose novice's garb she wore exclusively now, Tierney felt faint movement almost daily. When a day did pass without those sensations, she nearly became sick with worry. She wanted André's child more than anything else in the world. Indeed, she considered it her reason for living.

When she had written to the Reddings, she had been quite honest about her condition. She explained that she was new to the territory, that her "husband" was a merchant seaman. He had embarked on a transoceanic voyage some months ago, she wrote, and had not been heard from since. Tierney said she feared his impressment by the British, "or worse." In any case, her funds were running out and she was in great need of work.

The baby would not be due until August, she surmised,

and in the meantime, Mrs. Redding could be assured that she and her own new baby would be well cared for. If they found her services needed longer, perhaps the two babies would amuse one another through their early childhood. Pass Christian was, she understood, a remote area with few families and children.

Her letter had apparently been convincing, for Mrs. Redding's reply had come within the month. Could Mrs. Chambers come at once?

Tierney had so much to be thankful for, not the least of which was the Ursulines' respect for her private correspondence. As she readjusted the bodice of her burgundy gown for the last time, she again went over her mental list of what she would pack in the duffel. Her boots, missal, undergarments, miniatures, letters (two now, the vicar's and Mrs. Redding's), brooch, music box, topaz pendant, and on a whim, the sexy flesh-toned ensemble she had never worn. Even if she could never fit into it again, she reasoned, the gown and matching accessories were worth a small fortune.

Her other garments would be delivered to the St. Phillips Theater, donated as costumes. Tierney had never actually seen a play, and now regretted she had not thought to do so while still in London. André's gold coin would have easily stretched to cover such a frivolity. She sighed. Hoping one of her gowns would be seen on stage was the closest she would come to the theater now.

The black Ursuline smocks would be left behind, of course. Surprisingly, she had not ruined them. Perhaps the mother-to-be was finally growing up.

Sister Mercedes had given her farewell up in the dormitory. She had been notably shaking, her beads rustling, as she held back her tears. Her fear was that Tierney was going to be "too far removed" in Pass Christian to meet a nice young man and settle down. She was much too lovely, Sister Mercedes told her, to spend her life as a spinster nursery maid.

Tierney assured her lovable prefect that she would not be a world away. She had already crossed the ocean once, hadn't she? "I'll be back, Sister. I promise. And meanwhile, I'll write to you weekly."

Mother Superior was a different matter altogether. Seeing her off in the coach that waited at the curb on Chartres Street, the nun had never looked more austere or controlled.

"Tierney, you must write to us as soon as you are settled."

"Yes, Mother."

"And you are to keep aside monies sufficient to bring you back, should your return become necessary, desirable."

"Yes, Mother."

"You will continue in the faith?"

"Yes, Mother," thinking all the while about her grandmother's stoicism.

"And you are quite certain you do not want to leave a letter or message for Captain de Montfort, Tierney?"

"Quite, Mother. Only the sampler I made."

"If you insist. Well, child. I am happy to see you leave New Orleans. We love you, dear, and the convent will miss you."

"I will miss you too . . ." Tierney started.

"But with this war . . ." She held up a hand. "Oh, I know what the papers say. But one can never be too sure about these things. If we are invaded . . . well, I am sure you will be safe in Pass Christian." It was an unexpected display of emotion when the tall, thin woman bent to hug Tierney briefly and kiss her cheek.

As Tierney sat back in the carriage alone, she wept disconsolately. Once again, she was forced to leave those she loved.

The five-day journey by buckboard, flatboat, and coach was exhausting. The only respite had been crossing Lake Ponchartrain, and that only mildly comfortable.

Springtime was literally bursting forth in Louisiana, with riotous blossoms abounding, insects swarming, and reptiles and little furry animals bickering and scurrying well into the night. While crossing the lake, the roar of a bull alligator seemed dangerously close once, and nearly caused her to faint.

Otherwise, Tierney found the activity of nature around her delightful, and in spite of her wretched soreness, her other senses were awakened in joyful harmony. The honeysuckle and gardenias smelled heavenly and the wild array of color was not lost to her blurred vision.

The Reddings' estate was called Southwell, and as the carriage creaked up the mimosa-lined drive toward the huge house, Tierney hugged herself and closed her eyes. "I think we're home, baby," she whispered.

The mansion was not columned, as she had expected, but had instead the ornate ironwork she had seen scattered throughout New Orleans. This particular structure was three-storied pink stucco with an expansive portico along the outside of the entire first level, private grate-iron balconies opening from French doors about the second story, and beveled glass dormers on the third. It was lovely.

The house, built on a cliff over the beach, offered a breathtaking view of the Gulf of Mexico. There was little sound of the surf, however, what with the incessant chittering of frogs and cries of sea gulls, but Tierney could smell the sea as the light breeze carried it to her face.

A black butler, who much reminded Tierney of the Pinckney's footman, greeted her. "You be Miz Chambers?" he asked after a stiff bow.

"Yes, sir. Is Mrs. Redding home?"

"Yassum. She upstairs with Masta Jamey. Where yo' trunks, ma'am?"

"I brought only this duffel," Tierney replied uncomfortably. She knew she should be more assertive with the man —he was, after all, a mere slave. But she felt constrained, well aware of her own tenuous position as a mere servant in the huge household.

"Yassum, well, I'll jes' take your totebag on up. You be needin' anything, you call ol' Theodore. I be heres all the time."

"Thank you, Theodore."

He bowed again, and before ascending the gleaming marble stairs, called softly down the hallway to the left of the stairs. "Tessie! Tessie, come show Miz Chambers up to Miz Harriet. You hear me, gal?" he added, a bit more loudly.

"I'm comin'," returned a sultry voice.

Tessie, a beautifully proportioned mulatto about Tierney's age, curtsied when they entered the bedroom. "Miz Harriet, that nursemaid done arrived. Here she is . . ."

The slight woman remained seated before the gilt-framed mirror, and only after Tessie had been dismissed did she slowly turn around to face Tierney. She had pale blond hair that fell past her shoulders and bleached freckles. The fluffy gold dressing gown did little to conceal her bony frame, and only her liquid hazel eyes enhanced her drawn appearance.

"Mrs. Chambers," she began with forced enthusiasm, "how good of you to come so quickly!" Rising, she extended her hand. "I'm Harriet Redding, Jamey's mother."

The proffered hand was cold and limp in Tierney's grasp. Why hadn't she introduced herself as mistress of Southwell, Tierney wondered. And why was this woman so forlorn-looking and unsuitably attired? It was mid-afternoon.

"How do you do, Mrs. Redding. What a lovely home you have here."

"Thank you, dear. Now would you like to get settled first, or shall we visit the nursery? I do hope you'll like it here, Mrs. Chambers," she rushed on, "and my Jamey . . . Well, I just know that you will find him as adorable as we do. He's six months old now, and cutting his first tooth. A bit grouchy these days, I'm afraid, but . . ."

Tierney smiled reassuringly and, on impulse, took the woman's hand. "Let's go to him at once, then. I'm much more interested in meeting my little charge than in seeing my room."

The nursery, which lay across from Mrs. Redding's room and the master chamber, was delightfully furnished. A white wicker crib, cradle, and rocking chair were all complemented by bright red and yellow patchwork quilts, blankets, and padding. A rocking horse was already waiting in the corner for its master to learn to ride.

Tierney smiled. Her little one would never have such splendid accommodations, but she could well envision treasured visits to the little master's room to play with Jamey.

Jamey was soundly sleeping, a thumb firmly set in his rosy lips, the cane sugar tit on the floor, discarded there by the baby himself. Tierney reached down to retrieve it and peered down at the sleeping infant.

"He's beautiful, Mrs. Redding," she whispered. "You must consider yourself fortunate, indeed." The woman came toward the crib to stand by Tierney, and when the newcomer looked up, she saw tears glistening on the mother's lashes.

"Yes, he's a lamb. And when he is older . . ." The woman's words were silenced by another door creaking open, and a huge black woman bustled into the room, a robust black baby suckling noisily at her breast.

"Anything wrong, Miz Harriet?" she asked suspiciously.

"No, Mammy." Turning back to Tierney, she added, "Mrs. Chambers, this is Mammy Lou, our wet nurse. Mammy, come meet Mrs. Chambers. She is the nursemaid that Master and I told you would be coming soon."

"Soon 'nough, I 'spect," grumbled the black woman while glaring at the intruder.

Before Tierney could think of something to say to ease the growing tension, Jamey awoke with a start and yowled his irritation at having been disturbed. The Negro baby, upon hearing the cries of another, pulled away from his mother and let out a commiserative howl.

"I done tole you, Miz Harriet, when the chile sleeps, ain't no reason to go pokin' around him none," scolded Mammy over the din. "Y'all jes git outa here now. G'wan now!" she commanded as she dexterously lifted one screaming babe from his crib and lightly jiggled the other to calm his bruised pride.

As the two women left the nursery, they both glanced back to see Mammy Lou settled in the rocker, Jamey at a full breast and the bigger baby bounced on a knee. She smiled and clucked a scolding at their impervious lack of manners, and amazingly the babies calmed down immediately.

As they walked down the hall, Mrs. Redding exclaimed, "Why, you must be half-starved, Mrs. Chambers. I know how abominable the food is enroute from New Orleans. Would you care for a dinner or tea?"

"The tea would be lovely, thank you. Could you join me perhaps? We have so much to talk about . . ."

"I'm sorry, Mrs. Chambers, but I am not dressed to go down. You see, I haven't felt well lately, but perhaps this evening or in the morning we can talk," she offered apologetically.

Tierney, with an impulsive toss of her head, answered, "Oh, nonsense! Let's go back to your room first, get you dressed properly, and then we'll enjoy tea together."

Even to Tierney, the sudden lilt sounded more like children planning a tea party than two grown women about to discuss business.

Harriet Redding could think of no further excuse and said nothing when Tierney followed her back into the bedroom.

The young mistress was no more than twenty, Tierney guessed, and whatever ailed her was a problem of the spirit, not the body. Her own sudden enthusiasm seemed to affect her employer, for she invited Tierney to help her select a dress, and soon the two women were scattering gowns across the bed, chairs, and dresser.

"This one!" Tierney finally exclaimed. "It must look lovely with your eyes." It was yellow-sprigged muslin with gay little buttons and a trail of yellow primroses down the full skirt.

Midway through dressing Mrs. Redding's curls—Tierney was not very helpful with this part of the toilet, having only to brush her own willful locks all her life—the mistress threw up her hands. "Mrs. Chambers! It just occurred to me you might want to select some of my maternity gowns. You seem so spry, I'd nearly forgotten that you'll be in confinement yourself soon . . ."

Much later, the two descended the stairs, chatting busily.

"Mrs. Redding," Tierney began, sipping on the generously creamed and sugared tea. She was famished.

"Please do call me Harriet. You see, there are no other young women in Pass Christian, to speak of, and I get so . . . so lonely," she confessed. "I would consider it an honor to have you as a friend as well as Jamey's tutor."

"Nursemaid," corrected Tierney cheerfully. "Although I can read and write to a passing degree, I fear I am not nearly qualified to tutor. Even a baby!" she laughed. "But thank you, Harriet. I am in sore need of a friend myself. Please call me Tierney." She had almost slipped by saying that except for nuns she had not met any young women in the territory, but caught herself in time and devoured another piece of lemon cake.

"What I was saying, Harriet," she managed, "is that I don't quite understand why you and your husband decided to hire me. It seems to me that Mammy Lou is quite capable on her own."

Harriet giggled. "She's a marvel, isn't she? Don't worry about her, though. She is a slave, after all, and she won't be likely to forget it. It's simply that she resents any change in routine. She is slow to warm to new people. Everyone. Why, when I first married James—Mr. Redding, that is— you would not have believed the way she treated me! Barely answered me when I spoke, as though I didn't really exist. But she is wonderful to our Jamey! Treats him like her own little Bruce."

"So I have noticed," Tierney nodded. "I'm quite certain that she'll teach me a great deal about infants. Not that I'm ignorant," she assured quickly, more confidence in her voice than in her heart. "In England, I used to help with the children during Sunday school outings; and on holidays, the vicarage had special parties for the children. It was great fun. Of course, Salisbury is a long way from here," she sighed. "Those sugar tits are a great invention! The mothers in England would give an eye for a trinket to satisfy fretful babes. I never heard of them until I got here. In New Orleans, I did some volunteer work for Charity Hospital. Besides rolling bandages, we made hundreds of sugar tits with whittled cane and clean gauze."

The sun was dropping when Theodore entered and silently went about the parlor, lighting the lamps. The two young women were fast becoming friends, and one would have been hard put to decide who was more eager for the companionship. The conversation had turned to the timely subject of childbearing when James Redding came home. He stood in the foyer unnoticed for a few minutes before interrupting them. In the soft candlelight, his wife's eyes sparkled.

Harriet giggled suddenly at some private joke, and a lump caught in the man's throat. He had not seen his wife look or sound so vivacious in a long time. Over a year, in fact, he mused.

"Darling! It's so good to hear you laugh . . . And you look marvelous!"

As Harriet got up to greet him, Tierney studied the man. He was of medium height—short in comparison to André, she considered—but squarely built. His hair was the color of Tierney's own, but she could not focus well enough to determine the rest of his features.

"Tierney, I'd like you to meet my husband, Mr. Red-

ding." She led him by the hand into the parlor, her whole
face aglow. "James, this is Mrs. Chambers. Isn't she wonderful?"

The man laughed, embarrassed by his wife's unusual
gaiety. "Well, darling, Mrs. Chambers and I have hardly
had time to form any opinions of one another, now, have
we? But, Mrs. Chambers, I am very pleased to see you.
And if my wife is happy," he said with a broad smile,
"well, that is all that really matters to me."

CHAPTER SIXTEEN

The months sped by and before Tierney could adjust to
the wet and windy spring, a sultry humid summer descended upon the Gulf Coast.

It was not yet June, but already temperatures soared
above ninety and the moist air coming from the sea and
back swamps was stifling. If just one factor could be
eliminated, fumed Tierney, then she could manage quite
well. Just one thing—was that so much to ask? To be rid
of the wretched mosquitoes, the blazing heat, her swollen
ankles, Jamey's rash . . . anything would help!

It was with this in mind that she nearly jumped for joy
when a roll of thunder broke the heavy silence. A storm!
A marvelous summer tempest that would bring with it
cooling rains and cooler breezes. She could gladly put up
with tomorrow's higher humidity for a break in pace now.

The darkness quickly spread over the horizon and
Jamey, who was pulling himself up and into everything
within reach, squalled his disapproval. Bruce, already
walking, added to the nursery dissension by pulling a
stuffed rabbit from his diminutive master's hands. Tierney
was so relieved by the change in weather, she minded
neither child's ensuing tantrum.

Mammy Lou did, however, and came into the room with
arms akimbo. She looked at Tierney with a degree of
tolerant disapproval. It made the wet nurse happy to
know that no one—including a hired white woman—
could handle the children as well as she.

"Lawd, Lawd, cain't git nowheres without havin' to run
back heres and check up on these chillen! You g'wan
down to dinner, missy, and I'll handle the younguns now."

Tierney did not even remotely resent being ordered
about by Mammy Lou. The big woman knew how to
handle the babies to perfection, and besides, Tierney now

understood that her primary purpose for being at Southwell was to take care of Harriet, not Jamey.

As she went up the next flight toward her own room, she sighed aloud. These days she preferred resting to eating. It was not that she had grown too heavy or the babe too cumbersome. In fact, her lithe figure carried pregnancy amazingly well, but by late afternoon her ankles were oppressively large, and the heat did little to warrant a hearty appetite.

The room was small—about the size of André's cabin, she reflected—but she loved it. The two dormer windows faced the shoreline, and at night, when the breeze was nearly imperceptible, she could hear the waves. In the daytime, the light splashed throughout the room and brightly painted her own bentwood rocker and patchwork quilt.

But now, she thought, I can throw open the windows and let the cool breeze whip the whole place apart. I don't care, as long as that blessed sweet air reaches every corner.

She did not light either of her lamps. Rather, she leaned out of the third-story window and watched as the lightning shattered the dark sky over the water. When the rains turned from the heavy droplets to a stinging shower, she reluctantly pulled herself away and pulled the windows almost shut, allowing only cracks to send in wisps of air.

Tierney's thoughts were as tumultuous as the storm. She wondered where *La Reine de la Mer* sailed and how her captain fared. She missed André, to be sure, and at times anguished over what might have been. Still, she was thankful. In spite of the disagreeable climate, she liked her new homeland. She rarely thought of England anymore, and missed it even less. There was too much of the future in her days to reflect on the past.

The baby was healthy, of that she was sure. A little too energetic, she mused, as a boisterous thump was felt under her rib. She still hoped for a girl, and as she undressed, she patted her belly absently. As she stretched upon the bed wearing a voluminous silk nightgown from Harriet's maternity wardrobe, she turned her thoughts to Mammy Lou.

Bruce was every bit as delightful a baby as Jamey, and his soft fuzzy head was perfumed with the same talc as his master's. But despite the black child's robust health and generally happy disposition, the tides of fortune were more against him than her own illegitimate son or daughter. For little Bruce was a slave, born into servitude, and most likely he would die one.

Tierney's heart ached for Mammy Lou, but she was careful not to show it. Mammy was a proud woman, and would have scorned her unsolicited pity. Nonetheless, Tierney did pity the wet nurse because she knew that as soon as Bruce was weaned, he would be taken to the slave quarters to be raised by others. Except for Sundays, holidays, and emergencies, Mammy Lou would not be with her son anymore.

It might be years before Mammy could return to the slave huts herself. In a chilling sweep of instinctive fear, Tierney clutched at her abdomen.

Southwell was relatively small for a plantation. Tierney still found it difficult to believe that eighty thousand acres was a tiny parcel in the huge American territory, but so it was. Mr. Redding cultivated the regional cane, rice, and indigo, but in addition to these products, Southwell maintained a considerable fishing fleet. "Thus," he told Tierney, "should my crops fail, I can still reap the sea." The shrimp, crab, oysters, and clams seemed always in abundance, and Mr. Redding did not limit his catch to shellfish.

She learned more daily about plantation life, and the people who manned them. The reason, it turned out, that Harriet had not introduced herself as mistress of the estate was that Mr. Redding's mother, Angelique Redding, still lived and managed the household. "Angel," her son called her. Nothing could have been further from the truth, Tierney thought irritably.

The petite, gray-haired woman was the source of constant aggravation in the otherwise peaceful domicile. She badgered the servants incessantly and held only a slightly noticeable degree of respect for one—old Theodore. Theo had been her late husband's manservant, and he alone escaped Mrs. Redding's waspish tongue.

Her son James was at her beck and call whenever he was at home, and that was not often. Harriet, on the other hand, was always around but completely ignored. James Redding, at thirty-seven, had not been forgiven for bringing home his unwelcomed bride.

It was this that Tierney most bitterly resented. Harriet was shy and retiring enough without a shrewish mother-in-law to contend with. Tierney's pregnancy had not altogether subdued her temper, and she had openly remarked to Harriet that the older Mrs. Redding was "a born and bred bitch."

At this, Harriet had covered her ears in horror. She never could predict what Tierney would say or do next.

Thinking on it now, Tierney remembered when Angel had once remarked at dinner that she dearly wished her son had found such a spirited young girl for a wife, casting a meaningful glance at the brow-beaten daughter-in-law. Tierney, not to be taken in by such a double-edged stab, had stood and retorted, "Why, Madame, how generous of you! Especially since I overheard you just yesterday express doubt about my child's legitimate paternity, indeed, how *I* came to be, as well!" To the shock of everyone, Tierney then delivered a habitual toss of her head and left the room.

It was nothing short of a miracle that she was still employed at Southwell.

Her employment had, in any case, taken on more the feel of an extended visit than of a permanent post. She took her meals with the family, accompanied them on outings, and was more and more becoming a sister to Harriet. The young women were genuinely fond of one another, and Harriet's quiet nature balanced somewhat the still-mischievous Tierney.

Harriet had married James Redding when she was a mere girl of sixteen years. She had not then really known her husband, she admitted, but his patience and fortitude had eventually won her love. The marriage had not even been consummated in the first four months! When she confided this intimacy to Tierney, Tierney had, for once, been struck speechless.

Limiting lovemaking to just three occasions with André on board *La Reine* had been difficult enough for Tierney. To think that she and André themselves, unmarried, could not even stand a month of celibacy between England and America! How scandalous they had been! James Redding must certainly be a more stoic man than André de Montfort, and Harriet a far more virtuous lady than she.

But the Reddings were different in all ways, it seemed. It had taken Harriet nearly three years to become pregnant with Jamey, and now, according to an Orlean physician, she should expect no more. "I just thank God I had a son. It is the only accomplishment I shall ever have, I believe."

Harriet gently pressed Tierney for more details of her own marriage and husband. Surprisingly, Tierney was able to resist the temptation to be equally honest with her friend. It would have been such a relief to pour her heart out to someone, to get it all out in the open, if only to one female confidante. She would imagine telling Harriet the whole story: meeting her "prince" at the Silver Steed, posing as a boy, her scorn of the captain that grew into love. Everything! The beautiful gowns from Charleston and again in New Orleans, the handsome captain's rescue of her lost in the streets her first night in Louisiana . . . It was all such a thrilling romance to a girl of seventeen.

The possible consequences to such a disclosure, however, held Tierney back. Such shocking news at the very least might bring her abrupt dismissal from Southwell. But the worst result—that her child would be called a bastard—was uppermost in Tierney's mind.

Presently, Tierney sat up and stretched to rub her back. It would have been so nice to be Madame André de Montfort, and her waiting child to bear its true name . . .

Her stay in Pass Christian had so far been spent happily and speedily enough, but Tierney was growing impatient. She wanted the baby, now, to hold and cuddle and care for. But there was more she wanted, more she needed. "Oooh, that's impossible! And it must be against nature, a sin of some sort," she scolded herself as an unwelcomed longing for lovemaking spread through her limbs.

Tierney thought such sensations were preposterous, especially in her now pronounced condition. But of late, her thoughts turned frequently back to *La Reine de la Mer,* back to the master cabin, back to the berth where André held her in his arms. Sometimes, well into the night, she could almost see André's naked form and feel his heated breath on her neck. And as many rosaries as she would recite could not dispel her sensual memories of their bodies locked together.

Angrily, Tierney got up. After dressing again in one of Harriet's tent-sized confinement gowns, she plodded down the flights of stairs to the kitchen. Perhaps Bijou, the cook, would have some tempting morsels to soothe her frustration.

Tomorrow, she must apologize for absenting herself from supper. She could already imagine Angelique Redding's haughty reply.

It was unusual to receive a letter from Mother Superior. In fact, Tierney had heard only once before from her and that had been during her first month in Pass Christian. On the other hand, correspondence with Sister Mercedes was regular. "At least on her part," Tierney silently corrected. She was finding it increasingly difficult to post letters to the prefect. News of Jamey and the plantation was fine, she knew, but her most exciting news, the forthcoming birth of her own baby, had to be omitted from the letters. Invariably, Tierney would forget herself and slip. "I can feel the baby hiccough," or "August seems so long to wait . . ." and rewriting letters was such a bother!

But a letter from Mother Superior! What could possibly have happened? Tierney eagerly broke the seal as soon as she reached the beach below the house.

"My Dear Daughter," it began. The penmanship was perfect—small and cursive, but not elaborately so. It did not at all resemble her own rambling scribble . . . Why was it that all nuns' writing looked the same?

She read on. Mother Superior advised her that the British were now blockading the Eastern seaboard from Delaware to Georgia. Encounters had been concentrated about the Great Lakes region, and the fear was that once the Ohio Valley was lost—where was the Ohio Valley?—defeat was a grave possibility.

Tierney scanned the page. This war, which seemed too remote to bother with, was of keen interest to Mother Superior, but not Tierney.

Mother advised her to be cautious. The Indians were behaving suspiciously, she wrote; even the mild-mannered Choctaws were "imbibing heavily in spirits and roaming the streets in New Orleans." The Creek Nation, it was rumored, were agents of the British. "They are being bought, as in the Revolution," she warned.

Tierney chewed her lip absently. She had never heard of a Creek Nation. Moreover, what was so bloody awful about British domination? Remembering what little she knew about Belfast, she reconsidered and decided she would read the letter again before bed.

Meanwhile, was there any real news? An admonition to pray for peace . . . pray for the poor souls . . . Charity Hospital was inundated with fever patients . . . a letter from Captain de Montfort!

Tierney closed her eyes and waited for her trembling hands to calm. No use. She laid the letter on the sand where she sat, and weighted it with a few shells. She squinted at the blurred words.

> "Just a short note, dear. He inquired after your health, and that of the sisters. The captain was most generous in a donation to the order and school. . . . Very exciting, postmarked Singapore . . . Most regrettable that there is no forwarding address except Nantes, but can we not notify his sister, Madame Loren, of your new home? He left that information. . . ."

Tierney exclaimed angrily, and the sandpipers which pecked within an arm's length of her scattered. "Sure, and that would be a laugh! Write to his sister, and his beloved little fiancée would be waiting in Brittany with a dagger!" Over the months, Tierney had greatly enlarged upon what little she knew of André de Montfort's past and present paramours. But at this heated moment, had any of these women materialized, she would have attacked them as viciously as any she-cat, no matter her swollen belly!

> "Perhaps Sister Mercedes has already sent word to you of one of our former postulants, Amanda del Rindo Drake. Her engagement to Mr. Charles Bolier has been announced . . . The wedding is to be in August. We are all very happy for her, as I am sure you will be also, as she enters the blessed sacrament of matrimony . . . We hope that you continue to love and serve the Lord, that in all things He might be glorified . . ."

Tierney crumpled the letter. As she struggled to get back on her feet, she felt for the first time the full weight of her pregnancy.

CHAPTER SEVENTEEN

"Oh, Tierney, you mustn't! You really mustn't!" pleaded Harriet. "The baby could come any minute now, and it simply is not safe. And besides"—she sniffed on the verge of tears—"it's not proper. It is . . . it's indecent!"

"And who's to see me out on the beach? The fishes? They'll pay me no mind . . ." Harriet was right, of course. The baby was due any time, but that in itself was contributing to Tierney's stubbornness. She was not to be gainsayed.

"I've survived quite well, thank you. And I've been cooped up in the house nearly all summer. Surely a little walk on the beach won't kill us." She held up a hand at the women. "Now, listen. If by some miracle, this ornery babe wants to get born of a sudden, I'll let out a yell for help such as has never been heard in all of Louisiana and Mississippi put together. Old Theo and Mammy will get me back into the house in no time."

"But there is a mist gathering," enjoined Angelique, for once in accord with her daughter-in-law. "Now, be a sensible child for a change, and stay home."

There was genuine concern in the older woman's voice, and for a moment Tierney almost capitulated. The words might have been spoken by Nanna. But she shrugged and continued her ungainly descent of the porch steps. "If the scream doesn't bring them, I'll wave this yellow shawl like a Crown's flag!"

As she cautiously made her way down the drive, she giggled nervously at the thought of raising an English flag on this continent.

"Well, do stay in front of the house," called Harriet.

"I will!"

When she reached the sand dunes, Tierney sat down to catch her breath. A baby could be as restricting as a bedsheet binding, she thought glumly.

Late August. Only a year ago this week she had tiptoed into Nanna's room to find her lying so still ... The baby had been lying too still too. Mammy Lou and Harriet had both assured her this was natural. "Resting for the birth," they told her. She hoped they knew what they were talking about.

Everything appeared to be in order. Her "false" milk had started just yesterday, a sticky yellow fluid that stained her loose bodice. Pregnancy was a completely incredible experience. What with figures ballooning out of all imaginable proportion, ugly marks appearing here and there, and abominable little hairs growing on you in the most undesirable areas, it was a wonder carrying a baby nine months did not end more marriages. She shuddered at the thought of André frankly studying her now.

Getting back up to take her leisurely stroll was no piece of cake. Try as she might, she could not get from her haunches to her feet. "I must look like an overgrown jellyfish," she fumed. "I hope they aren't looking." Finally, bracing her arms to one side, she rolled to a kneeling position, then pushed herself to stand.

"Whew!" Absently brushing sand from her palms, she walked toward the overcast sunset. Tierney was trying to think of names for the baby. Sidney, perhaps, for a boy. André, even Andrew, was out of the question. She loved the name Paul. Paul Chambers? "Well, now, how would that look?" she scolded herself.

If it was the daughter she hoped for, Tierney would wait a day or so to name her. She might be like Tierney's Irish mother with golden wavy hair, or André with his straight thick mane of black, or—God forbid, she thought fervently—the baby might take after her and be bridled with the stubborn coppery curls. She would just have to wait and see about naming a little girl. . . .

As she contemplated the shells along her path, she remembered that Amanda and Charles had been married last week in the Cathedral of St. Louis. Tierney had been sent a personal invitation to the ceremony by Amanda. She searched the note that accompanied the embossed invitation for signs of the girl's former hostility or sarcasm, but there had been nothing to read between the lines. Amanda was quite obviously in a state of premarital bliss when she wrote it.

Before declining the invitation, Tierney had secretly considered putting in an appearance in all her bulging glory. But common sense prevailing, she sent a silver butter dish along with her regrets.

Actually, James Redding had purchased the gift and arranged to have it delivered during a business trip into the city. He could be so nice, she mused. A pity he spent so much time away from Harriet. He had even missed his son's first steps.

Tierney had assured Harriet time and again that her fears about his infidelity were unfounded. At first, Tierney had suspected that Harriet was right, that the mulatto Tessie was his consort. Now, however, she truly believed the man innocent of any wrongdoing; in fact, his mannerisms reminded her of Paul Mauriac.

"He's a man who is accustomed to bachelorhood, that's all," she soothed Harriet. "And his business is the very lifeblood of Southwell. You mustn't doubt him so!" She refrained from telling her friend that a decrease in bending to Angelique's supervision and perhaps an increase in Harriet's own romantic demands might do wonders.

Her own relationship with James Redding was unusual in itself. There was no salary; at least, there was none measurable. Her second week in Pass Christian, Tierney had asked for a word in private with the master. She had offered to forego regular recompense in lieu of free room and board, and generous free time. "When and if I need it, sir, that is, when my husband comes home and I return to New Orleans, I am certain we will come to some satisfactory agreement."

It was silently understood between James Redding and Tierney that he was keeping in his care a young unwed mother, and she fully appreciated both his compassion and discretion. Little else was said on the matter, but all that was required of Tierney was to entertain the year-old heir to Southwell—and that for only two hours each day.

Harriet was complacently happy with the arrangement; she had a trusted friend. Angelique suspected the truth, but shrugged it off as a slight eccentricity on the part of her son. The old woman secretly enjoyed having the girl about, anyway. Tierney reminded the woman of her own spirited youth, when as a bride, she and the first James

Redding had carved their own private world out of a wretchedly hostile frontier.

Bruce had been taken to the slave quarters, nearly a mile inland from the beach. Tierney could only imagine how Mammy must feel. Or *did* she still feel it? She had given birth to four others before little Bruce. Two of them still lived.

Tierney shivered and pulled the shawl more tightly about her shoulders. She had not kept track of time or distance, but estimated it was time to head back toward the house. "I'll just rest a bit first," she murmured aloud. A worrisome catch in her lower abdomen, "false pains" they were called, was starting again.

Today was the first break in hot weather since May, but the fine mist was beginning to take on an unseasonable chill. Something felt amiss, like that first night on the streets of New Orleans alone in the storm. Tierney was growing fidgety and peered into the fog to see nothing but a deserted stretch of beach and a powerless surf. The white wash was never more than a foot or so high except during foul weather. Mr. Redding had explained that this area of the Gulf was dotted with a string of miniature islands that broke the velocity and pattern of the waves. This afternoon, with the tide going out, the waves lapped the beach as timidly as a weak kitten laps cream.

"No storm at all," was her last sensible thought before a sudden blow to her head rendered her unconscious. She was dimly aware of pain and the sound of sand rustling, but the scream never reached her lips.

A mile west of Southwell, no one saw her body being dragged across the beach and into the pine forest.

Chinookseh had considered the matter for some time before actually deciding to abduct her. He lay in a moist bed of pine straw watching her walk down the beach, stretch her arms toward the gray, cloudy sky, and finally come to rest on the sandbunker not twenty yards from him.

Chinookseh was a warrior of twenty-four years of age, and not even during numerous raids on various white soldiers' posts east of Mississippi had he been close to capture by any white man. A great battle was now brewing—they would attack Fort Mims soon, and the

British gold would stave off the winter hunger that was coming. The young Indian did not flinch at the memories of blood and vengeance; such cowardice was not in his personality.

His reputation as a brave and knowledgeable man had quickly spread, and now in his own village he was honored with nods from the old men. He was called into the federation council. The Creek Federation—or Nation, as some called it—was comprised of over fifty Creek tribes that now spread from Georgia to Oklahoma, some eighty thousand men in all.

They, the Creeks, scorned their Choctaw, Cherokee, and Seminole brothers for capitulating to the white man's power, for already the mountains of Georgia, Tennessee, and the upper Mississippi Valley swarmed with these pale-faced madmen. First would come the fur trappers who depleted the wildlife for money, bargaining, sometimes fairly, with the Indian. The traders were the same breed, loners for the most part, exchanging spirited drink with red-skinned fools for the scant harvests. Finally the settlers would come—pushing, fencing, and mowing down the great forests.

But this was Chinookseh's land, and he did not intend to be pushed away.

In spite of his fighting prowess and agility on horseback, the young man had never brought a live enemy back to camp. The Indians, however, were quickly learning many vices of the white man: firearms, corn whiskey, and slavery, among them. His village, a good thirty miles into forests and swamps, was relatively poor. Only four hundred Kawita lived there. There were only three slaves, and none of them were white.

This woman with hair of cedar would add to his growing prestige. To be honest, he would have preferred a virgin with hair the color of honey and eyes the color of turquoise. But this one, with a look of harvest time, would do well. The time seemed ripe, he considered with some amusement.

He saw that she was heavy with child. Chinookseh hoped the woman was not stupid, for although he would find no immediate pleasure with his captive, he was glad she was near her time. With the right stars, the child would be born a male. To capture the camp's first white male would be a great honor.

Tierney slowly regained consciousness, and through the pounding in her head, heard a man singing. It was a peculiar incantation, like a druid or banshee, she thought. Then she remembered the beach, and her eyes flew open.

The trees overhead pointed menacing needles toward her and she struggled to scream. It was muffled, and Tierney froze at her own sound.

She was gagged, and the cloth tasted and smelled of mildew. Her hands and feet were securely bound, as was her body, strapped to a hide litter between two poles. She was being dragged, and as she shifted her weight to one side and leaned her head back, she could see the switch of the horse's tail.

Panicked, she wondered if he thought she was dead. No, of course not—he had cautiously wrapped her mouth to keep her quiet.

Tierney strained to see who the eerie singer was and where he was taking her. She peered helplessly into the dark woods and toward the black sky. Only on the clearest nights could Tierney see the stars, and her weeks on board *La Reine* had taught her very little.

After an eternity of breaking twigs and bouncing over rocks and ruts, the man halted and silently slipped down off the horse. In the sudden stillness, Tierney could hear him steal through the trees to a nearby running brook. He returned, then, unceremoniously dropping the litter from the animal's haunches, and led the beast to the water. Tierney heard the pony neigh appreciatively and the man speak softly in return. "I could do with a bit of water myself," she thought impotently.

She tried to concentrate on what was happening to her, but instead remembered swaying in the crow's nest with icy rain biting her hands and neck. She had survived that nightmare, hadn't she? But on that occasion, André had been there to rescue her. Tonight there was no one. "Just me and the babe," she thought with a start. Above all else, his child must survive whatever lay ahead. She owed André that much. Owed herself . . .

Her eyes blinked away the tears of despair that coursed

down the sides of her face. With the litter unhitched, she was flat on her back now, and the water trickled into her ears and crept into the hair above.

He was standing above her, a gourd of water in his left hand. With his right he motioned her to remain silent. She nodded her understanding and he cautiously untied the gag. Then he roughly lifted her head with his free hand, and proffered the cup of cold water.

When she had drunk her fill, Tierney sighed and lay back.

He was an Indian, all right, she thought morosely. Mother Superior had warned her, and others had too. "Be a sensible child for a change," Angelique had tried to tell her. When in heaven's name would she learn to listen to her betters? Not much chance to start listening now, she thought with wry amusement.

She could not understand a word he was saying. He was speaking in a low monotone, his brow creased in absolute earnest in the pale moonlight. Whatever he was saying, she thought fearfully, he was deadly serious about it.

Finding her voice, she whispered hoarsely, "Who are you? What do you want?"

His reply was equally unintelligible. "Ka-wee'ta," he said. He repeated it with "Kawita . . . Chinookseh," pointing to his bared breast. He wore a flannel shirt, but the sleeves were ripped off exposing smooth, powerful arms. The buttons were missing, as well, and it fell loosely open over the broad, hairless chest. He wore buckskin trousers and moccasins.

After saying "Chinookseh" and gesturing a few more times, Tierney realized he was giving her his name. He pointed to her.

"Tierney," she managed weakly.

Chinookseh was very pleased. The woman did not seem too stupid.

He walked back to his blanket roll, and pulled out a piece of jerky. Returning with this, he sat down next to the litter and held a piece of the dried meat under her nose. It smelled sour, and Tierney shook her head. She did not want to offend her captor, but she honestly thought she would retch if he put it to her lips.

Her nausea must have been readable, for the Indian shrugged and plopped all of it into his mouth. While he leisurely chewed the stuff, he took up again talking to her. Of course Tierney could not understand him, but she winced when he placed his hands, palms downward, on her stomach. No one, not even Harriet, had felt the baby within her.

As if aware of the foreigner's touch, the fetus gave a strong kick at his hands. Chinookseh pulled his hands away in surprise, and laughed softly. "Good," he said. Tierney did not know whether to cry out from joy or indignation, but she wisely chose to share his joke. She tremulously smiled and repeated, "Good!"

Tierney had mistakenly believed they were stopping for the night, and startled when she felt her stretcher being strapped to the horse. Chinookseh came back one more time to replace the gag, but Tierney set her lips firmly and shook her head. He understood the gesture and, uttering what could only have been a malicious threat, agreed to forego the precaution. She lay soundlessly for the rest of the long ride.

They arrived at the village near dawn. People were already up and about, with smoke curling out of nearly every hut. The children, however, were noticeably quiet and only older girls were seen carrying skins of water to and fro. In front of the long, low-lying hut which appeared to be the center of activity, a trussed pig roasted in a huge open fire. The aroma was unbearably delicious to Tierney.

There wasn't much time to think about it, however, as a shout rang out from her abductor. He was immediately answered with a hum of movement, shouts from other men, and curiosity spurred in the women and children. Chinookseh dragged her all the way to the open cooking pit in front of the longhouse. Then he happily leaped from the horse's back and clapped.

The Indians gathered in a circle about her, but held back at a respectful distance. For one ghastly second, Tierney imagined her own body bound and trussed and put up on the spit with the pig. She had heard of such atrocities. . . .

Fortunately, before her imagination took over her senses, Chinookseh appeared above her impishly grinning. He nimbly cut the leather straps that held her hands and feet, then loosed the straps that had secured her to the litter. She absently rubbed her numbed wrists and scraped her ankles together. The feet, at least, were none the worse for wear. Thank God she had thought to lace on her deck boots the afternoon before. . . .

A white-haired man came up to Chinookseh, merely glancing at Tierney as they spoke. Tierney strained to make some sense of the words, but it was to no avail. Suddenly, the young man began gesturing to her to stand up.

Tierney tried. At least on the beach, a crowd had not been there to gawk at her ungainly movements. "Instead of a jellyfish, now I feel like a turtle on its back," she thought. Some children tittered at the spectacle, and Tierney's temper might have gotten the best of her had not a wrenching pain jolted her already sore spine.

"Jesus, Mary, and Joseph," she cried in agony, "Won't one of you bloody heathens help me?" She searched her captor's face for some human sympathy, thinking he, at least, would lift her to her feet. Her back still burned with the effort of trying to brace her hands on the ground as she had on the beach.

For a moment, he looked as though he would lend assistance. He evidently thought better of it, however, and called a young woman—a child, really—out from the crowd.

"Melita!" he roared.

The girl inclined her head toward the white-haired elder, and after bowing similarly to Chinookseh, dropped to her knees beside the litter. First she fingered Tierney's matted hair, then put her forehead against Tierney's own. It was a peculiar gesture, surprising in its gentleness. Tierney dared not flinch. Melita spoke to the men in nearly a whisper. They nodded at her, and the girl turned back to Tierney, at last helping her to her feet.

Tierney was ushered into the long house and allowed to sit on a log bench in the corner of the room. There were no chairs.

The air in here was dank, but the barren dirt floors lent an impression of crude cleanliness. Tierney studied the skins of various animals that were strung to the walls as she breathed through parted lips to limit the foreign smells.

The men were coming in quietly, and each seemed to know his place on the four enormous logs that ran the length of the room; two logs were on either side of a loose circle of huge stones, apparently a fireplace during winter months. The hole in the hut's roof above the primitive hearth served as a chimney.

As the room filled, Tierney noticed the variety of dress before her. She had thought the savages inside the territory wore only loincloths and feathers. Many of them wore strings of beads, stones, shells, and dried nuts—but no feathers were in sight. Some wore buckskin, some were naked above the waist, and yet others wore hats. One very old man wore a long calico skirt and a shirt that reminded her of the one she had made for André.

She knew the meeting dealt with her being brought here, for Melita had long since disappeared. Tierney was the only woman in the room.

Since she could not decipher the discussion, she ignored them altogether. The pain was increasing steadily now, and she arched her back to ease the discomfort. Absently, she brushed at her boots, wondering what poor Harriet must be thinking at this hour. She estimated that she had been missing from Southwell now for some thirteen, maybe fourteen, hours.

There appeared no chance of rescue. Tierney poignantly regretted not having allowed Mother Superior to give André notice of her whereabouts. If nothing else, she should have admitted to the Ursulines she would bear his child. If she lived long enough, Tierney was confident she could devise an escape. "I've gotten myself in and out of scrapes before, haven't I?" She silently tried to bolster her spirits.

If she were to die—and that seemed a very real possibility—André had the right to know that a child of his was being helplessly cast to fate in a remote Indian camp. It was damned stupid of her not to have at least told Mr. Redding whom to contact should the child be orphaned. Not that even André would know where to look . . .

Her mental wanderings were disrupted by the argument. Tierney had been vaguely aware in the change from quiet discussion to mild disagreement. But now the air was positively charged with excitement. Chinookseh and another bigger Indian were heatedly quarreling. The white-haired man who had walked up with Chinookseh while she was still tied to the litter was presently shaking his head and holding Chinookseh's right forearm.

Before she could fathom the meaning of the dispute, the taller man sauntered over to where Tierney sat and pulled her by the hair to stand. She bit her lip to keep from screaming. The next thing Tierney saw was Chinookseh's jump between the man and herself, pushing him back toward the center of the room. The angry foe whipped out a broad-bladed knife, and Tierney did scream then.

Chinookseh ducked the blow, and came back with such speed that Tierney did not see him knock the knife out of the threatening man's hand. But she saw the taller one's arm reaching for her, and believing he still held the weapon, shrank back against the wall.

It happened so quickly! He grabbed at her neck, and as she heard the material rip at her bodice, she felt the water she had carried in her womb these long months break open. She was never quite certain whether her blood-chilling shriek was from fear or the shock of warm water gushing down her thighs.

One thing was certain. The sudden onset of Tierney's labor put a quick end to the fight. The Indian who had accosted her spat on the dirt floor and stalked out. The older man, evidently a leader, dismissed the rest of the gathering and the men trouped back to their homes. Chinookseh pushed Tierney back down on the log and ran from the room.

"Well, this is one hell of a fix!" she gasped. If a woman did come to her aid, it was doubtful she would understand a word of what was said. Tierney looked around desperately, slightly relieved that the cramps she felt were now as mild as an easy menses.

The girl, Melita, returned with two others. The women helped Tierney to get up, and together the four women walked out into the sunlight.

It was still early, but already the heat was rising in steamy waves from the moist ground. The women silently led her down well-worn paths, seemingly indifferent to the suffocating humidity.

They passed several chicken coops, a potter's wheel, and a primitive mill grind. Tierney was mildly surprised to see such domestic industry in an Indian camp, and speculated on the feasibility of an infirmary on the premises.

But instead, they took her to a tiny, one-room hut on the east end of the village. It was apparently Chinookseh's domicile, for he was inside eating his breakfast. Melita knelt down and rested her buttocks against her heels. She motioned Tierney to do the same. It was surprisingly comfortable.

The four women sat like this in silence. Finally, the young man finished his meal and, looking hard at Melita and then Tierney, left the hut.

The women began almost immediately to chatter, and laughed suddenly, apparently sharing a joke. Tierney failed to see the humor. The pain in her abdomen was worsening and now she was growing scared, a cold numbness spreading to her hands and chest. This was going to be the worst day of her life.

Harriet had assured her it would be. "I don't want to frighten you, Tierney. But *I* didn't know a thing before I had Jamey . . . You may as well prepare yourself, my dear . . . I feel sorry for James, of course, but I am truly relieved that Jamey will be the only one."

Tierney moaned. It was more from fear than pain, but the women took notice. One of them, a broad-faced woman with luminous black eyes, came over to where Tierney still sat on her haunches. The woman got on her hands and knees, and motioned Tierney to do the same. Then she hung her head down between her arms and raised her back, arching it like an angry cat. Tierney imitated the posture, feeling very foolish indeed. She knew she ought to be lying in a soft bed, with leather belts hitched to the post to pull on when the pains got bad.

She was surprised, however, to feel relief in both her abdomen and lower back when she stretched like the Indian woman. But she didn't stay like that for long. The teacher patted her bottom like a dog and stood up. She helped Tierney to her feet.

"Now what?" Tierney wondered unhappily. Were they amusing themselves with her antics? Another contraction rolled across her, and she cried out. They hushed her, shaking their heads adamantly and threatening to strike her. She would not be permitted to cry. . . .

The women walked her around, encouraging her to

kneel and arch whenever the pains seemed intolerable.
And they taught her to breathe . . . slowly, inhaling
through the nostrils and exhaling slowly through her
mouth. Slowly, in and out, in and out, throughout the
morning whenever the contractions came.

By early afternoon, Tierney was exhausted. But her
faith in the teacher's instruction was growing. So far, everything they had shown her to do was helping. She was beginning to feel like a trained monkey, aping every new exercise or posture the moon-faced woman demonstrated.
This one woman was far more useful than the others.

Tierney was hot and thirsty. They would not permit her
to drink water, but they sponged her face and gave her a
piece of sugar cane to suck. Once, when they weren't
looking, she cupped her hands into the water jar. But after
only two swallows, Tierney felt nauseous. She was sorry
she had disobeyed them.

After another hour or more of walking, arching, and
rhythmic breathing, Tierney grew drowsy. The woman
with keen understanding smiled knowingly, and motioned
her to lie down. A blanket covered the small pallet of
pinestraw and animal hides, and Tierney found the bed
remarkably comfortable. To her mild dismay, she realized
she was drifting off to sleep. It was heaven, however, deep
and peaceful.

She awoke with a scream. The women were gone and
Tierney panicked. Within seconds, though, two of them
returned still passive and unhurried. The teacher-woman
began to pant, gesticulating for Tierney to imitate. Tierney,
however, was too scared to pay attention. She was dying
from the piercing, all-encompassing agony.

She screamed again, and the woman slapped her face.
Hard.

Now they raised Tierney from her reclining position to
a squat. During the process, the pain miraculously disappeared. "What are you doing?" she demanded irritably.
"You want the child to be born on its head? I'll break the
poor thing's neck like this!" The Indians seemed wholly
unperturbed by her anger.

Another intense contraction suddenly racked her abdomen. The woman held Tierney's head between her hands
and panted into her face. This time, the pupil paid attention. Their eyes locked, and together they began the

quick breathing technique. Tierney was so engrossed in the red-skinned face before her, she barely felt Melita pull the already torn gown down her shoulders and over her hunched buttocks.

Once again she was released from the pain, but the reprieve lasted only a few seconds. Another contraction, longer this time, and another short rest. And so it went, Tierney squatting with the woman before her, the two united in breath and eye contact. Tierney trusted this ugly woman, certain that she was being saved from a hideous death.

Meanwhile, Melita quietly prepared for the arrival of the baby. A basin of warm water lay waiting, a mixture of scented bear oil and persimmon prepared to cleanse it. Raw cotton, soft deerskin, a blanket . . .

To her horror, Tierney suddenly felt she would defecate. A few drops of blood speckled the torn dress at her feet, but only the Indian noticed. Tierney shuddered. Would they let her go outside to empty her bowels? She must get up . . .

The women did not let her, however, and pushed her back to lie on the pallet. Although the contractions had ceased, Tierney's urge to bear down was overwhelming. She must, she thought, or expire from holding it back.

Both women positioned themselves between Tierney's legs, with Melita holding her quaking knees. Tierney grunted like a trapped animal and bore down. The two women exchanged a few words and then Tierney felt a slight sting, as quick and piercing as when André had taken her virginity. The pushing felt so good, and there was a kind of animal satisfaction . . .

At last, she felt the baby. A warm and wet head emerged, and Tierney lightly pressed her thighs about it to feel the wonder. Melita firmly pushed her legs back. The mother instinctively bore down again, and the child's shoulders, arms, torso, buttocks, and legs slipped out like a wet bar of soap.

"Let me see! Let me see!" Tierney was laughing and crying all at once, drunk with joy. The baby squealed back, and the sound stopped Tierney in mid-breath. Then Melita held up the child for Tierney to view.

A girl! Her long-awaited daughter! Hers . . . André's . . . Tierney wept deliriously, laughing all the while. A tear rolled down Melita's own face as she nestled the babe to Tierney's breast. The infant was still attached to the cord, but the new mother was so thrilled she barely noticed the women tying hemp and cutting it with a finely honed knife.

Melita handed her a damp cloth, and Tierney busily wiped at the tiny hands and face. The baby's face screwed up into a grimace at the unwelcomed attention, and she wailed at a deafening pitch. To Tierney, it was as melodious as her music box.

Melita took the baby from her minutes later, but reassuringly patted Tierney's hand. She would bring it back. She moved her palm in a circular motion, indicating that she would bathe the child.

When Melita handed her back, the baby smelled unidentifiably strange, but looked quite tidy. She was snugly rolled in the soft deerhide and slept contentedly. It had been a big day for mother and daughter. Melita tapped the baby's cheek to wake her as she put her back at Tierney's enlarged nipple. The baby mewed and struggled to find the teat, but it took some prodding on both women's part to adjust it securely. When the baby did begin to nurse, another cramp—milder than the others—contracted the shrinking womb. The older Indian woman, Moon-Face as Tierney silently called her, became busy again with the afterbirth.

It was a blissful few minutes before Chinookseh appeared in the doorway. He spoke to Melita, and whatever she told him was not well-received. Tierney believed he swore.

Before he left again, however, he walked over to Tierney and the infant and studied them both. His expression was blank. After he had gone, Tierney wondered at her own lack of embarrassment. She had lain motionless, easily allowing him to peruse her naked arms and breasts. Fortunately, the women had already disposed of the soiled bedclothes and draped a blanket over her hips. Shrugging off the curiosity, Tierney drifted back to sleep, the baby still in her arms.

Some time later she was awakened and was made to stand. Melita and one of the women who had visited that morning walked her back down the path. It was dusk. Tierney wondered if the camp was always this quiet or if she had merely missed the noises of day during her momentous labor and childbirthing. She walked slowly, deliberately.

A sling had been made for her, and the baby lay sleeping in the cocoon that rested against her left hip. It was suspended over her right shoulder, diagonally crossing her back and chest. Except for the sling, Tierney was naked above the waist. She was also barefoot. Her stockings, garter, and boys' boots were taken by the midwife as payment for her services. Tierney thought it was hardly adequate recompense for the woman's tireless work. She sighed, relieved that Harriet's apprehensions were unfounded.

Melita had ripped the remaining seam out of the bodice of Harriet's old dress and hitched the makeshift skirt around her waist with the remaining material. A rope held it in place. Tierney knew she must look a fright. Her hair tumbled in disarray over her bare shoulders and back. Her ribs protruded slightly over her now shrunken midriff, but her belly was still somewhat rounded and her navel seemed enlarged.

Despite all this, Tierney Chambers had never felt so intensely alive, so aware, and so primitively female. At seventeen, she was a woman.

CHAPTER EIGHTEEN

Paul watched from the helm. André paced the deck, absently slapping the rail as he scanned the horizon. The young man always seemed on the brink of change when summer ended. It was mid-September now, and he was as eager to return to New Orleans as he had been the year before, when docking in London. But the first mate knew only too well the reason for his anticipation this time around.

"You're as skittish as a spring colt, André!" he called out.

"Throw yourself to the sharks, why don't you?" André roared back in English.

"I tell you, you've nothing to worry about. The girl is safe and sound within the convent. I daresay she hasn't had one serious suitor. You did not leave her a tempting dowry, after all. And casket girls went out with log cabins. Tierney has waited for you," he teased. "I'd lay my life on it!"

André de Montfort laughed at his friend's taunting. He was probably right. Tierney was with the Ursulines, no doubt, and he would woo her properly this time. He had brought her a complete trousseau. A cedar-lined trunk beside his own held the delicate Chinese silk and the Belgian lace for her wedding gown, the emerald necklace and earrings, pearls, perfumes, everything. . . .

On impulse, he commanded Pelier to take over the navigation and called Paul to join him in his cabin.

He was restless. On land he would have raced a horse or caroused a bit to break the tension. On *La Reine de la Mer* there was little to do now except count the hours until they reached Louisiana.

* * *

It had been a rigorous year. After his return to London again, he had laid to home port for three weeks. It had taken every minute of that time to settle his affairs in Brittany. His first move was to revamp the deck to hold more cannon and armory. He had several carronade imported from Scotland, and two long Toms were secured at either end of the ship. The world was becoming even more unsettled as the war between America and Great Britain became more serious, and André wanted to assure his ship was not only the speediest, but capable of defending itself as well.

He sold his warehouses and waterfront buildings to Jens Nagel, and disposed of his father's estate through his brother-in-law, Jacques Loren. His sister would be able to keep as much of the property as she wanted, and what was sold would be divided equally between André and Françoise.

Fortunately, he had been spared breaking his engagement to Anne-Marie. The dainty mademoiselle imperiously announced she was tired of his preoccupation with business and had become betrothed to another. André, always the gallant around his lady fair, had feigned distress and remorse. No one except Paul knew just how relieved he felt.

He sailed out of Nantes a very wealthy, very unattached young man.

Napoleon's defeat was all but history by this time. Captain de Montfort determined to make the best of it, however, and decided to sail the world, reaping the profits of war before regular commerce could resume.

He sailed around the Cape of Good Hope and up through the Indian Ocean to his final journey to Goa and Calcutta. He instinctively knew he would never again see this strange land.

His next stop was China. André had never been that far east, and he had bypassed Australia because time was critical. André knew that as soon as Bonaparte's forces were smashed, Britain would turn all her resources into soundly defeating the United States. The captain wanted to arrive back in New Orleans before the Royal Navy could blockade the Gulf of Mexico, and so his world travels had to be at top speed. *La Reine de la Mer* would be put to the test.

They circumvented the maze of islands between Java and Borneo, stopping only twice to take on fresh water and produce. Then they sailed north and in only eight days' time, they put into Singapore.

His ship looked magnificent amid the Chinese junks, and it was here that de Montfort took a long-needed rest. The men had a two-week shoreleave, and all but one returned before setting across the Pacific. The toothless boatswain—the one who had kept Tierney from jumping ship that last night in London—had been strangled.

But André's first voyage to the Pacific Ocean was not a disappointment. To him, its beauty was boundless. Not trusting the summer monsoons, though, he decided against charting his own course and relied upon a two-hundred-year-old route.

A brief stopover in the Philippines was a welcomed change. The natives gave a memorable feast, and the women's choreographic achievements were only surpassed by their private performances. Soon after their departure, however, *La Reine* became bogged down in equatorial doldrums.

The ship lay dormant for days while André and Paul tried to determine another course. It was impossible to get with the wind, however. There was no wind. In a desperate attempt to free themselves of the motionless lethargy, André decided to heave ten tons of water and drench the canvas sails with more. It worked. The ship's draft was lessened by an inch, and the wet sails billowed in the almost imperceptible breeze. At long last, and at tremendous risk, *La Reine* had the weather gauge.

By the time he was able to steer out of the sleepy waters, André de Montfort had developed a new respect for the men working on the development of steam-powered vessels. He regretted the fact that someday his white-winged beauty would be a thing of the past, but there was no denying the advantages of the machine age.

La Reine put into Maui in the Hawaiian Islands only hours before the last of their drinking water was depleted. But as they restocked supplies for the next long leg of the voyage to the American continent, the captain forbade his men to go ashore during the two-day stopover. Visions of James Cook's murder here at the hands of natives made him overly cautious and irritable.

Cook, sailing the beautiful bark, *The Discovery*, had been bludgeoned to death in 1778, but as André grimly reminded Paul, "Three decades and more does not change a people's temperament, and this vicinity still has a reputation for thieving and violence."

The long haul from Maui to the settlement of San Francisco was relatively uneventful. André would not have put into the tiny port at all except he had kept his ship on a northerly route to avoid more delays. By the time he reached the frontier West Coast, he and the men were in need of more water and fresh meat.

The bay was quiet in the morning light. Only a few Russian fishing trawlers speckled the inlet. After refilling the ship's water supply and salting the game his sailors were finally able to bring down, they began the tedious southern descent.

They laid to port only once again before rounding the Horn. Here, as both the captain and first mate had expected, the weather was fierce. They battled for forty hours without a moment's rest to pass through the Straits of Magellan, and despite their efforts, a crew member was lost and *La Reine*'s foremast was split. Lightning struck her, sending the rigging down to crush the new boatswain.

André ordered a layover in San Julian for repairs, and then it was on to Rio de Janeiro. Here, a wealthy Portuguese baron offered de Montfort an unbelievable price for thirty percent of the ship's stores. They spent a full day unloading the cargo, and André exchanged the goods for pure gold bullion.

By this time, the Atlantic was boiling with her annual late-summer squalls. The repaired and pitch-replenished *La Reine* was up to the competition, however, and after a brief stop in Caracas to take on fresh citrus and bananas, they were on the final stretch to New Orleans.

"I hate that damned fruit," André muttered as he poured the Madeira. "It reeks, and it is not humanly possible to eliminate all the rats and vermin that come with it."

"Well, you said you wanted to fill the hold again after that drop in Rio," answered Paul.

It was true. Sometimes he wondered at his own fanaticism for profit. He could not think of how to adequately

invest all his monies now! But in the back of his mind,
André knew a man was never too rich, no matter whether
measured in health, wisdom, or bank notes. André
shrugged. He wanted all three. And Tierney Chambers . . .

Paul interrupted his thoughts. "Maybe the cats will take
care of it."

"What?"

"The cats you picked up in Caracas. There is one in
the ship's stores and another in the galley. They should
take care of the pests."

As if he understood the mention of cats, Taffey pricked
up his ears and barked. The dog was nearly full-grown,
and a real beauty. His coat had a silvery champagne-
colored sheen now. Only his long wavy ears were buff.
In almost every port of call, someone offered to buy him.
The Portuguese in Rio had offered far more than he was
worth, but André had not been tempted. He was taking
Taffey home to his mistress.

"I wonder if she is still wearing those damned boots,"
de Montfort absently mused.

Paul Mauriac was accustomed now to these seemingly
pointless statements. André had been irritable all the way
back to London, losing his temper over the slightest problem. By the time they reached Nantes, he had spilled his
innermost feelings to the faithful Mauriac.

The older man was not surprised. He was cautious,
however, in counseling his friend. It was he who suggested
the global voyage, "to let you think things out, lad."

André had confided that he had no doubts about his
love for Tierney. She was ever in his mind. What he could
not decide was whether or not to give up La Reine for
marriage to her. He was already married to the sea, he
thought, and he persisted in his belief that a man could
not have both.

Paul understood. He, too, loved sailing more than anything else in the world. But life could be lonely, and there
were many times when he regretted not having a wife,
children, a home of his own. Paul Mauriac agreed that
Tierney Chambers was the most darling girl he had ever
met, though he refrained from telling André that. The one
row they had had over her the year before was quite
enough. No sense spurring the young man's jealous ire.

"I still think you should have written to her . . . Prepared her for your return."

André glanced up anxiously. "I explained that to you! I knew I would reestablish myself here, but I didn't want to commit myself further. And by the time we reached Maui . . . Well, surely we're traveling faster than a letter from me would." André replenished his wineglass and leaned forward to convince himself, via the first mate, that he had been prudent in all decisions.

A cannon boomed in the distance, interrupting their conversation.

Pelier almost collided with the captain as he leaped down the hatch.

"Looks like an English bark, sir. A big one! Can't see what she's firing at, though. Never seen that flag before."

André grabbed the spyglass from the crewman and bounded up the steps. The defendant must be an American vessel, he thought. Or perhaps Spanish . . .

La Reine de la Mer was clipping along at several knots and would soon be upon them. He wasn't sure that he wanted to circumvent the fray, in any case, so he ordered the sails stayed as they were. He had been eager for some action for days, and it looked as though opportunity had reared its seductive head. Besides, if the battle was between the English and Americans, it was only his duty, he reflected with wry humor. Come hell or high water, he was about to make America his new home.

He ordered all hands on deck, commanding the gunners to be prepared. The merchant seamen quickly caught the spirit of the day, and with whoops of excitement, the cannons were powdered and stationed into position. They brought more ammunition and firearms from the hold, and then all was silent except for the heated exchange due north-northeast.

"Well, I'll be damned!" André whistled.

"What is it?" demanded Paul. "What is she flying?"

"It's Carthagenan."

Paul did not understand. Then the captain muttered, "We're in the Barataria Bay or thereabouts, aren't we?"

The first mate nodded. Then the truth hit him like a tidal wave. "Lafitte?" he whispered incredulously.

"I believe so . . ."

Jean Lafitte had already made a name for himself in the sailing world. He was jokingly referred to as a privateer, a professional like André. But Lafitte was better known as a latter-day pirate and smuggler, devil to many and saint to a few. He commanded over a thousand men, and both he and his brother, Pierre, were fast-growing legends. They haunted the waters of the Caribbean and the Gulf of Mexico, raiding Spanish vessels under the auspices of a commission from the rebellious little country, Carthagena. The pirates' stronghold was believed to be on the Baratarian coast, just southwest of New Orleans.

Jean Lafitte was only four years older than André, but *La Reine*'s captain had long envied and admired the other's genius. And now, as he studied the other proud vessel, the nerves in de Montfort's body sang in anticipation. This would be a memorable day.

"All sails aloft!"

The sleek ship bore down on the bark from the side opposite Lafitte. He would have to be careful, of course. The cannon must be fired at reasonably close range so as not to overshoot their mark and hit Lafitte. Then, too, Lafitte himself might mistake *La Reine* as enemy support and fire upon her. It was a risk de Montfort was willing to take. Just the idea of surrounding the British bark— André on one side, Lafitte on the other—was too enticing to miss.

The battle was disappointingly short, at least for the late arrivers. Once André wore ship, turning her in a half circle to aim her pivot guns and starboard quarter artillery at close range, the captain gave his order. "Now, men, pour it into them!"

La Reine got off only one good firing, but it hit the bark just above her bilge. "Thank God he directed it himself," mused Paul. He had rarely seen André so excited.

The bark, taken by surprise, returned the fire. Her crew must have panicked, however, for the shots were comically off target. Only one shot managed to hit them at all, and that at the topsail! It was shredded to bits, but that was merely token damage. The men of *La Reine* were laughing and cheering as the British vessel retreated and limped out of range.

"Ahoy!" It was the captain of the *Pride*, a splendid

ship nearly as gracefully proportioned as de Montfort's own. "Jean Lafitte here! Can you give me escort back to the coast? Those whoring scoundrels cracked my bow!"

"My pleasure, Lafitte!" André called back.

The crews of the *Pride* and *La Reine* were still raising havoc when the two young captains walked up the stairs. Even Mauriac was taking part in the revelry, and was now being expertly seduced by a bewitching Cajun woman.

"I believe in giving my men a good time," laughed Lafitte as two sailors pounced on one another, smashing a priceless Ming bowl to pieces during their fisticuffs.

"I keep the library up here. As you can see, it sometimes gets a little rough down there." As they entered, André looked about with open admiration. The high-ceilinged room was filled with leather-bound volumes, some so old they were hand-printed. There were gilt-framed pictures covering each wall, and on the uncoordinated chairs and tables lay an assortment of gold, silver, and china bric-a-brac. Sable and mink pelts littered the floors, apparently used as mere throw rugs.

"She's a fine one, your *Pride*," remarked André as his host proffered the snifter of cognac. It was strange, but he found himself slipping back and forth from French to English as he was wont to do with Mauriac. Lafitte seemed similarly at ease with either language.

"I thank you, Captain. Once I learn her ropes, I think I'll love her best of all my fleet. She's new, and I'm not quite used to her yet. As you witnessed this afternoon . . . Damned careless of me, really."

"Well, I for one enjoyed it! I've never been one for battles, basically because I am not willing to risk my life for some damned flag, or king, or emperor, or whatever the hell turns men's heads. But I had some fun today! Haven't been in these waters for some time now, and I was bored after nine months of sailing."

"You're a man after my own heart, de Montfort. Politics is just a decent name for thievery anyway. But what brings you back here? I've heard your name in New Orleans. You drive a hard bargain, if rumor's to be trusted."

André leaned back and laughed. Jean Lafitte, if a little

less than legend, was a man of spirit and a damned good host to boot. "I've come to live here. Sold my lot in Nantes, and I think I'm ready to settle down."

"You picked a good spot. Hell, I love New Orleans! I'd live there myself if they'd let me. They won't. A lot of 'em resent my business, and they all resent my prices. But they deal. *Mon Dieu,* do they deal! You'd be amazed . . ."

"Would I?" enjoined André, raising an eyebrow. The glints in both men's eyes read gold, and they chuckled amiably.

"Damned if I don't like you, man!" bellowed Lafitte, soundly slapping André's shoulder as they refilled their glasses.

"You've a fine ship yourself, you know. *La Reine de la Mer* is unusual, but she has a lot of class too. I always said we French could design the best. Those cocky English are highly overrated, and the Spanish barks are so ass-heavy, it's a wonder any stay afloat. You know what H.M.S. stands for?" Lafitte continued lightly.

André was puzzled at the obvious question. "His Majesty's Ship, what else?"

"Well, I've always said the letters stand for 'Hits Made o' Shit!' " Both men were just inebriated enough to find the pun funny, very funny, remembering their encounter that afternoon.

When they finally sobered a bit, André stood to take his leave. "I've got to round up my men. I want to be in New Orleans by noon on the morrow, and they've yet to sleep it off."

"You're welcome to stay, de Montfort. What's your hurry?"

André grinned. "A bit of Irish I left behind."

Lafitte looked at him quizzically, but did not press him. "Well, if you insist. I shall not forget your help today. If I can ever return the favor . . ."

"I'll let you know," finished André, shaking the pirate's hand.

CHAPTER NINETEEN

Mother Superior was still stunned. Captain de Montfort was darker than ever, his copper skin burnished a deep brown, making the blue of his eyes even more startling. He was also thinner. And the thick moustache and beard, although groomed, were decidedly menacing.

"To be quite frank, Captain, both Sister Mercedes and I tried to persuade Tierney to notify you. Or permit us to contact your sister in France. She was quite firmly set against it, you see. And we hadn't the authority . . ." She paused only a second. "You aren't exactly family, Captain."

André's jaw was tight. He was angry—with himself for not trying to contact her sooner and with this nun for failing to advise him of her whereabouts. Reason told him, however, that he would not have received word in time to stop her from leaving New Orleans, anyway. And a trip to Pass Christian seemed a mere inconvenience now that he had arrived.

"But we are quite worried now. The Reddings are a good family, we understand, but we haven't heard from Tierney in months. She has never been regular in her correspondence, but again, she has never been this late, either."

Looking up, André had to admit the old woman looked distraught.

"Under the circumstances, Captain," she continued, "I would consider it a personal favor if you would go to Pass Christian. The Reddings, Mr. and Mrs. James Redding, have a plantation. Tierney wrote that it is located directly on the coast, overlooking the beach. It shouldn't be hard to find. It's called Southwell . . ."

* * *

La Reine de la Mer edged into Bay St. Louis the following day. Paul was determined to accompany him by horseback to the plantation which lay some twenty miles east. But André convinced the first mate it would be best for him to greet Tierney alone.

"Besides," he argued, "I don't trust Pelier to put her back in New Orleans. We still have most of the cargo on board and those damned bananas are ready to rot," he laughed, forcing the humor he did not feel.

Mauriac finally relinquished and agreed to go back with André's promise that he would either return or send word within one week's time.

The captain was eager to get there. In fact, he had already procured the horse. It had nervously stood tethered to the rail all night. He hurriedly ticked off a few reminders to Paul. Which brokers to contact first, which ones to avoid . . . It wasn't necessary. Paul Mauriac was as capable as his captain, albeit more honest.

As a final thought, André whistled for the spaniel. He might need a bribe. . . .

The big roan was a splendid animal. After a few skittish starts, the horse began racing full speed down the beach, his hooves pounding the wet tidal sands. André had to stop short of the first mile to let Lord Taffey catch up.

"Come on, you overgrown pussycat!" he yelled. After that, the dog rode in the saddle unless André slowed the pace to a trot or stopped altogether to rest. It wasn't often. They rode hard and fast. Only when the pine copses along the beach offered fresh water rivulets did they drink and rest their fill.

By dusk, both horse and rider were sweaty, smelly, and tired. Had there been an inn, André would have stopped to clean himself up and order a good rubdown for his horse. But he passed only a few imposing mansions along the way. He was wearing riding breeches, boots, and the shirt Tierney had given him. He had a change of clothes in the saddlebag, of course, but in his current attire, he would not be well-received at any of these coastal palaces.

It was after dark by the time he found the pink mansion. He'd gotten a good description of the home from a New Orleans banker, and looking up the steep drive, he was certain that this was Southwell. André decided to walk the roan up to the front. The poor beast was shuddering with exhaustion.

André slowly slid down from the saddle. Although he was a capable horseman, he rarely had occasion to ride this long or this fast. He knew he looked like a highwayman, but he no longer cared. He was too exhausted, and by the time he reached the top of the drive he felt he had scaled a mountain. Wearily, he mounted the steps and raised the knocker.

An old Negro opened the doors, but upon seeing him, left only enough space for his own head. "Yassuh?" he asked suspiciously.

"Good evening. My name is André de Montfort. I am looking for a Miss Tierney Chambers. Do I have the right place?"

"I dunno, suh," he said, and shut the door in André's face.

The visitor was incensed. He knew damned well this was Southwell. The brass doormarker had the manor name engraved upon it! And if Tierney was not here, why the hell had he looked so wide-eyed at the mention of her name. He was about to pound his fist at the door when he heard a commotion coming from within. He leaned closer to the door and listened to the muffled voices.

Someone was running. A woman was crying, "My God, James, he might be the one! Pay the ransom. Pay it!"

Another woman's voice, vaguely French: "You are a bigger fool than your wife if you open that door . . ." The doorman was adding to the confusion, with "Look like a wild man to me, massa. An Indian, maybe, but he gots a beard and light eyes!"

In all of this, André strained to detect her voice. But it was hard to hear . . .

Finally, a deep sonorous voice boomed. "Quiet! All of you! Mother, take Harriet upstairs! She's going into hysterics again. I'll handle this. All of you, out!"

James Redding handed him another shotglass of whiskey, but André still didn't feel anything but shock. Tierney was gone.

Redding, having ordered the roan taken to the stables and the dog to the kitchen, had invited the disheveled man

into his study. There was no doubt but that this was a seafaring man, and at first, Redding had hoped he might perhaps have word of the missing girl's whereabouts, or at
least her husband, Mr. Chambers.

But as soon as de Montfort heard the news that Tierney
had not been seen or heard from in over four weeks, he
had looked stricken. "I presume, sir, that Mr. Chambers is
one of your crew?"

"I don't know what you mean, sir. There is no Mister
Chambers!"

Redding sighed. "I thought it might be so. She told us
she was married. You know, I suppose, that she is with
child, Captain. Or was, when she disappeared. Her time
was due . . ."

The captain had responded so violently to the news that
for a moment, Redding thought he might smash his fist
through the mantel. But André sank back into a chair and
muttered instead, "I had no idea . . . Damn me, what a
fool! I had no idea!"

"Then the child is yours." It was a simple statement.

"Yes. Yes, of course."

At that point, Harriet had breathlessly come into the
study. "James, I'm sorry. But I have to know! Does this
man know where she is?" Her voice rose tremulously.

"No, darling. I am afraid not. Sit down and let me
pour you a sherry." Turning back to André, he added,
"You see, sir, my wife and Tierney had grown quite
close. Harriet has been beside herself since the first
night . . ."

"Who are you?" Harriet suddenly demanded.

James Redding looked from his wife to the haggard sea
captain. The man appeared not to have heard the question,
and stared steadily into the candle's flame. He was absorbed in private thought, far removed from Southwell for
the time being.

James pressed the wineglass into his wife's trembling
hand. "This is Captain André de Montfort, sweetheart,"
he said softly. "Tierney's . . . husband."

"Husband? Then why—" But her words died at the grim
expression on her own husband's face.

"Have you any clues?" asked André, abruptly standing.

"None. I've posted several notices along the coast, offering a reward for her return or information leading to

her. All the families in this area, even the slaves, have a description of her. But so far, nothing."

"Has anyone searched?"

"Of course! I organized three search parties . . . A total of some sixty men including neighbors, my fishermen, and a few trustworthy slaves. We combed these beaches and woods for weeks."

André was not looking for a quarrel, but he was as demanding now as he was aboard his ship. "How far inland have you been?"

"Roughly twelve miles. In populated areas fifteen to twenty. There isn't much beyond there except swampland."

Harriet poured herself more sherry. She had been put to bed for three weeks. "Nervous collapse," said the doctor. She was only recently able to cope with Tierney's sudden disappearance, and the bearded visitor was something of an anticlimactic shock to her. "I should have stopped her that day," she said aloud.

"What happened, as far as you know?"

She told André about Tierney's growing apprehension over the birth, that the tedium of waiting out the last days had made her irritable and a bit impetuous. André winced.

He could well imagine her distress. Alone, thinking herself abandoned. Being the feisty lass he knew so well, she would not have given in to that depression, but paced until she found an answer. Only this time, instead of pacing *La Reine*'s deck, she walked a lonely stretch of isolated beach.

"The last time I saw her, she was sitting down there, in front of the house. She was trying to get up," Harriet blushed, "but with the baby and all, she had quite a time of it." Harriet looked up, the tears rolling down her pale face. "Oh, God! I even laughed then, she looked so funny. I went to get Mammy Lou. I was going to send her down there to help Tierney, but when I walked back out to the portico, she was already gone. I should have followed her then. But Mammy Lou and I could see her down the beach a way. We were sure she'd come back!" wept the woman.

Angelique heard the broken sobs and came into the room. The older woman was distraught herself, but for some inexplicable reason, the tragedy had caused her to pity her heretofore despised daughter-in-law. Presently, she put a shawl about Harriet's shoulders and gently urged her to stand.

"Come upstairs, dear. Jamey is fretful with this cold. He wants his mother right now, not Mammy."

When the women were gone, André began to pace himself, his deck strides covering the length of the room quickly. "Mr. Redding, be honest with me. What do you think has happened to Tierney?"

"I don't know, of course. But there are four possibilities, the way I see it. The first is the least likely—that Tierney is dead. The reason I don't believe it is that we would have uncovered her body by now."

"Drowned?"

"No, I think we can eliminate that altogether. Tierney would not have willingly gone into the water. She wanted that baby of hers to be strong and healthy. It was all she cared about, really. And the likelihood of her falling into the water is even more remote. As you know, the water is very shallow, not even waist-high for a hundred yards out.

"No, I don't think she has drowned. If she is dead— and as I said, I don't believe she is—then she was murdered."

André sat down. Redding seemed a sensible sort, and honest, as well. His own thoughts were running rampant. He still couldn't fathom losing Tierney in the first place, let alone the child. He leaned toward his host now, idly packing a pipe. "Well, what else, then?"

"Captain, the three other possibilities . . . They are all the same, really. Kidnapping. I'll give you my ideas in the same order. Most unlikely—but there is a chance— trappers. They're loners. An odd breed of men, if there ever was one. And they've been known to abduct women."

"Well?"

"There haven't been any trappers this far down for years now. They steer clear of other people generally, and when settlers move in, they move out. The trappers have all headed northward, back up with the Indians. Besides, Tierney would not have likely tempted one. A baby—and she was so obviously due—would have been a nuisance in the interior."

Offering André a light and selecting a cigar for himself, Redding continued. "The Indians are another possibility. There was that massacre at Fort Mims, Alabama, a few weeks back, and it's rumored they're all acting strangely with this white man's war going on."

"But she'd be dead!"

"Not necessarily. The Indians, Creeks, in particular, are building their own slave-trading business. I've heard they even keep a few for themselves. Occasionally, they steal some of the niggers from around these parts. At least, we think that's what happens. Never been caught . . ."

"Creeks, you say?" André fingered his beard. Indians. He had never been in direct contact with any of them before.

"Maybe. But they are pretty scarce too—around here. There is supposed to be a small band of them somewhere up in the bayou, but it's impossible to track them. A footprint disappears almost as quickly as it's made. Tierney would have been tempting, though," Redding considered. "Two slaves, you see. Not just one."

André grimaced and ran a hand over his eyes. Tierney a slave? The idea was too repulsive.

"And your final thought?" the captain asked, trying to shake the growing dread in his gut.

"Pirates. They steal along this shore from Dolphin Island to Mexico, and they're quite experienced at spiriting away innocent bystanders. Jean Lafitte and his men are a sordid lot, capable of anything. And Tierney would have been an easy target . . ."

"Easy target, yes," André mused aloud. He kept envisioning her caught in the rigging, his own men laughing and tormenting her. "But I don't believe Lafitte is responsible," he added listlessly.

"Why not?" Redding had thought the most likely criminals this band of smugglers.

"Because I had dinner with Jean Lafitte the night before last. Tierney wasn't there."

André did not see the shocked expression on Redding's face as the host stood up. What was he dealing with here?

"Did I hear you say you had some fishing vessels?" André suddenly asked, looking up.

Redding's face was inscrutable. He nodded.

"Could I have the use of one, sir? It would take me several days to get to my own, and I've wasted enough time getting back here!" he fumed. "As I say, I doubt Lafitte is our culprit, but since you strongly suspect him, it's

worth checking. I can be back on the Baratarian coast in a
day's time, with luck.

"If she is not there, I'll retrace the various ideas as you
have outlined them. I will find her, by God!"

James Redding immediately agreed to the plan. Before
leaving in the fishing sloop, however, André explained
briefly his need to get word of his whereabouts to Paul
Mauriac. Redding promised to get a message off the next
day.

Captain de Montfort remembered the deepwater channel
that led into secluded Barataria Bay. Back at the smuggler's fort, André went in search of Jean Lafitte, the "Bos"
his people called him. He had little trouble finding him,
for the lawless citizens here were eager to help the captain
who had assisted their leader a few days ago.

André explained as rapidly as he could what few facts
were available to him. The pirate assured him that Tierney
was not near Barataria, but suggested André search for her
himself if it would put his mind at ease. It was evident
that de Montfort was distracted with worry. "We don't
take white women," Lafitte continued carefully. "We have
enough trouble around here."

"I did not mean to sound so accusing, Jean. I believe
you. There isn't much chance of a woman that heavy with
child going unnoticed. In any event, Tierney Chambers,
had you seen her, would have warranted your attention.
She's a born troublemaker herself," he acknowledged
grimly, "or I should say, trouble follows that girl!"

Nonetheless, Lafitte sent for his lieutenants and ordered
a search of the area.

He returned to find de Montfort broodingly impatient.
He was motionless, and yet there was an air of attack
about him that virtually shook the room.

"I have an idea, André. If you are willing. I think your
friend may be right after all. The Indians are growing
bolder of late. My brother, Pierre, sometimes negotiates,
ah, transactions with the savages. If there is a Creek village somewhere near Pass Christian, I daresay he will know
its exact location. He has Indian contacts along the coast."

André spun around, anxiously nodding his consent.

"I'll get him," Lafitte answered, leaving the room again.

Pierre Lafitte appeared a few hours later. "Looking for me, Jean?" he asked none too pleasantly.

"*Oui*. Sit down. Pierre, this is Captain André de Montfort. I told you about him . . . the other day with that British bark. Captain," he gestured, "my brother."

"What's brewing?" asked the one, dismissing amenities with a wave of his hand.

After a brief description of Tierney and her disappearance, Pierre Lafitte broke in, "You're in luck, Captain. I've heard rumored that there is a white woman in Deer Run Bayou, a Kawita camp. It may be just a story, but the Creeks are a tight-mouthed bunch. Rarely brag, especially when there's no truth behind it. Don't know anything about a baby, though," he shrugged, "and heard nothing about her being knocked up."

André was too excited to take issue with Pierre Lafitte's choice of words. "I'll be ready to leave as soon as you give the word!"

"*Ah, non, monsieur*," he drawled, mockery in his tone. "I go alone, or I don't go."

"You sure that's wise, Pierre?" offered Jean. He lightly tossed a dart across the room, hitting the target dead center.

"*Oui, mon frère*," he answered, getting up. "There is only one way. As it is, I'll be bloody lucky to get out of there alive. My only 'acquaintance' is a big brute. They call him Oswatchee. If I show up at all, it had better be alone. Else they'll find my bones in the swamps in a hundred years or so . . ."

"But how—" started André.

"I'll think of something. If a white woman is there, I'll bring her back."

"When?" André was nearly frantic to be off himself in search of Tierney, but he knew Jean's brother was too irascible to start an argument. He could not conceal the edge in his voice, however.

Pierre Lafitte looked at André, but did not answer him. He merely shrugged, then turned to leave.

"Don't touch her, Pierre," warned the leader. "She's de Montfort's woman."

Before he slammed the door, he spat back, "You aren't the only Lafitte with breeding, Jean!"

There was little to do but wait, André realized. He had
no idea of how long this gloomy pirate would be gone, or
if, indeed, he would return with Tierney. Jean offered no
explanation for the obvious friction between him and his
brother, but graciously made arrangements for de Montfort's stay in the huge house. He was given free use of the
library, kitchen, and women.

The young captain strained to hide his dejection. Try
as he might, he could not feel comfortable, or sociable, or
optimistic. There was no returning to New Orleans now;
he could not return Redding's fishing rig, for that matter.
The man was immobilized until he knew something definite
from this rogue, Pierre.

André was too anxious to eat, and the women were just
so many models to him. That one's hands reminded him of
her . . . this one's legs . . . another's walk. None were a
temptation, and in his eyes, not one compared to Tierney's
unique beauty.

Taking several books back to his room, André scanned
a few pages but threw them aside in utter frustration. One
of the volumes fell to the floor, and when he reached to
pick it up, he found it open to a poem. With a jolt, he
remembered the cross-stitching the Ursulines had given
him. It was all Tierney left for him . . .

"The World Is Too Much with Us," a bitter reminder
of all that seemed lost to him now. Greed had its price,
and André de Montfort was finding this the most galling
lesson he had ever learned.

He buried his face in the pillow, and no one knew how
grievously he wept.

CHAPTER TWENTY

The night of Rosalie's birth, Melita and the other squaw had taken Tierney directly to the slave hut. It was located at the other end of the village, away from Chinookseh's abode. The mud-thatched cabin was long and narrow, like a miniature of the council meeting place.

They drew aside the bearskin that covered the hut's entrance, and Melita gently nudged her inside. Then they were gone.

Tierney looked around the dimly lit room, her arm protectively encircling the sling that held her newborn. She saw an old Negress bending over a pot that hung over the low fire in the middle of the room.

"Do you speak English?"

The woman looked up and gave her a toothless grin. "I sho' do, chile. Don't speak nothin' else, neither." Her voice was husky, but proud.

From a corner, Tierney heard a man's voice. "Lawd Almighty! It *is* a white lady, Birdie! I didn't believe you!" When he came out of the dark end of the room, Tierney nearly jumped with fright. He was monstrous in size, and blacker than old Theo. For the first time that day, Tierney consciously tried to cover her bared breasts.

He stopped short, and turned around as though embarrassed himself. "Dawn, honey, come here. Don't be shy now, you c'mon," he added with mock sternness. "We gots a new one here, and you has to pay your respects." He faced Tierney again, smiling sheepishly. "Hope you'll excuse her, ma'am. She scared of most peoples."

Out of the shadows emerged a voluptuous young woman. Except for a calf-length buckskin skirt, she was naked. Her face was an exaggeration of the Indian midwife, broader and flatter. Her long black hair fell below her waist.

"This here's my wife. I call her Beautiful Dawn."

"That's lovely," Tierney murmured. "Is it her real name?"

"I dunno, ma'am. She don't speak none."

For all her present dilemma, Tierney felt a twinge of sadness for the almond-eyed girl. "Is she one of theirs?" she asked, pointing in the direction of the camp center.

"No, ma'am!" he emphatically denied. "She's Seminole. From Georgia, like me, but ways south of my home. And the prettiest li'l Seminole there ever was . . ."

The big black was obviously enamored of his Indian bride, and the newcomer relaxed. This introduction was his way of assuring Tierney that he would not harm her, that he was not even interested in the idea.

"Hello, Dawn," she said at length. "I'm Tierney Chambers." She looked at the man expectantly.

"Sorry, ma'am. I was so wantin' to show you Dawn, I forgot to tell you who I am. I'm Jeb, ma'am. Big Jeb."

The baby awakened at that point, and Tierney settled herself near the fire. Carefully pulling the sling in front of her, she nestled the infant into a suckling position.

"Yo' milk in already?" asked the woman they called Birdie.

"I'm not sure," Tierney answered hesitantly. "It doesn't look right. Could I still have the false milk?"

"Yassum," the old Negress nodded with satisfaction. "Dat sound 'bout right. But don't worry none. 'Nother day or two, you be the land o' plenty for dat chile of yours. Meantime, he jest spit it up."

Tierney was aghast. "It's a girl," she managed, "and she hasn't spit up!"

"She will den. Gots to. Get up all dat poisen from de birthin'. No need to fret none. I raised more chillen dan you can count on yo' hands, missy. I knows what I say," she beamed. "What you name dat li'l gal?"

"I . . . I don't know." She looked at the woman again. It was hard to believe that this frail, wizened captive had ever been anyone's Mammy. She was about half Tierney's size. Although she was fully covered in her ragged clothes, Tierney imagined that the woman's breasts—if she ever had any—had shrunken away altogether. Her own were now round and firm. "André would never believe this," she mused inwardly. Only a year ago, she could remember his chiding laughter after the binding was discovered.

"You hungry, chile?" It was Birdie. Her voice had a soothing, almost hypnotic effect. Tierney had the distinct feeling this strange woman could read her thoughts. She looked at her dishing out the stew, a peculiar mixture of rice, fish, and a vegetable Tierney could not identify.

It tasted terrible, but the young woman was half-starved after her arduous day of giving birth. She disliked having to eat with her fingers, but this, too, was part of her new life.

After dinner, Birdie had helped her prepare a place of pine straw and animal skins for Tierney. It was in a far corner, away from the draft of the entrance and near Birdie's own pallet. All the huts were flea-infested, she was told, but she would get used to the vermin. "You jest call me, missy, you be needin' anything. You gonna need all de rest you can git."

Tierney was on the verge of tears, suddenly too sad to express anything more. Birdie stroked her hair, and spoke in her husky, sleepy voice. "You jest got dem blues, honey. It always happens dat way, but don't worry, chile. The Lawd gots His reasons. I knows."

The girl looked up at the old woman, searching for something beyond her own understanding. Why did Birdie seem so wise, so knowledgeable, when probably she had never known anything except hard work and pain?

Again, she was startled by the woman's perception with her next words. "Dat man o' yo's, missy. He gonna find you. You be all right, and dat baby of yo's be fine too. You jest gotta trust in de Lawd. He don't make Hisself easy to see, chile, but der's reasons for everthin'. I knows," she repeated. "Lawd, honey, don't you knows when I was a young gal I used to wonder 'bout His ways? Why I be born black-skinned, why I be white man's property? De Lawd give us lots o' hearts hurtin'. He give us hollerin' winds and rain and thunder, but he give us dose rainbows too. Don't you forget dat, chile. We all gots our rainbows . . ."

Tierney's own voice was almost reverent when she asked, "Birdie, can you see the future? Are you a soothsayer?"

Birdie chuckled softly and stroked the sleeping baby's foot. "Missy, my mama always tole me to say a li'l birdie tole me dat! Dat's how comes I got my name. But, chile, ain't no birds tellin' me nothin'. What I knows, de angels tells me!"

The old woman shuffled to her own bed then, still smiling. Tierney was oddly comforted by her presence, and sank back against the pallet, immune to the acrid odor and pestilence beneath her.

She had lain awake that first night, trying to think of a name for her lovely baby. Whether the infant was truly beautiful was a moot point—to her mother, she was perfect.

She had André's black hair, but it was wavy like Tierney's mother's. The eyes were dark blue, and Tierney hoped they would remain so. Her fair complexion, though, was very much like Tierney's. Sighing, Tierney gently kissed the little cheek. Perhaps she would be spared the freckles as well.

It was almost sunrise when she finally decided upon Rosalie Noel. "Roisin Dubh" was Gaelic for Little Dark Rose, and was also used as a mystical name for Ireland. Rosaleen was the accepted English form, usually, but Tierney preferred dropping the "n" because of the child's middle name. Noel seemed perfect for the child of a French sea captain conceived during the Christmas season . . .

They were smart, these Creek Indians.

On the very first day, Tierney had been put to work. She pounded clothes with large stones at the river. She fed and plucked chickens, and gathered eggs. She carried pig slops, heavy skins of water slung on a shoulder harness, and dragged freshly skinned animal hides to the curing poles. All this she did for four weeks, and Rosalie Noel was always at her side, happy to bounce at her mother's hip during the busy days. When the baby grew fretful and needed to be nursed, Tierney stopped whatever she was doing to feed her. No one seemed to mind.

But at three weeks, just when Rosalie was beginning to sleep through the night, Melita came back with Chinookseh. Tierney had had occasion to catch only glimpses of the two, and she had been so busy that she had not given the matter any thought. When they came that night, Tierney naïvely presumed they were only curious, visiting almost like friendly neighbors.

She was wrong. The couple had come for Rosalie Noel. Tierney had run to the corner of the room, her baby against her. She had never before felt so much like a trapped animal. She became hysterical, crying out for André, Paul, Nanna, anyone to help her.

Surprisingly, Chinookseh and Melita had not accosted her. They merely stood in the slave hut, waiting for Tierney's sobs to subside. Finally, Big Jeb came up to her and gently laid his hand on her shoulder.

"Miss Tierney, please rest yo'self. They only wants the baby at night. They'll bring her back in the mornin' for her feedin', sure as lightnin'. It's only to keeps you from tryin' to run at night when nobody's watchin' you. They knows you ain't goin' nowheres without that baby of yours. Every day, you'll have yo' baby at yo' side, just like always."

After several more minutes of Jeb's quiet persuasion, Tierney turned around. She felt so helpless!

She walked the dreaded paces back to the Indians, and carefully handed Rosalie Noel into Melita's arms. She looked at both of them, silently pleading for their mercy. Neither looked truly malicious. Melita was resolved to her duty, and her husband had a curious, sympathetic look about him.

Jeb had been right, of course. It was only a precaution against possible escape. Once, they even brought her back during the night. Rosalie had apparently awakened with a spasm of hiccoughing, and for all Melita's rocking and sugar tits, would not be quieted.

Tierney learned quickly that she was, indeed, a slave. Like any black on a plantation, she followed orders she could often not understand, and was therefore often thought to be stupid by her masters. She resented it bitterly, and felt she was less valuable to them than the horses the Indians rode without saddles. Like many high-spirited slaves she wanted to run away. But how?

"Jeb," she started late one night, "I don't understand why you are here. You could escape! They let Dawn stay with you, and no one watches us at night. Surely you could get away! You understand their language, you know their plans . . ."

"Miss Tierney, they don't know I understand them, and I don't never want them to. They think ol' Jeb is just another dumb nigger, and all I gots to have is my woman at night and I be happy," he laughed mirthlessly.

It was true. She felt sorry for the couple, furtively trying to comfort one another in the night when they thought she and Birdie slept. She shuddered. They were denied everything, it seemed—worst of all, their privacy.

"But I gots my plans too," he continued quietly. "Soon as I knows these swamps and woods as good as them, I'll make my break with my sweet Dawn. My biggest problem is figurin' on wheres to go. I cainst run back to Georgia, see, 'cause sho as I'm as black as they come, I'll get caught and sold again. Or lynched for them thinkin' me a runaway."

"How did you come to be here, Jeb?" She had always been curious, and supposed that he had run away from his white master.

"They got me. Plucked me right outa the fields one day when the foreman wasn't watchin'. Never did feel like such a fool ever! Don't believe nobody done seen or heard nothin'. They was so quick and quiet about it all." He shook his head as in disbelief still.

"Who was it? Chinookseh? Oswatchee?"

"No, ma'am. Wasn't none of these. I couldn't understand 'em back then, but I gots traded around plenty. I 'spect I done lived with more Indians in more camps than any man ever lived! It's been four years now, though, and I'm almost ready. Soon as I figures wheres to go . . ."

He told her how the others came to be here, as well. Dawn had been brought in about eight months before. He didn't know exactly where or when she had been apprehended, and admitted he probably never would. They held a council meeting as they had at Tierney's arrival, and then brought the deaf-mute to Jeb. They threw her onto the floor of the hut, making obscene gestures to him. He confided to Tierney that both he and his Seminole woman were glad there were no children. They did not want to breed more slaves for the Creeks.

Birdie had been sold off a plantation in Mississippi some

six years ago. The old master had died, and the heirs had no use for the aged woman. She had been sold for nearly nothing to a couple of trappers to cook and mend for them, but they had in turn traded her to this village for a barrel of fresh squash. She had then been the camp's first and only slave.

The first time Tierney was accosted, she had felt outrage, indignation, and her first shattering taste of hatred. Hatred, she immediately learned, was as all-consuming and ever-present as love. It was merely at the other end of the spectrum, like dark and light. Where love was glorious, hate was ignominious; where one was pure joy, the other was sheer hell; where there was once abandon and fulfillment, there was now coercion and pain.

It was Oswatchee, of course—the big murderous man who had tried to take Tierney her first day in the village.

She had been at the river, and rather than splash the baby as she pounded the smooth stones, Tierney had lay the child on a bed of pine needles where the sun would cast playful shadows against the big rocks. At four weeks, Rosalie was demonstrating an intense interest in color and movement.

Oswatchee had been on the opposite bank, watching Tierney's light chestnut curls shimmer in the noonday light, her breasts swinging invitingly with the movement of her work. She had seen him coming and her heart stopped. An Indian had never been less quiet or graceful!

He let out a grunt, and bounded across the shallow water stripping off his leather breeches all the while. Even with the advance warning, however, he had easily caught her as she bent to retrieve the baby. Squirming under his rude, probing hands, her revulsion and fear gave her strength, she brought her knee sharply into his groin. She snatched up the baby, and sobbing hysterically, ran back to the camp.

Now, a week later, she felt very little.

A council meeting had been called because of the incident. Rape was not condoned by the Kawitas, and was usually a punishable offense. This was the village's first encounter of the crime against a female slave, however, and there was much ado over how to handle it.

Big Jeb, after having extended his regrets that he could offer Tierney no protection, told her what information he had gleaned from the village gossip. Chinookseh, it seemed, had loaned Tierney to the village elders as common holding until such time as Melita bore him a son or he was eligible for a divorce, whichever came first. Jeb did not understand how the Indians kept track of time, but guessed that it would be another year or so before a divorce could be decreed.

Oswatchee, on the other hand, had offered to buy Tierney outright with gold. The man had accumulated personal wealth through clandestine dealings with smugglers and the British. That there was even the possibility of her being bought with English currency by an American Indian was too grossly ironic to contemplate.

Jeb did not offer to tell her that regardless of what happened to Tierney, the girl-child was Chinookseh's to keep whenever he chose to take her as his own. It would be left to him whether the child would be reared as another slave or an adopted daughter.

The black man did assure her that it was most unlikely that she would be hurt by Oswatchee again. The council had adjourned without a final vote as to whether she could be purchased now by his gold or remain a slave-at-large until Chinookseh's marriage was either blessed with a male child or ended. But Oswatchee was remonstrated for his deed, and warned against such unmanly acts again. It could bring him disgrace, it was said.

Neither Jeb nor Tierney realized they had the village women to thank for the verbal reprimand. Although the Creek women were forbidden in council, many men's votes were decided at home through their wives' influence, be it nagging or the ageless persuasion attributed to their sex.

Oswatchee was the most sought-after warrior in the village by maidens and would-be mothers-in-law. Tierney was not to interfere with their own domestic plans.

Unfortunately, Tierney took Jeb's assurances too seriously. And Oswatchee had tried to defile her again.

She had been sent into the nearby woods to gather the ripening muscadines. The morning was glum, a continuous cool drizzle signaling the end of warm weather. She left

Rosalie Noel with Birdie, who was inside the hut weaving baskets with her gnarled hands.

Unbeknownst to her, Oswatchee had followed Tierney, and when she made to return, he intercepted her in the narrow path.

She felt icy fear in the pit of her stomach, but thought quickly. "Perhaps if I don't act frightened," she told herself frantically, "he'll let me pass." Her mistake was in speaking too harshly, and in using ill-chosen words when he held her against her will. Calling upon coarse street language brought all the way from England, she hissed, "Oh, go work it! Stick it in your own arse!"

"You stupid woman." His words were quietly spoken, but deadly in import. If she had given the matter any consideration, it might have occurred to her that he understood and spoke English himself. He had English money, didn't he? But then it was too late. She had already insulted him, virtually challenged him.

Tierney backed away, slowly at first. He smiled easily, demonically, showing brilliant white teeth against his bronzed face. "He must scrub them with hickory root," she thought inanely. Her terror was mounting to blood-chilling heights, but she was unable to think clearly. She wondered vaguely if Jeb would think to take Rosalie Noel when he and Dawn made their escape. She hoped so. Better to be raised by a black man and Seminole woman than this . . .

It seemed an eternity, but he was on top of her within seconds. His face contorted into a gruesome mask above her, and Tierney at last found her wits to scream. But whatever noise she might have made was stifled by his violent, intruding hands. She was fighting now, however, and surprised him with her abrupt strength. She bit him.

He let out a yell himself, but wrenched her arms above her and positioned himself before she could inflict further pain. He muttered incredible oaths, swore in Kawita and English, and threatened further obscenities that she had never heard, even in English. She fought him throughout, and the man did not easily mete out any of the perversions he intended. He could only rub himself against her struggling body. When at last he achieved his grim satisfaction, he fell exhausted next to her on the sodden foot trail.

She lay deathly still, a cold determination coursing through her veins. At length, she was certain he slept.

She moved cautiously, rolling ever so slowly from beneath the dead weight of his arm. He didn't stir. Tierney squirmed out from what was left of the rope-hitched skirt, allowing his hand to remain poised in sleep on the material.

She stood silently, her bare limbs and stomach littered with bits of leaf and humus. She stood thus, barely breathing, for several minutes. She must be sure he slept!

Cold logic kept her from acting too quickly now. Every move must be predetermined, precise, and silent. Her bare feet were already accustomed to the feel of raw earth, and for weeks, the fawnlike movements of her captors had fascinated her. She put her study to good use now, imitating their stealth.

When finally she stood at his soft buckskin boot, she unconsciously held her breath altogether. Tierney felt enveloped in a dream world. The knife which lay inside the boot was as inviting, as soothing to her spirit, as had been the Ursuline walls. Blessed protection, she dimly perceived, an end to inner turmoil . . .

The woman was near rapture as she touched the blade, her lips parted, eyes glassy and breath faint. It had slid from beneath the buckskin beautifully. And now she held it. Loved it.

Oswatchee lay motionless, on his side, and though his shoulder looked vulnerable, she knew that it would never do. Neither would his broad back—too risky. His chest was out of reach. The throat! One swift plunge, below the beardless jaw and down toward the collarbone. Now she must be quick!

She raised her full height to make the violent descent. The blade was in midair, eerily glimmering in the hazy light when he grabbed her ankle. She dropped it in sheer, agonizing fright.

Tierney screamed. She screamed again. She screamed all the while she ran naked back into the camp, with Oswatchee's laughter following her like the devil incarnate.

Oswatchee was in trouble with his peers. The men had voted a public scorning; that was, Oswatchee would be made to stand before the entire native community, and members would be encouraged to fling insults at him, even pieces of trash. It was a most ignoble sentence, and although he was not exiled from the camp as Chinookseh had demanded, Oswatchee was most humiliated.

When the buckboard rolled into camp later that day, loaded with kegs of rum, it was a welcome respite for the camp's day-long tension. The villagers felt troubled at having ridiculed a prominent warrior, and Oswatchee himself was feeling despondent.

The white man who drove the vehicle brought two bolts of calico cotton as well. He had come into camp on the pretext of arranging with Oswatchee a consignment of woven wool that he, in turn, was to barter to the upland fur trappers.

The villagers, in return for the gifts of rum and calico, prepared a feast. Four pigs, a basket of catfish, and several chickens were put over the fires in their sudden generous mood, and much singing and dancing were enjoyed as the rum kegs were being emptied.

Tierney lay on her pallet, vaguely aware of the activity around her. She had lain in bed since her chilling return, not yet recovered from her traumatic encounter with the Indian. Rosalie had been brought only once for nursing, but her lactic reflexes had been altered by shock, and Melita soon carried the still-hungry babe to a nursing Kawita to care for her temporarily.

The other slaves were busy with the preparations of the impromptu celebration, and Tierney was alone. They had been solicitous to her, however, and Tierney subconsciously recalled a line once memorized. "Buried by strangers in foreign soil," dumbly reverberated in her otherwise vacant thoughts.

When she had first come screaming back to the hut, Jeb had discreetly absented himself from the vicinity for the women's ministrations.

Birdie crooned to her for a while, applying a smelly poultice to her many bruises. Dawn had gently dressed her in one of her own hide skirts, and it now lay loosely against Tierney's protruding hip bones.

Thus, lying in a semiconscious state of oblivion, Tierney did not stir when the first hut went up in flames. The night sky was glowing with a ghastly crimson light by the time Pierre Lafitte slipped into the slave hut. She did not hear him come in, but startled when she heard his voice.

"You Tierney Chambers, lady?" he whispered hoarsely.

She turned immediately, her nerves electrified, and tried to distinguish the shadowed figure. "Yes," she whispered back. "Who are you?" Tierney had intentionally blocked the memory of Oswatchee's voice, but now she strained to recollect it. The cracked whisper did not sound like the Indian's guttural obscenities but cautiously, she got up, prepared to run.

"Pierre Lafitte, mademoiselle!" he bowed with exaggeration. "And I believe you must be anxious to see one Captain André de Montfort!" Tierney thought surely she was hallucinating, but he rushed on. "Let's be off! Quiet, now. They are looking for me." He jerked his head toward the village center.

With a start, Tierney remembered Rosalie Noel was not here, and not with Chinookseh, either. She now smelled the acrid smoke, saw the flickering lights, and heard the roar of mounting panic. The full horror of the village aflame struck her senses.

"My baby!"

Pierre Lafitte rolled his eyes and swore under his breath. When he found Tierney alone he had presumed the child dead, and was now unwilling to accept further complications. It would not take the savages long to comprehend what was happening, and they would be swarming here in a few seconds.

"Where is it?" he asked testily.

"I don't know!" Hysteria was rising in the girl's voice. At this very moment, Lafitte knew the warriors were coming—that the baby had probably already suffocated with smoke.

Tierney read his thoughts. "No!" she cried. "I won't leave without her! I can find her," she wailed. "I can!"

He hushed her with a wave of his hand. Angry voices were fast approaching now. "Then I won't leave!" she broke in. "Go back alone. Tell André . . ." Her words were cut short by his sudden attack. He clamped one hand over her mouth, and dragged her bodily out of the hut, his other arm flung about her waist. The search had spread both east and west of the burning longhouse as he made to run.

The fires cast hideous shadows everywhere, but the smoke hindered his usually keen eyes. Pierre had left the horses tethered at the opposite end of camp. There would be no time to retrieve them now. "Hold still, God damn it!" he muttered into her ear. It was to no avail. The girl was fighting him like a madman, clawing his forearm, kicking, and alternately chewing his palm and spitting into it to make it slippery.

He managed to drag her as far as the nearest dense thicket before she broke away. He caught her within seconds, and spinning her back around, clipped her jaw in one short, but clean, blow. As she dropped to the ground, he swiftly jerked her limp body up and over his shoulder. The man was not overly tall, but he was strong and agile. Pierre Lafitte was experienced at both carrying contraband and making good his escape.

"Put me down," she managed weakly. It was still dark when Tierney regained consciousness, and he was only too happy to comply with her request. A hundred-pound burden could be devastatingly cumbersome after nearly an hour of racing in and out of copses, over brambles, and forging through mud.

"Where are you taking me?" she demanded, once on her feet.

"North," he answered her. "Then we shall cut back west and down the river by flatboat." He could see her clearly in the pale moonlight, her stark form abused, her eyes narrowed in thought. The foolish wench was calculating how to retrace their path to the camp—to a child almost certainly dead now.

"It is no use, mademoiselle," he offered gently. "You could never find your way. You've been unconscious hours now," he lied, "and I've not left any tracks. After I have returned you to your sea captain, we shall devise a plan to go back for your baby." This too was a lie. If any of the village survived the plunder, Pierre Lafitte, for one, would never risk a return.

Despite Tierney's haggard expression and bruised body, she made a tempting sight in the night shadows. Pierre Lafitte momentarily hated himself for even thinking it. "Here," he stated gruffly. "Take my coat."

She made no move to put on the proffered jacket, so

he put it on her himself, carefully buttoning it over her full breasts. The protection was as much for himself, he grimly conceded, as for her. She made no move to stop him, even when he tried to adjust the buckskin skirt from falling below her navel.

Neither did she respond when Lafitte told her they must continue their cautious journey. She was listening to Rosalie Noel. "She's awake," she said mindlessly. "The baby is hungry. I have to feed her now."

"This way," he croaked. Sympathy was not an integral part of his nature, and he was finding it difficult to acknowledge the depth of the emotion. His gullet ached with the effort of restrained sorrow for her. And guilt—his own. He should have looked for the baby. He should have looked.

Lafitte was nervous about his unwilling traveling companion. She was so grief-stricken she had stopped talking entirely. She didn't eat, either, and when he had found her she looked malnourished enough. But she followed him now, offering no further argument on the arduous journey afoot.

He cut west earlier than he had originally planned, partly because of his own exhaustion and partly because the girl's haunting eyes made him uneasy.

The trip downriver was even more morose. Tierney sat silently on the flat deck, her back straight and legs crossed as the Indians themselves sat. The wordless passenger was only slightly less grating on his nerves than the incessant chatter of the big oaf who guided the lumbering boat.

In New Orleans, Lafitte engaged a compatriate in smuggling to return them to Barataria Bay. Tierney, had she been aware of her surroundings, might have recognized *La Reine de la Mer,* which lay to port within sight and sound of the smaller craft. But the scraping of hull and *La Reine*'s lonely creaking went unheard by the victor of André's heart.

CHAPTER TWENTY-ONE

André de Montfort was beside himself. He had waited too many days for the braggart to return from the territory, and now, as Tierney was being ushered into the huge house, the captain's nerves were near snapping in despair.

He heard his name called from below, and then a muffled order barked out in French. André flung the door open and ran to the banister. He could not hear the two stories down over the pounding of his own heart, but warned himself against being too excited. He had gone through many false starts during the past few days.

This time, however, there was an unprecedented anticipation clutching his soul as he bounded down the stairs.

Tierney stood in the center of the large foyer, her cut and bared legs rigidly braced together. He followed his eyes up over the hideous skirt that barely concealed the bony knees and too-thin thighs, over the comically large coat that hung from her shoulders, to her face.

One side had been bruised nearly unrecognizable, and her lips were caked over with dust and cracked open in spots. Her hair was longer than he had ever seen it, but the disheveled mess was littered with mud, debris, and ash.

The entire room was filled with the heavy odors of soot and smoke and sweat emanating from both Pierre Lafitte and Tierney.

"*Mon Dieu!*" he choked in disbelief. "*Mon Dieu, mon Dieu . . .*"

Tierney stared at him out of vacant eyes. She did not recognize the lean, bearded man before her. She could still hear the baby, however. Rosalie Noel had been crying for so long . . . too hungry, she thought. She looked bleakly around her. If she followed the sound, she could find the baby. Her breasts ached unbearably, and the front of the man's coat was wet with overspilt milk.

She dazedly took some steps, but stopped. Tierney was terribly confused. The cries were distant. Rosalie must be outside somewhere . . . She said nothing when André gently took her hand, nor when he cautiously led her up the two flights to his room. He wanted to take her into his arms and carry her, but he knew she did not know him now. Above all else, he must not frighten her. She had obviously lived through enough hell to last a lifetime and beyond.

André insisted that only he administer to the newly arrived, abused houseguest. Lafitte's wenches mildly protested, assuring him that women could best attend now to her many needs. But he told the well-meaning gypsies to all go away. At their insistence, however, a bath was readied first.

He took these few minutes to seek out Pierre Lafitte.

The man was downstairs, drinking himself into a stupor. At André's urging, he briefly described to him the escape, and in slurred speech, admitted his only failure. The baby had been left behind. "I should have looked. Probably dead by now," he muttered. "It was a girl," he moaned miserably, laying his head heavily on folded arms.

André thanked him for his help, assuring him that Tierney alone was success enough. Then the heavy-hearted captain trudged back up the stairs to the woman he barely recognized.

After everyone was gone again, André tested the water. It was quite warm yet, but he knew it should be to properly cleanse her wounds and soothe her taut muscles.

She had not spoken a word, and even when he began to take off her tattered garb, she neither said not did anything. André kept up a continuous flow of conversation, unconsciously dotting the monologue with French.

"Tierney, what in God's name have they done to you? . . . You're trembling, darling. Are you cold? . . . *Ma petite,* can you ever forgive me? . . . Can you understand me, Tierney? Tierney, *mon coeur, ma chérie . . .*" And so it went, André trying not to grimace when yet another welt was uncovered, another rip detected in her once flawless skin.

Except for the slight shudder that periodically seemed to ripple over her entirely rigid form, Tierney did not move. Her lover thought he would have been relieved to see her squint again, or hear her weep. But he was desperate for recognition, or at least a sign that there was, indeed, a trace of sanity left in her.

He led her uninhibited to the enormous porcelain tub. "Here, *ma petite*," he whispered hoarsely. "A lovely bath for you. It's perfumed, *chérie*. Damask. Do you remember, my beloved?" He bent to swirl the water invitingly.

Tierney gasped. It was her first voluntary reflex; and though less than he had wished for, André felt a glimmer of hope.

"Does it frighten you, *petite*? Something happened in the water, yes? Or near it? Tierney, I am not asking you to remember that. Not now. You don't have to remember any of the ugly things, *chérie*. Remember the sweet," he quietly urged. "Damask. Remember how sweet it smells? Lean over the water. Smell it. If you don't want to get into it tonight, that is fine. But you will like it, Tierney. I promise."

She must have understood part of what he said, for she scooped some into her hands and brought it to her face. She breathed in the fragrance and closed her eyes to savor it, perhaps, or recall its scent. What water trickled from her hands did not disturb her.

At length, she stood up and faced him. His eyes were familiar. Nothing else. Deep blue—the color of sky at twilight. In the distance, she heard Rosalie Noel again, but this time the sound did not confuse her. A violent pain shattered her dreamlike state.

"André?" she cried brokenly. "Sweet Jesus, André, is it you?" she whimpered, seizing both his hands.

This time it was the man who was unable to speak. Tears rolled unchecked down his drawn face, and he could barely restrain himself from clutching her to him. He silently swore never to let her out of his reach again.

The strength of her hands biting into his own was surprising, and he finally managed to find his voice. "Tierney. Oh, thank God. You know me, *ma chérie*. I thought . . ." But his words were quickly extinguished by her sudden frenzy.

"The baby, André! We have to go back. She's waiting

there. The savages . . . They'll, God only knows what
they might do to her now! Let's go back, André. I can
find her, I know it. Don't look at me like that, you fool!
Our baby, I'm telling you, we have to leave."

He tried vainly to calm her, assure her they would go
back for the baby, but she could not be persuaded to listen. Her raving reached an ear-splitting pitch.

"Not later, you bastard! Now! Every minute we waste
could . . . could be her last!" she screeched. "Where is
Paul?" she demanded. "He will take me, if you refuse.
Where is he? Where is the ship?"

"In New Orleans," he answered quietly. It stung him
to the core that Tierney would ask for Paul Mauriac, now,
of all times.

"And where the hell are we, André? Have you abducted
me as well? I should have known! You're beasts, every
last one of you! Men," she spat, "I hope they all burn in
hell, their bloody spikes along with them!"

At last she could spend her pent-up fury. She struck
at him savagely, swearing nonsensically. She bit, kicked
him, pounded her flailing fists at his chest, arms, and face.
He took the blows absently, only remorse piercing his
conscience. There were more than surface wounds to be
seen here, and he digested the full weight of the horrors
she had been subjected to in as stoic a manner as was
humanly possible.

When she finally fell against him, naked, exhausted, and
weeping at last, he put his arms around her. The long-
awaited embrace was far removed from the image André
had conjured while crossing the Pacific.

She permitted him to lift her into the scented water.
Scattered pictures of her bath in Charleston, Mother Superior, and Nanna flitted about her memory like so many
mindless butterflies. She could not bear to think of André
directly, nor their child.

He bathed her thoroughly, but tenderly. He washed
the long tendrils of hair until their natural spring and
color became familiar to his touch. When he dried her,
she smiled tentatively. But so enraptured was he at this
first sign of happiness that he unwittingly became less
gentle with the huge linen towel. When he patted her
swollen breasts, she groaned with the pain.

"Aaah, God! It has been four days now since I had her

to me. My milk," she wept, "it must be spoiling in me. Rosalie Noel is such a patient little thing," she mused aloud, a pathetic wistfulness in her voice.

André was afraid she might become hysterical again. He would dutifully go out and search for this child of theirs, to be sure, but Tierney's recovery was uppermost in his mind. He hastily sent for tea. She still refused food, and anything as strong as wine or brandy would surely make her retch. Before pouring the tea, however, he dropped some opiate into the cup.

"It's awfully bitter," she coughed. "I must have grown accustomed to the root and bark teas the Indians drink. Sassafras, I think."

"That and the fact that I asked them to steep it for a long time. Here, *chérie*, add more honey. It will nourish you."

It wasn't long before Tierney felt the effects of the drug, coupled with so many sleepless nights. She was too drowsy to even appreciate the soft silk sheets and down-filled satin quilt that André drew up to her shoulders. Under different circumstances, she would have luxuriated in stretching out the full length of the high fourposter bed.

Before dropping into the much-needed slumber, Tierney talked about Rosalie. She had longed to tell someone how very exciting new motherhood was to her, and there had been no one to whom she could truly pour out her heart. The infant had been her only joy for nearly six infinitely trying weeks. Now, in the induced relaxation of the opiate, she felt idyllic peace. What could be more poignant than a new mother sharing these singular interests with the new father.

"I named her Rosalie Noel, André. Do you like it? It means 'little dark rose,' and of course, I never forgot our Christmas on board *La Reine de la Mer*. Rosalie Noel . . . it suits her perfectly. She looks like you, André," she murmured sleepily. "Jet black hair—it's wavy—and your eyes. But her complexion is very fair. She has the most exquisite little face . . . André?"

"*Oui, ma petite*. I am here." He took her hand, gently kissing each fingertip.

"I call her that sometimes," she sighed. "*Ma petite* . . . I was so afraid I, we, would never see you again. You'll love her, André. Our little dark rose . . . You shall worship her!"

Sleep overtook Tierney at last. André got up from where he had knelt by the bed. He rubbed the back of his neck, trying to make some plans for their future. It was certain now that he could not leave her again.

Would she settle in New Orleans, or would this, too, be painful—wondering if somewhere in the vast Louisiana territory their daughter traveled with a pack of heathens? André de Montfort had to agree with Lafitte. It was highly improbable that the infant survived the fire, let alone the revenge of the Creeks once Tierney's escape was made known.

He poured a tall glass of brandy and lifted it to his lips. It was hard to imagine himself a father, even if it had been only a fleeting and unfulfilled moment in the span of his life. He looked back at the sleeping form.

Tierney, once washed and powdered, looked rested and renewed. Except for her enlarged bosom and excessive bruises, she might be the same girl he had brought down from the crow's nest . . .

As he refilled the glass, he heard her groan. He rushed over to find her still asleep, but unconsciously clutching her breasts. He carefully pulled back the sheet. It was wet.

Some milk was evidently forcing its way out of her engorged, reddened nipples. He felt them lightly and they were feverish to the touch. He winced, realizing how painful they must be for the feeling to penetrate the liberal doses of opiate he had given her. He could not remember Tierney ever complaining before, and despite her numerous tender spots now, she had admitted only the soreness caused by the interruption in nursing.

André had naïvely assumed that this was part of her mental anguish. Now he saw her physical distress as well. He pulled the sheet away from her entirely, and stared.

On impulse, he lay down beside her, though fully clothed. He lightly traced the two pink lines that etched sharply across her lower abdomen, cutting diagonally above the triangular patch of auburn hair. They were permanent reminders of the child she had truly borne him, one he might never see. Ever so tenderly, he kissed the two scars.

Then he crept up closer to her face, careful not to

disturb her, lest she awaken. But Tierney slept soundly. Except for an occasional moan, she did not stir. She seemed barely to breathe at all.

A short spurt of bluish milk dotted his hand. He had intended to reach up and stroke the ever-unruly hair away from her face, but instead he unthinkingly tasted the opaque liquid.

He considered the matter, but only briefly. Cautiously he moved his lips to cover one hardened nipple. Afraid to hurt her, he did not suck at all, but merely tongued it. In seconds, the stored milk flowed freely from the taut breast into his mouth. Loving her, he did not moralize over his action, but drank in the sensual warmth without thought.

Already the strain of her recent experiences and the lack of use had affected the nourishing supply. In less than two minutes, her breast checked its flow. He gently moved over to kiss the other, aware only of its subtle sweetness.

Afterward, he lay back against the pillow. There was no guilt, no remonstrations, but any thinking man would wonder at such uncommon intimacy. Tierney had not moved during the brief episode, but she now breathed in deeply, more naturally. He was unaccountably proud that he could so simply comfort her. The once woodenlike, hot bosom was now soft and supple. The pleasure had not been erotic; it had been a much deeper sensuality, and an emotional discovery.

Concern for her firstborn was uppermost in her mind, would always be. It was purely instinctive, a poignant reminder to André de Montfort that much had changed since he had last seen Tierney.

He vowed that he would find this "little dark rose." Rosalie Noel, if she lived, would have her God-given mother and father!

CHAPTER TWENTY-TWO

"I will marry you, André. I suppose it is what I have wanted. But not until we find Rosalie Noel!"

André paced the parlor, and stopped. He was furious.

These silly Ursulines were well-meaning enough, but they were all, in truth, just so many interfering old biddies, he fumed. Couldn't they see his logic? Oh, yes! Mother Superior assured him they were trying to persuade Tierney to marry him and be done with it.

"But, Captain de Montfort," the old nun had said, "you know as well as we that she has a mind of her own."

Mon Dieu, that was the understatement of the century! He had been so certain that Tierney would not tell the nuns the truth. He had presumed Tierney would also want a quiet ceremony before returning here. They could have, with some persuasion, talked some poor padre into it. But, no; this thick-headed one would have no part of it.

He slammed his hand down on the table in frustration. He had been a fool to bring her back here. He should have let her beg him until she was blue in the face. Even Paul had believed bringing her back was a mistake.

"Milady, this is nothing short of blackmail! You know I am doing everything in my power to find our daughter. Our daughter! Are you listening, Tierney? Yours and mine. Rosalie has us both now. Why can't you and I be together, at least?"

At Tierney's insistence, they had left Lafitte's the very next day and gone back to Southwell. Her return to Pass Christian had been nothing short of a homecoming.

Harriet Redding had wept and laughed hysterically, kissing her like a long-lost sister. Angelique had carried on almost as dramatically, with Mammy Lou in the midst of all of it, dabbing her eyes and blowing her nose every other minute.

The clamorous welcome was good for Tierney. After many tears and much embracing, she had gone upstairs with Mammy and the younger Mrs. Redding to dress for dinner.

"Mammy Lou, you go with Miss Tierney and help her," Harriet said gaily. "I can manage alone." Kissing Tierney again, she added, "Do cheer up, dear. If your handsome husband could arrange your escape, I just know he will find your little girl."

Seeing Jamey again had been a heart-rending experience. The milk in her breasts had all but disappeared, but they were still tender. She still had not been able to explain why, upon awakening that first morning in Barataria, she had felt such relief. Then, seeing the familiar baby, her breasts had felt near bursting again; but even Tierney knew that this time it was her imagination. The milk was no longer replenishing itself.

Mammy Lou led her weeping up to her old room.

"Now, missy, you gots to stop this bawlin'. Yo' man don't deserve it a-tall. He come back, jest lak I knows he would. He gonna find that chile, now, don't you worry none."

"Oh, Mammy!" she sighed. "I just cannot help it. My Rosalie Noel, alone out there with those savages! They took her from me, Mammy Lou. At night, so I wouldn't try to run . . . That's why I don't have her with me now!" she cried. "Oh, God, Mammy! I know how you feel with Bruce gone. I've been a slave now too. But as God is my judge, I would give anything to trade places with you, Mammy! I would! I'd be able to see her Sundays . . ."

The big Negress held her tightly, soothing Tierney as best she could. Only another childless mother would have fully understood the scene in the little room with dormer windows.

When she finally joined the others in the dining hall, Tierney was dressed in the one Madame Richet gown she had kept. The beige ensemble flowed enticingly about her long legs, and snugly held her rounded bust. In spite of himself, André caught his breath.

Mammy Lou had insisted she look "decent" for her

man, and the gaudy dresses that Lafitte's women had
donated were poor in comparison. She had also made
Tierney scrub her face, and "git rid of them troublesome
tears." Although her face still had fading reminders of
Oswatchee's beating, her eyes sparkled a dewy green and
her complexion fairly glowed from the brisk washing.

Presently, looking across the convent parlor to her
stubborn chin and narrowed eyes, André had to chuckle.
It tested his patience to beg her, to have her here again,
to be sure. But she was safe again, and the Ursulines'
routine of prayer, regular meals, and rest was obviously
agreeing with Tierney.

It had been almost a month now; and except for the
constant worry over Rosalie, she was fast recovering from
the ordeal.

"Well, have your way then. I surrender to you, mademoiselle," he said, sweeping into a low bow. "First, I find
Rosalie. Then I have you, m'dear. But be prepared. I shan't
be put off an hour after I drop her into your lap!"

Tierney grinned. It was a small victory, she knew.
When they had first parted in January of this year, Tierney
had promised herself that André de Montfort would, upon
his return, want her. "Well, he does," she told herself,
"and although things are mightily changed, he still will
have to work for my hand!"

Beyond this idle conceit was the perpetual fear that once
married, André would relax—become complacent with his
new life, and because it would be easier to enter New
Orleans society without the embarrassment of Rosalie
Noel's inexplicably premature arrival, the search for the
child might dwindle to mere conversation between the two
of them. Tierney did not want conversation; she wanted
action.

Their first night at Southwell, Tierney had begun to
formulate her plans. A trek back to the bayou was first
on the agenda, but she had to think what her best approach
might be.

When André followed her the two flights of stairs up
to her little room that faced the surf, she let him believe
he would be permitted to stay.

"Thank you for seeing me to my room, André. Good
night."

"And where am I to sleep?" he demanded in a whisper.

"I presume Mr. Redding has provided you a bed. If not, talk to Theodore. He will manage something." But as she put her hand on the doorknob, André covered it with his own.

"*Chérie*, it is all right. They think we are married. I told them we were." He smiled confidently.

"Well, you lied then! We are not married. Now go downstairs before we start to bicker and disrupt the household."

He was embarrassed and insulted by her sudden animosity. "Well, Miss Chambers," he countered drily, "would you object to telling me why it was so different last night? I slept beside you, and you started no argument either then or this morning."

"Yes, I'll tell you, Captain," she replied testily. "Last night was different because last night was different!"

In spite of himself, he had to laugh.

Tierney stamped her foot in frustration. "It was different because first of all, I was in no state to know any better and you know it! Secondly, you drugged me, didn't you? How could I protest when I could not even think clearly. And," she snapped, "last night was different because you kept all your clothes on!"

"I'd keep them on again, *chérie*, if that is what you want . . . I've no intention of seducing you. I wouldn't even attempt it, after . . ."

"I don't believe you, André de Montfort! The way you have stared at me all night in this silly dress, well, your intentions could not have been more obvious if I'd been stark naked down there!" she accused.

André could not argue the point. He had been hard tested not to embrace her all evening, but in truth, he would not have laid a hand on her tonight. He wanted to be near her, was afraid to let her out of his sight. But he had already dismissed the idea of any lovemaking. Tierney would be unapproachable for months.

The dog, Taffey, had remembered his mistress almost immediately. The next day, as they strolled Southwell's gardens with the spaniel at their heels, Tierney confided her plans to André. They must leave for the Indian camp at once.

"Absolutely not!" he commanded. "I forbid it. Tierney, you evidently have not yet regained all your senses. The idea of your going back into that jungle is outrageous! Are you mad?"

"Not yet. But I will be," she threatened. "I have already explained it to you. I must go, even more than you, André. No one else will know where to look. She is probably with Melita and Chinookseh. If not, Birdie and Jeb will be able to tell me where to find her. The slave hut didn't burn, I tell you! They, at least, can tell us what has happened."

"I have already said no. I am going upcountry myself. James has some neighbors who are willing to accompany us. And Paul . . ."

"Oh, dear God!" she cried in exasperation. "Will you listen to me? You are the one who is mad, André, if you cannot see the sense in what I say. I know the village. I know where to look and how! I can pick up their trail if they have gone. I know the squaws who might be nursing the baby. And I know who to kill if Rosalie Noel is dead," she ended bitterly. "Oswatchee!"

Not only did Tierney insist upon going, but she also determined it would be best if only she and André went into the dense bayou. "Any more would be noticed, André. They could trap us. Two traveling alone will be less suspicious."

"And how do you propose we do it?"

"We will disguise ourselves as trappers, of course."

"Oh, of course! I almost forgot that you are a master of disguise. A veritable Jeanne d'Arc!"

"Do listen to me, André," she pleaded. "I saw two trappers come into camp once. They didn't stir up any trouble at all." Tierney was lying. There had been no fur trappers in the weeks she spent with the Creeks. But she was desperate. If she didn't go herself and others returned without her baby, she would never be certain Rosalie Noel was not there; indeed, she would not have been sure that a search had been conducted at all. Tierney had grown suspicious of everyone now, and even André de Montfort was not an exception.

"Besides, it is our responsibility, André. No one else's. Rosalie is yours and mine. Not the Reddings', not Paul's, not Lafitte's . . ."

"It just isn't safe—or sane," he argued. "I promise you that we men . . ."

"What's the matter with you, André?" she hissed. "Are you afraid? Is the great fearless sea captain too frightened to forge into unknown land—a fish out of water, so to speak? Well, I am not!

"You forget I am the self-same girl who left her homeland not knowing what to expect or where I was going! I've got guts, André! And you can nay me now, but know that if you won't take me back there, I will go alone. I swear to God, André, I'll die before I'll let some willy-nilly man keep me back from what I know I must do!"

And so, through her incessant demanding, nagging, pleading, and conniving over a two-day period, Tierney Chambers and the captain set off for Bay St. Louis.

To make the departure simpler, the couple allowed the Reddings to assume they were returning to New Orleans, via *La Reine de la Mer*. True enough, *La Reine* awaited them at the bay.

Tierney had not admitted to anyone that she had never ridden a horse, and in fact, had been frightened of them most of her life. André had asked her if there was a problem when they first started out on the beach that morning. Tierney had attributed the difficulty to the bay mare and the fact that she had never straddled a horse. "I've always used a lady's saddle," she told him. It never ceased to surprise her how easily she could lie.

If necessity is, indeed, the mother of invention, determination, then, is its sire. Within a few miles, Tierney had come to grips with the animal and the animal with her. There was no doubt: the rider was also master.

Recruiting Paul for the bizarre expedition had been Tierney's one concession. It was ludicrous, of course. Two men, wholly inexperienced at dealing with natives—at least, American natives—and a bold, but oftimes foolish, girl. Pelier and several of the others had wanted to go, but André de Montfort thought that an entire crew of merchant seamen tracking through swamps and forest was unthinkable.

Tierney wore a rather elaborate costume of buckskin breeches, jacket, and moccasins. The ensemble was completed by the coonskin hat Paul had included. "In New Orleans they tell me it's virtually the trademark of Indian fighters and trappers alike. Andy Jackson, have you heard about him, André? Interesting fellow . . . Even Jackson wears one.

"Tierney, lass, you are a sight for sore eyes!" Paul exclaimed when she returned from André's cabin to the deck. Everyone turned to see her, and those who remembered the voyage from London to Charleston the year before were greatly amused. In spite of the gravity of the situation, no one could help but compare the girl in buckskin with her hair up under a raccoon's tail to the naïve little "cabin boy" on that memorable trip.

André rode his great roan that had been stabled those two weeks at Southwell; Harriet had given Tierney the use of her own skittish mare that was very well groomed, but seldom ridden; and Paul had brought a larger, dappled mare from New Orleans that was overly nervous from her hours at sea.

The trio headed north by northwest on a little known trail used by Pierre Lafitte and some of his trusted men. Although it was long and arduous, it was the nearest route by which goods could be shuffled between the settlement and a ship. There were no other deepwater inlets in a hundred-mile stretch of shallow coastal waters, and Lafitte had suggested that retracing his and Tierney's path from New Orleans, upriver, and east again, would be impossible for even the most astute tracker.

Paul and the captain had dressed less elaborately, wearing work clothes and pea jackets. They did, however, strap on their cutlasses. Without exchanging a word, both remembered that violent encounter off the coast of Greece. Rescue of the Turk's daughter had cost a dozen lives and more maiming. Neither man wanted to wager on the outcome of what lay ahead.

Looking at Tierney now, dressed in a lovely gown of brown velvet with silver trim, it would have been impossible to explain to a stranger their eerie return to Deer Run Bayou.

"A penny for your thoughts," she teased.

André chuckled and nodded toward Mother Superior's office. "It would cost you more than a penny, *ma chérie*. And with all these agents of the Lord about, I daresay I could not collect my price . . ."

* * *

There had been no need for his worry, as it turned out. He raised his cutlass only once, and that for a copperhead snake that had crawled from one of the vacant huts.

Pierre Lafitte's prediction was accurate, if disappointing to Tierney. The Indians had gone, leaving only a *talla-hassee*, an abandoned settlement. André had not seen as much damage as Lafitte would have him believe. Perhaps he had been tipping the rum himself that night.

Less than a third of the village was burned. Neverthe-less, not a soul remained. They had packed everything and left. Except for charred remnants and those huts that stood empty, not a trace of the Creeks remained.

There were three fresh mounds, however. Victims of the fire. One was small.

"Tierney, no!" he had begged.

"Get away from me, you bloody coward! Both of you!"

It was as gruesome a scene as he had ever witnessed. Tierney on her knees, desperately clawing at the soft pile of dirt. She babbled, often incoherently, throughout. "It is not Rosalie Noel!" she wept. "I'm sure. But I must see for myself. Oh, Mum . . . Da, forgive me. I have to know! A fire, dear God, why a fire?" she screamed. "She has been baptized, André. I baptized her myself . . . down there, at the river where, where . . . Still and all, she must have a Christian burial. You can see that, can't you? Nanna?"

And then the blankets. Both he and Paul had grabbed her, never thinking she could reach the corpse so quickly. They had believed all along that she would give up the maniacal digging. But it was a shallow grave. Too shallow.

"Let go of me," she growled, an unearthly glint emanat-ing through her dirt- and tear-streaked face. "Get your hands away!" She clutched at a corner of the wrap and pulled. The tiny body tumbled out, Tierney issued a ma-cabre scream, and Paul vomited.

It was not Rosalie Noel.

Tierney rocked back and forth all the while the men reburied the poor Creek innocent. *"Confiteor Deo, omni-potenti . . ."* she mumbled. *"Mea culpa, mea culpa . . ."*

It was later, on the return to Bay St. Louis, that she asked to be taken to the convent on Chartres and Ursuline streets in New Orleans.

* * *

"You are quite sure that you want to marry me?" she asked for the second time. André was daydreaming again. She had never noticed that about him before. Of course, back then, he had his charts and sextant to moon over . . .

"Quite, milady," he answered cheerfully. "But if you mean to say I can pay you court in the meanwhile, then I demand at least a kiss."

It was very odd, but she had not kissed him even innocently since his return to Louisiana. He could understand her hesitation. Between marks on her body and her frenzied attack of him that first night at the pirate's cove, there was little doubt in André's mind of the sordid ravaging she had survived.

Whether or not Rosalie Noel was ever found, André de Montfort knew that one day he would have the singular pleasure of killing the savage Oswatchee.

"A kiss?" she asked tremulously.

"*Oui, mon couer.* A little symbol of your affection that I might take with me on the morrow."

"Tomorrow? Where are you going?"

"Upriver. My first riverboat ride on the Mississippi. I wish you could come, my love. Ah, but we aren't married," he chided, seeing a new spark of interest.

"Why?" she continued, ignoring his teasing. "Have you heard something?"

"No," admitted André. "Nothing specific. But these steam vessels have my curiosity up now that I may be selling *La Reine.* And there are rumors of a Creek federation powwow up by a place called Natchez . . ."

Tierney flew across the room into his arms. Her kiss was simple gratitude at first, but with André's gentle persuasion, it became something more.

CHAPTER TWENTY-THREE

"As a friend, child, I am talking to you as a friend. I don't think you are being fair to him, or yourself, for that matter."

Tierney pulled the sable-lined cloak tightly around her shoulders. It was December already, and although the day was bright, it was abominably cold. Father Donavan did not mind the chill, apparently, for he had suggested the walk in the garden himself, and now he looked at her expectantly.

"Yes, Father. I understand how you feel about it. André had been kind, too kind, really," she sighed, feeling the dark rich fur of her collar. "But none of you seem to understand how I feel. Mother Superior and Sister Mercedes both have tried to persuade me to marry him now, but I can't. Marriage is my only trump card left. If I play it before Rosalie Noel is found, I feel certain I will never see her again!"

The aging priest persisted. "That is precisely what I mean, Tierney Chambers! Your attitude is most unfair. You are assuming that the captain will grow derelict in his paternal duty. A dangerous assumption, lass. It has the earmarks of suspicion, distrust, and infidelity. 'Tis no way to start a marriage." He turned his palm upward in a helpless gesture. "Aah, perhaps you're right, Tierney girl. You should not marry him at all, at all. That's the way of it, I suppose. And I thought, silly old man that I am, that God in His omniscience had bound the two of you together as surely as He ordered the rivers to run into the seas. Tierney, lass, an aging priest is a fool, indeed," he sighed, shaking his head.

Tierney fell hook, line, and sinker for the bait. Not marry him? At all, at all . . . That is not what she had in mind. "But, Father Donavan!" she exclaimed, "I want to marry him. I love him!"

"Do you now?" he asked pointedly. "And that is a bit hard to believe! Sure, you've made the man suffer, Tierney. And I don't know but that he deserved a pinch of it. But this? To demand what may not be possible, what may not be in God's holy plan?"

The girl turned her head, not willing to listen to more.

"You'll hear me out, Tierney, that you will! For ye have no earthly father, now, do ye?" The old man's brogue was growing thick with emotion. "So listen, though ye may not have a mind to. That child of yours, God bless her, may never be found. Tierney, I tell ye for ye own good. The truth of it is, ye don't know! None of us do, dear. But ye mustn't be blinded to what ye're doin' to him with your love for Rosalie."

Tierney sank onto the garden's stone bench, where she and André had once argued.

Father Donavan gently patted her shoulder. "Now, now. I don't mean to be cruel, lass. But ye must see, the way ye've been treating the man—yer uppity ways, sendin' him upriver one minute, down the next, inland east, west, and all between, and him trying to establish his own business in these troubled times—well, daughter, ye mustn't run him amuck so. The poor man is making his penance in more ways than ye'll ever know. But ye keep this up, girl . . . I'm warnin' ye, if he does find his daughter he will resent her for all ye're puttin' her so far above yer love of him all the months, years, betwixt the searchin' and the findin'!"

Tierney was tired. She was tired of struggling, tired of her plans, tired of her own almighty stubbornness. Perhaps they were right. All of them.

Her eighteenth birthday was today, and she felt that for all her experiences, she was growing duller by the day, not wiser. Heaven only knew that she had all her life acted on impulse, disregarding the good advice of older and more worldly-wise individuals. Father Donavan had struck a chord in her, and his words rang true.

Presently, though, Tierney thought about the coming evening. André would come for her at seven o'clock. Mother Superior had not even balked at the suggestion that he be allowed to take her out tonight, alone. They were going to celebrate her birthday at a luxurious restaurant, attend the theater for a special Christmas Eve presentation, and end the long night at midnight mass at the Cathedral of St. Louis.

She was not as excited as she might have expected. Eighteen was considered the age for young women to miraculously mature. Tierney felt as old as Methuselah one day and wet behind the ears the next. Today, she was certain, would not create any overnight changes in temperament.

"Tierney?" It was Sister Mercedes calling and lightly tapping on her door. "Are you there, dear?"

She opened the door to the merry-eyed prefect. "Hello, Sister. Please come in," she said listlessly.

"Why so glum?" the nun chided. "Christmas Eve? Your birthday? Cheer up now! There is a surprise waiting for you downstairs."

Tierney followed Sister Mercedes back down to the parlor with little enthusiasm. "Probably flowers again," she grumbled as she dragged her fingertips along the banister.

What awaited her was not one surprise, but an entire wagonload of presents. Despite her day-long gloom, Tierney became as excited as a child beneath the tree. André had sent packages upon packages, all wrapped differently. Some were in foil, some in tissue, some even boxed in gingham, silks, and satin. The most intriguing gift, however, was a large box all covered in gay little hard candies of multiple shapes and colors, each glued to the box itself!

All the sisters were gathered about, nearly as excited as Tierney herself. André had not forgotten them, either. There were four smoked hams, a dressed turkey, a wheel of aged cheddar, baskets of fruit, and a case of champagne. They tittered self-consciously at the last gift, but most were silently thankful that the Holy Father had never denounced occasional tipping.

The candy-covered box had a little note attached: "I dare you to open this first!" Tierney tore into it immediately.

Mother Superior stood patiently to the side, watching her toss the multicolored candies to the giggling young postulants and novices. Youthful indulgence was not encouraged, but it was a relief to hear Tierney laugh and

look a little more like her old self. Besides, the little
postulants were no more than sixteen and seventeen years
old themselves, for the most part.

"Oh, that rogue!" she finally exclaimed, exasperated.
"It's all candy. Look! The box is full of it . . . He's such
a terrible tease sometimes." To everyone's amazement, the
spirited Miss Chambers was pouting.

Only Mother Superior knew the full meaning of this
nonsense. She and the sea captain had become comrades
in arms of late. The nun cleared her throat to keep from
laughing.

"Tierney, don't tell us you haven't the virtue of per-
severance! We have all come to think of you as a young
woman rare in persistence, in determination, and in righteous fortitude . . ." she chided, much to the amusement of
everyone. It was rare to see the sober woman tease.

"Oh, all right, Mother!" Tierney laughed. "But I feel
like such a ninny kneeling here, raking through a box of
candies. Do you think he just plays me the fool, or is
there more than sugar in here?" Tierney looked at the
robed matron suspiciously. "You know, don't you!"

Mother Superior refused to say. "I suggest you get back
to work," was her only comment.

It took several minutes to find it, and only Sister Mercedes's curiosity had matched Tierney's own. It was an
enormous solitaire diamond set in a thin band of gold, a
sizable emerald on either side of the exquisite gem. Tierney caught her breath and fell back on her buttocks in
the middle of the parlor floor. Sister Mercedes's beads
clacked together as she bent to inspect the ring.

A thread was attached to the band leading beneath yet
more candies. In seconds Tierney was back up, eagerly
pulling the card out at the other end of the string. Her
fingers trembled as she read:

Mon petit cœur,
   *The emeralds are your eyes that precede my every
thought. The diamond is a symbol of your many
tears, those I cannot bear to see and, yet, cannot
dismiss.*
   My beloved, ma chérie, *if you wear this ring tonight, I shall know we are to be married within a
fortnight, and I shall rejoice. If you choose not to*

wear it, so be it. I will remain patiently yours for the asking.

Forever and in All Ways,
André

Tierney was silent.

The remaining armloads of gifts were carried up the two flights to her dormitory. They nearly filled her room, and as Tierney lifted, unwrapped, and tore tissue, the ring was ever on her mind.

The gifts ranged from porcelain figurines and teacups to silk stockings and lace garters. Sister Mercedes and two awestruck novices left in utter disbelief. There were velvet gowns of brocade, silk, and satin. Madame Richet had now adjusted one of her sewing frames permanently to Tierney's measurements; this, at André's insistence. He had sent two complete riding habits too. One was dove gray with black trim and the other was hunter's green with gold.

The jewelry was equally impressive. Topaz earrings and a bracelet to match her first pendant, a cameo brooch and ring, three strands of pearls, painted china pins and buttons, and pear-shaped diamond earrings with black pearls at the lobe piece, a dinner ring of clustered sapphires, and much more.

It was a magnificent array of finery, and Tierney could not imagine wealth enough to afford such extravagance. With all this before her, she wondered bleakly why Rosalie Noel could not simply be bought back. As far as she could tell, what lay at her feet was at least a king's ransom!

She tried to shake her returning gloom, but it seemed to no avail. "I ought to be wallowing in conceit, not self-pity," she scolded herself. "Or at the very least, preparing to dress. He'll be here in less than two hours. But here I sit, the world's greatest dimwit, impervious to it all." It did not occur to her that she might be spoiled.

Suddenly she espied an obscure package, long and flat under a tower of tissue and emptied boxes. She picked it up and shook it, trying to guess at the contents. She was not eager to open the very last gift, and considered saving it for Christmas morning. As usual, however, curiosity got the best of her.

It was a garment, to be sure, but unlike any she had

ever seen. The material was exquisite sea-green silk, heavily embroidered in gold, silver, and white threads. The collar was almost like those the priests wore, but it opened a bit at the throat.

The dress buttoned up the front like a coat, but the closures were diminutive and matched the green material to perfection. "There must be a hundred," she mused holding it up now. Tierney did not take the time to count them all, but they ran the entire length of it from neck to hem.

A sheer silk slip of some sort was included as well. She had never seen anything like it. The undershift had long narrow sleeves, and its color was a translucent silver. It was breathtaking, like softspun dew from a meadow in the first light of day.

White pantaloons completed the lingerie, but they were so odd, Tierney chuckled. They were not gathered at the calf or knee. Instead, these fell to her ankles and were open-bottomed like a man's trousers!

Tierney was excited again, and presently hurried down the hall to bathe. Although the good sisters had sent up ample hot water, one difference in convent life was attending to a lady's toilette. One managed to bathe, perfume, and dress alone. Not that this was a problem for Tierney. All her life she had done quite well without the personal service of maids, and wondered now if she could really live comfortably any other way.

She slipped into the long silvery chemise and then hurriedly adjusted the outer gown on her shoulders. The dress, once buttoned, snugly encased her slim shoulders and back, and though closed to her throat, the design gracefully contoured her now enticing bustline.

Below the waist, the skirt flared somewhat, emphasizing Tierney's flat stomach, but adding another dimension to her rather narrow hips. To her dismay, the side seams were open along the calf almost to her knee. Tierney clucked irritably. She had felt so exotic in this peculiar gown, and now there was not time to mend the split seams. There was barely time to change into another gown!

As she bent to undo the buttons, she examined the tear.

It was no tear, at all; it was intentional. She stood up abruptly, pondering the reason. Certainly no decent woman could go out in public with less than a nightgown on underneath it! The sheer silk beneath gave a liberal view of her legs. Then it occurred to her that the long pantaloons were really trousers to be worn under the transparent silver.

She quickly donned them.

Standing to adjust the entire ensemble, she tried to imagine the total effect of everything put together. The sleeves of the outer garment were as pontifical as the collar, sweeping wide at the wrists. But here too the shiny silk of the tight long-sleeved undergarment was deceptively modest. Her slender arms appeared flatteringly dramatic.

Tierney hurriedly slipped into the matching satin slippers, and ran a comb through her hair. Mirrors were not permitted in the convent, since vanity was considered highly improper for a nun, but she did have her little music box with the small oval mirror inside. As she propped it on the table to adjust the last article, a silver-studded satin hair ribbon, the tinkling of "Greensleeves" sent pleasant little ripples up her spine.

The mirror was not much use. Tierney's vision was such that she could, at very close range, focus on an eye, her cheek, her lips—but never all her face at once. "Let's hope I will do," she shrugged. After dabbing jasmine fragrance at her throat, wrist, and temples, she was ready.

The ring lay open on her bedstand. It complemented perfectly this unique gown, of course, for André had so intended it. "Why, I daresay that man planned for me to wear this dress, as well!" she exclaimed aloud. It had been at the bottom of it all, in the least likely box. The ring in the first, the dress in the last; it struck her that André, understanding her love of costumes, actually anticipated her liking this combination best. Thinking on it, Tierney wished she had time to change altogether. "He has no right to think he knows me so well!" she sighed, feigning annoyance. She was actually very pleased.

Tierney could hear Sister Mercedes bustling up the hall. "He's here!" Tierney cried, and slipping the ring on her finger, she flung open the door before Sister even reached it.

"My goodness! You're all ready, Tierney. This is an occasion, isn't it?" she beamed, spying the ring. "Well, get your wrap, dear. It's quite cold out there. And you will be gone late into the night . . . Tsk, tsk, child! Your cloak! Where is it amid all your new finery?"

As they walked down the hall, the prefect whispered, "I daresay your Captain de Montfort has on raiment nearly as splendid as your own."

Tierney glided down the last flight of steps, and André stood waiting in the foyer. He was always amazed when on those rare occasions Tierney demonstrated the grace and poise of a highborn aristocrat. Now, with her regal bearing in the Mandarin gown, he was spellbound.

It was not until he lifted her into the landau—recently purchased and styled in the same black and gold as his beloved ship—that André noticed the ring. His knees went weak with the discovery and his heart raced before he rudely reminded himself that she was, after all, a saucy little girl who had stolen his senses.

"Darling," he started awkwardly, now beside her in the dark intimacy of the carriage, "you have quite exceeded my expectations. You look magnificent, Tierney! Truly!"

She had hoped for "beautiful" or "lovely"—something a bit more feminine than magnificent, but his flattery would do. "At least for the present," she smugly decided. Someday, he would find her all things.

"Thank you, André. But you really should not have been so extravagant with me . . . *Mon Dieu!*" she teased, tapping her wrist against her brow, "the convent will never be the same. You should have seen Mother Superior's face. A display of such worldly wealth could turn the novices' hearts." She giggled to think of the lace garters that two of them had seen.

To André, it was worth far more than he had spent to hear her girlish laughter. If her persistent worry over Rosalie Noel could be diminished, even periodically, then all he was capable of giving her made him richer a thousandfold.

"Tierney," he whispered, kissing her ringed hand, "you have made me the happiest man on all the earth tonight."

Wordlessly, she moved close to him and, encircling his neck in her slender arms, kissed him passionately. It was not a passion born of lust, but rather, of hope. She loved him almost as a child might, trusting and looking for answers to questions not even voiced.

André knew Tierney, he thought, and timid she was not. Yet something in her present manner, tremulous and hesitant, gave him a new sense of awesome proportion, a yoke of protection he would willingly wear.

Something in the nearness of her, however, her moist lips and jasmined throat, gave way to instinct and he groaned into her luxuriously silky hair. When he could not endure his own response any longer, he took one of her hands and laid it upon his straining breeches.

She withdrew from him immediately.

"We are not married yet!" she scolded in a whisper.

"I just did not want you to forget," he chuckled good-naturedly. He did not truly expect her to reciprocate tonight. What could he expect with her living among virgin nuns now? He knew her, and he remembered vividly their too few encounters on board ship. It would take logistical genius, however, to seduce her now, before the wedding.

But the wedding night, aah! That would be superb . . . He would be generous with champagne, hire musicians for the courtyard below their balcony, deliver a masterful massage with scented oils he had procured in the Orient, and put to very good use his own persuasive nature.

"What are you grinning about?" she demanded. "You look like the cat swallowing the canary."

"Very close, milady. Very close."

They were seated in the dining hall, but the table was actually in a small alcove in La Maison, surrounded by exotic hanging ferns and potted shrubbery. It was very secluded, nearly a room within a room. From their table, Tierney could hear orchestral music drifting in from the ballroom. She could also hear the tinkling of a fountain nearby, hidden by the foliage.

The garçon was discreet, appearing soundlessly to fill wine goblets and replenish hors d'oeuvres, and occasionally taking orders from André in muted French. Tierney was too excited to try to make out any of the words.

"All these people, André! This is no mere restaurant. Why, there must be over a hundred people in the ballroom alone!"

"It is not much of a crowd, really. Most people are at

home tonight." He had nearly made the faux pas of saying "with their children," but caught himself in time. A slip like that could spoil her whole evening!

"Several of the gentlemen here are government people, I understand," he continued. "They are to take to Washington information regarding the vulnerability of New Orleans, and also reports of any Indian uprisings." There! He had done it, and after just cautioning himself against saying anything to upset her. Dear God, the very word "Indian" might set her off.

He could not tell whether she had not heard him, or if she, too, was consciously trying to avoid topics that would hurt them. All she said was, "And the ladies, milord? Are they from Washington as well?"

"No, *ma petite*. Women do not often travel great distances, present company excluded, of course," he added. "These are local girls, either engaged, married, or accompanied tonight by anxious mothers and fathers. There are not many women here, as you can see."

Tierney knew that what women were here tonight had already taken note of her gown. In spite of her haughtiness in the coach, she now felt conspicuous even in their private corner. "André, I know I am not the most fastidious woman in the world, nor the most fashionable. But I cannot help observing how they looked at me. What am I wearing, a nightrobe?" she asked in a low voice.

"Darling, they are looking at you with envy. It is a Mandarin gown that I had made for you in China. It fits you to perfection," he smiled, staring appreciatively at the rise and fall of her breasts beneath the enveloping silk. "You are most beautiful, Tierney," he ended huskily.

After dinner, Tierney confessed to André that she had never been inside a real ballroom and would very much like to see the dancing and hear the orchestra play. He conceded any young woman should appreciate the finer enjoyments of life, "Especially one who will soon be married and entering New Orleans society," he added, amused at the idea of Tierney's first dance. He would have preferred, naturally, a ball in honor of his bride-to-be. La Maison, although selective and appealing to the town's most prestigious families, was still a public gathering place. It did splendidly, however, and Tierney was relaxed enough to enjoy herself. Had it really been a private party for her eighteenth birthday, he was sure she would have felt ill-at-ease. La Maison's orchestration was the perfect introduction to gala affairs.

"Whatever are they doing, André? I have never seen anything so glorious! And the music . . ." Tierney's eyes alternately squinted to focus on the swirling dancers and grew wide upon hearing a thrilling crescendo in the panoply of sound.

Her escort drank in the sight of her so transformed by the momentum and motion. "It is called the waltz, milady. It is a modern dance, and the first civilized dance that permits a man to openly embrace a woman." André did not often want to dance, although he did so expertly. But now, the music vibrated through him. He could feel Tierney's lithe body in his arms already . . . "May I?" he queried, bestowing a courtly bow.

At first Tierney was very shy, and to her utter disgrace, stepped upon her partner's feet several times. After the third swirl around the room, however, she caught the natural grandeur of Mozart's style and with André's innate sense of timing, was floating and twirling with the best of them.

To her amazement and André's mild chagrin, she found herself the focal point of several men's attention. Tierney had never had an opportunity to turn men's heads, and she gloried in this new experience. Even timid Charles Bolier, her solitary suitor, had never had his arms about her. Now, all of a sudden, she found herself swung around the ballroom by not less than five gentlemen. Only one was old, about fifty, she guessed, and two were quite attractive.

Her dress did not sway to the music as the properly skirted designs did, but the dancing did display a show of the sheer silver and her trousered calves. The ladies were evidently bewildered by the spectacle, for they started to gather in small groups, refusing to dance for long intervals. They stood aghast, but distinctly interested which greatly amused their company of gentlemen partners and the sea captain who stood back to watch them all.

André had an eye for women, as evidenced by the lovely copper-haired girl who glided past him, enraptured by her first ball. He also had an eye for fashion, and he knew within the week the ladies of New Orleans would be clamoring for Oriental styles. He chuckled to himself. Although he had proudly displayed the gown for Madame Richet to admire, Tierney's dress would remain an original. For all the modiste's pleading, André would not permit her to copy it except by memory.

He also noted that those gentlemen who, either by wives or jealous companions, were unable to request a turn with Tierney were as mesmerized by the girl in green as were her actual partners. Knowing she now wore the ring, André did not so much resent their attentions as he basked in them. Tierney Chambers was his alone; "forever and always," he told himself.

Enough was enough, however, and now he made his way to the refreshment table where Tierney stood with three dawdling admirers.

"We have missed the theater, my sweet," he whispered into her ear. "Don't reproach me, you little vixen. You have been *la femme fatale* this night, and you enjoyed every unfaithful minute of it!"

Tierney took his teasing seriously, and once seated back in the landau, she began to weep quietly. They were early for midnight mass, but as the vehicle drew close to the great cathedral, the choir's rehearsal drifted to them through the foggy air.

André, believing Tierney lost in reminiscing her first waltz, turned at last to comment on the distant singing. His throat tightened when he saw the tears glistening her lashes and trickling down her face. Fearing again that Tierney's thoughts were back to the child conceived during the yuletide, he swept her into his arms.

"Darling," he urged, "please try to be happy."

"I was happy," she commiserated, "until I realized you were right! I was cheeky tonight with all those men. I . . . I don't know what came over me!" she stammered. "André, I cannot blame you if you won't forgive me! You called me unfaithful, and I have been. Not with Oswatchee . . . that was not my fault. But tonight, I was flirting!"

André laughed aloud, relief flooding him. Tierney sat back at once, gaping at him in bewilderment.

"Aren't you angry?" she sputtered.

"No, of course not! Darling, if men fall at your feet I

cannot blame them. But I am not angry. I rather enjoyed watching you spin about."

"But you have not said a word to me since we left there!" she accused.

André, still chuckling, leaned forward and ordered the coachman to drive the square until the cathedral doors were swung open. Settling back in the seat, he studied his future wife with obvious amusement. She delighted him. With her constant change of temperament, she rivaled the seas in variety.

Now she was pouting and this too was a facet of her personality hitherto undetected. She was as enchanting a girl as he had ever met.

"Why the scowl?" he chided. "Have I offended you?"

In exasperation, Tierney threw up her hands. "You're the very devil to figure, André de Montfort! I thought you were jealous . . . I wanted you to be pea green with jealousy," she sulked.

"Then your crying just now, that was just play-acting?" he asked incredulously.

"Yes," she said after a moment's hesitation. She could not resist asking, "How was I?"

"A fine performance, Miss Chambers!" he exclaimed, still not sure whether or not she was serious. "And you do not feel guilty or unfaithful?" he prodded.

Her answer was quick and tart. "Certainly not. Why should I, for heaven's sake!"

Mass was glorious with the candles brightening every corner, and the altar splendidly arrayed in gold and white. André escorted Tierney up the aisle to take the Eucharist, although he himself did not take the sacrament. It had been eight years since his last visit to church, and although he was by no means a devout man, Captain de Montfort was enough a Catholic to decline communion if not certainly in a state of grace.

Walking Tierney down the center of the high-domed building led his thoughts to the other sacrament he was about to undertake very soon, Holy Matrimony. For reasons unknown, he decided he would make his penance within the next few days.

The cathedral was filled with Christmas worshipers, and

it was so crowded that he was privately grateful that they were detained by acquaintances after the service had ended. Over a resounding chorus of *"Venite Adoremus,"* Tierney espied her old antagonist, Amanda. Amanda, she excitedly whispered, had left the convent and was now married to Mr. Charles Bolier, also an acquaintance although she did not explain how she knew him.

After mass, the two young women happily embraced. "Something tantamount to a miracle must have changed these two," he mused silently. "They used to have their claws bared." The newlyweds were well-matched, he thought: she, talkative and reedy-voiced; he, pudgy and quiet as a dormouse.

Madame Deneuve hailed André just as he lifted Tierney into the carriage. The elderly woman was certainly vivacious, despite her use of a silver-tipped cane.

"Well, hello, young man! I had heard you were in New Orleans," she called gaily. When André returned the greeting, he mumbled to Tierney. *"Je regrette, chérie.* But there is someone here you would enjoy meeting. Will you step down again?"

After the introductions, Madame Deneuve expressed her relief at having finally met the lovely Miss Chambers. "You told me about her last year, Captain! Surely you remember. And then poor Charles, he was quite smitten with you, my dear," she gently chided. Then pointedly looking at André from head to foot, she chucked Tierney's chin and to both young people's amazement, winked. "You did the right thing, my dear. Captain de Montfort is by far the better catch . . ."

After nearly rolling with laughter in the privacy of the coach for several minutes, Tierney and André recovered themselves. But the brief lapse into hilarity was like a good tonic. They had only laughed together like that a few times before, and those times seemed long ago.

Presently, however, each sobered and allowed the long evening to steal over them. There was much to think about, do together, and still say to one another. As yet, they had consciously avoided uncomfortable things. Now, each privately considered their most unforgettable problem, Rosalie Noel.

Did she live? Where? How would they go about finding her? Would she, once found, suffer for her parents' scandalous behavior and her own illegitimate birth? These questions and more crackled like gunfire in each one's mind, and yet, they could not speak of these things.

Not tonight . . .

CHAPTER TWENTY-FOUR

The banns had been posted the day after Christmas, but discreetly, in the vestibule of the cathedral and in the convent chapel where the wedding was to be held. It was believed best, by all concerned except Tierney, that publishing them more widely would be inappropriate.

"But I am proud to be marrying him!" stammered the bride, looking beseechingly at Mother Superior and then Sister Mercedes. Both remained stalwart.

"Yes, dear. And you should be. Captain de Montfort is a wonderful, caring man. Any young girl would be esteemed. But," Mother Superior asserted, "there are unusual circumstances here, and well you know it!"

It was the first and only time Tierney ever saw the nun blush. The faint coloring beneath the coif made Tierney remorseful. She had certainly embarrassed enough people already: Dear Paul Mauriac for having beguiled him in the first place; the Reddings, for having told them that ridiculous story about her husband impressed by the British; and now these good-hearted sisters—she had unwittingly put them in a preposterous position as well.

So Tierney Chambers had meekly yielded once again to common sense and the judgment of others.

The ceremony was a quiet one in the chapel at four o'clock in the afternoon, and what an unlikely gathering it was too!

Now, sitting in the townhouse that André had procured as their temporary home, Tierney blinked into the crackling fire. She sipped wistfully at her cordial, feeling oddly at rest and restless all in the same breath.

The little chapel had had a marvelous air of quietude this afternoon. There were the seasonal crimson and white poinsettias at the simple altar, and every candle glowed peacefully, a few flickering near the robust Irish priest.

Bemused, Tierney leaned into the velvet high-backed chair and smiled. It was a rare occasion, to be certain.

The austere and propitious Ursulines gathered in the front pews poised as in vespers, and at the back stood the shuffling and ill-at-ease merchant seamen from *La Reine de la Mer*, the former to mistily watch their darling girl take sacred vows, and the latter to witness their admired sea captain take his fatal dive. The wedding brought together one of the most ill-matched gatherings the convent would ever see.

Father Donavan too had been an intrinsic part of the montage of personalities present, his brogue thick with the emotions of trust in the Almighty and of gratitude that the two were finally bound in wedlock. In his considered opinion, the young couple before him would require continued benign intercession.

The captain, dressed in highly polished boots and finely woven dark blue wool with a white polished cravat, looked magnificent. He took his vows as though swearing his allegiance, his voice filling every nook of the tiny arched room. His tone was decisive, determined, and infinitely self-assured.

Tierney, on the other hand, had temporarily lost her spunk, her voice trembling and hands visibly shaking. Father Donavan had never seen a woman look quite so lovely, despite her nervousness. She had worn a satin gown of delicate blue, "powder blue" introduced only recently in the French courts. The afternoon sunlight had filtered through the chapel's solitary stained-glass window high above the altar, and it spread an ethereal glow upon Tierney's face, hair, and gown. The gold light played upon her head, making the hair nearly flame beneath the modest lace mantilla. The gold melted to rose as it enlightened her face. Her high forehead fairly radiated, her eyes shone holly green and her long lashes sparkled gilt amid the thick dark of brow and lash.

Father Donavan had caught his breath when she uttered her solemn vows, for he startled at a sudden, even more pronounced radiance when she swore before God and man, "till death do us part." Had he been a more superstitious man, he would have thought he had seen an aura, a halo, about Tierney's head.

But Tierney, still staring into the fire and absently

stroking Taffey's head as he lay draped across her lap, was not privy to the priest's impressions of the wedding. She was absorbed in her own.

André, she knew, had been fully aware of his commitment today. He would love and honor her "forever and always," as he had resonantly added to the ceremonial vows himself. What a marvel he was! Sometimes Tierney believed that André felt things more deeply than she, but in time she hoped she would understand the man as well as she understood herself.

At this, she paused. How well did she know herself? She felt as though most of her life had raced beneath her feet and high above her head, as the world spins of no personal volition and the skies are ever out of reach. Her first sense of self-determination had accompanied her to Southwell. All before that had simply happened. Even her cabin boy stratagem had seemed to sweep her along, impetuosity—not her own reasoning—ruling the game.

Since the birth of her daughter, however, she had grown substantially assertive, and stubbornness now was more resolute and less impulsive. So what was to happen now, as Madame de Montfort? She would love him, surely; honor him, always; but obey? That was not a promise forthrightly given, for in the depths of her soul, Tierney knew that if obeying André was to forfeit finding Rosalie Noel, she would resign herself to disobedience. As Tierney dreamt before the fire, therefore, she knew from the outset that her vows might be broken or, at the very least, marred.

"How very beautiful you are!" André said, returning to the parlor.

Gingerly picking up the sleeping spaniel, he added, "And you, Lord Taffey, may feel quite beautiful, but you spoil my view." The dog gave his master a doleful look and crept beneath Tierney's chair.

Making to pull a heavily padded leather chair and ottoman next to her, André asked, "Shall I join you, *ma petite*? Or shall we retire? The evening grows late."

A familiar warmth spread up Tierney's spine. She had been thinking on it for days—their marital union so long postponed. It had been over a year since she had felt the passion, the glory, the total surrender of being with him as one. She smiled hesitantly and longingly glanced back to the embers still glowing. "I am tired, I think," she demurred. "Shall we go upstairs, *monsieur*?"

"*Oui, madame*," he responded quietly. André had not known what to expect on this, their first night as man and wife. The girl with diminutive breasts and eager slim hips was an eternity removed from the introspective woman before him now.

"Shall I dismiss Annette or would you like to go ahead of me and have her help you undress?" André had adamantly refused the purchase of slaves, despite his neighbors' protestations. And Tierney, having experienced the reality of it herself, was in enthusiastic agreement. The de Montforts had a modest number of paid servants: a housekeeper, butler, cook, and two housemaids. The coachmen and stable boy lived in back of the house, above the livery. Except for the hostlers and housekeeper, Mrs. de Mateo, the servants had homes of their own.

"Do let Annette go home," she replied. "I believe you once said yourself that a discriminating man can best see to a lady's needs."

Some of André's carefully laid plans had gone awry. The weather was foul, for one thing—raining and cold. That, in turn, had canceled his retaining musicians for the courtyard below. Only a beast would have insisted the men remain to play, so he had paid them half of what he had originally offered, promising the rest when an occasion would warrant their return.

The remainder of his plans—at least those he could remember now as overwhelming excitement surged through him—were working out well. The wine was chilled, he had bathed with Tierney in a magnificent sunken tub adjacent to their bedroom, and now she lay enticingly before him, a sheer, beige gown all that stood between him and the realization of all he had been anticipating.

He held a check on himself, however, preferring to increase her somewhat reticent passion and to agonizingly heighten his own. He poured the fragrant champagne into two stemmed crystals and approached her. She sat up, the cut of negligee exposing one firm breast almost entirely, and accepted the glass he offered. "Shall we toast?" she giggled nervously.

"To our infinite joy, tonight and always," he said. As

Tierney sipped the champagne, André glanced at an un-
obtrusive box which lay on the floor beside their bed. It
was filled with aromatic oils: sandalwood, jasmine, musk,
damask, myrcia, and myrrh.

"Do you remember, *ma petite,* when I massaged your
battered little person the night of the gale on the Atlantic?"
he began hoarsely. "Do you remember the scent of cloves,
and how good that made you feel?"

"Yes," she purred. "It felt very good. Indecent"—she
smiled impishly—"but very good." Her eyes were wide
in expectancy, unconsciously fluttering now and then in
response to her quickening pulse.

"Darling, since you found it so, ah, soothing," he continued, "I have decided to make you feel that way again.
Tonight."

Tierney closed her eyes altogether, and would have
spilled her champagne had not her husband deftly put
it on the bedstand. She nearly giggled again, not from
nervousness, but in relief. Her stay with the nuns, albeit
brief, had inhibited to a large extent her own willful nature. Now, however, she could take heart in the fact that
she was married, and whatever marital bliss lay ahead
was sanctioned. It was the first time Tierney had considered one of the primary advantages of matrimony—sex
without guilt or shame.

An inkling of darkness sent evil wisps, ghostlike,
through her otherwise happy thoughts. Oswatchee had
been willful too, and lusty, and—abominable. She would
not think of him, of that! No, she would not . . .

When she opened her eyes again, she found André fully
undressed at the foot of the bed. He had dimmed every
lamp, and only one long-tapered candle burned at the bedside, casting its soft light on the white silk canopy above.
"Yes," she whispered in a barely audible voice, "I would
be pleased. Honored. I have longed for your touch,
André."

She did not protest when he wordlessly, tenderly, lifted
her and removed the sheer nightgown. He lay her down
again, and opened a small vial. He poured the candescent
oil into his palm and the sensuous fragrance filled the
still air.

If his hands were weather-worn and leathery, his touch
was not. He smoothed the oil over her feet, ankles and

calves, unhurriedly caressing each inch of her flesh. By the time he reached her thighs, Tierney was already unconsciously squirming beneath him.

André knew women, and to what they best responded. He teasingly, but lovingly, moved his hands away from her legs to her soft, supple stomach. Tierney's eyes flew open in surprise. He had seemingly overlooked her most anxious parts. She was too embarrassed, however, to remind him.

André ruefully told himself that he deserved an award for his patience and restraint. But he was intent upon bringing his new bride to the heights of sensual awareness, and nothing—not even his own pulsating demands—would interfere with that purpose or hasten its arrival. He had waited this long . . .

Now, as he nimbly applied the intoxicating scent to her hard brown nipples, alabaster breasts and throat, he felt he might surrender to his own needs. He was almost in pain.

What André could not realize, and would never understand, was that the mind and body of the woman beneath him were raging against one another. Her body, taut with excitement and thrilling to his every movement, was causing her considerable consternation.

Was this how she would always feel? The delicious physical sensation blotting out all memory, all other desires? Some things were more important than marital pleasure, of greater value altogether. Tierney's body writhed in expectation, her throat groaned for release, and yet her mind battled for attention. The Indians, the camp, Rosalie Noel alone in their pagan ways . . .

André could not sense her turmoil. He could only feel her and hear her, and he was no longer able to quell his own nature. He fell upon her, fiercely kissing for her response. He had stopped battling himself, and now demanded his wife reciprocate. His searching tongue commanded it.

An ugly vision spread before Tierney's tightly closed eyes. He was standing above her, his reddish brown skin oddly contrasting the drizzling sky above. She opened her mouth to scream, but he tried to force himself upon her. . . .

To Tierney's horror and André's profound embarrassment, she gagged as though to vomit.

He sat up immediately, too stupefied to speak. *Mon Dieu*, he had merely been kissing her! What on earth . . . ?

Tierney lay weeping brokenly, her back now turned to him. She had not retched really, but her own embarrassment was enormous. "Oh, André!" she cried. "I have spoiled everything! I am sorry, my love . . . my dear, dear love. How could I let myself think such gruesome, such hideous, such vile, unspeakable things! Dear Lord in heaven, what is wrong with me?" Her oil-glistening body lay crouched as in fear, and sobs racked her slender frame from head to foot. Her lustrous long hair covered her face and scattered across the pillow, its wild disorder seeming to reflect Tierney's tumultuous thoughts.

André was moved to a pity so overwhelming that his own frustration vanished. He was now concerned only for Tierney. "My wife," he thought incredulously. "My lovely young wife can never forget."

He reached over and brushed the hair away from her face. "Tierney, love. *Chérie.* Don't apologize. Don't. You've spoiled nothing, *ma petite*. Come now, come here, into my arms! You have nothing to fear, nothing . . ."

The cathedral bells tolled midnight and each ring punctuated the rhythmic sounds of rain against windows in the French quarter. André rocked her gently, in much the same way he had the night of her nightmares of fire aboard his ship. Her tears subsided and he ceased his sweet lullabies he had been singing to her.

At his urging, Tierney had finally been able to put into words her two terrifying episodes with Oswatchee. The bastard had come very close to ruining forever a normal relationship between Tierney and André as man and wife. He could well understand the girl's sudden remembrance of sadism.

André sighed. The incident had most definitely smashed André's hopes of ever introducing his wife to the more subtle nuances of eroticism. Those experiences lay behind him now, and hopefully he would limit memories of such intense delight to occasional dreams of his past worldly adventures. There was another thought, however . . .

"Well, darling," he gently chided, "we have the rest

of our lives to make love. The marriage will not be the less if we forego consummating our vows tonight."

"But that is unheard of!" she argued, her innate stubbornness back in her voice. "You are my husband now, André, and naturally, you must . . ."

"Oh, but I mustn't," he chuckled. "I do not want to hurt you, or frighten you, or force you, or sicken you again. Not ever again, Tierney," he added soberly. "No one will hurt you. I swear it."

Tierney gazed into his eyes steadily. He was absolutely sincere, and she breathed his breath, content merely with the closeness of him.

"But I do demand a kiss, Madame de Montfort. You are my wife, and as such, I'll take no argument from you," he stated with mock severity.

"Of course, milord!" she giggled, all thoughts of Oswatchee fading. Tierney tentatively pressed her lips to his, and was puzzled when he drew away from her.

"I shan't kiss you on your sweet mouth again tonight, *petite*," he said determinedly, now putting her back down against the pillows and snuffing the candle.

"But I don't know what you mean," she laughed. Tierney was puzzled by his current teasing.

"You'll know soon enough, madame," he whispered as he moved next to her under the covers. "And remember what I said . . . no argument."

And so, Tierney on her wedding night was led to a glorious new plane of experience; unexpected, and so twice more enjoyed. Her ecstasy was exceeded only by André's own.

To the man's welcomed surprise, he too was surfeited with arousal and climactic release: her softness, her scent, her dreamy submissiveness, combined with his sensitivity in a near-perfect union.

Part 3

A TIME OF DETERMINATION

CHAPTER TWENTY-FIVE

The rain seemed interminable. It was already late March, and as Tierney blankly stared outside into the grayness, her nerves grew taut as bowstrings. The baby would be seven months old next week, and still there was no sign, no word of Rosalie Noel. She fought her mounting despair with rising temper.

"It's inconceivable to me that the whole of this nation's navy is a mere sixteen ships!" André declared. It was his considered opinion that with a war waged against a nation an ocean away it was bald-faced lunacy not to have amassed a larger fleet.

"I agree with you, of course, André, but this is a young country. There aren't the resources here for the much-needed naval power. And you must admit that what men and fleet they do have are among the finest. Look at Chauncey, Perry, Porter . . . any of them! These are able men. The Americans make maximum use of their little gunboats, as well, not rated with the fleet of sixteen vessels," Paul remarked.

They had discussed it so often of late that Tierney had lost all interest in their talk of war. Paul, in particular, was becoming a nuisance. He seemed to be present whenever André managed to be home. And the talk was less and less about recovering the baby. The war, it seemed, was all that mattered to all of Louisiana, all of this stupid country!

"Over five-hundred privateers are already involved in the effort, Paul. And many of those are only valuable for coastal defense or as ship runners. Why, my *Reine*, ah, she's worthy of much more with her speed and tonnage— to say nothing of her rating since refitting her in Nantes."

"But you risk so much, André! And to what end? You sold your other vessels while we were there. Except for these few riverboats, steamboats—whatever the devil you call them—you have only *La Reine* left. Pah! You must see the foolishness of surrendering her to the Americans."

Tierney slowly withdrew from the window. The French quarter, which was not French at all, but Spanish in design, according to André, was spattered with the seasonal mud. A foolhardy coachman was bogged in the mire on the street below, beating the poor animals as if they themselves had chosen the muddy route to travel. Tierney shuddered as she turned away. She wondered what the floor of an Indian hut was like in this kind of weather.

"I have no intention of surrendering her to anyone," André was arguing. "But if I am to even maintain my worth, I will have to start running some of these damned blockades. And why not gain my letter of marque or a naval commission to boot? I tell you, man, if the United States is to succeed in this madness, it will take hundreds more ships and men like—"

"Like you, André?" Tierney's quiet interruption startled them. The men had quite forgotten that she was still in the room. They both looked at her now and simultaneously noticed how thin she had grown again; the dark smudges under her eyes gave her a sickly, almost sepulchral, pallor.

"Darling, do come join us here. Sit with me, Tierney." André attempted one of his most persuasive smiles. "You'll wear a path on the carpet if you don't light somewhere," he gently teased. He had brought the Turkish carpet from the ship and put it here in the library for her.

Tierney was unmoved. She had not focused on his smile or even listened to the loving tone in his voice. Her own voice was quiet, but it hissed unbecomingly. "Why, André, what a noble man you are. To think on it! A man without a country volunteering his skill, his prowess to the most patriotic of all causes—a war. A war whose cause, incidentally, no one has been able to adequately explain to me! But do go, beloved. By all means, do go! For God and country!"

André was already on his feet, angrily crossing the room to where she stood rigidly clasping her hands to the back of a chair, her knuckles white with strain. "That is quite enough of your empty prattle, Tierney. You may be excused!"

"Oh, dear. Have I said something offensive? Why, I did not intend it so. I simply meant to comment on your valor. Certainly it takes greater courage to face the Royal Navy than a band of thieving savages. By far, milord," she whined sweetly.

"Enough, I said! Take your leave, woman, before I . . ." His shouting was cut short by her throaty response.

"Before you do what, André? Strike me? I assure you, *monsieur*, that I would not even feel it. And if I did, pray God, it would at least affirm to me that I am still alive!" Her eyes flickered cruelly. "Have you noticed, milord? I'm quite the corpse beneath the sheets of late . . ."

He shook her roughly, swearing vehemently in his own language. Pulling her to the side of the chair, he shoved her over the arm and pinned her into it. They stared at one another, their angry breathing the only break of silence. Paul Mauriac had taken his leave without notice, and they could now hear his harried orders to Pedro, the stable boy.

André abruptly released his grip on Tierney's arms, and walked stiffly toward the marble-topped mahogany cabinet at the far end of the room. "Care to join me?" he asked rigidly, pouring a liberal glass of brandy.

Tierney, who had nuzzled her burning cheek into the cool corner of the wing-backed chair, murmured her assent.

"Sherry?" he offered.

"Brandy."

When she raised her head to sip the fiery intoxicant, she looked vacantly over his shoulder.

"Look at me, damn you!"

She did. His blue eyes were as dark as thunderclouds, and she hurriedly wished he would drink himself into a stupor.

"I will not tolerate your insolence, Tierney," he began quietly. "Nor are you to ever again address me so brashly before a guest."

"A guest?" she interrupted, an ugly smirk crossing her face. "Paul, a guest? Why, I thought he was a member of the family."

"Enough, I say!" Secretly, André was pleased by this

particular turn in conversation. "Do his frequent visits annoy you, then?"

Unthinkingly, Tierney replied, "I am sick of the very sight of Paul Mauriac!" She did not notice that as her husband turned to look toward the fire, he looked relieved.

"Well, then," he drily commented after a moment, bringing his chair to face her, "I'll see to it that he doesn't stop by so often. Nonetheless, do not treat me so insultingly again. Not in the presence of others—not when we are alone."

Tierney promised herself that she would become more careful in the future. She could push her husband only so far.

The brandy had stopped burning, and now smoothly slid over her tongue in short, rapid sips. She unceremoniously swung her legs over the arm of the chair and curled herself comfortably with her legs tucked underneath her. In response, André pulled off his boots and stretched his legs across to rest on Tierney's chair, his stockinged feet on the cushion by her hip.

They were thus arranged when Mrs. de Mateo appeared in the entrance. The housekeeper was a middle-aged widow, overpaid for her work, and so she did not carry gossip. But she was enough of a romantic to appreciate being in the home of newlyweds, and in fact, was vicariously aroused by glimpses of intimacy such as she now espied. They seemed such a devoted couple, in spite of their little spats. Mrs. de Mateo coughed demurely to announce her arrival.

Tierney immediately made to sit up and gather some semblance of decorum, but André rudely pressed his foot against her thighs to detain her. Rather than struggle so obviously, she chose to stay put and suffer the embarrassment.

"Tea, madame?" The housekeeper's voice throbbed heavily with a Spanish accent, and Tierney was struck anew with the odd mixture of her surroundings here in New Orleans.

"Yes, please. A light tea. We will take it in here, señora. Oh, and please include some of those delectable little candies I brought home yesterday."

"Candy?" he asked after Mrs. de Mateo was gone. "I didn't realize you had such a fondness for sweets."

"I don't really," Tierney shrugged. "Didn't I tell you about that funny little man?" Her face brightened a bit, so André encouraged her.

"No, *chérie*. You told me that you and Annette went shopping yesterday, but not where you went nor whom you met. Who is this funny little man?"

"I don't know." It was so typical of Tierney to bring up a subject and then lead it to a seemingly blank end that André could not suppress a laugh. She put down her wineglass and drummed her fingertips irritably. "Well, what I mean is that I do not know the man's real name. People call him the Chevalier."

"I have heard of him. Is he as odd as they say?" The man was one of the diehard French, an *emigré*, who lived to prepare impotent rebellions for a return to French rule. After more than a decade of their futile efforts, the rebels were fast becoming a thing of the past. The Chevalier, however, clung to his old world dreams, and was the subject of friendly gossip.

Tierney sat upright and leaned forward eagerly. At times, she struck a chord in her husband's heart that was bittersweet with pain. Now was just such an occasion, her face enlivened and childlike. "Oh, yes! Yes, he is very odd, Captain," she rambled on, oblivious to the slip in address. "He looks as though he stepped right out of the last century. He wears a powdered wig and—what is this?" she asked quickly, grasping her hair back behind her neck.

"Queue?"

"That is it! Queue. He wears one. And long silk stockings and knee breeches, and a very lacy shirtfront and high-heeled slippers with silver buckles. Can you imagine that, André?"

"No!" he laughed with mock surprise. Tierney may have been too young, but de Montfort remembered well the style so popular during his youth.

"But that's not all. Believe it or not, he carries a real live monkey around on his back. Truly! And a dog—not nearly so handsome as Taffey—follows his heels all day," she added rather weakly. The monkey, after all, was the crux of the Chevalier's absurdities.

"Well?" he teased.

She looked at him blankly for several seconds. "Oh, of

course. The candy! I was getting to that," she asserted.
"He runs a little sweetmeat shop on Chartres Street near
Dumaine. Cakes of all description, but these candies . . .
Well, you'll just have to eat one. He calls them 'pralines,'
and Annette says they are becoming quite popular here.
But the Chevalier has said he will never disclose the
recipe, not even on his deathbed!" she ended dramatically.

The teacart rattled as it was rolled from the dining room
toward the library. André reluctantly put his boots back
on, and stood to stretch. He smiled. "These pralines of
yours are delicious, I am sure, *ma petite.*"

The rain had stopped, and a beautiful sunset etched
rays across the multicolored carpet as the little mulatto
maid cleared the cart away. Her name was Suzette, and
she was the product of a third generation of *gens de
couleur librés,* free colored. Suzette's birth and baptismal
records, her marriage certificate when she chose to marry,
would be designated f.w.c.—free woman of color.

The *Code Noir,* or Black Code as it was becoming
known, had been written almost a hundred years before.
Although it firmly regulated the practice of slavery, it
was liberal in that it provided for the protection of freemen. Suzette, and others like her, would never have to
worry about being enslaved again nor would her progeny
unless she broke the law by marrying a slave herself.
The Black Code was the most progressive document of
its kind.

Tierney, upon first learning of the two-sided *Code Noir,*
had asked what protection it would afford Big Jeb if, in
fact, he were ever able to escape the Creeks with his
wife, Dawn. "Unfortunately, sweetheart, Jeb would still
be considered a runaway slave, not properly freed. He'd
be put on the auction block or returned to his former
master if caught." When she asked what would happen
to Dawn in that event, André had shrugged. "She would
not be sold as a slave, to be sure. But neither would anyone hire her. A deaf-mute is of little value."

Presently, with Suzette gone as quietly as she had
come, Tierney inquired after his opinion of the pralines.

"Too sweet for my palate," he answered distractedly.

André subscribed to both newspapers—*The Louisiana*

Gazette for news of the war, and *Le Moniteur de la Louisiane* for business notices and bills of lading. He suddenly dropped the French newspaper and commented, "Drinking water is going up to fifty cents a hogshead. I wish this city could arrange a more suitable delivery system. I don't mind the expense so much, but buying our water from the back of a wagon is a damned nuisance!"

"How much does fifty cents come to?" she asked, not realizing how silly her question sounded. Figuring the price on the hogshead was too complex for her.

André answered her patiently. "Water, *ma chérie*, now costs more than a penny per bucket. Almost two cents."

Tierney was too shocked to reply. Although she was wealthy beyond her wildest imagination, she had not forgotten her brief poverty in London. Tuppence for a bucket of water was criminal. They had to buy water not only for drinking, but washing, as well. The courtyard well water was not potable, and that which was bought still had to be filtered through pourous stone or purified with charcoal or lime. She wondered glumly why the Spaniards had built all these New Orleans wells in the first place. None was of any use, André told her.

She unconsciously began wondering how much more water they would require for all the baby's napkins, once Rosalie Noel came home. Tierney refused to believe that she was gone forever. Somehow, sometime, their baby would be safe and sound with her own parents. She barely heard André describe the story he had just read in the Gazette.

"He bought the vessel in Paris, and after refitting her, christened her the *True-Blooded Yankee*. *Mon Dieu*, what a good name. In any case, he sailed out of Paris a year ago this week, and proceeded to carry out a month-long tirade along the coasts of Scotland and Ireland. Took twenty-seven British vessels as prizes!" André gave a low whistle. "If nothing else, these American privateers are costing Your Majesty a small fortune in trade."

"I don't care," she sighed. "He isn't my king anymore. And I don't care about the rest, either."

André looked up from his reading and searched her face. Tierney met his gaze steadily, and at length managed to say, "Go, André. I did mean that earlier. Take

your *Reine* and do what you will in this war. I truly do
not care."

"Let's talk about it," he said.

Well past supper, the couple retired to their bedroom.
Mrs. de Mateo had been given the night off, and decided
to spend it with her younger sister and her five children.
André and Tierney were alone.

They reached what amounted to a disappointing com-
promise, at least for André. It was his own suggestion,
however, and he could hardly hold his wife responsible.
La Reine de la Mer would sail again, and this time under
the American stars and stripes. But she would be captained
by Paul Mauriac. Pelier would remain in his present ca-
pacity or promoted to first mate, depending upon the
new captain's wish. If Paul did want to recruit another
first mate, it would not prove difficult. New Orleans now
had an estimated twenty-thousand permanent residents,
and the transient population of traders, rivermen, and
sailors often more than doubled that number.

André resolved to stay in Louisiana. He might travel
the sixty miles from New Orleans to the open Gulf and
see the crew off on its first transoceanic voyage without
him, but that was all. Knowing he would remain at home,
Tierney enthusiastically agreed to her husband's plans to
volunteer his services to the militia or naval station here.

In the meantime, he would continue to build his newly
founded business, de Montfort Shipping, Ltd. To date, he
had not been able to procure any new fully rigged ships.
The war had temporarily precluded reasonable prices, and
André, although eager for more ships, was not fool
enough to pay twice their value. The line, therefore, consisted only of four river barges, six keelboats, seven flat-
boats, two steam passenger ferries, and one pirogue for
personal use.

He had turned a handsome deal, spending only seven
thousand dollars for the lot of it, not including the steam
engines. These, he knew, were a waste of money and effort.
Finding experienced rivermen to navigate them was a
nuisance, and engine repairs were slow and costly. But
de Montfort was confident that in the near future, these
steam-powered vessels would become his most profitable
venture.

Until that time, he could take some measure of pride in the flats and keelboats. His first purchase, in particular, was rewarding. *Lucy Girl,* a sixty-eight foot keelboat, carried up to seventy tons. Fully loaded, she was expected to make the trip from New Orleans to Ohio Falls near Louisville in just fourteen weeks. Even for spring, it was remarkable time. Her captain, Jake Reilly, was a big, beefy, second-generation American of Irish descent. He had a fierce temper. Jake wore the heavy spiked brogans, so popular with men of the river, and sported a red turkey feather in his coarse black hair. Although decidedly enamored of his "good old Nongela," a rye whiskey that would burn a hole in most men's guts, Jake was a good sort. On his own admission, he knew the Mississippi "like the back o' me hand," and swore its mud coursed through his veins. But the Irish, André decided, were an unpredictable lot.

Tierney was no exception. He puzzled over her now, as she lay sleeping. They rarely got into bed together anymore, for Tierney either felt overly tired and turned in before him, or complained she was restless and would not sleep at all.

Tonight, for the first time in weeks, they had come up to the room holding hands, Annette had left a steaming bath for her mistress, and it was Tierney's suggestion that if she hurried, the water would be warm enough for him to bathe also. When he came back into the bedroom, André found her already asleep.

"I ought to wake her, blast her!" he muttered as he let the towel drop at his feet. He was constantly vexed by her of late.

After their wedding night, she had warmed delightfully, and they had made love almost immediately upon waking the next morning. For a while, at least, their sexual reunion was mutually fulfilling. She never mentioned Oswatchee again, so he wondered what was at the root of her current behavior.

During the past month, Tierney had grown increasingly frigid. She never actually denied him his nuptial rights, but between her inaccessibility and total lack of response on those rare nights they did undress together, she managed to present an overwhelming problem.

The more remote she became, the more frustrated she made him. He desired her madly, and those nights when

she restlessly stayed away from the room until dawn, he
thrashed about the empty bed swearing she had cast a
spell over him. In rational moments, he knew it was
absurd, of course, but his visit to a bordello only the week
before had nearly convinced him.

He had procured a rather buxom brunette who put him
in mind of some very satisfactory London wench he had
bedded. But several days ago, the Creole beauty had not
nearly gratified him. She was very willing; indeed, decidedly adventurous. But André could not display any real
interest, and abruptly left the woman, to her disappointment and his own bewilderment. He had refused to believe
himself impotent, however, but the very idea infuriated
him, for even at sea rarely had he felt so desperate.

Now thinking on it, he burned with anger and passion
for Tierney. He paced the bedside, trying to decide what
to do. He had no desire to drink himself to sleep, and in
frustration, confusion, and sympathy for his wife, he
looked down at her. The vision of her arrival at Lafitte's
fort was permanently engraved in his memory.

In sheer resentment, André struck his fist against the
bedpost and turned to go downstairs. A dull book was
sometimes a good sleeping tonic—failing that, there was
always the cognac.

"Don't leave, *mon capitaine*."

He swung around and then stood stone still, eyeing her
in disbelief. She wore a white cambric gown gathered at
the neck and a matching nightcap bound about her curls,
but she was a vision of perfection to him. The one lamp
still burning softened the thinness of her face and her
eyes glowed becomingly. Suddenly, she giggled and fell
back against the pillows.

"Oh, André! You do make quite a sight with your legs
spread so! Are we expecting a storm at sea?" she teased.

By the time he grabbed her, she was still struggling to
untie the gown. Her hair was already down.

CHAPTER TWENTY-SIX

"What are their names? These 'agents', as you call them."
Tierney could not dispel her suspicions. She had seen
enough of Louisiana's riffraff to distrust strangers, especially supposed Indian fighters. For all she knew, one of these
men might abscond with the baby himself, demanding an
ungodly ransom that could not be met. How much that
would amount to, she could only wonder.

"Does it matter? If you must know, their names are Ike
Davies, Joe Tinder, and a young one, James Bowie. Now,
does that change anything, madame? You have not heard
of any of them, have you?" Tierney shook her head, and
he continued. "Nor had I, *ma petite*. But I have it on good
word that each is reliable."

"Whose good word?"

"Governor Claiborne, for one. He recommended Tinder. Davies was referred to me by one of the *Gazette*'s
reporters, and I met with him personally three nights in
a row at La Bourse de Maspero. He's the best according
to many there."

She was mollified. Certainly the governor would not
have recommended a recalcitrant to André. And Maspero's Exchange—or La Bourse, as the French said—was
the most well-respected coffeehouse in all of New Orleans. It was the meeting place of the town's elite writers,
politicians, and businessmen. For many years, even the
mail was delivered there.

"But what of this young one, James?"

"Bowie. He is one of Lafitte's protégés. Perhaps eighteen
years old. But very clever, I'm told, and quick as a whip."

André was lighting a cigar from a nearby lamp. "You
don't trust the Lafittes, do you, Tierney?" he asked, still
trying to get an even burn on the tip of his tobacco. To

himself, he noted that had he remembered how damnably wet this climate was, he would never have settled here.

"They are pirates, André. After all . . ." she shrugged. Jean and Pierre Lafitte, although once popular enough to be considered demigods, had fallen from grace. Their command of Barataria was felt at all levels, and even their most loyal advocates resented the cost of goods rerouted through Lafitte's hands. Merchants now complained openly and bitterly, begging relief from the government.

"Gambi and Cut Nose are pirates, most certainly. And so are many of Jean's men. But Jean Lafitte himself is a smuggler. There is a difference, *ma chérie*. I daresay some ladies in London who purchased the silks I sold to Levitz —at the very time I met you, I might add—would accuse your loving husband of being a pirate. And, 'after all,' " he mimicked, "have you forgotten that Pierre Lafitte saved your life?"

"How could I when you remind me so often!" she cried. "André, you know I barely remember him. Four days I traveled with him, you say. And all I remember is he bowed to me. Yes! A wide sweeping bow in the slave hut. I remember I wanted to laugh at him. It all seemed so preposterous! And the fire—I remember that. Trying to go back for Rosalie Noel . . . I recall nothing else," she ended weakly. "Nothing until I recognized you behind that beard."

"I should have shaved." He wanted to say more, but he could not find the words. It seemed every conversation they held started innocently enough, but ended regrettably, painfully.

Tierney sighed heavily. "Yes. You should have thought to shave, I suppose."

The three agents were retained at five thousand dollars apiece. Upon locating the child, another ten thousand would follow. At first, André worried over giving that amount to the youth, Bowie, but Lafitte had insisted on keeping all but one thousand in his strongbox at Barataria. He would return it; had no real need of it himself. But he knew his men and their weakness with money in their pockets.

The five-thousand dollar reward was also posted along

the riverfront at Tchoupitoulas Street, and in the Swamp —a six-block area that had earned for New Orleans the name "City of Sin." This was the haunt of the Mississippi's most notorious rivermen and fighters, and although many a murderous event transpired among them, these were the heartiest of upriver travelers.

As could be expected, de Montfort got many false leads from would-be collectors. He always followed them; however, he soon put a stop to the nonsense by adding to the posters that the man collecting the money would have to accompany him on the search. Then, for the most part, only the serious-minded rivermen brought him information of the baby's possible whereabouts.

Whenever André did travel on yet another futile search, he dressed as a frontiersman. He wore the buckskin breeches and boots, the rough linsey-woolsey shirts and eventually, even the coonskin hat. The Indians, it was discovered, were less wary of a backwoodsman than of a well-dressed emigré. All Tierney's pleas to accompany him were to no avail—André de Montfort was adamant about it. Her frantic clawing at the shallow grave on his first trip into the interior was too garish to ever forget.

Sometimes he would go up or down the river on one of his barges, but most often, he would travel in his light and speedy pirogue. He learned to speak a few rudimentary Indian phrases to ensure his survival, as well as to communicate with them. Joe Tinder taught him Natchez and Biloxi, but it was the old priest, Father Donavan, who instructed him in the basic words and mannerisms of the Creeks. The Kawita tribe, he was told, was the most reasonable in all the Creek Federation.

Despite this, cooperation was virtually impossible. News traveled fast these days among the many tribes, and even in the Louisiana territory, Southern Indians knew that in the Northern frontier of this white man's war, Indians were growing famous for their exploits alongside the British. It was true. In Canada the red men outnumbered the British regulars three to one, and although their support posed a supply problem for the Crown, their fighting was ferocious. Many battles were decided by the impact of Indian strength.

Tecumseh, the most gallant and widely renowned Indian leader, had been killed. Even among the Americans, his fame was fast growing to legend. To make matters worse, Tecumseh had visited the Southern tribes the year before his death, and a new ethnocentricism was developing in the natives.

The terrain was new to de Montfort, but of necessity he quickly learned the trails, campsites, and inland roads as well as he knew the river now. He was already as accomplished on horseback as he had always been on the deck of a ship. He kept his first horse, the big roan stallion he called Sire, for stud. Now he was riding an ugly but sturdier beast he simply named Animal.

Besides the exotic foliage abounding throughout lower Louisiana, there were many weird plants with peculiar properties. Two, in particular, were helpful in his travels. There was a type of grass called *semper virens,* and a drop of its juices instantly froze water. The Indians, it was said, used it widely, but André would not drink it melted or chew the ice. Rather, he applied ice chips to soothe the numerous insect bites that were a continual nuisance in this country. Even in the city, the mosquitoes and pestilence were nearly overwhelming, for open sewers along every street were their breeding grounds.

Another plant, viperine, or goat's tongue, had an even more unusual propensity. Its juices reportedly healed wounds almost immediately upon applying the sticky substance from its leaves and stalk. There was a myth about a warrior, Blood Sucker, who once in battle received four fatal wounds in the chest and stomach. It was said that the Indian stuffed viperine leaves in them—the bleeding stopped, the battle was won, and by the time the warrior returned to his home camp, the scars had vanished.

André could almost believe that folktale after having been grazed in the shoulder by a stray arrow. The viperine did stop the bleeding, and there was virtually no pain. He was forty miles west of Natchez when the arrow struck. The tracker on this particular expedition, a half-breed himself, insisted it was a Comanche flint, but the culprit was not found.

Neither was Rosalie Noel. That had been a month ago.

* * *

"I must speak to Madame de Montfort," he insisted. "It is a matter concerning her husband. *Por favor, señora.* Wake her at once!"

Mrs. de Mateo peered suspiciously around the door at the stranger. It was past eleven o'clock, and her mistress had long since retired in what the housekeeper called one of her "black Irish moods."

"*Uno momento.* Wait here." She latched the door between them, and leaned against it a moment. Why was it that a seemingly respectable couple like her employers had such peculiar callers, and at such indecent hours! She crossed herself then, and walked the one flight to Madame's room.

Tierney's heart raced as she quickly threw on a dress over her nightgown and slid her bare toes into the low-heeled slippers. She thought to grab a shawl—the nights were cool and she might have to meet André—but in her frenzy, she forgot to take off her nightcap.

When she reached the foyer, she recklessly threw open the door and commanded the messenger to step in. He was sallow-skinned and reedy, but his voice was gentle, almost apologetic. He took off his hat.

"Ike Davies, ma'am. Hate to bother you at this time of night, lady, but it's about your husband. I took a skiff downriver to hurry things up a little, give you time . . ."

"Mr. Davies," she hastily broke in, "do tell me what this is all about. André. Has he been injured?" Her voice rose unsteadily. "Has he been shot?"

"No, ma'am. He's down with the fever. Blackwater fever. Ain't rightly sure how he's doing now, but he was just starting the shakes when I hopped the skiff. Thought maybe you'd want to rustle up a doctor. He's gonna be a mighty sick man come morning. But he's strong. Strongest emigré I ever did meet! So don't worry too much, missus. Just wanted to warn you, is all."

Tierney tapped her foot furiously, lost in thought. Malaria was the devil's own doing, and the City of Dead was filled with its victims, many of whom had been strong immigrants. If only the disease were familiar to her! Old remedies used widely for a number of other maladies were reportedly useless with this swamp fever. She would find something. She must. If André were to die . . . "I mustn't even think it!" she admonished.

"Ma'am?" Davies looked exhausted. He might have been on the brink of collapse himself.

Tierney forced herself to remain calm. "What time will they bring him home?"

"Couple more hours, I expect."

"Thank you, Mr. Davies. I appreciate your bringing me advance notice. You look very tired yourself, sir. If you please, go back to my livery now and ask Rafael to come at once. The boy, Pedro, will bed your horse. You are welcome to spend the night there. Good night, Mr. Davies. And again, thank you."

When Jake Reilly carried in André, dawn was breaking through the low river mist. The doctor, a young physician recently arrived from Savannah, was already at the three-story brick town house. Tierney was dressed fully now, and when Annette arrived to the household confusion, Mrs. de Mateo retired to the third floor to rest.

He was delirious already, muttering French through clenched teeth and staring at his wife through glassy, un-recognizing eyes. They put him on the long table in the kitchen.

Dr. Friedham immediately stripped him of the linsey-woolsey, buckskins, and boots, and began fingering the man's neck, armpits, and elbows. Tierney gasped at the sight of those areas that were not sun-darkened. His flesh was tinged with blue, and his lips were nearly purple.

"Madame, I would suggest you leave now. There is nothing for you to do at the moment. I shall call you . . ."

"There is no need to call me, Doctor. I will not leave. Don't worry. I do not swoon, sir."

He glanced up at the green-eyed woman and determined there would be no point in arguing with her. He only hoped she would not become sick herself. Her stubborn expression was deceiving—she looked very pale. Perhaps anemic, he thought harriedly.

"If you insist." Looking now at the huge boatman, he asked, "When did he first complain of feeling ill?"

"The captain didn't complain at all until a little while before sunset yesterday." Reilly stroked his beard thoughtfully. "Come to think of it, Doc, he did rub his neck a lot yesterday morning. His eyes, too. Kept scrunching 'em up and shaking his head like he couldn't see right. I asked him about it, and he just said he'd been on the river too long."

"Were you in the marshlands at all?" he asked, now examining the groin and kneejoints.

"Not me. But him and that Injun fighter, Ike, was in the swamps. Last week, seems to me. I met them up Natchez way. Said they wanted me to take them as far as St. Louis. Me and ol' *Lucy Girl* was bound for Ohio Falls. Captain de Montfort don't even know we turned her around. He's gonna be powerful mad if I don't get this cargo back upstream and pronto! Think I might take my leave now, Doc?"

Suddenly, the stricken man appeared to choke and lose his breath altogether. Before the doctor could do anything, Jake grabbed André by his hair and shoved his head off the table. The patient vomited a vile black substance and fell faint, his breathing rapid and shallow. Tierney grasped his limp head, and rested it on the table once more,

Jake Reilly grinned broadly and winked at the young doctor. "Might have told you that was comin', Doc. You'd best hurry with your examination here, 'cause pretty soon he's gonna loose the other end!"

A red-faced Friedham managed, "Thank you, I know that. Didn't you say you were pressed for time?"

"Yes, sir, I did," he beamed. Turning to Tierney, he put one ham-sized hand on her shoulder. "Don't fret too much, ma'am. Your husband'll be okay. Had the Blackwater myself some years back, and I pulled through. And the captain's got a lot more to live for than I did. Yes, ma'am, that's the gospel truth."

Tierney felt oddly relieved by his few words, and when he had gone, put herself and the doctor to the test.

"Is it blackwater fever, Doctor?"

"Madame, it's too early to tell. It is a tertian ague, I am almost certain. But there are many types, and we will just have to wait. There is Continual Tertian, Bastard or Spurious Tertian, Endemic—I think that is most likely."

"How will I know which it is, and what are the various treatments?"

He looked up at her in surprise. She could be no more than eighteen, he surmised. How could a woman—and a young one, at that—retain the answers that had taken him years of study to learn himself? It was ridiculous! The

brief list of possibilities he had ticked off had been to
stifle her, not urge more interrogation. And yet, something
in her manner bespoke absolute confidence.

Before he could answer her, however, André began to
shake much more violently than before. "Let's get this
man covered."

Tierney had Annette bring her several blankets while
she busied herself in the kitchen with pots of water. If the
doctor would not require any boiled water for André, she
needed some herself. Some strongly brewed tea would be
a welcomed lift. She had not slept since the day before,
and despite the tension, she was exceedingly tired already.

Jake's predictions came true. Dr. Friedham was silently
pleased with Tierney's efficiency and emotional restraint.
Here was no wilting violet, thank God.

"They will have to be burned," he said, nodding toward
the soiled bedclothes. "They are contaminated."

"Then burn them we shall," she said, whisking them
into the courtyard beyond. When she returned, André appeared to be sleeping soundly. Without a glance toward
the young physician, she caressed his face, smoothed his
hair back, and tenderly kissed his brow. It was cold and
dry. "We must get him up to bed," she said.

"Madame de Montfort, I must tell you that that would
be unwise. Attending him here will be quite difficult
enough. There's no need for you to unnecessarily tire
yourself running stairs. I assure you, your husband does
not know the difference."

"He will, Doctor. And I won't have my husband in the
kitchen like some backdoor servant. I'll get the stable boy
to help you."

For the first time that morning, the doctor smiled. He
had a crooked, boyish grin. "I'm glad you follow my instructions to the letter, Madame. As I was saying, we
must get him up to bed."

"Speaking of instructions, Doctor, we haven't . . ."

"I know, I know," he interjected impatiently. "You
want detailed instructions of symptoms and various remedies. I haven't forgotten. Get your stable hand. I'll teach
you as we work."

At ten o'clock, André opened his eyes and recognized
Tierney. *"Mon coeur,"* he whispered. Then his teeth began

to chatter and the tremors again racked his body. The doctor explained that if there appeared any blood or sediment in his water, she was to contact him immediately.

"There may be periods when he is totally lucid, and will insist he is fully recovered. But do not permit him any solid food or allow him out of bed."

"I know, Dr. Friedham. If he is free of delirium for the next two days, he has the . . . the Quartan Ague?" He nodded, and she continued. "And then he will go back into fits on the fourth day." She repeated to him the signs of each ailment and also recited his suggested preparations for each. "I think I understand now," she finally nodded.

He bowed slightly and squeezed her hand. "I am quite certain you do, Madame de Montfort. You make a remarkable pupil."

The doctor left shortly before noon, promising to return the same evening.

Tierney left André resting in a state of oblivion. His hands twitched spasmodically, but that was all. She awakened the still-sleeping Mrs. de Mateo and ordered her to accompany Annette to the apothecary on Chartres Street. The order was complex, so she copied down Dr. Friedham's list for the pharmacist. She would keep her original notes and particular concoctions for future reference.

The two servants left, carrying the precious piece of paper. The list consisted of: emetic tartar, half ounce; rob of elder, four ounces; Peruvian bark, one ounce; licorice, one ounce; camomile flowers in powder, ten drams; extract of lesser centaury and jelliflowers powder, two drams each; salt of wormwood, four drams; and spirit of sulphur, four scruples. Tierney was determined to have all these ingredients so that, once the disease was firmly diagnosed, she would be prepared.

She would need fennel, but that posed no problem whatsoever. She cultivated the fragrant herb for calmative teas and used the fleshy stalks to brush her teeth. The seeds, too, she used in one of her grandmother's cookie recipes.

Tierney also had the needed epsom salts, and the fennel and lemon syrup he had recommended she could prepare while the two maids were gone. Suzette, the diminutive mulatto, would scour the kitchen and prepare the water-gruel fattened with butter.

The day was unbearably hot and Tierney was finally reduced to wearing only her shift as she administered to her husband on the second floor. Fortunately, their bedroom opened on the courtyard—or patio, as it was popularly called—and she was spared the further stench of the street gutters at the front of the house. After each spell, always more violent than the last, Tierney would sponge-bathe André from head to foot and carefully cover his body in new sheets and blankets. Despite the oppressive heat, the helpless man appeared to be freezing.

Twice she had to send Annette to the marketplace for more bedding, and finally she was compelled to beg assistance from the commander of the naval station, Daniel T. Patterson. Within three hours of her message, a wagon carrying twenty new blankets and even more linen arrived from naval supply. She did not question the navy's generosity, but made a mental note to someday properly repay them.

Her greatest dilemma was in delaying any treatments until the type of fever he suffered was made evident. The doctor had warned her that blackwater fever was local jargon for a number of agues, and administering the wrong medication in haste might do more harm than good. Nonetheless, Tierney intuitively spooned him the fennel water and bark tea after each bout. She knew he could lose only so much body fluid before he would die anyway.

When Dr. Friedham came back that night, she had bathed herself, put on a fresh muslin dress, and quickly downed more tea and a cup of custard before his arrival.

The doctor openly admired her day's nursing. The patient was still delirious and intermittently racked with chills, but the disease had not degenerated him further. His pulse, though spasmodic at times, was quite strong, and for the most part, his breathing was more regular than it had been that morning.

In the sickroom, the aromatic fennel water at his bedstand was sweet-smelling. At his inquiry, Tierney explained to the doctor that she was now sending the bedclothes away to be burned, and the bricked courtyard had since been swept and scrubbed.

"But didn't your hostler object to carrying the soiled linens himself?" he asked doubtfully.

"Oh, yes. Rafael played quite the high and mighty at first." She saw his raised eyebrows and finished. "I told him either he cleared away what I said, when I said, and how I said . . . or he could clear himself out within the quarter hour!"

The young man could not suppress a laugh, but Tierney's eyes flickered dangerously. She was still furious with Rafael.

"I suspect it is the tertiary form. We should know tomorrow if the febrile—fever—takes over. In the meantime, it is most fortunate that the urine has remained clear."

After he left, Dr. Friedham had a fleeting hope that his patient would die. He was a bachelor himself, and could use a wife and helpmate like Tierney de Montfort. But this was a momentary lapse, and he shrugged off the unholy thought.

It had been a very long day, and he was tired.

The house was quiet. Annette had kindly volunteered to stay in the spare apartment next to Mrs. de Mateo upstairs. But everyone had long since retired for the night.

Tierney was exhausted, but restless. She walked aimlessly around the room, wishing that someone other than herself, someone more capable, could attend to André. Paul Mauriac would know what to do, if he were here. In the current stillness of the late hour, she felt her self-confidence slipping.

La Reine was en route to France again. Europe was suffused with a new eagerness for American trade. If all went well, the ship would be back in New Orleans in late September, and that now seemed an eternity away. Before he fell ill, André was always checking the newspapers for any word of his ship encountering British blockades.

Well, she thought, perhaps Paul's absence was the will of divine Providence. She stopped her idle pacing and pulled the *prie-dieu* to the bedside. She fingered the pearl rosary strand that André had bought for her in Charleston her first night in America.

Was it really possible that so much had happened to her, to André, to them, in so little time? She felt as though

she had already lived a lifetime, and it seemed to her
that time grew shorter, more precious with every passing
day.

"In the name of the Father, and of the Son, and of the
Holy Ghost . . ." Before the first prayer was directed to
Our Lady of Sorrows, Tierney slumped forward on her
folded arms. She slept on her knees until the cries of the
first morning's birds.

CHAPTER TWENTY-SEVEN

Within two weeks André recovered.

The fever had once gone as high as one hundred and five, and Dr. Friedham had worried over permanent damage to his nervous system, but when the fever broke and the profuse sweating began, the patient made a determined effort to recuperate fully. His appetite was exceedingly poor so that every mouthful of food required tremendous willpower. Tierney had lost even more weight herself and to her husband, she looked pathetically thin.

He insisted that she take her meals with him during his convalescence, and he persuaded her to build an appetite as well. She also napped with him, and during the cool evenings, the couple snuggled together and discovered a new kind of peace and unity.

Now was just such a time.

"I love you," she said simply.

"Ah, *ma chérie,*" he sighed, pushing the long coppery tendrils of hair from her face. He traced her brow and nose, and lightly continued his fingertips across her lips and down to her throat. Her skin went gooseflesh and her nipples puckered appreciably. "You are more than my love, *mon cœur.* I feel you are my very life!" He rolled over suddenly and swept her into a passionate embrace. His intense, unexpected desire for Tierney might have conquered his lingering weakness, but she pushed him back.

"André, you aren't well enough yet. Soon, darling, but not now." She sat up and coyly gave him a child's kiss. He made a face at her, and she laughingly swept from under the sheet and put on a robe. She felt singularly jovial now that he was gaining back his strength.

The weight of knowing she might have lost him only days before had been a trial of strength as well as spirit, and now she silently congratulated herself on her show of fortitude. "How about a lemonade to cool you off, Captain?" she asked brightly.

"If I can't have you, *ma petite*, I'll take a brandy." He leaned against the fresh pillow contentedly, for he had already decided he was quite well enough for sex.

"No brandy. Dr. Friedham says you may have beer, but no hard liquor for another month."

"Dr. Friedham, Dr. Friedham," he mocked impatiently. "Always Dr. Friedham! You know I don't like brew, Tierney. More to the point, we don't stock any in the house."

"We do now," she enjoined smugly as she sauntered out of the room.

"See to it that you don't throw it in my face this time!" he called behind her.

She returned dutifully with a tray carrying a mug of cool beer for her husband and the lemon drink for herself. Tierney made quite a ceremony of serving him the refreshment, imitating her distress and nervousness at the Silver Steed. André laughed, delighted by her nonsense. He quickly sobered, however, when she threatened to really toss the stuff in his face again in her true-to-life reenactment of the scene.

"That's enough now!" he said. "Now, Tierney . . . Don't do anything foolish!" When she still did not desist in her teasing, he challenged her. "Listen to me, *ma petite*. Back in London I had neither the time nor the wherewithal to deal with a cocky lass proper. I do tonight!"

Tierney capitulated, knowing full well he meant it, even if it necessitated a chase around the house to catch her. If he were not so weak, she considered, the sport would be fun.

After they had finished their drinks and idle chatter, the two settled down comfortably together in bed. It seemed only minutes after falling to sleep that Tierney felt she was again in the master cabin on board *La Reine de la Mer*. Lavender-colored dolphins played happily alongside the portholes in crystal-clear waters, and she was miraculously transported through the glass to join them in their play. Their chittering became a melody as they led her beneath the waves to the sandy white bottom.

There she found a multitude of treasures. A chest lay

open, and pearls, glittering gems, and gold goblets spilled onto the sand. Tierney searched the cache and found among the many valuables Nanna's brooch and the miniatures of her parents. However, it was a topaz pendant that caught her fancy. A doleful-eyed dolphin delivered it into her hand from his snub-nosed mouth. He was smiling. Tierney climbed onto his back, then, and he whisked her back to the surface.

André was inside the cabin, and she could see him clearly. He beckoned her to come back inside with him. He smiled at her dreamily, his white teeth startling against the dark of his face. She moved forward slowly and passed through the glass again effortlessly into a soft, velvetlike embrace.

Water droplets glistened on her bare shoulders and melted against his warm flesh. He wrapped them together in a cloth such as she had never seen before. He spoke to her then, in a muted indiscernible language that sent rivulets of pleasure down her spine.

When she awakened, André was carefully fondling her, although the sheet was inhibiting his progress. The linen bound them as tightly as a cocoon. She gave him a pensive smile. "If you are going to persist, is there at least some way that I may be of assistance?"

He grinned rather wickedly and said, "My dear wife, yes! And if you do not know how, then surely I have failed you as a teacher!" He whipped the sheet out from beneath them and eagerly pulled Tierney on top of him.

When they had finished their lovemaking to their mutual satisfaction, Tierney rolled to her side and propped herself on one elbow. "Why, André de Montfort," she exclaimed. "I don't believe you are sick at all. You're just plain lazy!"

He was happy with himself and her. "And you, milady, have grown very sassy while I've been out of sorts." Presently he pulled her down to snuggle and secured her against him, one leg thrown over both of hers. "And I'm not at all sure but that I don't like it," he said.

The next day was a momentous one in the lives of Tierney and André de Montfort, as well as for all New Orleans.

Pierre Lafitte had been arrested. He had been captured

the night before at the Royal Street Smithy, owned by the
Lafitte brothers. The report André read at the breakfast
table said he was bound in chains, to be held without
bond at the Calaboose, the city's jailhouse located on St.
Peter between Chartres and Royal streets.

André slammed the paper down on the table, over-
turning Tierney's teacup.

"My God! What's wrong? It's not the ship, is it?"

"I told Jean that business over rewards for the governor's capture was pushing the issue too far," he growled,
flicking his hand at the news story. Tierney picked up the
Gazette and saw instantly the headline that had so incensed
her husband.

Sometime earlier, Governor Claiborne, thwarted by indecision on the part of local legislators and spurred by
angry bankers and businessmen, had offered a reward of
five hundred dollars for the capture and delivery of Jean
Lafitte. The Baratarian Bos, realizing how preposterous
the scheme was, had posted counter-offers throughout the
city. In flowery language and much tongue-in-cheek, Lafitte had offered three times that sum for Governor Claiborne's deliverance to him at Grande Terre in the obscure
bay.

All of New Orleans had enjoyed the joke, all, that was,
except for the governor. He was deadly serious, and Pierre's
arrest the night before was solid proof of it.

There was no stopping André from throwing himself
full force back into rigorous activity now. The most Tierney could think to do was persuade him to take her along
on this, his first day out in more than a fortnight.

Rafael brought around the smaller phaeton carriage and
the couple set out alone. The morning was typically humid, but the streets were filled with inordinately irritable
carriage, dray, and buckboard drivers. André himself was
in a foul mood and Tierney dared not intervene in the
several traffic arguments he initiated on his way to the
Cabildo.

The first person he determined to see was the district
attorney, John R. Grymes. Rather than witness what she
suspected would be a nasty confrontation, Tierney pleaded
a headache and told him she would remain in the carriage.

Across the street from the government house were the
pillories. There were two culprits on public display today;

one an ill-kempt old white man, probably a town drunk, and the other a freed black youth. She stared, trying to make out the words on the placards that were suspended from their necks. The placards would tell passers-by their names and offenses. The old one called out an obscenity and she quickly looked away, embarrassed.

André had been gone less than fifteen minutes now, but it seemed to Tierney much longer. Finally, she climbed down from the vehicle intent on making the Stations of the Cross in the cathedral just beyond the Cabildo. A group of people were coming toward her, taking up all of the boarded banquette.

"Tierney!" a woman called, hurrying down the side-walk. "Tierney, dear!" It was Harriet Redding, coming toward her spritely, with arms outstretched. With her was James and his mother, Angelique. "My dear, how exciting to run across you! Where is that marvelous man you call a husband?" She blanched while still kissing her friend. "Oh, my!" she apologized, quite upset now. "I didn't mean that the way it sounded, Tierney."

Tierney laughed briefly and gave her an easy hug. "Good heavens, Harriet. If you and I held everything we said literally, we'd be in a fine fix, now wouldn't we?" She kissed Angelique affectionately, and Mr. Redding bowed politely.

"Where is the captain?" he said.

"He's looking for the district attorney, I believe."

Redding looked uncomfortable. "No trouble, I hope."

Tierney shook her head and started to explain her husband's impromptu mission, but Harriet burst in, "What an exciting day for James to bring us all to New Orleans! Have you heard about the arrest? It's a good thing they're finally doing something about these pirates, James says." She looked up at her husband in unabashed admiration, as though he himself had apprehended the elusive smuggler.

Tierney felt obliged to say something in Pierre's defense. "Well, it is not Jean Lafitte they have caught. It is his brother, and he can hardly be held responsible—"

Harriet broke in, eager to make amends. "Of course, darling. And Pierre Lafitte did rescue you, after all. None of us will ever forget that, my dear. Perhaps he will only be fined."

"How is little Jamey?" Tierney asked, anxious to end the conversation about the Robin Hood rogues.

Angelique beamed, at last aroused to speak. "He is a splendid child! The image of my own James."

"He's almost two now," Harriet added. "Quite a well-behaved little boy. Quiet and even-tempered. Well, most of the time," she laughed.

"And Bruce?" Tierney asked innocently.

"Who?" Harriet was genuinely puzzled.

"Mammy Lou's baby, Bruce. How is he doing now?"

Harriet shrugged and Angelique looked away. James had already crossed the street to get a closer look at the men pinned at the pillories. "He is all right, I suppose," the young woman responded at length. "The house servants tell me that he is an overly big child, and tends to be a bit rowdy. But don't worry, dear. If he doesn't calm down by the time he's old enough to be put in the fields, James will sell him. Speaking of slaves," she continued, "that is why we're here. There is an auction today down on Camp Street. James usually has to travel some thirty miles farther to St. John's Parish," Harriet sighed. "I'll never understand why they banned the importation of slaves. Why, it used to be you could get one for two hundred dollars or less. Now they cost eight hundred. Sometimes a thousand or more!"

"Perhaps we shall see you there," Tierney suggested in a tight voice.

"I thought Captain de Montfort did not allow slaves in your household," her friend answered incredulously.

"He doesn't."

Within minutes after the Redding trio departed, André reappeared. He hoisted himself back up onto the carriage and took up the reins. A sweat had broken out over his face, and Tierney suggested that they return home. "No," he said flatly. "I'm going to the Calaboose. I want to talk to Lafitte himself."

She did not argue. "Well, what happened? Did you see the district attorney?"

He nodded and told her that Grymes insisted he knew nothing of the arrest. "He is as shocked as the rest of us. Claiborne refuses to listen to Grymes's counsel, and the mayor is conveniently unavailable."

On Peter Street, a crowd of people had already merged

upon the jailhouse. It was orderly enough, but choked with traffic. André turned the carriage around and left Tierney parked on Royal. "Wait here," he commanded, and then disappeared into the crowd.

He returned very shortly, however, and in a state of complete vexation. He obviously had been denied a visit with Pierre Lafitte.

As he silently joined her again, she decided to try and break the tension. "*Monsieur*, if you would be so kind and if you have no other destination in mind, please direct us now to Camp Street."

"Whatever for?" he asked irritably.

"There is a slave auction today." At his dark scowl, she added, "Oh, André. I know how you feel. But I've never seen an actual sale."

"Morbid curiosity, my little witch?"

"No. It's more than that, although I don't deny that I am curious. I just have this feeling . . . I can't forget that I was a slave, too, for a short time. And it's changed me somehow . . ."

Eight slaves were to be put on the block today. She searched the gathering for Harriet, not at all certain she really wanted to see her. The Redding party had either bought the first two sold and were already gone, or they had not yet arrived.

Once André had accepted his wife's dubious request, he guided her forward through the crowd until they came upon the front of the hastily constructed platform. There, in full view of Tierney's nearsightedness, was a frail-looking black woman with three children, one a mere infant. The auctioneer was evidently having difficulty in bartering her. At his shouting, a male child—about five years old, Tierney guessed—shrank behind his mother's skirts. The third child, a toddler, stood wide-eyed with his mouth open.

"Four hundred dollars!" the man shouted indignantly. "Why you're crazier than a backwoods polecat!" The crowd tittered, and he continued, encouraged now.

"Lizzie here ain't much to look at, I'll admit. But she's only twenty and has got a lot of hard-working years left in her. She's been a house nigger lately and can cook and clean. But she has picked tobacco too!"

"Four-fifty," someone yelled.

The auctioneer appeared not to have heard. "You ladies out there ought to encourage your scoundrel husbands to buy this family. Lizzie ain't never been no man's mistress." He looked at the silent woman scornfully. "Ain't likely she ever will be neither!" More laughter was heard, more bids.

"Her husband was a big ape!" he shouted anxiously, still not happy with the amounts he heard bid. "And these here children—all boys, mind you—are gonna be as big as their daddy soon." He grabbed the oldest from behind his mother's skirts and held him up before the crowd. The mother glared, but still said nothing. The crowd roared with delight when the little boy, terrified, wet on the auctioneer's arm.

"Five hundred!" another offered. And so it went until finally the auctioneer enticed the going price to seven. When the gavel sounded and "Sold!" was shouted, Tierney shuddered.

"Let's go," she mumbled. As they shouldered their way back toward the carriage, however, Tierney stopped short. Another slave was on the block now, and the salesman was yelling, "A runaway, but a mighty fine buck. His old master don't want to pay the price to bring him back to Georgia and wants him sold." Tierney couldn't see, but she turned and pushed herself back toward the platform, blindly elbowing the people around her.

"His master said he never had any problems with this nigger before, and swears he's tame enough!" the man was saying. "He's got burn scars on his hands and forearm, but on his own admission, says he got 'em fighting a fire and not by being mistreated. Strong man, this one! What am I bid?"

Tierney's heart pounded frantically, and she barely heard herself call, "Jeb!" The black man looked up, but apparently did not see her.

"What am I bid," the auctioneer repeated.

Tierney screamed, "Twelve hundred!"

The crowd shuffled and murmured their surprise. The afternoon was not a loss if the bidding went high and spirits picked up. The slave dealer grinned his pleasure and peered down at the little lady who had so generously opened the sale.

"Twelve-fifty," a man shouted from the back.

"Thirteen hundred!" Tierney put in. André had rejoined her now, and roughly pulled her around to face him.

"What in the hell do you think you are doing?" he shouted.

"André! It's Jeb—Big Jeb. The one I lived with," she started, but at the shocked expression on several nearby faces, she lowered her voice. "I told you about him, André. He may know where Rosalie Noel is. I must have him. We'll set him free right away, of course!" She looked up and offered fourteen hundred and fifty dollars, overbidding the last offer she had heard.

"Not at these prices, he won't go free! I'm not a complete idiot!" André exploded. But it was André's own bid of eighteen hundred dollars that was the final sale price for Jeb.

Tierney clapped and called out to him, and it was only then that the black man looked up and recognized his new owner. "Miz Tierney!" he cried, relief and incredulity written on his face.

The ride back to the town house was chaotic, tears interspersed with their laughter. Jeb did not know the exact relocation of the Kawita village, but he was certain that they were headed due north-northeast when he made good his escape. The last he had seen of the baby was then, and he assured her that the child was being well cared for.

"But didn't they know that my escape was planned and the village destruction lay on my head?" she asked worriedly. André glanced at her in surprise. It was the first time it had occurred to him that Tierney blamed herself for the fire.

"Them Creeks ain't fools, ma'am. Sure they knowed. But they ain't crazy, Miz Tierney. Nobody wants to hurt that baby of yours!"

The ugly memory of the death of one of the Kawitas's own children flashed in front of her. She hung her head down. At length she asked, "Why didn't you run during the fire, Jeb? Everything was so confused then."

"That's jest it. It was so mixed up I couldn't find Dawn in time. Pardon, Miz Tierney, but that night was pure hell."

Tierney could well imagine the frenzy. "Where is Dawn?" she asked, suddenly reminded of his treasured Indian consort.

Jeb looked away before he answered. His voice was so low, she had to strain to hear him. "She wouldn't come, Miz Tierney. All that time I thought she loved me, but when the time came to leave, she wanted to stay with them. We was on the trail, headed north, and she hung back when I decided to run. I tried to carry her, make her come with me. But she kicked and bit me, fought me like a wildcat. Can you picture my sweet Dawn actin' like that?" he asked, finally facing her again.

Tierney was too stricken to speak, and Jeb continued. "Cain't say as I blame her, I guess. Them Kawita was more like her own than an ugly buck like me."

She reached over to him and patted his hand. "Perhaps it is best, Jeb," was all she could say.

As they pulled the carriage into their drive, Tierney asked about Birdie. "Dead," he answered. "An old woman like that couldn't have made that trek no-how." Tierney was strangely comforted, thinking of Birdie at last with her angels.

Tierney's insides were all a-flutter when she went into the house. She ordered high tea to be delivered to the dining room, poured a brandy for André, and a sherry for herself in the meantime.

André took the opportunity for a private word with Jeb in the coach house. While Rafael groomed the animals, de Montfort led the black man over to a corner. He eyed him levelly until finally Jeb coughed uncomfortably.

"What you told my wife . . . Is it true, Jeb? Is the child still alive?"

"Yes, massa. Last I seen, Rosie was fine."

"I'm not your master. You may call me Captain." André's cheek twitched. He had not prepared himself for this eventuality, and only hoped the man proved worthy.

"I paid a handsome price for you, Jeb," he said. "Eighteen hundred, to be exact."

"Yes, suh, Cap'n. I knows."

"Well, then. I have in mind paying you a salary of one hundred and twenty-five dollars per month, one hundred of which I will retain. In eighteen months you will be a clear man, free to go and do as you please. Does that sound fair to you?"

Jeb's mouth dropped open, but he quickly recovered. The man was obviously not a Southerner, and probably an abolitionist in the bargain. "Mighty fair, Cap'n. Mighty fair!"

In truth, André would have preferred some argument. He paid his boatmen two hundred, and house servants a hundred and a half monthly. But he supposed Jeb was in no position to argue. "What sort of work to you do, Jeb?"

"I was a field hand, Cap'n, but I 'spect I can do any work you want me to do."

Tierney had not exaggerated her description of Jeb's size. He was taller than André by an inch, and broader. "Do you have anything against learning the river, Jeb?" When he answered he would do any work required of him, André added, "Fine. You start tomorrow loading cargo. If all goes well, perhaps you'll skipper one of my barges someday."

Pierre Lafitte remained in jail.

His brother retained two lawyers at twenty thousand dollars each. One of the attorneys was John Randolph Grymes, who resigned his post as the city's district attorney to accept the substantial fee; the other, Edward Livingston, was a highly esteemed barrister. Their combined talents failed to have Pierre Lafitte released—even on bond.

Jean Lafitte was enraged with Governor Claiborne's obstinacy, but for all the smuggler's money and influence he was unable to free his brother. The Baratarians, as a whole, were becoming edgy. Two of Lafitte's finest lieutenants, Dominique You and René Beluche, were reportedly considering an attempt to rescue the expelled emperor, Napoleon Bonaparte, from the island of Elba.

To make matters worse, the British had nearly completed a blockade of the Gulf and were engendering spurious uprisings among the Southern Indians. Some declared that in addition to the war with Britain, America was also at war with the Creek Nation. War Department reports from Washington were nebulous on the Indian issue.

In the north, Commodore Perry had won a decisive

victory as early as 1813, but now, since Napoleon's abdication of his throne this spring, the British had launched an enormous offensive. Naval battles read like a chess match with the United States and Great Britain taking one another's ships like so many chessmen. It remained unclear who was winning this war.

It was in the spirit of just this pandemonium that the de Montforts received word that a treaty with the Creeks was being negotiated at Fort Jackson, a newly created stronghold at the crossing of the Coosa and Tallapoosa rivers in Alabama. In early August, after the treaty had been signed, André left for Mobile. There were rumors of white captives being freed there.

The day after André left, a young man appeared at the de Montfort's front steps. He sounded the knocker and Suzette, their quiet colored servant, opened the door. "Jim Bowie," he announced. "I understand that the captain has left New Orleans already, but will you please tell his missus I'm here?"

CHAPTER TWENTY-EIGHT

"Do come in, Mr. Bowie."

He was a big lad, and seemed very self-assured in spite of his age.

Suzette had disappeared, so as Tierney led him into the parlor, she called for Mrs. de Mateo to bring in some light refreshment.

"Ma'am, I don't mean to intrude, but I figured you'd want to know any information I've come across."

"That's quite true. I'm glad you have come." As Tierney poured a lemonade for him, he flashed her a smile. He was obviously accustomed to stronger drink, but Tierney was not about to offer it without her husband being home. She couldn't help smiling back at him, however.

"Well, ma'am," he began without further encouragement, "it's like this. The captain told me about the slave y'all bought some weeks back, and that he was with the Injuns that's got your baby girl. I heard that he says they were headed north by northeast. The way I figure it, that must be up the Natchez Trace someways, if they were going in that direction leaving Deer Run Bayou."

He stopped talking to empty his glass, but continued as soon as he plunked it back on the table. "So I've been talking to some recent travelers of the Trace, asking questions and the like. Nobody knows anything about a white baby, or Creek slaves of any way, shape, or form."

He stuffed a teacake into his mouth then, and Tierney nearly jumped in anticipation. She wondered what he was driving at, but held her tongue. This protégé of Lafitte hardly needed prompting.

"But," he emphasized on the last swallow, "a couple did tell me about a newly built Creek village up near the Tombigbee River. Not right on the river, mind you, but near a smaller creek that runs into it."

"How long has the settlement been there?" Tierney asked suddenly, her mind racing ahead to a vision of haphazardly grouped huts.

"Don't know for sure, ma'am," he answered easily. "But one old trader swears it couldn't be a year even since it was built. Says he saw them choppin' the trees for it. Could be this is just a wild goose chase, Mrs. de Montfort, because it seems to me that territory is Choctaw land. Mighty strange for the Creeks to build there. It happens, though," he added thoughtfully. "I reckon these tribes can't keep their boundaries straight what with new treaties and white settlers traipsing through and all."

Tierney stood up and walked to the window overlooking the street. It would rain again tomorrow, she thought, or maybe this afternoon. "Well, we certainly must check the village," she said.

"I thought you'd see it that way, ma'am," he beamed, standing now to take his leave. "I just wanted to get yours or the captain's okay on it."

"When do we start?" She turned to face him, a look of barely restrained excitement about her.

Jim Bowie sat down again abruptly. "We, ma'am?"

"Yes, of course. I'll need to know the time we will be setting off. I have to prepare, instruct the servants . . . But the sooner, the better, as far as I am concerned."

"No, ma'am!" he said emphatically. "I'm afraid I can't do that, Mrs. de Montfort. It's too dangerous on the Trace for a woman like you!" Tierney's eyes burned furiously and the young man could have sworn they changed colors. But it did not matter to him how angry she got. "Your husband would near kill me if I was to let you come," he offered, hoping to soothe her ruffled feathers.

Tierney studied him. She calculated he must have been at least a year younger than herself, and she was not going to be deterred by a mere stripling. She had to decide, therefore, what her best strategy would be. There was bribery. She could offer him more than André's ten thousand, although how she would pay the debt would have to be considered later. But she instinctively knew that money was not the sole issue here. The boy was seeking glory as well.

Perhaps feminine wiles would work—he was certainly young enough to be flattered by such trickery. "My dear young man," she began sweetly. "You must realize that it is my daughter for whom we are searching. I assure you, I shall not be in your way. Indeed, I shall be quite helpful. I too understand the markings of an Indian trail," she lied smoothly, "and am familiar with their customs."

He sat in the chair unmoved.

"Sir, you mustn't forget that I lived among the very tribe we are seeking. I shall recognize whether this village is, in fact, the one which has my baby!"

"Sorry, ma'am," he drawled, standing once more. "If you'd like, maybe we'd best wait until your husband gets back to settle this." He picked up his hat.

Tierney literally blocked his way. "Mr. Bowie!" she cried imperiously. "We will not wait, and we will leave tomorrow. I do not need your permission, nor my husband's, where my child is concerned!

"I've disguised myself as a man before, and will do so again—with or without your help. You've already mentioned where this village is. Along the Natchez Trace, in the vicinity of its crossing with the Tombigbee River," she repeated. She was grateful that she had a good memory for his words, at least, for she truly had no idea of where such a place might be.

"So, Mr. Bowie," she continued testily, "if you forbid me to accompany you, I shall go alone. That," she added frankly, "will most assuredly anger Captain de Montfort! But, you understand, it is not I that the captain will kill. Do I make myself clear now, Mr. Bowie?"

The young man was bewildered. It had all seemed so innocent. The lemonade, her sweet voice . . . All in all, de Montfort had on his hands a bitch for a wife!

"Ma'am, I just gotta say I think you're downright crazy!" he said, putting his coonskin cap on his bright-colored hair. "But you got me over a barrel, that's for sure. We'll start out at dawn. You say you got an outfit to disguise yourself as a boy, ma'am?"

"I do," she lied again. André had gotten rid of her buckskins after that gruesome return to Deer Run Bayou. He told her then that he never wanted to see her dressed as a man again. Well, he wouldn't. She would return before her husband could get back from Alabama, of that she was certain. Perhaps they would all be together for Rosalie Noel's first birthday!

After Bowie left, she quickly put her plans into action. She called Annette to join her, and together they set out for a day in the city with Rafael driving. Their first stop was the Ursuline convent. She visited regularly with Mother Superior and Sister Mercedes, and except during André's illness, had not missed a weekly visit. Now, she must somehow explain her absence for the next few weeks. Tierney told the nuns that she would be joining André in Mobile, at his request.

She had to tell someone the truth of it, however, and Annette was chosen as confidante. The maid was to tell only André what she had done, and that, only if he were to return early or if she did not return within the month.

"Oh, madame!" the nervous girl whispered in the back of the carriage, "you mustn't do this! Really, you mustn't! *Mon Dieu*, if something were to happen . . ."

"Oh, don't be such a willy-nilly, Annette. Nothing is going to happen! If we find Rosalie Noel, I have every intention of regaining her without a fight. I happen to know that these Indians will trade, so I am bringing my jewels."

"*Non, madame!*"

"*Oui, mademoiselle*," she teased. "Once I have seen her, I will have Mr. Bowie deliver the bribe. I don't believe they would recognize me, but I shan't chance it by doing or saying anything to draw attention to myself."

They ended their outing by going into the canal district, whereupon Rafael looked askance at the ladies in his charge, but he said nothing. He had distrusted Madame de Montfort since she had threatened to dismiss him over the burning of sheets.

Tierney found a young boy—an octoroon, she guessed —about her size, and paid him to buy the required costume. She couldn't risk being recognized by one of André's boatmen or dock handlers, and she wasn't even certain that the shop she chose was not one of her husband's storefronts.

Later that night, as Annette helped her try on the clothes, she knew her days of easily being mistaken for a male were behind her. Her hips, though still slender, were shapely now, and the buckskin breeches were tight across the buttocks and loose at the waist. Moreover, her breasts were round and full and not easily disguised.

André had put the fear of God into her about using binding, saying it could destroy them and keep her from nursing again.

She paused momentarily, wondering why she was not with child again. Perhaps marriage itself did something to one. It had taken Harriet two years after her marriage to James Redding. Or, like Harriet, perhaps something had happened to her during her first childbirth. Rosalie Noel, then, would be her only one. Tierney bit back the tears that threatened.

"Go downstairs and bring me that foot pillow from the study," she told Annette. "Perhaps if I look a bit paunchy . . . Please hurry. I have to get a good night's sleep."

Sleep didn't come, however. She lay awake all night, trying to picture the baby she had not seen for so many months. Try as she might, she could only see the six-week-old infant she had left behind. Imagining André's reception of the child he had never seen at all was even more difficult.

Before the first light of dawn, Tierney dressed herself again and picked up the leather pouch that held her only worldly possessions of great worth, the jewelry her husband had given so generously. On impulse, she opened the bag and removed the topaz pendant and put it back into her dresser drawer.

Fortunately, Mrs. de Mateo was a sound sleeper, and Rafael was going deaf. She hoped the groom's hand, Rafael's son, was still young enough to slumber childlike. Jeb had gone upriver, but had he been home, she would have gladly included him in the conspiracy. If there were anyone she felt she could trust without question, it was Jeb.

As she led Animal from his stall into the courtyard, she felt confident that no one had seen her. Annette would come early this morning and tell the household that the mistress had been suddenly called to join her husband.

No one would have seen her leave had not Mrs. de Mateo suffered a particularly difficult night with her stomach ulcer. She heard Tierney up and about, and later watched the captain's wife leave the courtyard. Mrs. de Mateo would direct a novena to St. Jude, patron of hopeless cases.

* * *

"Your hair!" Bowie exclaimed as he approached her riding a big white gelding.

"I know," Tierney sighed, touching the shorn edges along her neck. "My maid refused to cut it, so I had to do it myself. Is it too awful?"

He grinned. "Ma'am, between that belly you're wearin' and your skinny white neck stickin' out like that, you do make a, ah . . ."

"Never mind, Mr. Bowie," she said irritably, urging Animal to a trot. "Let's be off!"

After ferrying across Lake Pontchartrain, they followed a path alongside the Pearl River. Then, after several days along the riverbank, they would pick up the Natchez Trace at the Choctaw agency located at Jackson, Mississippi, where they could resupply.

The traveling was miserable. It rained intermittently each day, and the trail was difficult under the best conditions. The only break in the monotony of the trip was setting camp each night and ten minutes of pistol practice every morning. Bowie insisted that Tierney at least know how to handle a gun in the event that she would need it. The scout had seen enough accidents in his travels to know that there were no guarantees of safety, no way of ensuring that even he would survive it. If something happened to him, and he prayed God nothing would, it would be almost impossible for the young woman to make it back to civilization.

Her aim was dangerously off, however, despite his patient instruction. He suspected the girl was blind as a bat, but he never said anything to her about it. Tierney was posing no problems, really. She did not complain at all.

They called one another by their given names now: Jim and Tierney. But she should have tendered the warning in his voice on the fifth day out when he cried, "Tierney!"

She had slid from the saddle to check her mount's hind foot, for Animal had suddenly stopped and refused her command to "Gee-yup!" Under other circumstances, or had her vision been better, nothing might have happened. But as she reached down to lift the horse's foot, the copperhead struck.

Before she knew exactly what had happened, the young man leaped down and grabbed the snake's tail, swinging it high over their heads. Tierney felt she would never forget that sight—the snake whirling in circles and when Jim had built up enough momentum, cracking it like a bull-whip against a pinetree. After it slumped to the ground, either stunned or already dead, he shot off its head.

He whipped a knife out from his belt and took her hand. The bite was at her wrist, below the thumb. He unceremoniously made a crosslike incision with the blade and began sucking the wound. Tierney fainted.

"I thought you were tough!" he teased as she regained consciousness. She was pale and shaking, but Bowie felt confident he had gotten the venom out soon enough. "You're lucky, Tierney. Another inch and that sneaky bastard would've hit a blood vessel. There wouldn't have been a thing in this world I'd've been able to do then."

"Jim, how can I ever thank you?" She leaned against the trunk of a tree, feeling nauseous and cold at the same time.

"You can thank me by not arguing none. I'm taking you back. I was plum loco to have brought you in the first place. It's my fault."

She opened her eyes to protest. "Jim, you mustn't say that! Don't even think it." Tierney felt like going to bed for a week, but she struggled to overcome the weakness. "And we shouldn't turn back now. I can make it! I'm just a little shaken. But another hour or so, and I'll feel fine." She wished she felt as confident as she sounded, but in truth she felt miserable. Her head ached, and the fright of it all left her feeling totally drained.

It seemed so quiet now—like nothing had happened to disturb the peaceful setting. Tierney recalled her other narrow escapes, and how innocent they had seemed at the time, never heeding others' advice. The vicar had warned her about London . . . the shopkeeper once she was there offered advice . . . Mother Superior had told her to be wary of Indians . . . Angelique had begged her to stay inside that afternoon . . .

And André himself had ordered her to stay below the night she ended up in the crow's nest. He ordered her to stay home now, and leave finding Rosalie to him. Perhaps she should have listened this time; he'd be furious if he found out. Besides, even God seemed to be warning her with the portent of the snake.

Still, Tierney was not one to obey, and not one to quit. But it was only a half-hearted response when she finally repeated, "I can make it, Jim. Just give me a few more minutes, all right?" She strained to see his face then, but he looked away.

He plucked a weed from the ground and chewed it absently. Except for the chirping of birds and water rushing over the rocks in the nearby stream, it was silent. Even the horses seemed to be waiting for something. At length, Jim said, "I'll grant you that, ma'am. You probably *would* make it. But I can't take you there, Tierney." He looked at her again, his boyish face very sober as he spoke to her between his hunched knees. "You see, ma'am, I'm finding it damned hard being alone out here with a woman like you. You're the craziest, prettiest lady I ever run across. And you being married and all," he faltered, looking now at the sky between the pines. "It just wouldn't do to fall in love with you. I feel I'm already sunk, you know?"

She chided herself for being insensitive to anyone but herself. Hadn't she felt the same infatuation for Paul? And maybe Jim, at the same age as when she had fallen in love with André, felt the even greater turmoil and pain of true love, newly discovered. No, she could not ask any more of him.

Tierney did not say anything, and her silence told him she understood. They sat there, leaning against opposite trees, for a long time. Finally, he stood up. "Sun'll be down pretty soon. I'll make up camp, and we'll start back in the morning. You oughta rest, anyway."

During the night, her body ached and her teeth chattered uncontrollably. Her young escort moved her closer to the small fire and then lay down next to her back, giving her more warmth. She permitted him to do so, and dreamily remembered lying alongside the length of Paul Mauriac when he lay unconscious on *La Reine de la Mer*. It seemed so long ago. . . . Once when Bowie thought she slept, he kissed her on the back of her neck, softly and tenderly. Tierney permitted that too.

The next day, Jim went back to calling her Mrs. de Montfort, and sometimes just plain "missus." Tierney responded by calling him Bowie.

The six days back to New Orleans was far more tiring than the journey out.

André returned in bad humor the last week of August. He had met with no further information in Mobile, and it seemed as though every succeeding futile trip to recover his daughter made him more embittered, more enraged.

Mrs. de Mateo, in an effort to ensure her household position, told him everything she knew about his wife's escapade into Mississippi—from the borrowing of Animal to James Bowie's abrupt return of his wife because of a snakebite. Tierney was visiting the Ursulines at the moment of his arrival.

When she returned, the murderous look she received from André made her want to run from him. But instead, she walked up to him and tried to bestow a kiss.

"Don't play the innocent with me, you conniving little shrew!" he boomed, gripping her by her short hair.

"André!" she gasped. "You'll hurt me!"

"And well I might! You've disobeyed me for the last time, madame." Tierney felt certain the servants were all eavesdropping and she burned with shame. She struck out a hand to free her hair from his angry grasp.

It was then that André saw the ugly scar on her wrist by Bowie's knife. He released her immediately, the reality of her near death overwhelming all else. "I'll kill him, by God," he said in a flat, deadly tone.

"You do," Tierney enjoined, finally regaining her wits, "and I will leave you. I'll go somewhere you'll never find me!"

"You wouldn't dare! Not as long as there is some chance I'll find the baby. You would not risk leaving . . ."

"Test me, André!" she spat.

"Get out of here! Go up to your room, Tierney—now!" he thundered.

She considered continuing the argument from behind her winged-back chair, but thought better of it. She fled from the room, humiliated by his tyrannical reception of her and her own cowardice.

* * *

Captain de Montfort found the cub Indian fighter at
Le Cafes des Exiles on the corner of Royal and St. Ann
streets where Bowie was negotiating with a young Frenchman to accompany him back to Mississippi for part of
the ransom. This time, however, he planned to go up the
river to Natchez and follow the Trace from there to the
Tombigbee River. It was a longer route, but probably
faster and definitely safer.

His face blanched when he saw de Montfort, but he
casually excused himself to the surprised Frenchman and
met André halfway across the room.

"I ought to kill you!" the angry one began.

"Yes, sir," Bowie replied quietly. "You ought. Mind
if we discuss this out in the street, though? No need inviting a score of men into this."

The younger man had the innate good sense to take
what he considered a justifiable brow-beating, and when
the captain summarily dismissed him from further service,
Bowie humbly offered to repay the four thousand that
Jean Lafitte still held in the strongbox at Grande Terre.

"No, Jim. You're a young fool, but you meant no
harm," de Montfort admitted. "And no one knows my
wife's wily maneuvers better than I. I don't like the mark
you left on her, but you did save her life." Just like
Pierre Lafitte, he thought bitterly. For some unconscionable reason, de Montfort deeply resented the assistance
of other men in the affairs of his wife.

Bowie left with a sincere apology and a shake of the
captain's hand.

André shook his head as he took his mount. Damned
if he didn't like the kid, after all.

CHAPTER TWENTY-NINE

André was still in low spirits. Tierney attributed it to the long effects of a recovery from blackwater fever combined with his failure to locate the child. Failure, she knew, was no kind stranger to André de Montfort.

André felt compelled to pursue Bowie's lead into the Mississippi Territory. It could be another false hope, but he had talked the matter over with Jeb, who felt it was a reasonable relocation site for the Kawita tribe.

Unfortunately, he felt equally compelled to stay in New Orleans, and this ambivalence alone was driving him to distraction. He had visions of the city being sacked during his absence, and Tierney, alone again, faced with her greatest fear—fire.

Close upon his departure from Mobile, he learned of a British encampment at Pensacola, in Spanish Florida. That was on the doorstep of the Louisiana territory, and after delivering the news to the governor, Colonel George Ross of the U.S. Army, 44th regiment, and Master-Commandant Daniel T. Patterson of the naval station in a private meeting at La Bourse, André grew more anxious daily. He knew that New Orleans was the only worthwhile target for a southern invasion. It was only a matter of time, and he wished now that he had never let his grand ship out of his sight.

It was in this frame of mind that de Montfort received word from Jean Lafitte. The written message was decidedly urgent, although vague. He left for Grande Terre in Barataria at once, telling Tierney only that he would probably be gone several days. He told her quite adamantly she was to do "nothing" until he returned.

They spoke in their native French. "Take a look at it,"

Lafitte said once they were alone in the privacy of the upstairs library. "I think they are serious!"

André studied the proposal in silence.

H.M.S. *Sophie* had located the deepwater channel into Barataria Bay, and Captain Nicholas Lockyear had delivered his commander's message three days ago. Colonel Edward Nichols, the man who had only recently taken Pensacola, was offering Jean Lafitte a commission of captaincy in the Royal Navy, amnesty for all Baratarians, and considerable lands once the British victory over New Orleans was won. As a bonus, Lafitte was being offered thirty thousand sterling pounds for his immediate acceptance and assistance in the attack.

It was a generous proposal, and appeared to have been made in good faith. André's nerves thrilled as he read it. He might have been tempted himself simply by the challenge it offered. And Jean Lafitte was cut of the same cloth —politics was merely a matter of expediency. André de Montfort wavered, however. His life had changed so dramatically over the past year that he was beginning to feel the faint stirrings of patriotism. A fight was a fight, to be sure, but he preferred fighting against the British.

"What have you decided?" he finally asked.

Lafitte smiled and leaned forward with a brandy snifter for his friend. "Nothing yet. The pompous louts say I haven't a choice, really. They will attack Grande Terre before New Orleans if I decline their offer," he chuckled.

"You think you can defeat their forces then?"

"No," the smuggler answered soberly. "Not defeat them, unless they are foolish enough to charge here without more support. At the moment, they have only a few hundred men and we outnumber them three to one. It will take them several weeks to organize a larger fleet, and in that event, I can't imagine their navy would be foolhardy enough to bother with Grande Terre." He lit an enormous cigar, and continued. "They must know I'd warn Patterson. And no one knows this bay and the back bayou like I do! If they entered with a considerable force, we'd scatter back toward the swamps; they'd give chase, and by the time they knew what was upon them, our own navy could have the channels blocked!"

"Our own navy?" André asked in surprise.

"My friend, it may be difficult for you to understand—

I'm not sure that I understand it myself, really—but I've grown very fond of this land. Americans are a bullish lot, and greedy. But I like them, and I prefer America to all other countries, including our old girl, France."

At that, the two men raised their glasses to "the old girl," and sat quietly a moment, each lost in his own thoughts.

"It seems," Lafitte began again quietly, "that I must leave Louisiana."

André de Montfort said nothing. Jean was right.

"I hear rumors that the United States is preparing an attack against me as well. Either direction I take may be disastrous. I'll fare, no matter. But some of these cut-throats . . ." he muttered, jerking a thumb toward the window, "Well, I would hate to see a return to real piracy. I am a just man, André."

"I know that." André had been witness to a Baratarian trial of a man who was accused of needlessly murdering two Cubans. Lafitte found him guilty and hanged him. "You feel responsible for these people."

The host shifted in his chair and poured more cognac. "Not very," he admitted with a sardonic chuckle. "They will get along without me—they have before. But they're so damned unruly without a strong arm to direct them. Some would cut out the heart of another over a sou! One of my lieutenants, Gambi, is the worst of the lot. In fact, I've often thought 'the mad Italian' was coined for him. He'll meet a sorry end. . . ."

"When did you say you would get word back to them?" André asked. Lafitte, he feared, was becoming morose.

"I told Lockyear to give me two weeks to think it over. But there is nothing to consider as far as the English are concerned. I'd find fighting alongside them unconscionable. But I have a trump card here," he said, tapping the letter that offered conspiratorial reward.

"I thought we'd get around to that." André grinned. "What is it that I can do for you?"

It was sound, it was politic, and it was bribery. Captain de Montfort arrived back in New Orleans late the following night. Tierney sensed the undercurrent of tension in her husband's seemingly relaxed demeanor, but the more she pleaded with him for an explanation, the more tight-lipped he became.

"Ma chérie," he teased, "you have a very pretty nose for one that has grown so long. But why don't you see if it can shrink back to its original size. I liked it better before."

"You're being unfair, André! I have a right to know what is happening. Especially where our daughter is concerned . . ."

"It has nothing whatsoever to do with Rosalie," he broke in. "Do you think me so cruel that for one minute I would keep from you anything regarding the child?" His face was set in rigidly drawn lines, and Tierney immediately regretted her subtle accusation.

But what else was important enough for all this secrecy? "What then?" she inquired, less anxious than before.

André looked at her, noticing her own furrowed brow and drawn lips. Nothing she wore of late brightened her, and her cheeks were colorless. Only her eyes put life into her. They were clear and wide now, he mused. She looked bored. "I will tell you only that it is a matter regarding Pierre Lafitte," he finally answered.

Tierney shrugged, as if wholly unconcerned with the man's fate. "I am going to bed," was all she had to say.

Governor Claiborne was incredulous of the news. He neither believed the British wanted the Baratarian horde, nor that Jean Lafitte was seriously offering his own men to the American forces. The packet of documents that purported both issues were, in the opinion of the governor, forged papers to induce him to release the Lafitte he had already captured.

André de Montfort used his innate business acumen, however, and even Claiborne grew uncertain. "Sir," he began, "I believe it would be foolhardy, indeed, to summarily dismiss Lafitte's message based only on your own suspicions and admitted prejudice. I reported to you only last week the activities of the British marines and fleet near Pensacola. I know for a fact that the ship *Sophie* was there last month, the very same ship, sir, that Lafitte refers to in his letter to you."

"Did you see the *Sophie* personally, captain, or any other evidence of an English force during your meeting with the pirate?"

Honesty was oftimes the best tool in negotiating a sale,

and de Montfort rarely found it wise to tell bald-faced lies. "No, governor, I did not. The British were already back in the Gulf."

"Why, then, do you believe this nonsense?" Claiborne angrily tossed the documents back on his desk.

André leaned forward and retrieved the papers. He thumbed through them as he spoke. "Governor Claiborne, as a privateer myself, I can tell you that forged documents are a mark of the merchant captain's trade. I've used them broadly myself—most recently against the British, I might add.

"My own forgeries are virtually impossible to detect. I have a fine hand," he continued, lifting his palm and smiling. The governor tentatively returned the smile and nodded.

"What I am telling you, Governor Claiborne, is that even the finely-drawn forgery of Jean Lafitte would not be foolproof. And I am willing to swear to you that these, sir," he said earnestly, waving the documents over the desk, "are genuine!"

Claiborne leaned back into his chair, unconvinced. He was a young man himself, no older than Jean Lafitte. He had been only twenty-two years of age when President Thomas Jefferson appointed him governor of the new, vast territory. For more than a decade now, he had been responsible for an area larger than all of the states put together, and alone he had tackled what would have been insurmountable problems for a lesser man.

Still, piracy remained his most imposing dilemma. Early in his career, he had written to Washington, requesting support in his efforts to do away with the Baratarians. "I have denounced smuggling as dishonest," he reported, "and very generally a reply, in substance, would be returned: 'That is impossible, for my grandfather (or my father, or my husband) was . . . a great smuggler, and he was always esteemed an honest man.'"

The French captain could not read the other's thoughts, however, so he added, "You know, *monsieur*, that Lafitte has heard of your plans to attack his fort. He had nothing to risk in agreeing to the British proposal and turning this information over to you. *Au contraire*, he had much to gain by cooperating with them."

At this, the governor lifted his heavy eyebrows and absently toyed with the curls that were plastered to his forehead. The planned raid was in the strictest confidence of a very few. He wondered who among his cabinet was leaking information to the pirates.

"I see," he answered noncommittally. "Well, Captain de Montfort, I thank you for your time and cooperation. Of course, the decision is not ultimately mine alone. But I assure you, I will bring the matter before the council. Jean Lafitte will have my answer before the week is out . . ."

Two days later, the special committee met together in a private chamber of the legislature. The day was blustery for early September, and high winds shot bullets of rain against every structure in the riverside town.

The windows of the chamber were closed. The men were restless and irritable. Heavy cigar smoke circled aimlessly toward the high ceiling only to drift down again to smart their eyes.

After much heated discussion, a vote was taken. Colonel Ross and the naval commander, Patterson, were given approval to carry on with their raid. The general consensus was that even if the documents were bona fide evidence of an impending British attack on New Orleans, that battle would be months away yet. Jean Lafitte's support, along with several hundred Baratarians, would be negligible, they thought—if any support, indeed, might be mustered. Meanwhile, the release of Pierre Lafitte in return for the valuable information was preposterous.

The vote, however, was by no means unanimous. Governor Claiborne himself admitted he found a clear-cut decision impossible to reach, but he too conceded on the attack. It had been in the making too long to cancel at this late hour. The booty alone would be worth a small fortune, and the local naval station and militia needed all the supply they could get their hands on, to say nothing of prize ships captured.

After several hours of deliberation, then, the grumbling, apprehensive body of men dispersed. They went back out into the foul weather, bent on getting to their respective homes as quickly as possible. The roads would soon be a sea of mud.

* * *

"Oh, but you will, *señora*," Tierney threatened. "You see, I have only now decided how to repay you for breaking confidence with me. When you told my husband about my trip with Mr. Bowie, I intended then to someday even our little score." Her eyes flashed wildly at the housekeeper. "Put it on!"

André had been impossible to live with since his trip to Grande Terre, and altogether unapproachable since his meeting with the governor two days ago. He had been awaiting word back on Pierre Lafitte's fate, and Tierney could no longer stand the tension. She knew that the legislators would not bother telling André de Montfort of their decision if it were less than hoped for. They were not foolish enough to risk him warning Jean Lafitte. Sometimes Tierney wondered who was really the most naïve, André or herself!

"*Madre de Diós*," Mrs. de Mateo whimpered. "It is a great sin!"

"Then you'd best keep your mouth closed and do whatever I tell you. You wouldn't want to die before saying your penance, would you?"

The Spanish matron was dumbstruck. Perhaps, she thought, she should simply give up her post here before the crazy mistress led her to her grave. But Mrs. de Mateo's sister, poor fool that she was with five children and no husband, needed the money that Captain de Montfort paid her. "The weather, madame," she shrugged. "It is *muy malo . . .*"

"*Si, señora*. It is foul. Just call me Lady Macbeth," she teased, narrowing her eyes wickedly. Suddenly Tierney laughed. In spite of her serious intentions, she had to admit that the woman looked frightfully funny. Mrs. de Mateo wore an enormous religious habit over her working clothes, and the coif and veil were big too, nearly covering her eyes. She imagined her own costume—"borrowed" without permission as well—looked less bizarre, since she gauged a proper size for herself and chose an oversized one for her accomplice.

"But, madame," Mrs. de Mateo argued weakly, "your husband! What if he should discover us?"

Tierney impatiently started down the stairs. "Come along now. I've already explained to you, Mrs. de Mateo.

Rafael has taken him in the landau to some meeting. He
told us not to wait supper on him. And if, by chance, he
arrives home before us, then we shall explain to him that
one of your nieces became ill and we have been there,
at your sister's home."

Jeb waited outside on the dray he had brought from the
docks. He was hunched forward, a poncho covering all but
his face.

"Carry this," Tierney commanded hurriedly. The oil
lantern offered little lumination, but it was better than
nothing at all as they walked across the wobbly planks
that helped cover the flooding sewers.

"*Ay, que terrible!*" the older woman mourned. "We
will get very wet."

"There is a tarp in the buckboard. Don't be such a
scaredy-cat!" Tierney and Jeb together got the matron
settled on the seat, and after arranging themselves, Jeb
began to urge the horses forward into the mire. Fortunately, it was not yet cold and only the continuous rain made
the going rough.

When they reached the Calaboose, Tierney quickly went
over their instructions. Jeb was to remain outside as long
as necessary. Mrs. de Mateo was reminded to keep absolutely silent. She was only to walk with Tierney and stay
close.

The front room of the jailhouse was quiet. Only one
lamp flickered, casting tall, dull shadows upon the walls.
The attendant, a stout little man with a startling black
moustache, was nodding over a cup of coffee when the
two women entered.

He jumped up immediately and gestured as though to
remove a hat, although he wore none. "Ladies! Ah . . .
Sisters, beg pardon. May I help you?" he asked, still
stunned.

"Good evening," Tierney murmured smoothly, her eyes
cast down. "I certainly hope you can help us, kind sir."

She walked toward his desk, keeping the wavering servant in tow. "Sir, I would introduce myself. I am Sister
Dominique and this is my traveling companion, Sister
Marie Ann. We have come to see my brother, and are
told he is here. Pierre Lafitte."

"Lafitte!" The man gulped loudly, and looked around

the room, as if a superior might materialize to handle the request.

"He is not your prisoner?" she inquired innocently. "I thought surely . . ."

"Oh, yes! Yes, Sister, he is here. But I am sorry—no visitors. Absolutely no one, Sister Dominique. The governor himself . . ."

Tierney held up her hand to stifle his speech and dropped her head. Her own voice was quivering when she spoke. "I understand, sir. My brother—my brothers—are guilty of many sins. I know that." She looked up, tears swimming in her eyes. "But surely you can make an exception! We have come a long way, sir, Sister and I. And it is my understanding that Pierre will never again see the light of day." She clutched her beads piteously, gathering courage. Or so it seemed. "You see, it is not secular matters that concern me, but his very soul!"

The jailor was growing dismayed. "I have no knowledge of a Lafitte sister," he said.

"No, of course, you would not know," Tierney murmured obligingly. "It is humiliating to explain, sir. I was so young when we were sent, but there was no room in my father's home for scapegrace sons—or a daughter," she ended miserably.

"My good Sister!" the man exclaimed, thoroughly embarrassed by the nun's sad admission. "I must apologize. I meant no implied distrust of you!" He crossed himself quickly now, and came around from his desk. "I beg your forgiveness, Sister Dominique," he mumbled nervously. "Please wait here. A final visit from you might comfort the poor man, and exceptions are not unheard of . . . But I must ask you not to advise anyone of your visit."

"Of course. Only a special dispensation made my journey possible. It may relieve you to know that ours is a very strict cloister and idle conversation is forbidden. As a rule, we speak only to praise our Savior, Our Lord, Jesus Christ."

"Amen," he enjoined, reaching for the brass key ring above the doorway. As he left, Tierney hoped that the prisoner would not show any surprise at the sudden appearance of a ficticious sibling. If she were caught . . .

Her anxiety diminished somewhat when the jailkeeper

came back into the room smiling. "Sister, he is most contrite to learn that news of his arrest reached you. But he begs to see you. It is a miracle, Sister. The change in him! I have never seen Pierre Lafitte humbled!"

"Only the Almighty can work miracles, monsieur," Tierney admonished. She felt growing confidence, and plucked at Mrs. de Mateo's sleeve. "Come along, Sister. The hour grows late."

"She'll have to wait out here."

Tierney stopped short. She had not planned on this difficulty. "But she must accompany me!" she said, a bit too loudly. "We are not permitted to go into public alone. Not even for corporal works of mercy."

"I am sorry, Sister. I am breaking a rule already by letting you see him. But no prisoner can have more than one visitor at a time. No one." The fat little man seemed closed to further negotiation.

Tierney wept, partly from fright and partly for dramatic effect. "Then I cannot go in either. It is against our rules."

"Sister," he began impatiently, "you forget that I am breaking a rule too. Surely you can this once."

She brought her head up indignantly. "Yours is a secular regulation. Mine are sacred vows. There is a difference!"

The jailor thought to himself that for one who was usually sworn to silence, Sister Dominique had a quick tongue. He shrugged. He was not prepared to argue with a nun all night; the sooner it all was over, the sooner he could take his nightly snooze. And the less likely he would be caught breaking regulations . . . "Well, all right, then," he said finally. "But you will both have to leave within a quarter hour."

When they entered his nearby cell, the man she barely remembered stared at her a moment then rushed forward to embrace her. Tierney nearly lost her balance.

"*Ma petite sœur*," he cried, "my beautiful little sister!" Tierney discreetly stepped on his toe, indicating that was quite enough of a display, and he held her back from him, smiling as though she were a beatific vision.

The jailer was touched by the prisoner's show of emotion, and before locking the door behind him, called, "Remember, Sister. Fifteen minutes."

"God bless you," she answered.

They listened as his footsteps retreated back down the hall until they heard the other iron door being closed.

Pierre Lafitte held his arms up and turned around, his excitement barely in check. Mrs. de Mateo groaned and slumped down to sit on the solitary bunk. She quickly noticed the bedding was flea-infested, but she no longer cared.

"*Mon Dieu!*" he exclaimed in a hushed voice as he turned back toward the younger woman. "Are you who I think you are?" He was obviously delighted, but a little disbelieving.

"The same. It's Tierney."

"Who sent you? Does your husband . . ."

At this, the seated woman groaned again and Tierney snapped her fingers to silence her. "No one sent me, *monsieur*. There is little time for explanation now. We must act quickly, and I need your help!"

The pirate permitted himself a chuckle. "At your service, madame," he bowed.

"It has been simple up until this point," Tierney told him. "But now I don't know what to do! I have brought my housekeeper, as you can see . . ." Mrs. de Mateo was fervently saying her beads. "She is dressed as a nun, but she has on regular clothes under it, and her costume will be worn by you when we leave."

"Yes?"

"Yes. But now I have to find a way to get her back outside, dressed as herself. Do you understand?"

The Spanish woman stopped her prayers in mid-breath and fell against the wall, her mouth open in absolute shock. Up until this moment, she believed they were really visiting the criminal, not helping him to escape!

Lafitte gave a low whistle. "Madame, I sincerely appreciate your assistance. But you have brought me a half-baked cake. I will have to think about this," he said, absently rubbing his wrists.

"We are really quite lucky," Tierney offered hopefully. "I expected to find you in chains."

"Sam came back here to tidy up a bit and took the harness with him. He didn't want you thinking I've been abused."

"Have you?" she asked with genuine concern.

The pirate shook his head. "Not really. I am well-fed, and I exercise myself pacing and lifting my arms—quite an achievement in chains! But I have lived to escape, and tonight . . . Quite clever to use Captain Dominique's name, madame. I knew immediately it was to be tonight."

"I hadn't considered the name," Tierney admitted. "It is merely a coincidence." They both fell silent then, and she took in her surroundings.

The room was small and rectangular, smaller than her dormitory space at the convent. The stained stucco walls were thick and reinforced with broad beams, and the floor was stone. A fetid odor of urine and sweat hung in the air. Tierney wondered what it must be like to live weeks, months, in solitary confinement. Pierre Lafitte looked well, considering his present habitat.

The silence seemed interminable, and the minutes stretched out mercilessly. Tierney stood quite still, allowing Pierre to lose himself in concentration.

Mrs. de Mateo thought she would shriek over such foolish waste of time. "*Por favor, señor.* Have you not thought of how we can all get back out?"

Pierre shifted uncomfortably. He had been standing since the pair arrived, and presently he sat down next to the frightened housekeeper. "I think, *señora,* we shall do this . . ."

The plan was to temporarily leave Mrs. de Mateo behind. They would cover her with the blanket, simulating the prisoner asleep, and the robed pair would depart as quietly as the original couple had come. Minutes later, Pierre would steal back inside, knock poor Sam unconscious—he promised Tierney he would not kill him— and free the waiting woman.

When the jailor reappeared to lead the ladies out, all was in order. Pierre was stooped over as Tierney had previously instructed Mrs. de Mateo to do, and the keeper did not even give the nun a second glance. He did, however, look doubtfully toward the hunched body on the bunk. The candle nearby had been snuffed out, and only Sam's lantern shed any light into the room.

"Asleep?" he asked suspiciously.

"No, not yet. But my brother is exhausted," sighed Tierney, edging toward the hall. "I thank you for allowing me to see him. I will remember you in my prayers. You have been so kind . . ." These were the first honest words Tierney had said to him all evening.

"Thank you, Sister Dominique. I'd appreciate that." Looking once again toward the figure on the bed, he said, "Still and all, I think I better put those chains back on. Pardon my saying, Sister, but that brother of yours is a sly one."

At that, Mrs. de Mateo could no longer contain herself. She screamed and jumped up. Pierre doubled up his fists, and before the jailor could register anything but shock, the prisoner struck him on the head. He slid to the floor, and Pierre pushed the rest of him inside. "He will come to in a minute or so," he said angrily. "Get your servant!"

Tierney grabbed the still-terrified woman and shoved her into the hall. Lafitte made quick work of locking up the cell and the odd trio ran down the hall, the costumed man swearing at his skirts all the while.

An hour later they were riding down Cypress, moving in the direction of Tchoupitoulas Street, where various river-craft were tied. The rain had finally stopped. Nonetheless, the streets were nearly impassable and the getaway had been painfully slow. It was late, but here in the Swamp District, the city was alive with people. Drunken rivermen sang and brawled along the muddy streets, and the high-pitched laughter of the whores punctuated the night air.

Here, in front of the House of Rest for Weary Boat-men, Pierre Lafitte—minus his costume—decided to get off the buckboard. He turned to Tierney.

"Consider it a favor, Monsieur Lafitte," she teased. "A favor returned."

He kissed her then, long and ardently. Despite his malodorous clothes and hair, Tierney found the intimacy surprisingly pleasant. She did not fight him, even when she heard the housekeeper's gasp.

When he broke away from her, he was smiling broadly. "Madame," he announced, "I congratulate you on having successfully stolen my person away from the hands of treachery. But tonight, you have stolen my heart away as well."

CHAPTER THIRTY

"Where were you last night, Tierney?"

For the first time since leaving her childhood behind, Tierney was finding it very uncomfortable to lie. She glanced timidly at her husband, and knew he sensed her sudden attack of conscience. André was in no mood for nonsense.

"I have already told you. Mrs. de Mateo's niece was quite sick, and we spent a good part of the night nursing her. That is why I have given her today off to spend upstairs in bed. The poor woman needs the rest." It was no good. Try as she might, Tierney did not sound convincing even to herself.

"Poor woman, indeed! I have already gone up to see her myself, Tierney. She is nearly in a state of shock!" André pulled a chair close to the dressing table where Tierney pretended to administer her toilette. He sat down. The night had been a wretched one for him. He learned the preparations for the raid on Barataria were still underway, and he dreaded bearing such gloomy tidings to Jean.

Tierney absently toyed with her short curls, trying to determine why her husband was sitting there so patiently. It made her very nervous, and presently she wished he would behave in a more typically stormy fashion.

"I know about Pierre Lafitte's escape last night," he stated flatly.

Tierney started and dropped her hairbrush. She wondered frantically how news of this nature had traveled so fast. It was not yet seven o'clock in the morning.

"The police have already been here," he prompted, his voice still calm.

So she had been found out, and so soon! Her silence alone had been an admission of guilt. Had she gathered her wits quickly enough, she might have stayed off her husband's intuition. Fool! she thought. She might have at least made a pretense of surprise at news of the escape. It was too late now, however. Tierney cast her eyes down into her lap and asked, "Am I to be hanged, then?"

André felt an inane urge to throw back his head and laugh at her aloud. She was still so childish at times, and he adored her for it. But now, with all hell breaking loose, was not the time to behave flippantly.

"No, you little imp. You shan't be hanged unless you are stupid enough to look so damned guilty in front of others! The police were here to question me. Fortunately, I have a solid alibi. I was with Mayor Girod last night."

André stood up and stretched. He had already shaved and was fully dressed. A knot formed in her throat as she looked up at him. "Put on your clothes, little witch, and come down to breakfast before I beat you within an inch of your life," he threatened mildly. "Annette is fixing an omelette for us."

Tierney ate more heartily than she had in months. She was uncomfortably full by the time they took up their conversation again.

"Whatever your intentions, Tierney," he began, "and I don't doubt but that they were good, you have risked a great deal by last night's behavior. More than you can imagine," he emphasized in all earnestness. "There is at stake our well-being, yours and mine; for what chance would we have if news of this leaked out? I'll tell you what could happen," he said, not giving pause for her answer, "At the very least, we might be forced to leave Louisiana—and then what chance would we have of re-covering the baby?" Tierney winced. He was absolutely right. "Or we might yet be tried and prosecuted for con-spiracy against the government. Neither of us yet is a naturalized citizen of this country, madame. We could be sentenced to imprisonment, even death."

He stopped to be sure he had her complete attention before continuing. "You have also risked the honest in-tentions of Jean Lafitte. He is at this very moment offering his forces to the defense of New Orleans. By his brother's escape last night, in all probability you have thwarted that forthright effort; thereby threatening the security of this city—of this very land!" he told her.

Tierney's mouth dropped open in disbelief. "Oh, André," she giggled at last, "you are teasing me. Surely you are!"

André explained to Tierney all that had been transpiring over the past several weeks: the British takeover of Spanish Florida in the west; the Royal Navy's offer to the Baratarians and their admitted plan to invade New Orleans; Jean Lafitte's counter-proposal in support of the United States; and finally, in André's own opinion, how vital the pirates' support would be in determining an American victory in a battle over New Orleans.

Tierney stood up, aghast. "Oh, darling!" she cried, covering her face with her hands. "I am so sorry. I am so very stupid! I believed that you wanted to see Pierre escape. I . . . I thought I would be helping," she choked out.

André pulled her into his lap then, and kissed her wet face, stroking the damp curls behind her ears. When at last he had calmed her down, he smiled at her. It was a tender smile, and only then did Tierney realize how much she had missed his gentleness of late.

"I have to admit, *ma petite,* I am beginning to believe you can accomplish anything you set your heart on. And adventure does put the bloom back in your face, so all is not lost. However did you manage your little escapade last night? It must have been incredible . . ." He could no longer disguise his pride and curiosity.

Much later, and after an interlude of mid-morning abandon in the privacy of their bedroom, André left once again for the pirates' cove at Grande Terre. He would take the more difficult backwater route in his speedy pirogue. No time could be wasted.

"I'll be glad when Paul returns," he remarked to her before leaving. "He is bringing a young man, Hans Nagel. I only hope the lad has his father's head for business. I need the help. Between personal trips hither and yon, my business is going to hell!"

Tierney sat up, suddenly alert. "André, I could learn . . ."

"Don't even start that, Tierney," he responded instantly. He dropped a kiss on her forehead and left.

Captain de Montfort was too late.

By the time he met with Jean Lafitte again and returned

to New Orleans to repeat the pirate's offer of cooperation
—in spite of his brother's uncanny escape—the raiding
party was already destined for Grande Terre. It was September 16, 1814.

The Baratarians, over one thousand strong, prepared to
fight, thinking all the while that before them lay a British
attack. When the American flag was sighted, however,
Bos Lafitte knew at once his hope for amnesty had gone
awry.

He immediately ordered a retreat, and the cunning Baratarians disappeared back into the swamps like so many
waterfront rats. Only eighty men were captured, and those
without a struggle. Neither Jean nor Pierre Lafitte was
among them.

The success of the raid, then, was measured in the loot
seized. The American forces brought back as prizes ten
large vessels and the warehouse stores. These supplies from
Lafitte's stores alone were worth over a half million dollars. What neither Commander Patterson nor Colonel Ross
realized was that these "front" warehouses held only a
portion of the Baratarians' booty and Jean Lafitte's own
personal wealth. There were other warehouses hidden in
the back bayou and many more Baratarian ships at sea.

Nonetheless, the Americans retired back to New Orleans
believing they had finally squelched the blight of piracy in
Louisiana.

The reaction of New Orleans' citizenry was mixed. Many
were appalled by news of the raid, and believed those men
held captive should be released immediately. Even those
who were delighted with the economic boon of returned
stolen or "lost" goods were quick to demand their release.
An even bigger issue was the return of Lafitte's ships. A
swelling number of citizens believed the navy had out-
rightly stolen them.

Governor Claiborne was not to be persuaded by public
opinion, however. The captured Baratarians were promptly crammed into the Calaboose, and the prize vessels were
held for an auction that would be announced as soon as
tempers grew more moderate again.

Captain and Madame de Montfort held their opinions of
the raid to themselves. The matter of Pierre Lafitte's inexplicable escape was fast taking on the proportions of
local legend, with mythical powers being attributed to the

brothers Lafitte. André and Tierney could not have been more pleased with the mystery. And for the time being, at least, the young couple put aside the problems of their neighbors.

La Reine de la Mer came home the last week in September.

CHAPTER THIRTY-ONE

Tierney was preparing for her first party ever. After a joyous reunion of the trio, she threw herself into a flurry of activity to arrange a proper reception for Paul Mauriac.

It was a small gathering, really, but for Tierney, it seemed an enormous undertaking. Twelve invitations were sent out, and they included Mr. and Mrs. James Redding and James's mother, Angelique. Charles and Amanda Bolier were also invited, and so was Dr. Peter Friedham. The rest were business associates of André—a local banker and his wife, a broker and his fiancée, and an engineer whom André had befriended, Major A. Lacarrier Latour. Attorney Edward Livingston, although invited, would not be able to attend.

When she received Mr. Livingston's regrets, Tierney quickly sent out two other invitations. One was to Master-Commandant Daniel Patterson and the other went to his army alternate, Colonel George Ross. Despite mixed feelings since the raid at Grande Terre, it was not difficult to persuade André that the ranking officers should be included. Their presence would lay to rest any lingering suspicion surrounding the de Montforts and the escape of one Lafitte from the hands of the law.

The guest of honor, of course, was Paul. Young Hans Nagel, however, would also be formally introduced as the new assistant manager of the de Montfort shipping line.

Tierney paid particular attention to the menu. A delicious seafood gumbo, a dish which André attributed to French bouillabaisse and the Creole imagination, was to be the first course, followed by a fruit sherbet to wash the palate. Ham, pheasant en crème, and Beef Wellington would follow with a rice pilaf and vegetables. Cold clams, shrimp, and oysters would be available throughout, and the servants were told there were to be no fewer than

three hot platters of fresh breads and rolls at any time.
The dessert would be an assortment of blancmange,
peach flambé, and French pastries.

In order to assure herself that the meal would be prepared and served properly, Tierney procured two additional servants, Suzette's twin sister and Mrs. de Mateo's
oldest niece.

When she was satisfied that the dinner was in good
hands (the mulatto girl was a genius in the kitchen),
Tierney set about deciding her gown. She told her husband
that she would feel too conspicuous in the green Mandarin
ensemble, and that her others seemed too drab for such
a splendid occasion.

André knew only too well that this was Tierney's first
affair and was happy to suggest that she have a new gown
made. Madame Richet was expecting her, and would spare
no expense in fitting something appropriate for the wife
of handsome André de Montfort.

The gown finally chosen was of a striped satin material,
pale gold interspersed with narrow stripes of darker gold.
It was high-waisted and low-cut. The leg-o'-mutton sleeves
were the paler shade throughout, with dark gold accentuat-
ing the cuffs and sleeve band. A detachable cape was made
of matching dark gold velvet and lined with the satin
stripes. Though simple in design, the mildly contrasting
colors and material were breathtaking. Tierney was most
pleased and secretly admired the daring décolletage.

By the third week of October that year, the evenings
grew decidedly chilly. As luck would have it, it also
rained the night of Tierney's party. Those guests with
ladies in their company would arrive early enough to dress
with the hostess, for no lady of New Orleans in her right
mind braved the mud in her finery.

The Reddings arrived first, and would stay the night.
The guest bedrooms had already been prepared for them,
but Harriet and Tierney excitedly dressed together while
James adjourned with André for a brandy in the study.
Angelique complained of being travel-weary and arthritic,
and so was shown to her room to rest.

"Darling!" Harriet cried when she saw Tierney's gown.
"It is magnificent!" She looked at her friend in obvious
admiration. "You are so beautiful anyway, dear . . . And
after all you've been through too."

Tierney's eyes shadowed momentarily. She did not want to spoil this evening by remembering any of it. Not the Indians, not the searches, not even Rosalie Noel. "You've always been too generous with me, Harriet."

"Well, see mine then!" Harriet hurried across the hall to the room where she and her husband would stay and returned shortly with her dress, a dark blue velvet trimmed with white fur.

After much ado over buttons and arranging of skirts, Annette came in to dress the ladies' hair. She was able to work wonders with the pale long hair of Harriet Redding, sweeping it high from her neck and braiding the very top into a crown effect. The only ringlets were bare illusions of curl at each temple. All three women were impressed with the result.

The petite maid clucked irritably at Tierney's unevenly cropped hair. The best she was able to achieve took further clipping and scented pomade. A handsomely tooled miniature gold tiara was all that kept her mistress from looking totally at odds with the beautiful gown.

Annette stood behind her at the mirror, chewing her lip in frustration.

"Thank you." Tierney nodded at the image behind her. "It looks fine, Annette. Now please see if our other guest would like your assistance."

The maid left then, murmuring to herself. In a few moments they overheard her chatting pleasantly in French with Angelique. Tierney, giggling, explained how the young girl had balked at cutting her hair herself when she had made her last trip into the Mississippi territory with a scout to find the baby.

Harriet merely smiled in response, but when Tierney asked her to lock the chain around her throat, she felt compelled to speak. "However will you manage this, dear?" she asked quietly. "The baby, I mean. Surely here in New Orleans—these people who will be here tonight—there will be questions! How on earth will you explain it if your daughter is returned to you?" Privately, the woman thought it would be best for all concerned if the child were never found. Such a complicated ordeal, and such an uncivilized background for a white baby!

The topaz sparkled enticingly above Tierney's neat cleavage. She put her hand over the jewel protectively, as if it must not be soiled by the conversation taking place. "I don't know, Harriet," she answered slowly. "I honestly don't know."

The next guests arrived simultaneously. Charles and Amanda came, and on their heels was the broker, Frank Rubio and his fiancée, Maria San Bernardo del Gato. Maria and her dueña quietly removed themselves to the Reddings' guest room to dress the young lady.

Much later, after all the guests had arrived and dressed, the dinner party commenced. Paul and Hans arrived together as planned, and were the last arrivals, as Tierney hoped they would be.

The only surprise in the menu was escargots in garlic butter, which Suzette had thoughtfully included and served before the gumbo. Everyone except Angelique seemed to enjoy the various courses. The old woman looked to be in a sour disposition. She said nothing, and ate very little.

The surprise in table conversation carried much more impact than Tierney's surprise at the amended menu. It happened during dessert. Tierney was just selecting a pastry when she heard someone ask, "Any word yet on your daughter, Captain?" It was the young naval officer, Daniel Patterson. André answered him over the ring of Harriet's fork clattering to her plate.

"Nothing definitive, sir. We hear a great many rumors, of course, but they seem to be unfounded," André said smoothly. "Thank you for inquiring."

A hush fell over the table then, as guests tried to digest the innocent remarks just made. Very few persons in New Orleans were aware of a child between Captain and Madame de Montfort. How could they? To their knowledge, the couple had not yet been married a year!

Patterson sensed he had somehow committed a faux pas, and attempted to make up for it over the cordials and coffee. He asked the newcomer, Hans Nagel, for a personal account of Europe's reaction to Napoleon's fall from power and the collapse of his empire. While the conversation was of interest to the men, the ladies present were still unsettled over the previous discussion.

When at last the company all adjourned to the parlor, André asked Tierney to entertain them at the pianoforte. The guests all politely joined in his request.

"I'm not really practiced," Tierney apologized. "You

see, Mr. Mauriac only recently brought it back from Europe for us. It is a wedding gift from him."

"Belated, to be sure," Paul laughed, "but with all the same hopes I had on your wedding day."

Tierney settled down to play after Paul's strange remark, and gave a pleasant, if not brilliant, performance. When she ended the brief recital, a polite applause rippled over the room. Dr. Friedham, however, clapped rather loudly for such a mediocre presentation. Shortly after that, he explained that he had a rather difficult case at Charity Hospital and unhappily took his leave.

Tierney and André both saw him to the courtyard where he had stabled his horse. The rain had finally ended, and the faint glow of carondelet oil lamps made everything glisten. After the doctor waved good-bye and left through the side gate, the only sound was that of water dripping from the eaves onto brick. It offered them a moment's surcease, and they stood with their arms entwined several seconds before André spoke.

"*Mon cœur*," he began quietly. "There is something I have meant to tell you, but until tonight, the moment never seemed right. I want you to know that as far as I am concerned, as far as this whole damned world is concerned, that you and I were married on the day we set sail out of London. November first, in the year of our Lord, eighteen hundred and twelve. Do you remember that day, *chérie*?"

"How could I forget it?" she responded.

André held her closer. "What is in your heart, Tierney, I cannot begin to control. Wish that I might," he whispered urgently. "But I have the marriage document to prove how I feel, if prove it I must."

Tierney pushed away from him, her mind chaotic in surprise. "How, André? Witnessed by whom?"

He explained to her that as soon as he learned of the baby he had never seen, he had made a false entry into the ship's logbook, verifying the date. He did not tell her that his log alone was sacred to him, and that only after hours of introspection had he altered *La Reine*'s records. During his latest trip to London, Paul Mauriac had procured a legitimate certificate (he did not mention the cost of bribing the magistrate), on André's orders. Paul had also witnessed it, of course. It only required Tierney's own hand now.

"And what of the second witness?" she asked.

Her husband grinned. "A fellow by the name of Tom Hall. The very same who saved your position at the Silver Steed once, and ordered you away the night you nearly drowned me in ale!"

"Jesus, Mary, and Joseph!" Tierney cried. It was all she could think to say.

"I know you don't like it, Tierney. I wish it were otherwise. But do be a sensible girl, *chérie*. We can't very well introduce a daughter who is older than the marriage itself. It wouldn't be fair to Rosalie!"

"Rosalie Noel seems like a mere dream to me now. We might never find her," she said tonelessly.

André swept her back into his arms and kissed her determinedly. *"Mais si,* we shall find her!"

When they walked back inside, Tierney's teeth chattered from chill and nerves. André immediately made his way back to the gathering while Tierney surreptitiously downed a sherry. The evening, she knew, had not become a disaster over one mysterious remark. Not yet.

With the amenities of dinner and entertainment over, the men were all eager to retreat to cigars and brandy again in the study. Tierney, therefore, was left to see to the ladies still in the parlor.

The discussion for some time dwelt on the forthcoming October masquerade ball. Tierney was not familiar with the local custom, but quickly realized that it was of great significance here in New Orleans. The ball, she learned, would be at the St. Philips Theater. A new theater, Le Thêatre d'Orléans, had only recently opened and was the town's most splendid auditorium, but the ballroom had not yet been built.

The banker's wife, a rather plump woman by the name of Mrs. Hudson, admitted in hushed tones that she would come as the first lady, Dolly Madison. "Such a remarkable woman. So brave!" Mrs. Hudson exclaimed. "Why, I do believe she was the only person with a head on her shoulders when the British invaded Washington this summer! As a matter of fact, our own noble Constitution would have burned if it had not been for that dear woman!"

Other suggestions for unique costumes were made. Empress Josephine still held the lead over Cleopatra, despite the fall of the empire. Tierney asked if Anne Boleyn or Jeanne d'Arc were popular heroines, and was told that no one had been seen as Anne Boleyn in years.

As might have been expected, the masquerade chatter eventually died down and gave way to the matter desperately pressing on each one's mind. Surprisingly it was the exotic-looking Spanish girl, Maria, who brought the topic back into focus. The soon-to-be-married señorita had been ostensibly quiet all evening, her dark luminous eyes dreaming of things beyond the present. But even she, with only an elementary comprehension of English, had caught the thrilling undercurrent at the dinner table.

"Pardon me, señora," she said softly, "but did they speak of a baby? You have a child?"

The fire crackled suddenly and Harriet jumped.

"Yes. Captain de Montfort and I have a little daughter. Rosalie Noel. She has been missing for some time now."

"*Lo siento mucho*," the girl murmured. "I am very sad for you."

"Thank you," Tierney responded sincerely.

Amanda was speechless. She had only half-listened at the supper table, and presumed they were speaking of someone else's child.

Mrs. Hudson, all enthusiasm again, asked how old the child was. Tierney closed her eyes for a second, trying to imagine once again her baby of fourteen months of age. "She had her first birthday last month."

"Oh, my!" Mrs. Hudson was so excited over a possible scandal that the pearls about her neck actually quivered. "I was given the understanding that you were married only recently . . ."

Tierney began, "Well, that isn't quite the truth, actually."

Harriet was between running from the room and swooning. She just knew something like this would happen! Amanda, meanwhile, was calculating months, and when she arrived at the conclusion that Tierney was actually pregnant while at the Ursuline convent, her eyes bugged out most unbecomingly.

Tierney took in the various expressions about the room as best she could, and decided she must fully explain it now if the story were ever to be believed. "You see, I only married André in the Church last January. Our first wedding, the November the year before that, was just a civil ceremony, nothing in the eyes of God."

The former postulant finally found her voice. "This is incredible! Do you mean to say that you were already married when you were seeing my Charles?" Her voice had the most annoying pitch Tierney had ever known. Mrs. Hudson smiled. This was becoming the most interesting discovery she had made in quite some time.

"Yes, dear," Tierney said smoothly. "That is what I mean. Only once I arrived in New Orleans, I decided that marrying André back in London had been a dire mistake. We had some difficulty adjusting, and a winter voyage was not the ideal circumstance for getting to know one another as man and wife. Surely you understand that, Amanda. You haven't been married that long yourself!" Both women blushed knowing the subject now at hand was sex.

"Of course I understand that," she said uncomfortably. "What I cannot comprehend is why you did not have the marriage blessed immediately when you arrived here, or why it was a civil ceremony in the first place. That was extremely unwise!"

"Amanda, please do calm down. I will explain it to you. I was born a Catholic, but I was raised a Protestant. I had no feelings for either whatsoever until André sent me there. He wanted me to think twice before I left him altogether. I never saw Charles seriously. Certainly he must have told you that. But he was the only person who lived outside the walls kind enough to visit me. It was never as you imagined, Amanda. No one was courting me. Courting!" she laughed softly. "I never wanted to marry or see another man in that respect again!"

Amanda leaned back into the sofa cushions. "Charles always said there was nothing serious between you," she remarked thoughtfully. "But I thought he was just saying that to be kind. I suspected that he had fallen in love with you."

Tierney offered the ladies some sherry—she felt she might need one. Fortunately, all the women wanted a drink too. "Of course, I didn't realize I was with child at the time," she continued as she poured. "And when I did find out, I was too stunned to think properly. I felt I had to get away. André was God-knows-where on the high seas, and I knew that as far as the religious community was concerned, a civil marriage was no marriage at all." That wasn't quite fair to the Ursulines, Tierney knew. They would have been glad to permit her to spend her confinement there. "I was afraid I would scandalize everyone, you see. For I had made it quite clear that the captain and I were not married. I was a fool," she admitted sadly. "Only when André came back to see if I still wanted a separation, did he learn about the baby."

Presently, Angelique spoke. It was practically the first time she had said anything all evening. "Yes, ladies, Madame de Montfort was a little fool, and a little too young to come to grips with her life. I tried to tell her myself! Mind you, before marrying my late husband, I too was a Catholic. But," she sighed, lifting her palms upward, "I fell in love with a Protestant, a Presbyterian, to be precise. We settled on a civil ceremony, and I can tell you all that I have always felt quite properly wed. Certainly no one can call my dear James a bastard!" Harriet was appalled by her mother-in-law speaking so bluntly, but Angelique ignored the gasp.

"I tried to tell you, didn't I, dear?" she asked, searching Tierney's face. Tierney was so grateful for the older woman's smooth deception that she crossed the room toward her. "Yes, you did, Angelique," she answered quietly, kissing the woman's cheek. "And I was too foolish to listen . . ."

The conversation in the study was of far greater consequence than talk of marriages and missing offspring.

On the day that the local military forces had raided Grande Terre and seized the eighty Baratarians, about one hundred and fifty miles farther east along the Gulf of Mexico, the British had launched their first assault on the American territory. Four British vessels, under the command of Captain Sir William H. Percy, moved over Mobile. Days had been spent maneuvering the ships in the shallow harbor; and in the end, only H.M.S. the *Sophie* and the *Hermes* got within firing range of the fort.

Meanwhile, the British landed forces consisting of only sixty marines and one hundred Indians under the command of Major Edward Nicholls. These troops, which had come ashore unnoticed the twelfth of September, landed at the rear of Fort Bowyer in Mobile.

The American forces were ready, and the combined land and naval efforts on the part of the British cost the Crown far more than it gained. The crew of the *Hermes* alone suffered twenty-five casualties, and when she ran aground in the shoals, her captain was forced to blow her up.

Paul Mauriac had been too late and too far south to be of any real assistance, but he did give chase to the *Sophie* who was desperately trying to catch up with her sister ships in retreat.

"What of the land forces?" Frank Rubio wanted to know.

Colonel Ross replied. "I received a dispatch only Tuesday last. It seems Major Nicholls and his assortment disappeared east, back into Spanish territory."

"What has me bothered," André rejoined, "is that the British attack on Mobile may be just a feint. To give us false encouragement, you see, having made such a weak display there. I feel that Lafitte's information is correct." He looked pointedly at both of the officers in the room. "The Crown must be planning a major attack on New Orleans itself!"

"We know that, André," answered Patterson. "But how?"

The engineer, Latour, spoke up. "Precisely, gentlemen. It would not make much sense to deploy their forces directly from the Gulf. The British surely cannot be seriously contemplating a naval attack from the river! It would be of no use to them at all unless they could devastate us from the north, cutting off our supplies and communication with the interior."

They considered this idea for some time. Only Hans Nagel seemed indifferent to the matter. He was studying the many trade journals that lay about André's office.

At length, Colonel Ross stood up and stretched. "I fully expect that General Andrew Jackson will be put in charge of defense over the entire territory—both Mississippi and Louisiana. He is a fierce man. Fierce, impatient, and doesn't give an unholy damn for awaiting instructions from Washington. General Jackson is precisely who we need!"

CHAPTER THIRTY-TWO

Dixie. The name was coined for New Orleans, and the sturdy rivermen were the first to call the Crescent City by the odd name. A decade earlier when the Americans took over the territory and rough-hewn town, a local bank had issued its first American currency. They were ten-dollar bank notes printed in English on one side, and French on the other. "Dix" notes soon became commonly referred to as "dixies." The nickname lasted long after the bank notes went out of circulation, and would some day go hand in hand with a new generation of American people. It would mean much more, and no one would remember those original ten-dollar banknotes.

Andrew Jackson arrived here on the second day in December. Colonel Ross's description had been an accurate one. The general now commanded all of the forces in the entire Southern region. And he was, as the colonel had put it, "a fierce man."

Presently, he had about five thousand troops under him. He brought two thousand of these men with him into New Orleans. The rest he had deployed in Mobile and Baton Rouge to defend those cities, or be called upon as needed.

"Have you met him?" Tierney asked excitedly. "What is he like?"

Tierney was already in bed, covered in flannel from head to foot. She even wore a bedjacket. But she was wide awake, and André grinned at her. She might as well be a virgin cabin boy all over again.

"Please," she begged. "Don't tease!"

"Yes, I met him," he began as he unbuttoned his shirt. "He seems confident enough, I think, but very keen on the local battalions proving their worth. It seems none

compare with his backwoods riflemen, and I, for one," he
grunted, pulling off his boots, "don't doubt it."

"Does he look like Mr. Henry?" she asked.

"Who?" André did not know what in the devil she was
talking about, and said as much.

"Oh, you remember. The red-haired gentleman who
came to the masquerade ball as General Jackson."

"No." André laughed. "He doesn't look anything like
Mr. Henry." He jumped on her then, squeezing her legs
with his own and pinning her arms down. "So it's the
general's looks you are interested in, eh, my pretty?"

"Get under the covers!" she squealed. "You are such
an idiot sometimes! And you are a lunatic not to wear at
least a nightshirt when it's as cold as this!" she scolded.

After her husband was settled comfortably beside her,
he continued. "He is very tall, *chérie*. Taller than I, although he does wear thicker boots," he teased. "And
very handsome. But, *ma petite*, it is of no use to the ladies.
I am told he is very much in love with his own wife,
Rachel. Quite a scandalous affair, that one!" he quipped.
Then he gave Tierney a wink. "Want to hear about it?"

"Oh, *you*," she said accusingly, and snuffed out the
candle.

The next morning, André awoke in a very sober mood.
He was engrossed in the newspapers throughout breakfast, so much so that he didn't seem to notice his coffee
mug being refilled by Suzette. He was usually gracious
to the servants, especially upon awakening.

When he did speak, it seemed to Tierney he was merely
thinking aloud. "There are four initial objectives," he was
saying. "The first is to upgrade what defenses we already
have. Fort St. Philip could send us our first warning from
the south, and Fort St. Leon might be able to delay an
attack on the city." He looked up then, remembering his
wife was listening.

"Do you recall that point on the river, English Turn,
where we lost the wind and were delayed so long on our
approach to New Orleans?" Tierney nodded, but she did
not truly remember it. She only remembered being dis-
consolate over having to leave André and Paul when she
first arrived here. "Well, that is where Fort St. Leon is
located, at English Turn. It might be crucial . . ."

Tierney did not pay very close attention as he described

the importance of troop position, possible inland routes for an attack, and obstructing the bayous. She was, however, alerted to the mention of Jean and Pierre Lafitte.

"It's foolish of him, really. Not accepting the aid of those 'hellish banditi,' as he likes to refer to them. The Baratarians are his most valuable allies in gathering intelligence and learning the terrain.

"Major Latour, you remember him from our party? He's drawing some excellent maps for the general. He's the best. Latour was trained in Napoleon's army. But the maps would be that much finer if Lafitte were able to help . . ."

Presently, during a discourse on the pros and cons of army regulars versus state militia and local battalions, Suzette came in, bobbed a curtsy and announced, "Monsieur, Jeb is in the courtyard. He begs a word with you."

Tierney and André looked up in surprise, then at one another.

"Show him in, please," Tierney said.

Suzette threw a brief, quizzical glance at the seated couple, then soundlessly walked away. A few minutes later, the big man walked in.

"What is it, Jeb? Is there a problem down at the docks?"

"No, Cap'n," he answered, looking around uncomfortably. He would have preferred seeing the boss alone, outside. "I come to ask a favor, suh. I need my papers, suh. Now. I'll come back," he continued nervously, "but there's somethin' else I jest gotta do for the time bein'. There's a lot of freemen down there." He gestured toward the streets at large. "And they's doin' more than me about this war! I want to sign up for Daquin's battalion, Cap'n, if you can see my way of it."

Tierney felt her throat constrict. There was something about Jeb that reminded her of Paul Mauriac, though they were worlds apart.

André tried to conceal his pleasure. "Fine, Jeb! That's just fine. I'm sorry I didn't think of it myself. I've heard nothing but praise for the colored battalions, both Major La Coste's and Louis Daquin's." He stood up and gripped the other's hand. "A gentlemen's agreement then. You'll finish your year with me after the war. We'll go down to the courthouse this afternoon."

The two men left the dining room and walked back toward the kitchen. Tierney overheard Jeb remark, "I jest can't believe I'm gonna carry a gun!" She heard her husband's reply, "It's a crazy world, all right," and the two chuckle on their way to the courtyard.

Jackson wasted no time in putting the entire city to work. The legislature, notoriously slow to move in any direction, was quickly denied thwarting any of the general's plans. Thoroughly disgusted with the local government, Jackson soon declared martial law.

New Orleans had not been asleep, however. They had a montage of battalions, easily distinguished by race and class, but all able-bodied and disciplined men nonetheless. Besides the two battalions of black soldiers there was a battalion organized by Major Jean Plauche, which was comprised of the sons and brothers of New Orleans' aristocracy. It was this group to which André had offered his services.

There were also "The New Orleans Sharpshooters," men of brawn and skill who worked the rivers and frontier paths, commanded by Major Thomas Beale. General David Morgan led the Louisiana militia, and an enterprising man by the name of Pierre Jugeat had organized a battalion of Choctaw Indians.

These and more were put into immediate service by Old Hickory. New Orleans, the general conceded, was relatively easy to defend. Located on a bit of dry land on the east bank of the great Mississippi, it was surrounded by inland lakes and snake-infested swamps. Other than the waterways, most of which were either hidden or too shallow to navigate, there were only two stretches of dry land that might allow the passage of enemy troops.

The first led from Lake Borgne to the west of New Orleans. The Chef Menteur road, as it was called, was relatively dry but it narrowed to only one hundred yards along some places. This, however, would be the most likely route for an overland invasion, and Jackson quickly sent the first battalion there—those freed blacks under the command of Pierre La Coste.

The other dry route was singularly doubtful. It led into New Orleans from the south directly on the river's east bank. If the British were to start the raid from the south of New Orleans, however, they would most probably travel on the water—not next to it.

Able-bodied citizens and slaves, not otherwise employed in the war effort, were ordered to obstruct the many bayous leading into the city by whatever means were available. These people spent days of hard labor chopping trees and shovelling the wet mud.

Jackson sent the state militia down to English Turn on the river. He kept the battalion that Jeb had joined, the Indians, and Beale's sharpshooters within the city limits. The rich man's battalion was sent north to guard the forts along Lake Pontchartrain, but André was not among them.

Hans Nagel had taken an apartment in the warehouse district, but Paul Mauriac and the crew were living on board *La Reine*. Consequently, Paul was a frequent guest for supper in the town house. The men talked incessantly about defense, strategy, supplies, and ammunition. Tonight was no exception, and Tierney nibbled at her meal absently while they talked.

"I talked with Patterson down at the naval station," André said between bites. "Seems they are having a great deal of difficulty in manning the gunboats. I volunteered myself for duty on the *Louisiana,* and tentatively put you and some of our crew in the service of the *Carolina.* What do you say, my man?"

Paul finished his wine before answering. "I say fine. I'm growing fat and bored awaiting a merchant voyage. So are the men," he added irritably.

"It won't be much of a voyage, I'm afraid," André admitted. "Jackson does not anticipate taking them into the Gulf. He's ordered Patterson to load them down with artillery and heavy cannon. He intends to bombard the enemy from the river if they get within any distance of the city."

"That's fine too. The crew are quite fit for doing battle. I've had to threaten Pelier with walking the plank!" He chuckled, continuing, "So the angry general has finally conceded to meet with Jean Lafitte, eh?" Paul was not personally acquainted with either of the giants, but so much was said of both men, he felt he did know them.

André smiled apprehensively. "Yes, they finally met earlier this week. It was no easy task, I can tell you. By the time Jackson agreed, Jean was so enraged by the general's rude treatment that he refused. It cost Edward Livingston a few more hairs on his head to pull the two together."

"Well, what happened?" Tierney asked, suddenly interested. It was the first she had heard of the tête-à-tête.

"General Jackson was surprised, I think. He was expecting Lafitte to be a gruesome sort—a reincarnation of Blackbeard. But Jean was at his most polished, diplomatic self. I believe the general was actually jealous when he learned that Jean is fluent in English, French, Spanish, and Italian—as well-educated as any nobleman. Jackson himself is not very academic. He's more of the self-educated type.

"But they are both alike, in my opinion. They display the same qualities of leadership, personal strength, stamina, integrity—each in his own way, of course. And they are both mightily conceited. They each have absolute faith in their own talents.

"All taken into account, I would say they will get along famously. That is, unless one grows too overbearing and bruises the other one's ego."

Paul stood up and kissed the top of Tierney's head. "Thank you, lass. The meal was outstanding, as always. *Au revoir, petite*." Before he left, he asked André about the forthcoming Baratarian support.

"They will be everywhere," André replied. "Some will participate in the ground action, and many of them will be on board the *Carolina* and *Louisiana* with us. They are a brand of men you'll not likely meet again, my friend."

"*Ma chérie*," he said gently. "I promise you that I will be back as soon as it is humanly possible. As it is, I've left headquarters far more often than necessary. Patterson deserves more than my mouth backing him!"

She wasn't listening. She pretended sudden interest in a cigar burn on the carpet, and knelt down to inspect it more carefully.

"Tierney, please do get up! I cannot force you to understand, but I shall not have you *look* so obstinate!" He waited a few seconds for her to respond, then literally pulled her to her feet.

"*Mon Dieu!* You can be more stubborn than a jackass!"

he exploded, shaking her by the shoulders. "Listen, it's important. They've landed!"

At last André had her attention. It was a mere whisper. "Where are they?"

"About nine miles from here. The Villeré Plantation. The owner's son escaped only this morning to spread the alert. It's only because the lad had sense enough to tell them we have fifteen thousand troops here that they haven't already attacked. But when the British do find out our numbers . . ."

"How many troops are in New Orleans?" she asked, her voice rising.

André looked at her thoughtfully a moment before answering. "About twenty-one hundred is all. But as soon as General Coffee's troops from Baton Rouge and Hind's Mississippi Dragoons get in position, we will have more."

Tierney slumped into a chair. "The Villeré Plantation . . . Isn't that south?" She didn't wait for his reply. "I thought you said that was the least likely, André!"

In spite of himself he grinned. She had listened more closely over the past few weeks than she had led them to believe. "C'est la vie!" he said, trying to make light of it now that she was upset.

"C'est la vie, my foot! I thought all the bayous had been blocked! How did they get in?" she demanded.

"The Bienvenue Bayou. Some fool overlooked it," he responded, angry again over such stupidity. It all might have been avoided. Carelessness was responsible for more needless deaths than all other reasons combined, he thought.

"When will you be back?" she asked dismally. She had not seen Jeb or Paul in over a week.

"As soon as I can be, darling."

"By Christmas, then?"

"Not likely," he admitted, moving to kiss her. "I'll wish you a happy nineteenth birthday now, ma petite. Mrs. de Mateo is holding your gift, but you mustn't pester her for it early. None of your tricks now, Tierney. Promise?"

Tears streamed down her face unchecked, and she was unable to speak.

"Promise?" he repeated.

She caught her breath raggedly and nodded.

"Ah, that's my good girl!" he said cheerfully. If the

British broke within the city limits, he would somehow get back. But he did not tell her that.

When he kissed her full on the mouth, she clung to him briefly. Her pride would not allow more than that, for she could not have borne his fighting her to leave.

Tierney had lain awake most of the night. She watched a heavy fog settle over the streets, saw the early-morning rain sweep it away, and then paced her room as another fog moved in again to block the dawn.

Annette had graciously agreed to stay overnight until André's return: Tierney swore she would go mad alone in the house with Mrs. de Mateo.

"Did you hear anything last night?" Tierney asked as soon as she saw the maid that morning.

"*Non, madame.* I slept very well."

"Well, I heard it. Cannonade in the distance. Something is happening, something dreadful. I just know it."

Annette dismissed it as "nerves" and an overactive imagination, but the housekeeper had second thoughts on the matter. It seemed to her that Madame de Montfort had a third eye—perhaps a third ear as well!

Suzette arrived early that morning, and when Tierney came down to breakfast, all her favorite dishes awaited her. Creamed eggs with thyme, pork pudding, and an enticing array of pastries and muffins.

Mrs. de Mateo and the two younger women all hovered in the doorway, waiting expectantly. When Tierney just looked at them quizzically, they wished her happy birthday and many happy returns.

"I'd completely forgotten my birthday!" she cried before biting into a cheese pastry. It was not quite true— she had hoped and even half-expected André to surprise her. But the three women were attempting to make an occasion of it, and that alone cheered her.

"Please sit down with me, do. I hate eating alone." The two white women hesitantly pulled up chairs, but Suzette turned back toward the kitchen. "Oh, for heaven's sake, Suzette! Don't make me order you to join us!"

Annette and Mrs. de Mateo looked at one another in embarrassment, but said nothing.

"*Oui, madame,*" the mulatto curtsied slightly. "But I will get more plates now."

As Tierney finished her second cup of tea, she asked if any coffee had been made. Mrs. de Mateo got up immediately. She was hoping the mistress would ask, as she herself was not fond of English tea.

"Ah, ladies," Tierney sighed as the coffee cups were filled. "Such a dismal Christmas Eve. I think we need a bit of cheer, don't you?"

All of them agreed, and it was during their second leisurely cups of brandy-laced coffee that the tension really eased. For once the feminine chitchat swept past color and national origin, and the four contentedly nibbled and drank.

Presently, an uproar from the courtyard jolted everyone's nerves. Mrs. de Mateo mumbled something unintelligible, thinking the British were on their very doorsteps, but Tierney screamed, "My God! Something has happened to André!" She did not believe the dog, Taffey, would set up such a commotion otherwise.

It was Jeb.

Two of Daquin's soldiers brought him on horseback. He was conscious, but Tierney could see that he had taken a bayonet in the thigh, and was still losing blood.

"Get him upstairs," she directed the men. "Rafael, bring Dr. Friedham at once!" After settling him on the bed, she ordered Suzette to cut away the dirty bandages while she gathered some more. When the leg was cleansed and a tourniquet applied, there was not much left that the women could do. He fell into a fitful sleep while Suzette wrapped the clean bandage.

Tierney went to the kitchen to start the herb and beef teas herself.

It was midafternoon before the doctor arrived, and Tierney flew at him immediately with accusations.

"Mrs. de Montfort," he replied wearily, "Jeb is not the only man who was wounded last night . . ."

"André?" she cried out.

"As far as I know, your husband is fine, madame."

She was so relieved that she said nothing as she led the man upstairs. Suzette started to leave the room when Dr. Friedham and Tierney came in, saying that she would be within hearing range if called.

"Stay here," Dr. Friedham broke in. "Mrs. de Montfort, I'll see you downstairs after the examination."

Tierney bristled slightly at being ordered about in her own house, but realizing he might be right, she went quietly back to the kitchen. *"Señora,"* the housekeeper began when Tierney entered. "I almost forgot . . . there was so much happening . . ."

"Well, what is it?" she asked impatiently, still a little irked with the doctor.

"The birthday present from your husband, *niña.*" It was an affectionate word for Mrs. de Mateo to use, and Tierney was momentarily taken back. *"Su Biblia.* Your family Bible," she said softly, handing the large leather-tooled volume to her mistress.

Tierney studied the outside. It had brass reinforcements at the corners and binding, and engraved in gold was *Bible Sacré.* The lower left-hand cover was also inlaid with gold and read, "Bernadette Claire de Montfort, la cinquème juin, 1758." It had been his grandmother's wedding gift, then!

She opened it quickly, and folded out the enormous parchment paper sewn within Genesis. She scanned the entries of births, baptisms, and deaths until her eyes fell upon hers and André's names. In his own hand, her husband had listed their marriage. It was dated November first, eighteen hundred and twelve. A line beneath it designated the birth of their firstborn, Rosalie Noel de Montfort. Tierney began to weep quietly now, and Mrs. de Mateo discreetly left the room.

A few minutes later, she heard Dr. Friedham coming down the stairs. "I'll meet you in the parlor, Doctor," Tierney called. She hurried to the kitchen and put a cold, damp cloth against her eyes and patted a bit of flour on her nose before joining him.

"How is Jeb?" she asked as she entered the room.

"You did a fine job, Mrs. de Montfort. I knew you would. There is not much I can do beyond your ministrations. I removed the tourniquet—the bleeding has stopped. If it should begin again, send for me. In the meanwhile, feed him easily digestible foods and change the dressing twice daily."

"He will get well, then?"

"Certainly! He has lost a quantity of blood, but he is strong as a bull, really. You can move him to the stables now if you'd like."

Tierney drew herself up indignantly. "I'll do no such thing, Dr. Friedham."

The doctor looked at her in surprise. "I meant no offense, madame. But you do have him directly across from your own room! And the master of the house is not even here. Surely the captain . . ."

"Doctor," she retorted testily, "let me assure you that I am quite safe with Jeb. And I would certainly have Captain de Montfort's approval were he here!"

The poor physician was too shocked to reply. Mumbling something about leaving pain medication with the servant girl, he quickly took his leave.

Tierney, however, was not much needed, as it turned out. Suzette left early and returned with her things, saying she would stay until Jeb recovered. She overlooked her mistress's beef brew and camomile tea, and prepared her own concoctions for the suffering man.

An alert went out that afternoon demanding that all able men direct themselves to General Jackson's camp for the hurried construction of a wall eight miles below the city. Rafael and the boy left immediately.

Tierney felt something was terribly amiss, as she tried desperately to sleep that night. Never had she spent such a lonely holiday, and Christmas Day promised to be no brighter. She wished herself back two years to a night on board *La Reine de la Mer,* with warm breezes and the rich melody of the French sailors singing under a starlit sky.

Yes, something was very eerie about this night. No one knew yet about the landing of yet more troops at the Villeré plantation and the swelling of enemy forces there.

Moreover, no one could know that thousands of miles away in a town called Ghent, a treaty was signed to end the War of 1812.

CHAPTER THIRTY-THREE

Four days later the *Carolina* was struck, and because she was loaded with such heavy artillery, she quickly caught fire and exploded. Her sister ship, the *Louisiana,* was only a few hundred yards upriver.

As soon as André saw the gunboat's distress he bounded over the side and began to swim. Despite the urgency, he took slow and steady strokes. The British now had their cannon trained on the *Louisiana,* but she was just short of range. Nonetheless, the Americans made fast work of towing their remaining vessel completely out of firing distance.

The grapeshot pricked the water all around André. He kept his wits about him, however, and when a second explosion blasted the air and water, he swam underwater until the stray debris fell back into the river.

He was farther downriver than he had anticipated by the time he surfaced again. There was smoke and burning wreckage everywhere. "Paul!" he shouted. "Paul!"

The victims who were still conscious were swimming toward the west bank, away from British artillery. Paul Mauriac was not among them. André began frantically upturning the dead bodies that floated here and there. One was the hideously burned form of his man, Pelier. He was just starting to haul the body toward shore when he heard a faint cry.

Letting loose of the body, André turned in the water. "Paul?"

The sound was only barely discernible. It might have been the creaking of the demolished vessel, but André swam blindly back into the current. After minutes of agonizing search, he finally found his friend, semiconscious and clinging to a beam of wreckage.

* * *

The first crisis when news reached the town house of yet another patient being brought in was Jeb unceremoniously announcing he must return to the line.

Suzette tried to literally hold him down, but with a roar of anger, Jeb threw her off. Tierney sped up the stairs upon hearing the commotion. When she entered, the mulatto was glaring angrily at the big black man.

"Madame," she explained furiously, "this overgrown ape has decided he is ready to go back and fight. Tell him how stupid he is!"

Tierney took in the situation and shrugged helplessly. "Let him go, then, if that's what he wants." Suzette threw her a resentful glance, and Jeb, with a self-satisfied expression on his face, got up. Halfway to the door, without the benefit of either lady to assist him, he collapsed in a dead faint.

Suzette rushed forward, but looked up when she heard the other laugh. "I thought that would happen," she said matter-of-factly. "Suzette, the longer you know a man, the more you begin to understand what children they can be. It's much easier to let them prove themselves fools than to tell them they are fools. And like children, it is easier to trick them than to order them about."

The maid gave Tierney a rare smile. They waited then, for Jeb was far too heavy to lift. When he came to a moment later, they helped a much-aggravated man back to his bed and soothed him with another dose of painkiller.

Hans Nagel and Dr. Friedham brought Paul in at dusk. André could not be spared again, and was back on the *Louisiana* in anticipation of the final battle. Sir Edward Pakenham, brother-in-law to the Duke of Wellington, had at long last arrived with the remainder of his troops. A bigger attack was expected at any moment.

Young Nagel had come to Louisiana entirely unprepared to walk into the midst of this war and had kept to himself, close to the business district until today. But when Captain de Montfort summoned him, he went immediately and agreed to take responsibility for Mauriac and be of whatever assistance possible to Tierney. "Upon your life," the captain had charged him.

Tierney thanked Hans and told him to go back to his apartment. The last thing she needed was a namby-pamby foreigner on her hands, she thought irritably. It was unusual for the woman to feel so dispassionate, but rarely had she felt so distressed while surrounded by friends.

Paul lay deathly still. When Dr. Friedham saw the fearful expression on Tierney's face, he quickly explained he had already administered a heavy injection of morphia.

"Is he badly burned, Doctor?" she asked, wincing at the sight of his back.

"Not as badly as he might have been. A powder keg exploded from behind him, igniting his jacket. Fortunately, the impact sent him into the water almost as quickly. The burns could have been much worse. I'm more concerned about infection or damage to the nerves and spinal column. I fear he has damaged several vertebrae," he added, shaking his head.

"What does that mean?"

"Paralysis of the lower extremities."

Tierney held her hands to her face. "His legs?" she cried. "You mean Paul might never walk again?"

"It is far too early to say yet, Mrs. de Montfort. I'm sorry," he added. "I did not intend to frighten you."

By the next morning, Paul Mauriac was lucid. Tierney explained to him what little she had learned of what happened—everything except the possibility of losing the use of his legs.

"I thought it was André," the old first mate murmured. "He should have stayed where he was, but your husband, Tierney, is a reckless man. Very reckless." he muttered as another spasm of pain renewed its attack.

"You are all reckless," Tierney replied in exasperation. She knew changing the linen dressing on his back would cause Paul much more anguish. But the fact that he could feel pain, Dr. Friedham told her, was a good sign.

"My dear lass, you are not one to go about calling kettles black," he mocked as she lifted the gauze.

On New Year's Day, after Suzette's careful ministrations and with the doctor's approval, Jeb left. He was limping heavily, but there was no talking him out of it. Tierney gave him Animal to ride the eight miles back to the front line.

Jeb arrived after noontime, and was amazed to see all the changes. The wall Jackson had ordered begun on Christmas Eve was now eight feet high, reinforced another five feet on the American side. It spanned the six-hundred yard plain entirely, and had been further expanded another two hundred yards into the swamp at the far left. In addition, another wall was under construction two miles closer to the city limits in the event that the British overcame the first.

Reporting to Major Daquin, he learned he had missed this morning's skirmish by only an hour.

"Wish you'd been here to see it!" one of his compatriots hailed him. "We tore 'em apart!"

"Caught by su'prise, huh?"

"Yassuh! Ol' Hickory, he jest started reviewin' the troops when them redcoats busted through the fog." The man stretched out on a cotton bale and grinned up at Jeb.

"What's these bales doin' here?"

"Thought you'd ask, brother. They's beds now," he laughed. "They was cannon support, but when them guns got to blazin' so did the cotton! Had to pull 'em and pack mud under the big guns. Gen'l says they's beds now," he repeated, slapping the bale beneath him.

"Plum crazy to use cotton bales in the first place," Jeb commented drily. "Any fool should have realized the hazard with hot artillery."

"That ain't nothin!" his friend laughed anew. "The redcoats was usin' barrels of raw sugar under theirs. Things got 'sticky' you might say, after we shot those barrels full o' holes. And when it started rainin' about ten this mornin . . . Well, suh, them British might as well been swimmin' in molasses!"

Jeb fell against the cotton bale laughing so hard that his sides ached. His disappointment at having missed the action, the throbbing of his leg, and his desire for the unapproachable Suzette were temporarily forgotten.

Captain de Montfort felt as though he might smother. The *Louisiana* was not nearly so large as his *Reine*, and was so overcrowded with men and ammunition that the waterline was dangerously high along her beams. There wasn't a single stretch of open deck to be paced. Every inch was so cluttered with cannonballs, powder, and grapeshot that one had to literally walk through a maze.

Seated in the cabin with Patterson and several Baratarian lieutenants was no better. The room reeked of cigar smoke, stale spitoons and rum.

"Captain Dominque, You gave a good account of himself the other day," Patterson was telling the others. "Ripped apart several British batteries according to the general."

There was a hum of agreement regarding the Frenchman's fighting prowess, and one of Lafitte's men began recounting some of You's exploits under Napoleon. While the men continued talking, Patterson got up and presently strode up behind de Montfort. "Patience, Captain. That is the game we play."

"Playing by redcoat rules, I might add," growled André. "This quiet is so deceptive . . . What does Jackson think?" he asked turning to the naval commander.

"He is rechecking the lines in the north and St. John Bayou. Perhaps these skirmishes down here are just to distract us." The man shrugged. "But our intelligence sources indicate that the Villeré plantation is their only campsite."

"Any estimates on their numbers?"

"Between seven and nine thousand, we think, against our own five, so we can't risk taking an offensive position. Those damned mud-packed logs we call our wall are all that is stopping them. I know you want more to do, André. That action the other day only whetted our appetites. But there is nothing we can do beyond waiting."

"Major Latour is starting to build a line on the west bank, isn't he? Would it be possible for me to go there and work on it?"

"No, sir," the officer responded. "I want you here. Believe it or not, I need you here!"

His tall, handsome subordinate did not look pleased. In an effort to change the subject, Patterson lightly asked, "Have you heard the latest on Jackson's tantrum today?"

André accepted his dull fate for the time being and took up the bait. "No. What has the general's dander up now?"

"The Kentucky militia finally arrived," he chuckled, "but without any guns. Not a damned rifle among them!"

Mon Dieu! André exclaimed.

"That isn't exactly how General Jackson put it, Captain. He said, and I quote, 'I don't believe it. By God, I have never seen a Kentuckian without a gun and a pack of cards and a bottle of whiskey in my life!' Then he sent a search party back into Dixie to dig up some weaponry. So far, all they have come up with are a few Spanish muskets and some other relics . . ."

"Did the Kentucky troops forget their cards and whiskey as well?" André grinned.

"Not on your life, Captain! They wouldn't come completely unprepared . . . Speaking of which, are you game for a go at whist?"

"Mention chess and you have a bargain, sir."

The long-awaited final battle began on a mist-laden dawn, January the eighth. The British advanced their troops in the pre-morning darkness when General Sir Pakenham fired a rocket to signal the move.

As the last singing reverberation of the rocket ended, a sudden breeze arose and swept clean the mist. Stretching as far as the eye could see, wave upon wave of British regulars marched along the narrow plain between the wood and river. Only the occasional green of a British rifleman's jacket broke the sea of white-belted redcoats.

The Americans were ready. Their brilliant commander had finally resolved that the area to the north was under no threat and had brought back with him the remaining troops. La Coste's colored battalion stood man-to-man with Jeb's troops, still holding the center. To the Americans' right flank, along the river, were positioned Plauche's sons of New Orleans, guarding the levy beyond. And on the left flank, the Kentucky militia, armed with an odd assortment of pistols, muskets, and rifles, gave added strength to Coffee's regulars and the Choctaws hidden in the cypress swamp. All along the wall, the Americans stood four men deep, shoulder to shoulder.

When the British came across the five-hundred-yard range, General Jackson ordered the firing of his twelve cannon. Hundreds of Britons fell, but their countrymen marched over them, advancing toward the mud-banked wall like an army of fire ants. As soon as they came within rifle range, the Americans were ordered to cease firing several cannon. Old Hickory didn't want the powder smoke to burn the dead-eye accuracy of his sharpshooters' eyes.

"Keep an eye for mounted troops, men!" he shouted. "Aim just above the breastplate on those redcoats. Ready . . . aim . . . fire!" An orange flame of fire crackled forth as the Americans fired their rifles simultaneously along the entire six-hundred-yard length of wall.

The first rifles fired, and those men retreated to fourth position, allowing the second line of Americans to shoot. Then the third. Then the fourth. Then the first again, all in unison, so that a steady fusillade of bullets tore into the British columns.

Sir Pakenham, seeing the distress and suffering of men on his right flank, raced toward General Keane and commanded him and his troops to their aid. Pakenham's horse was quickly shot out from under him. He grabbed another mount, but before he could even swing the beast around, he caught fatal shots in his neck and stomach. Meanwhile, Keane watched the fall of his commander with horror. He raced not toward the right as ordered, but back toward the river. There he ordered the 93rd Highlanders Regiment to cut across the field to the right column. Then American bullets found their mark in Keane, and he fell, blessedly unconscious of the devastation around him. With the entire right flank of the British army now leaderless, the stealthy Choctaws moved upon those remaining in bloody hand-to-hand assault.

On the far side of the wall, near the river, the British met with false encouragement. They succeeded in mounting a small bunker before the eight-foot enclosure, and though some managed to actually reach the wall, they died in their vain attempt to climb across to the Americans on the other side.

The Highlanders now, with bagpipes blaring, marched across the battlefield under Keane's ill-conceived orders. Over five hundred brave Scots thereby met their end and with them, their own commander, Colonel Dale. The melee was nearly complete.

The British left flank, discouraged and terrified with terror beyond expression at the loss of Colonel Rennie, and the smell of death all around them, began to retreat. The center columns, under fire from both the American wall and their own artillery at their backs, had already begun a frenzied withdrawal.

The one remaining commander, General Lambert, had kept to the rear with one third of the army in reserve. When he saw another third of his men dead and dying, and the rest running back in speechless horror, there was nothing to do but sound an official retreat.

Hearing this, General Andrew Jackson mounted the wall and stared into the field beyond. A red carpet of blood and over two thousand strewn bodies awaited his eyes. Not a little shaken, Jackson ordered a cease fire. His own losses had been seven men killed and another six wounded.

It was only eight-thirty in the morning.

"They've quit firing!" André shouted above the din of cannon.

"Only the east bank!" Patterson returned. "Over here, Morgan's troops are getting the hell kicked out of them. That fool Morgan! If he had listened to Latour, his defense wouldn't be so goddamned weak . . ."

The *Louisiana* continued her bombardment of British rank and file, careful to keep the guns pointed well below the American line. The British commander on this side of the river, William Thornton, had earned his marks the summer before at the Battle of Bladensburg, and rallied his men forward. When the Americans were forced to retreat a few miles further upriver, the gunboat was forced to stop shelling lest she injure her own.

Thornton, however, was wounded and was forced to give his command to a young lieutenant. But even the less seasoned officer was able to keep his men moving. The Americans under Morgan were presently encouraged by a resounding chorus of cheers from their friends on the gunboat and the opposite bank, and finally stopped their retreat to stand their ground. By this time, however, the British had dropped the chase to await further orders from the east bank of the river.

It was late afternoon by the time Jackson received word that the surviving General Lambert was requesting a formal announcement of cease fire. He needed to bury his dead, he wrote. Jackson had the uncanny presence of mind to permit a cease fire only on the east bank, and not the west where Morgan's troops were still under threat.

As expected, Lambert ordered his troops on the west bank withdrawn that night. The Americans now could wait again, but this time they knew that without a doubt, they were the victors.

The following morning, British regulars went forth unarmed to retrieve their dead and dying compatriots. It was only then that they learned from the Americans of the incredibly few numbers lost on the other side of the wall. They carried their wounded back to the Villeré plantation, wholly disheartened, to exhausted surgeons who worked desperately to stave off more fatalities.

Those who could travel began the bitter trek back through the bayou to Lake Borgne. Lady Pakenham, thinking her husband would be the new governor of Louisiana, awaited Sir Pakenham on board a British man-of-war at the mouth of the lake. She went temporarily berserk when her beloved was delivered to the ship, his body preserved in a keg of rum.

The Victory Ball two weeks later was a glorious affair. The men wore military uniforms or dressed in cutaway coats with long tails. They all wore white kid gloves and carried the famous dueling weapons, and rapiers, called colchemardes, on their hips. The ladies were splendidly arrayed in a rainbow of colors, glittering in their finest jewels.

General Jackson had already sent a special dispatch to Washington alerting the government of the resounding victory of the Battle of New Orleans. The message, in part, read:

> *Captains Dominique and Beluche, lately commanding privateers at Barataria, with part of their former crews and many brave citizens of New Orleans, were stationed at Batteries Three and Four. The general cannot avoid giving his warm approbation of the manner in which these gentlemen have uniformly conducted themselves while under his command, and of the gallantry with which they have redeemed the pledge they gave at the opening of the campaign to defend the country. The brothers Lafitte have exhibited the same courage and fidelity, and the general promises that the government shall be duly apprised of their conduct."*

Thus, many of the Baratarians mingled freely with the socialites of New Orleans for the first time in many years. Everyone, it seemed, was on friendly terms, including Governor Claiborne who raised a toast to his former arch-enemy, Jean Lafitte.

Tierney had worn her green Chinese ensemble, only this time she basked in the curious and envious stares. She felt wondrously happy as she and André privately celebrated their belated first anniversary, teasing one another about having managed to arrange such an occasion twice every year.

Pierre Lafitte, looking nearly as magnificent as his brother, came up and requested a dance with her. André grinned, knowing these two had something to celebrate as well, and walked toward the group of men to his right.

Jean was standing with the governor and several other dignitaries as André sauntered toward them. Governor Claiborne was introducing Lafitte around when it so happened that the recently arrived General de Flaugeac turned away. To make matters worse, General Coffee hesitated several seconds before extending his hand to Lafitte. Jean was thoroughly angered by the gesture, and haughtily declared, "Yes, general. I am Lafitte, the pirate!" Without another word, he turned on his heel and strode away.

André de Montfort realized from that moment on that someday, Jean Lafitte would once again be considered an enemy of the American people. He watched Tierney laughingly waltz around the room in Pierre's arms, and fleetingly regretted he had ever set foot in New Orleans.

CHAPTER THIRTY-FOUR

Washington received news of the victory of New Orleans in early February. Ten days later President Madison was delivered a copy of the Treaty of Ghent, written the previous December. The document was approved by the president almost immediately.

It was late March, however, before Andrew Jackson withdrew his troops from New Orleans. To make matters more tedious, he had kept the city under martial law for the duration, thereby retaining command over every volunteer.

"I'll be ruined!" André roared when he was finally released from duty. "I can't blame young Nagel either. There has been little chance for him to accomplish anything without you or I to guide him."

Paul was managing admirably to walk with the aid of a cane now, and settled himself across from André's desk. He smiled tolerantly at the younger man. "You'll do quite well, André. You always have. You've a better head on your shoulders than your father, and that's going a ways."

The compliment put him in better humor. "Well, I think first I shall have to sell *La Reine*. She'll bring a fair price and recoup half my losses. I'll miss her, my friend, as well you know. But . . ." he sighed. There was nothing he could say that Paul Mauriac did not already understand. "Would you mind training Hans properly, Paul? I have to throw myself headlong into finding Rosalie Noel before Tierney goes mad. She's grown so quiet—I think she fears the child is dead." André looked down at his hands. What if the baby had been killed—or lost without a trace?

"Of course," the former first mate agreed quietly, "first on your list should be finding your daughter. Tierney is a lovely girl, but she has grown so melancholy over the past few weeks I fear she'll be a changed woman soon. And not one changed for the better," he warned.

Paul had been staying in the town house with Tierney since his injury, and felt her current period of despondency was fast becoming a sickness. Tierney had refused all along her husband's desire to build a fine home of their own high on the bluff overlooking the river. This, she had confessed to Paul over a year ago, was her only trump card left. She would not settle here permanently until the child was found alive or proved dead.

More recently, Tierney put further self-restrictions on her comfort. She went out daily, but only to attend morning mass at the cathedral. On Sundays she wore a heavy black veil, explaining only that she had committed a sin of pride. In her own home, she limited herself only to her bedroom and the study for "private reflection." During André's absence she had taken to receiving her meals upstairs alone.

On this, André's first day home, she seemed to be making an enormous attempt to behave normally. She even greeted her husband with an affectionate kiss. But Paul sensed it was a false and tiring bravado for the sake of her husband.

After a strangely unsettling supper together in the dining hall, the young couple retired to their room. It was only then that André realized the extent of his wife's disturbance. Tierney undressed quietly and slipped into bed without a word. André was talking, but not of Rosalie Noel.

"The most ridiculous aspect of the entire campaign was not that the war had already ended, but that no one won! After three years, not a blessed thing has changed. The borders have not moved an inch and trade will simply resume normally. Of course, those damned tariffs that American merchants were forced to pay by both England and France were part of the reason the United States declared war in the first place, but those practices have long since ended. The whole matter might have been quickly resolved without any bloodshed years ago! What was it all for?" he muttered irritably, reaching for the lamp.

"I have to leave you, André."

He stopped turning down the lamp and looked up

quickly. His wife's voice had been strangely soft, but he could tell by her face she was deadly earnest. She looked as though she had been carved from alabaster. Only her eyes glittered, but they too had an eerie quality about them.

"*Mon cœur*, what are you saying?" The skin on his neck prickled in fearful anticipation. He had never felt so helpless as this—like a drowning man. "What have I done, Tierney, that you should leave me?"

She closed her eyes and spoke slowly, determinedly. "You have done nothing, André. You have been good to me—too good, really. That may be part of it . . ." she said blankly. But her next statement, made effortlessly and without a trace of emotion, caused André to sit down. "I love you, yes. But I must go. Very soon."

"But why?" he whispered, taking her hand now. It was cold and listless.

"André, I know why we haven't found the baby. I am the reason. I am being punished, and we cannot allow Rosalie Noel to suffer because of my sins. I know you will be a good father, André. I know it. Once I am gone, you will find her."

He could not listen to any more of it. "You're talking nonsense! You don't know what you are saying!"

"Yes, I do," she answered tonelessly. "The night of the ball, André, I forgot about her. I pretended Rosalie Noel had never been born. And that wasn't the only time—I've done it several times. It's a great sin to deny a gift from God, André. And that is what our daughter is, a blessed gift.

"As soon as I leave, you will find her. I would rather have you keep her and raise her alone—deny myself ever seeing her—than to have her live the rest of her life among heathens."

André jumped up, not believing what he was hearing. "Stop it!" he shouted. "You are guilty of nothing. If anyone is to blame, it is I! For having left you alone in the first place, for not having married you before I took you to my bed—against your will! For being fool enough to circle the world thinking I could forget you! Tierney!" he cried, lifting her and crushing her to him. "I'll never let you go! Never! And I will find our daughter and lay to rest forever any doubts you have about deserving Rosalie Noel. Let me prove it!"

"Let go of me," she said dully. "Let me be." When she lay back down, she turned her face away from him. "Turn down the lamp, please. I want to sleep." Tierney smiled tentatively into her pillow. If anyone could find their baby, it was André. She'd known the joys of motherhood for such precious little time, it was hard to believe she could know them again. But André had instilled in her a thread of hope, small but much needed. She slept more soundly than she had in months.

André set out the next morning before either the city or his wife awakened. He wrote a letter to Paul Mauriac, and then he left. He had considered asking Jeb to accompany him because of his knowledge of the territory and the language, but decided against it. Besides the fact that the black man's freedom would be in jeopardy, they would make a conspicuous pair.

Now, as André set out in the pre-dawn darkness, he was relieved to be going alone. The war, the men he had lost, the sale of *La Reine* all weighed heavily upon him, and he welcomed a period of solitude.

Spring came early that year, and buds poked out from the multitude of flowering trees and shrubs along the muddy banks of the great river, but André didn't seem to notice. He took his horse with him and rode upriver on one of his own keelboats.

The journey was a quiet one. Jake Reilly and the other boatmen intuitively knew the captain was in no temperament for river travel gaiety, and as far as Natchez, Jake declined every offer to wrestle for the turkey feather he wore. "Next time, fellas!" he called. "Be back down this way in a couple of months, and then you can put your money up to have ol' Jake tear the pants off you!"

The Mississippi swelled with the early spring rains eliminating the problem of scraping bottom or running aground. But the currents in some places made for hard travel all the way to Natchez. Here, André wished his men well on the rest of their journey.

"Where you goin', Cap'n?" Jake asked. "Never did say."

"Mississippi. Tennessee, maybe. Even Georgia. I'm not sure, to tell you the truth. But I'll be back, so you boys behave yourselves," he said good-naturedly. "No cheating on the cargo, and do your fighting, gambling, and whoring where you won't get caught, understand?" The men laughed, and waved their good-byes.

The days grew warmer and the insects more plentiful, but every day spent traveling the Natchez Trace brought more hope, more tranquility to the man. He rode Animal at a leisurely pace now, at last enjoying the natural beauty of forest and trail. The untamed land had a beauty and mystique of its own: not so thrilling as the open sea, perhaps, but wondrous all the same.

Next month he would be thirty-one, old enough to truly want now the warmth and security of a home and family. Tierney. Ah, Tierney! What a remarkable woman she really was. The world might take little notice of her stubborn little ways or the beauty he saw in her, but so much the better. André wanted her all to himself, always had . . . her mention of leaving him was unthinkable, and he wondered briefly if that were one of her ruses. . . .

Once he found the Tombigbee River, it was not hard to pick up the narrow trail. It led from the riverbank about four miles south of the Trace and west again. The path was marked by tiny splotches of white, about three inches from the ground, painted on the pine trees.

It was past noontime when he found the Creek trail. André had no idea how far into the dense interior it led, but better to arrive late into the village than risk making camp on their own trail without their consent. He could only go on the popular belief that, since the latest treaties had been signed, the Creeks were no longer hostile. Nonetheless, he was armed.

Less than two hundred yards into the trail he heard the faint sound of movement beyond. Careful attention told him it was a horse, probably with a rider. There were no sounds of shoed hoofs or clinking bridle. André waited, his hand cautiously resting on his pistol.

They saw one another at the same time. It occurred to the trespasser that the Indian approaching him had been aware of his presence for some time, for he showed no surprise.

Chinookseh patted his pony's cheek and spoke soothingly. From this position, he could quickly unsheath his knife and spring if necessary. Perhaps the white man was lost, for he had no utensils, no drygoods, nothing of any value to trade, it seemed.

He sat up now, and waited for the other to speak.

André studied him carefully, but he could read nothing from the Indian's face. He suddenly wished that he had encouraged Tierney to talk about these people so that he might understand more fully what lay in store. To his consternation, he could not recall a single word of Creek the old priest had taught him. "I am Captain André de Montfort. I have come for my daughter, Rosalie Noel. Do you have her?" André knew he sounded ridiculous, but could think of nothing else to say. "Fool!" he thought angrily. "I should have brought a breed."

Wordlessly, the Indian turned his back on the white man, evidently a sign of trust. He began retracing his tracks, and André obediently, silently, followed.

Chinookseh was learning English, but he felt very awkward in the white man's tongue. Since Oswatchee's death at Horseshoe Bend, however, the village was in desperate need of an English-speaking member for their encounters with settlers and requirements at the trading posts along the Trace. Chinookseh was thinking furiously in his own language.

He had formally adopted Lilalee immediately after the fire. Uneasily, he noticed the similarity between the little girl and this man with the piercing blue eyes.

The two riders came upon a small clearing. In the distance was the village, but André's eyes were riveted toward the children at play. His heart, pounding in his ears, competed with their screams and laughter.

The Indian slipped from his horse and held a hand up to André. "Stay," he ordered.

Only the oldest among them were fully clothed. André searched the little ones, trying to identify his own, and failing that, trying to spot a female child of about one and a half years old. André was not at all sure how big that should be.

One child, sitting apart from the quick-legged ones, sat with its back to André busily stacking flat stones. It was this child whom the Indian approached.

"Lilalee!" he heard the native call. "Lilalee!" he repeated, more loudly and cheerfully.

The little one, a girl, jumped up and promptly fell back, smacking her bare bottom on the small pile of stones. She cried, and reached her arms up to the Indian.

Chinookseh gathered her in his arms. When finally she calmed, he held her high over his head and tossed her, a game she obviously loved. The little girl was still giggling when he carried her slowly toward André.

Chinookseh thought his heart might burst. It was best, he knew, for his woman punished the child for the slightest reason. Since the birth of their son, Melita had no room in her soul for his Lilalee.

The little girl had enormous blue eyes. Her hair, her face, everything, struck André so strongly that his hands trembled.

The Indian murmured to her in a language unknown, and the child studied the stranger curiously. "Father," the man said aloud and firmly handed her up to André. It was only then that the toddler understood, and she strongly voiced her disapproval. She cried out and wriggled frantically in the strange man's arms.

Chinookseh did not look back. He swung himself onto his horse and sped toward the village, Lilalee's cries for him ringing in his ears.

"Ook-say! Ook-say!"

André held her firmly to his chest, but she fought him furiously. "Ook-say!" she wept, her tears soaking through to his own skin. By the time he reached the open field near the river, Rosalie Noel had spent her fury and slept soundly, crooked in her father's arm.

André's own heart ached, but for so many reasons it was impossible for him to unravel his thoughts. The Indian must have been her father in the village, for despite his expressionless face, his tenderness with Rosalie bespoke love. And André hurt for his daughter too. This living, breathing, weeping little person was at long last real to him—his own flesh and blood. But he was nothing to her; at least, not yet.

André looked down into the sleeping face and smiled. Ever so lightly, he kissed his little girl for the first time.

The trip home was riotous.

The captain knew nothing about children, and was not

in the least prepared for the multitude of crises that took place.

First of all, she was naked. Except for André's shirt which she threw down every few minutes, causing them to stop, she remained so until they reached Fort Jackson, which was halfway back to New Orleans. And she was not cautious about many of her personal habits. André soon learned that if she wiggled her feet decidedly, it meant they must stop, or else . . . Even so, Rosalie slept quite soundly in the saddle, not quite without accident.

The biggest problems, however, came at night. Lilalee, he soon determined, rhymed satisfactorily with Rosalie if he placed emphasis on the second syllable, and so he quickly took to calling her that. A name she would respond to, though, did not deter her from trying to run away back to "Ook-say." André was painfully aware that the baby awaited her rescue by the Indians, and failing that, she was just stubborn enough to try going on her own.

Setting up camp, then, was nightmarish for the new father. If he took his eyes away from her longer than a minute, Rosalie would disappear. He lost one week's worth of sleep worrying over her sneaking away while he slept before he came upon a solution.

One night, a few days out of the fort, he pretended to let her go. It was dusk when she stumbled into the copse along the Trace, heading north in a direction opposite the Creek village and their own destination. As expected, the very fact that he did not pursue her made her pause several times and look back at him questioningly. Her captor appeared not to notice.

When it grew dark, he heard her call out. He realized that by this time her stubby little legs would not carry her much farther. She called "Ook-say" over and over again. He waited.

André had coached her for days now to say "Papa," but Rosalie either could not form the word or refused to say it. André did not know which. Presently, her call for the Indian gave way to crying. It was a petulant cry at first, but soon became fearful crying, and finally hysterical screams. Her father ran into the woods, fearful now himself, and called her name. She did not answer. Suddenly the crying stopped altogether, and panic seized him.

He strained to see in the moonlit shadows and made his way hopefully toward where he believed he had last heard her. He prayed inwardly, hoping for once God really listened.

He found her a few moments later. She was sitting in a pool of silver light, bright-eyed and content, sucking her thumb. André felt like a fool, not for the first time, and decided it was time to scold his saucy daughter. But before he could say a word, Rosalie pulled her thumb out and with an angelic smile, stuttered, "Pa-pa. Pa-pa." The baby held her arms out to him.

By the time they reached New Orleans, André was completely enamored of her charms. Never mind that she insisted on taking off all her new clothes. Never mind that she ate like a little heathen, pulling food from her mouth to inspect it again and licking dirty fingers. Never mind that she bit the boatman who brought them downriver from Natchez. Rosalie Noel was beautiful, and she was his.

She rarely called for the Indian anymore, only every other day or so, whereas before, it had seemed every other minute. André had also switched slowly from rhyming her name with Lilalee to the correct pronunciation of Rosalie. The baby did not seem to notice the subtle transition.

Occasionally, André forgot himself and spoke to her in French. It was difficult enough, he believed, for her to learn one new language, so he made a concentrated effort to use only English. André knew that for Tierney's sake, it must be Rosalie's primary language.

Jeb was working near the dock, overseeing a lumber shipment, when André walked up to him carrying the wide-eyed little girl.

"Cap'n de Montfort!" he cried. "Good to see you, suh! Mighty good . . . Hey, there, li'l Rosie! What you been up to with your Daddy? You ride that big ol' muddy river with him, chile?" Rosalie giggled and playfully caught at the finger he crooked at her.

"Yassuh," Jeb said, turning back to the captain, "Miz Tierney gonna be powerful happy to see this chile of hers again! Be happy to see you both, safe and home."

"Thank you, Jeb. I think it's about time we took her to

her mother. But where are Hans and Mr. Mauriac? Everything has gone well, hasn't it?"

"Yes, Cap'n. Everythin's jest fine. Mr. Mauriac and the other gentleman done gone to the auction. Ship auction, Cap'n," he said, waving toward the south levy.

So *La Reine de la Mer* really would be sold, after all. Her captain hoped Jean Lafitte could meet her price, or forfeit reclaiming one of his own for her. André felt a momentary twinge of regret, but nothing more. His little girl was playing with his hair, and it felt too good to waste much time on regrets. Besides, he shrugged, one day he would have another fine ship to call his own.

Animal had enjoyed a fine rest tethered to the flatboat's rail all the way from Natchez. Presently returned to his familiar surroundings, the horse eagerly trotted toward his comfortable stall and Rafael's loving care.

When they rounded the corner and came into the courtyard, André shouted his arrival. Everyone raced to the kitchen door at once, but Tierney pushed herself forward. Her blood thundered in her ears, and she longed to run toward them. André set the child barefoot on the patio bricks, hoping she would run to her mother.

She did not. Rosalie Noel was having an unprecedented attack of shyness, and leaned closer into the man's sturdy legs, her hands clasped on one knee.

To André's amazement, Tierney put her arms around him and kissed him full on the lips before anything else. Their tiny daughter stared up at them curiously. Then her mother smiled down at her and slowly sat down, crossing her legs Indian-style. Rosalie responded with a timid smile.

The captain looked down at the woman and child at his feet, and drank in a full measure of pride. He said nothing, but listened carefully to the words his wife was saying. Her voice was as soft as rose petals.

"Rosalie Noel, mine! What a big girl you've grown to be! And so pretty too. Come here, lamb," she said, gesturing with her hand as she had seen when the Creeks bade her come. Suddenly, it seemed only yesterday. The few words she had learned were fresh again in her memory.

Rosalie peered teasingly between André's legs. When Tierney repeated a command to come, this time using Kawita, the tot sobered and stared at her mother intently.

"Lee-tah?" the little one queried at length.

"Not Melita, lovey. Mama. Come, Rosalie," she said again in English. Her voice was still soft, but the inflection was firm.

Without warning, Rosalie shot out from between his legs and toddled happily toward her mother. Tierney caught her up in her arms just as she started to stumble on the uneven bricks, and hugged her gingerly. To the mother's tremendous relief, the baby allowed the hug and contentedly snuggled against her chest to suck her thumb.

The trio remained poised in the courtyard, André standing above his wife and daughter for a long time. Tierney finally allowed herself the tears of joy.

CHAPTER THIRTY-FIVE

"Well, all I can say," Tierney said, struggling to hold still the two-year-old, "is that you are an overgrown fool, Suzette, and your head is bigger than what's inside it!"

Rosalie was impatient to be off, but her mother clucked at her, and she tried very hard to stand quietly while the second braid was being plaited. Papa would be leaving for work very soon, and she must hurry down the big stairs to breakfast with him.

"Madame, he is a full-blooded Negro!" she answered the mistress worriedly. "Our children would be *griffe*."

"Do you love Jeb, dear? You don't have to admit it, you know. I can tell. And he is very much in love with you, Suzette. I think it is a pity you refuse him when you feel so strongly about him. But," she added, patting Rosalie's behind to send her down now, "it is your decision. No one else can live your life. As André once told me regarding Jean Lafitte's slave trading, 'I cannot be another man's conscience.' Nor can I, Suzette."

The mulatto girl was on the verge of crying. "You don't understand, Madame. My father was a gentleman planter, a white man! He gave me an education almost as fine as his legal daughters. For one such as me, Madame de Montfort, marrying a black man is a step down, beneath my station. You do not understand," Suzette moaned.

"Oh, but I do understand. Let me tell you a little story. Where I come from, it is every bit as much frowned upon to intermarry. Moreso, perhaps. But my father, an Englishman, fell in love with my mother, an Irish commoner. He married her, in spite of the many protests of friends and family, and knowing fully well he was forfeiting a promising career."

"It isn't the same," Suzette sighed. "The English and Irish belong to the same race."

"Don't tell them that," Tierney remarked wryly. She stood up to join her family downstairs. "I understand far more than you realize, Suzette. If you don't marry Jeb out of love for him, what chance do you have for a happy life? You know better than I what happens to beautiful mulatto and quadroon women—they become mistresses to white men, desperately hoping it will miraculously end in marriage. But marriage is not part of the bargain. You live your last years well off, I suppose, with nice little homes of your own. But it is surely a lonely way to spend old age. Lonely, indeed. Is that what you want, Suzette?"

"Non, madame," she wept. What Tierney said was true. As was customary, her mother had already been approached by "respectable gentlemen" requesting the lovely girl's hand in an *affaire du cœur*. As was also proper, Suzette was still a virgin.

Tierney stroked her soft brown curls before going downstairs. "I know you will make the right decision, dear. I was afraid also. But with some gentle prodding, I married the captain. And I couldn't be happier . . ."

Tuesday night was the opening of a play new to New Orleans, the comedy *Nanine* by Voltaire, at the Théâtre d'Orléans. Tuesdays and Saturdays full dress was always obligatory, but tonight was a special occasion—at least for the de Montforts.

Earlier that morning, Tierney had summarily announced it was time to start building a mansion, high on the bluff as her husband had always planned. She was tired of le Vieux Carré, she said, and did not want to spend another sweltering summer in the city with its stinking open sewers.

"A fine time you pick, Madame!" André had bellowed. "I have tried since our wedding to have you agree to that; but, no, you wanted to stay here until we were 'settled,' you argued. Now, all at once, when my funds couldn't be lower or my business demands higher, you want me to build a mansion for you! Tierney, you never cease to amaze me. Your propensity for bad timing exceeds my imagination . . ."

Tierney reached over and covered his mouth with her palm. "Shush, will you?"

He waited silently, planning already how he might overcome her next argument.

"You will just have to work harder, Captain," she said impishly, "much harder. You'll have another hungry mouth to feed soon. And where shall we put our son, if not in a new home?"

Wordlessly, André swept her into his arms and carried her upstairs.

Now, as they dressed for the theater, neither could conceal the adoration in one anothers' eyes. André was more relaxed, more loving than she had ever seen him. Tierney did not pretend to understand the workings of the universe, or even of her own heart. But she knew that beneath it all, there must be a divine plan—some reason for her being here, some purpose behind all the tribulations, all the joys.

"André, did I ever tell you about Birdie?" she asked as they started down the stairs.

He locked his arm in hers and smiled. "Tell me," he said. André de Montfort already knew, but this would not be the last time his wife spoke of rainbows.

Rosalie Noel looked across the room to where Mary Eileen was busily arranging flowers.

Her sister looked nothing like her. "Where did you get that cornsilk hair?" they would ask her. "Even your eyes are different," people would tell the two girls. Mary Eileen was different. She was fair and petite, her slate gray eyes contrasted becomingly with her magnolia white skin; but most of all, Mary Eileen was different from Rosalie because she was a quiet child, calm and content.

Rosalie did not understand where her sister's placid disposition came from. The blond hair, she knew, was reminiscent of their grandmother, Kathleen Tierney Chambers. Mama had given her firstborn the miniatures of their grandparents, and a brooch that had belonged to their great-grandmother to Mary Eileen. She would never part with the topaz pendant.

That was probably a good thing about the brooch, Rosalie considered as she studied the younger girl now. Perhaps Mary Eileen took after the old woman in temperament. Mama used to say her Nanna was very devout, which was odd, the girls thought, because their great-grandmother had been a Protestant.

Mary Eileen was devout too. In fact, if she had not already declared her betrothal to Jim Redding, Rosalie would not have been in the least surprised if her sister entered the convent. She was always studying or praying or working, it seemed.

Presently, Rosalie Noel got up and walked out to the veranda. She was extremely restless as spring stretched its colorful, warm wings over the Mississippi delta. Rosalie would be seventeen this summer.

She wanted to go somewhere, do something, be with someone! Someone young, handsome, and as daring as she. Unfortunately, none of the neighboring young men appealed to her. If only Papa did not need her! She was certain, however, that he did. Papa was still a strikingly handsome man despite his age. His dark complexion was weather-lined, and his temples had a trace of silver, but Rosalie proudly believed that this only lent character.

But ever since Mama's death, some four years ago, Papa had frequent bouts of melancholy. Occasionally, he even became completely despondent. Papa said it was the way Mama died that was so hard for him to accept. A common fever took her. Their mother, he said, had looked Death in the face so many times, she must not have taken his last visit seriously.

When he was in one of these dark moods, he would spend a lot of time in his study, staring endlessly at her portrait. The portrait was one of the few things about which his daughters agreed. They thought it was gauche. The artist had painted her so vividly that the girls were invariably startled by it: her eyes wide, her cheeks flushed, and her lips slightly parted as if she might speak at any moment. It was indecent, really. The worst part was that Mama was wearing a ridiculous costume of a brilliant green shade, embroidered with gold. Papa said it was a Mandarin gown he had brought to her from China, and knowing this, the girls were even more embarrassed. Papa loved the painting, though, and Rosalie and Mary Eileen were only grateful he kept it in his private study.

Holidays were bad times for Papa. The family was quite large now, considering Aunt Françoise had come from France with her five children after the death of her own spouse. Uncle Paul, who was just like family, had finally married a Creole woman, so his three boys were still young. But all the children underfoot and gay laughter of friends did not seem to cheer him. Christmas Eve was worst of all. Once a year, on this night, even Uncle Paul got drunk!

Papa was happiest, it seemed, when he visited Mother Superior regarding the de Montfort girls' educations. The nuns never had trouble with Mary Eileen—she was a star student. Rosalie Noel—they called her by both names, as Mama had—was a different matter. Rosalie did not mean to cause trouble. It seemed to follow her—or catch up with her, as the case might be.

If a conference were called to take some disciplinary measures with his strong-willed daughter, it started with an unpleasant lecture and ended with Rosalie being sent into the hall while Papa and Mother Superior had "a private word." On these occasions, laughter was invariably heard echoing through the heavy office door.

Mary Eileen thought it sacrilege for Papa to laugh so boisterously and even smoke cigars within the convent walls, but Rosalie loved these moments of hearing her father enjoy himself so. Rosalie knew that the plump, merry-eyed nun had been her mother's prefect many years ago when Mama had actually lived here. She often wondered just what secrets Papa and Mother Superior shared about Mama, and suspected that it was reminiscing over a saucy young girl and a dashing young sea captain that took up their "private words," and not discipline. Someday, she hoped her father would tell her the entire story behind their romance. . . .

If Rosalie Noel had inherited her mother's impetuosity and her father's good looks, she had from them both a certain sensuality, an undercurrent of excitement. Now her manner was deceptively quiet as she leaned against the ivy-covered column and peered below to the teeming river.

New Orleans was a city bursting with life. The steamboats rolled steadily up- and downstream, carrying with them a universe of personalities. There were businessmen, dance-hall girls, gamblers, politicians, actors and actresses, and even cowboys. Rosalie wanted desperately to be with all of them.

Thinking of freckle-faced Jim Redding (his insipid mother called him Jamey, for God's sake!) and Mary Eileen irritated Rosalie Noel. Jim was all right, she supposed, and very well off. He would inherit Southwell—slaves too, of course. But Rosalie would have liked her little sister to be a bit more spirited. She could think of nothing more dull than of knowing for years in advance whom you would marry.

With a decided toss of her long black hair, Rosalie descended the wide veranda steps to the manicured lawn below. She paced a few moments, and then ran for the stables. Papa had never developed an interest in plantations, but in addition to his shipping line, he owned a fabulous horse-breeding ranch. The family had the pick of its finest offspring. Her own mount was of Arabian stock, and Rosalie called him Pirate. Papa thought the name was silly, but of all her favorite childhood stories, Rosalie liked the ones about pirates the best. Her own parents had actually known some, according to the servants.

Old Rafael was snoring outside the back building when she ran up. He seemed to do little else these days, she thought sadly. She slowed her pace, lest Pedro see her behaving like a little boy. Rosalie was a quickly maturing young woman, and she was well aware of the fact.

Before Rosalie was able to break into a canter, she saw her father's carriage coming up the long drive. She reined Pirate around and, despite both hers and the horse's desire to race free, urged him gently down the drive. Rosalie dared not let Papa see her being reckless for he was never too depressed to discipline his daughters.

As she drew up alongside him, he ordered the driver to halt. "I'll get out here," he told him. "Thank you, Tim."

Rosalie could not suppress her own excitement at seeing her father's cheerful expression.

"Mind if I walk along with you, sweetheart? You can take Pirate out in a few minutes, but there is something I'd like to tell you."

"Of course, Papa! What is it? I've never seen you this happy over a contract . . ."

"Calm down," he chuckled, "and let me get the words out. I have purchased a ship, Rosalie."

The girl's merriment subsided. There was nothing so remarkable about a ship.

"Do you remember my telling you about my finest vessel, *Le Reine de la Mer*?"

Rosalie nodded. Mama had talked about that ship too. Papa had brought her to America on that one.

"And do you remember Uncle Paul and I talking about the ships being built these days in Baltimore? Clippers, they call them. Well, I have just today purchased one. She'll be ready next month."

"Congratulations, Papa."

André looked up at his daughter affectionately, remembering his first ride with her down the Natchez Trace. "Rosalie," he said quietly, "I'll be leaving for a while.

I'm sailing *Mon Cœur* myself. It has been a long time for your Papa on the open seas, but he needs a change of scenery. Do you understand, *petite*?"

Lord, did she ever, she thought in exasperation. Suddenly, another thought struck her. "Papa, I am happy for you. Truly. But could I come with you, Papa? Could I?" she pleaded. "I promise I shan't be in your way. I'll be out of school next month—forever!" she added a little too gaily. "And Uncle Paul will be here. Why, Mary Eileen could even stay with Aunt Françoise and lend a hand with the children. She's never a bother to anyone, Papa. Mary Eileen is so good!" she said sincerely. "In fact, you ought to take me! I'm the one always in trouble, you know," she teased.

André put his hand on hers and smiled. "Not this time, daughter. I must go alone. But soon, Rosalie, I will take you. We'll travel to New York, London, Paris, Venice— you'll see it all. I promise."

Papa never made promises lightly, and Rosalie was mollified. She could use this summer alone with Mary Eileen to put some spunk into her. The poor girl could use it, Rosalie thought.

"What did you say you were calling her, Papa?" she asked as they reached the steps.

"Mon Coeur," he answered.

"My Heart? Why, Papa?"

"Just a name, sweetheart," he said quietly.